Venser is
He doesn't w

Fear and dread shriveled like paper in the ... swelled. The Weaver King had erred in pushing him at this particular moment, for Venser had reached his limit. There were too many people making too many demands on him. Planeswalkers and archmages aside, Venser's own sense of duty and the guilt from shirking that duty were more than enough to spur him to action. The Weaver King's exhortations appealed to his weakness, that childish desire that told him to hide his head and wait for the danger to pass. It was a compelling notion no matter how irrational, but Venser would no longer be compelled. Windgrace would never succumb to such a ploy, nor Jodah, nor Radha, and Jhoira least of all.

Venser gritted his teeth and stabbed his fingers in deliberate, measured motion. The ambulator whirred to life under his fingers. A film of yellow energy crawled up the dais and over the arms of the chair, slowly covering Venser in a gleaming skin of crackling light.

Stay. Do not leave. I forbid it. Rest . . .

"I will not rest," Venser said, "until my work is done."

. . . but he's the only one who can.

Scott McGough ushers in new author Timothy Sanders, and together they continue the adventure first started in *Time Spiral*.

EXPERIENCE THE MAGIC

Time Spiral Cycle · Book II

Scott McGough and Timothy Sanders

Time Spiral Cycle, Book II
PLANAR CHAOS

©2007 Wizards of the Coast, Inc.

All characters in this book are fictitious. Any resemblance to actual persons, living or dead, is purely coincidental.

This book is protected under the copyright laws of the United States of America. Any reproduction or unauthorized use of the material or artwork contained herein is prohibited without the express written permission of Wizards of the Coast, Inc.

Published by Wizards of the Coast, Inc. MAGIC: THE GATHERING, WIZARDS OF THE COAST, and their respective logos are trademarks of Wizards of the Coast, Inc., in the U.S.A. and other countries.

All Wizards of the Coast characters, character names, and the distinctive likenesses thereof are property of Wizards of the Coast, Inc.

Printed in the U.S.A.

The sale of this book without its cover has not been authorized by the publisher. If you purchased this book without a cover, you should be aware that neither the author nor the publisher has received payment for this "stripped book."

Cover art by Daren Bader
First Printing: January 2007

9 8 7 6 5 4 3 2 1

ISBN: 978-0-7869-4249-7
620-95915740-001-EN

U.S., CANADA,
ASIA, PACIFIC, & LATIN AMERICA
Wizards of the Coast, Inc.
P.O. Box 707
Renton, WA 98057-0707
+1-800-324-6496

EUROPEAN HEADQUARTERS
Hasbro UK Ltd
Caswell Way
Newport, Gwent NP9 0YH
GREAT BRITAIN
Save this address for your records.

Visit our web site at www.wizards.com

Dedication

This book is dedicated to
Cathy, Erin, Jon, Barb, Gabrielle, and Jim,
whose generosity in allowing me to crash in their homes made its
successful completion not only possible, but enjoyable.
Thanks again, my friends.

—Scott McGough

This is for Karin,
who patiently supports all my mad schemes
and listens to my crazy plots.

—Timothy Sanders

Acknowledgments

Scott McGough would like to acknowledge the following
individuals for their invaluable input:

- Jeff Grubb, for his outstanding, inspiring, and bar-setting Magic fiction as well as his excellent advice on how to put the great character he created to good use
- Susan Morris, whose steady hand and patience made the near-impossible slightly less painful and a great deal more manageable
- Al, Dan, Johnny, Silas, Trixie, and the rest of the gang down at the Gem

Timothy Sanders would like to acknowledge:

- Susan J. Morris for being an awesome editor and for always having a patient explanation for a new author
- Scott McGough for being a willing co-conspirator and providing the voice of experience as I slogged through the weeds of plot development
- John Delaney for his many suggestions and improvements and for batting cleanup on all my loose threads
- Brady Dommermuth for always having another suggestion that was *slightly* more evil than what we had already done to the poor characters
- All the people involved in making *Magic: The Gathering* what it is today and especially those who decided to take a chance with a pair of new authors

Venser stood on the acid-steaming sands of Shiv. He winced in the stinging wind as he faced the howling mass of goblins, orcs, slivers, and reptilian viashino raging toward him. The horde's diverse membership was unified by a shared disposition—feral, desperate, and wild-eyed—and the shared purpose of tearing Venser and his party limb from limb. The marauders rolled across the sand like a great wave, closing the gap between them and their prey. Not for the first time, Venser decided his life had been far more manageable before he left Urborg.

Not that things in his homeland were ever easy for him. Venser was an artificer, a maker of machines in a land where artifact-hating monsters scoured the swamps for machines to destroy. Venser had never wavered from his life's work, designing, building, and testing his devices as often as he could. He scavenged raw materials from a toxic junkyard and learned to avoid the fen's native dangers as well as the fanatical beasts who would kill him on sight for his endeavors. It was a dangerous way to live in one of the most dangerous places in the world.

But life in Urborg seemed like a good night's sleep compared to the past few days. Since Jhoira and Teferi had found him, Venser had been violently ripped from his home, hurled across wide expanses of space and time, and attacked by an ancient, godlike dragon. He had seen a magical tear in reality itself and watched as the wizard who created that tear healed it. He had witnessed two halves of a broken continent reassembled by planetary-scale magic, seen noble warriors come to ignoble ends, and been bullied by a lady barbarian. Now, in the face of an advancing horde on the seams of the restored land of Shiv, Venser struggled with the obvious fact that his troubles were only beginning.

His party must have seemed easy pickings to the approaching mob, numbering four with only one warrior. Venser and Jhoira were artificers, and though both were young and strong, neither was especially well armed or battle-tested. The planeswalker Teferi had strong magic, but he was still dazed from his recent efforts and bleeding from a solid blow to the head. Only Corus, the huge viashino lizard-man, was trained and ready for close combat. Corus had already bested one of the mob's leaders, but he could not fight a gang of fifty and protect his human charges all at once.

The viashino warrior stood rigidly atop the sand, his eyes narrow and his sharp tongue slicing the air. Teferi had sunk to his knees nearby, his bald head and his dark, handsome features marred by a stream of blood trickling down from his split scalp. The master wizard's eyes were glassy and vacant, and his lips moved as he muttered, seemingly unaware of his current surroundings.

Venser turned to Jhoira, as he had done so often during the past few days. She was a native of this harsh land, a Shivan from the nomadic Ghitu tribe. She was slight of build but wiry and strong, her body shaped and tempered by years of roaming the desert. Her people placed special significance on artifice, on forging metal and building tools. This shared interest made Jhoira the only like-minded person he had seen in weeks. Even when Venser put Jhoira's kind nature and considerable beauty aside, her keen eye and insightful mind made her precious to him. She was the only stable thing he'd found among the chaos that surrounded them, a haven of clear, calm thinking.

Venser's eye was also drawn to the star-shaped gem Jhoira

wore on a chain around her neck. The gem was a powerstone, a crystalline battery that contained vast amounts of raw, magical energy. Venser had two similar stones in his belt pack that had powered his creations for years, but he knew that even combined his were less potent than a single facet of Jhoira's mana star.

Jhoira noticed him watching her and slowly turned to face him, taking her stern gaze away from the clamoring mob. Venser felt the wave of dizzying vertigo that always hit him when Jhoira's eyes found his. She seemed so young, at least a decade younger than Venser himself, but something in her was also old, vast, and wise. She carried herself and spoke with the confidence of a mature and experienced world traveler rather than the fresh-faced nineteen-year-old academic she appeared to be.

Now Jhoira's eyes were tired and profoundly sad. "I'm out of ideas, Venser."

Recent experience had taught Venser the value of thinking and speaking quickly. "I see two options, myself. Run or fight."

"Can't run," Jhoira said. "Corus could dive under the sand and swim rings around them, but he couldn't carry us along. We'd be overwhelmed on the surface before we take twenty steps."

"Then we fight," Venser said, without any of the confidence or conviction he knew such a statement required. He gestured at Teferi. "Can he create another barrier? Or transport us out of here?"

Jhoira's expression soured. "Possibly. But Teferi and his power are unreliable right now."

"We could try to bring him around—"

"Unreliable," Jhoira said, "in that I choose not to rely on them."

"Oh." Venser paused. "What about Corus? Does he know any spells that might help?"

"You could ask him yourself," Corus said, "because he's standing right here. And he'd answer, 'no.' I'm a frontline warrior, little builder, and we prefer to get our hands dirty."

Venser gulped slightly, but he eyed the mana star Corus wore and said, "What about that?"

Corus puffed air through his nostrils. "I never needed it. The planeswalker insisted."

"How about you, Jhoira? You've got your mana star, plus you were born and raised here. You must know some survival spells."

"I do." Jhoira smiled a little, perhaps charmed by his earnest faith in her. "But not on the scale we need to keep that lot at bay." She pointed to the feral goblins, orcs, and viashino. They were close enough now to make out distinct figures—soon, they would be close enough to do far more. "The magic here is as dried up as it is everywhere else."

"Shiv is whole now," Venser said. "And the part that came back is as fresh as it was three hundred years ago. Can't you feel it? I'm not even from here. I've never cast a spell. But even I can tell there's power here." It was true—Venser felt he was standing on a mountain as the edge of a major thunderstorm rolled past. The air was humming, and it tingled on his skin.

Jhoira's eyes sparked to life. She regarded Venser intently. "No," she said. "I don't feel anything." She turned to the viashino. "Corus?"

The big lizard shook his head. "Nothing."

Jhoira turned back to Venser. "But you do. You feel it."

Venser hesitated, unnerved by Jhoira's expression. Then he nodded.

Teferi's eyes cleared. He blinked, locked eyes with Venser, and said, "Venser's right. It surges along the boundary line. Plenty of mana for the next . . . few . . . hours . . . as it balances back out. . . ."

"Teferi," Jhoira said. The wizard's eyes rolled back up into his head, and his chin lowered once more, his jaw working as he mumbled silently.

"Hear that?" Venser said. "There's mana here. Teferi the planeswalker agrees with me." He was beaming triumphantly, but Jhoira regarded him and Teferi both as if they were merely interesting specimens on display.

"So he does. But I say again, Teferi is not reliable." She extended her hands, one each to Venser and Corus. "I may be able to protect us in the short term, but I'll need both of you to help." She gestured. "Please take my hands."

Venser eagerly stepped forward and clasped his fingers around Jhoira's palm. Corus hesitated for a moment and said, "What do you have in mind?"

"The Ghitu glass storm," Jhoira said. To Venser, she added, "A defensive spell, albeit a very aggressive one. It'll bloody them and keep them at bay, but it won't kill them."

"Unless they charge right through it," Corus said.

"In which case it will shred them," Jhoira said. "At this point that's a risk I'm willing to take."

"Seconded," Venser said. Corus hissed at him.

"I don't like Ghitu rituals," the viashino said. "They tend to consume those who perform them."

Jhoira's hand remained extended, as steady as a mountain. "I will take steps to avoid that. I mean to save us, not sacrifice us."

"And it's not like you have a better option," Venser said. "Burn up in the spell or get torn up by the mob."

Corus's tongue flicked the air. "I can escape any time I like."

"Then do so," Jhoira said, anger flaring across her elegant features, "or take my hand. But whichever you choose, do it now."

Corus hissed again, but he stepped forward and enveloped Jhoira's hand in his own.

"Should I take Teferi's hand?" Venser asked.

"Don't bother," Jhoira said. She turned her back to the wizard on the ground, forcing Venser and Corus to do the same. Jhoira raised her arms over her head, taking Venser's and Corus's hands with them, and began speaking in the throaty tones and clipped cadence of her native Ghitu tongue.

A hot wind kicked up, peppering their faces with sand. Jhoira's coarse, brown hair rose and writhed like an uncountable mass of snakes. Venser felt warmth building between his palm and Jhoira's and an unsettling internal wrench as something vital flowed from his body into hers.

Jhoira's spell sounded more like a song, a haunting melody that could echo for miles across the desert wastes. Grit swirled above the surface of the sand, a rushing river of dust and air that cut a wide arcing swath between Jhoira and the leading edge of the ragged mob.

Tiny needles of sand began to accrete inside the stream of air, each dart growing larger and longer as the wind hurled it back and forth. The stream expanded and settled into a cloud on the surface of the desert, and soon that cloud was full of long, sharp-edged diamonds of tightly packed sand. The diamonds flashed, glowing first red, then white as their fine silicate particles melted, fused, and flowed together. As these molten missiles cooled, they hardened and shattered, producing countless multifaceted shards of razor-sharp glass.

Venser wondered if the frenzied goblins and viashino even saw the cloudbank in their path. He started to voice his concern when a searing galvanic shock shot up his arm and slammed into his spine, forcing him to clench his teeth so tightly he was sure he felt them crack.

Venser's entire body went rigid as he choked on the pain. The surge ran back down his arm to his palm. He saw Jhoira through a gauzy, white haze, her body also convulsed, and her face likewise contorted. Corus had been right, and now they were all doomed— the Ghitu glass storm had consumed them after all.

Venser endured for a few moments. He registered the fact that he was still alive, and as the pain leveled off he also realized he was not going to die—at least not right now and not from Jhoira's spell. He continued to view Jhoira herself and to feel her hand in his. He also saw her struggling to regain control of her body, straining to flex her rigid muscles. Though the near-blinding agony remained, Venser quickly adjusted to it, calmly thinking through the searing sensation pressing in on his body from all sides. He needed to break the circuit somehow, to interrupt the flow of magical energy that was fueling Jhoira's spell.

Something clicked and popped between their palms, then the Ghitu woman shouted as she tore her hand from Venser's. Jhoira pulled free with such force that she staggered forward and fell. She swung toward Corus, who had not released her hand, toppling awkwardly. She barely managed to get her free arm under her in time to keep her face from hitting the sand.

Smoke curled from Corus's palm as he opened his grip. Jhoira fell heavily onto her side. She drew in a lungful of acrid air and sand, then fell into a violent fit of coughing.

The huge viashino dropped to his knees. Corus craned his long neck up, peering through double-lidded eyes at the approaching mob. When he spoke, his voice was slow and heavy. "Ghitu," he said, "what have you done?"

Venser took a step toward Jhoira, but Corus was in the way. The viashino twisted his massive head, bared his fangs, and growled at Venser. "Leave her," he said. "It's not safe."

Venser stopped. With Corus on his knees, Venser had a clear view over the viashino's massive shoulder. Jhoira crouched a mere step away from Corus, her knees curled under her as she tried to sit up. Venser looked past Jhoira, to the spot where her spell cloud and the Shivan horde had met.

The glass storm covered the desert before him, stretching out as far as he could see in all directions. It was as if the misty sky itself had descended to engulf the entire surface of northern Shiv. All of the blasted flatlands and countless rolling dunes were now hidden under a broad expanse of buzzing glass fragments, a billowing mass that rose almost a mile into the air.

Venser looked more closely and gasped. There were dozens, perhaps hundreds of shapes within the great mass of slivered crystal, vague outlines of bodies in all shapes and sizes: lean, tall viashino with their sharp scales on end, stunted goblins bearing cudgels and rocks in their stubby limbs, hulking orcs with their too-broad shoulders and comically puny heads, wedge-shaped slivers with lashing double tails.

The living shapes inside the glass storm did not maintain their discrete outlines for long. As Venser watched and the feral Shivans screamed, the wind-driven glass reduced the horde first to ragged, featureless forms, then on to a fine, red mist. This crimson tinge slowly spread across the cloud until its center shone with the soft, pink glow of a sunrise. As the last of the agonized cries faded, the brittle, crackling sound of glass striking glass continued.

Its purpose fulfilled, the storm's frenzy only increased. Venser found himself unable to do anything but stare and fight for breath.

"What have you done?" Corus spoke again, softer now.

"Not this." Jhoira still spoke through her cough. "I couldn't have. I'm not capable."

"And yet." Corus sneered. His tongue lashed angrily, and he left his accusation unfinished, allowing the nearby carnage to speak for him.

"Surges," Teferi muttered. Only the whites of his eyes showed, and he did not raise his chin. "All along the border."

Corus twisted and hissed at the wizard. "Disaster follows you, Planeswalker," he said. "I've come to expect that." He turned back to Jhoira. "But you . . . you swore to restore Shiv, to heal our homeland. And I trusted you."

"She has," Venser said. "She brought it back just as she said she would. And in case you missed it, she just saved us all. That mob would have eaten us alive. It's not her fault the mana is unstable."

"A fine welcome home," Corus spat. He reached forward and hoisted Jhoira up with both hands clamped tight on her shoulders, lifting her to his face. "Those are viashino lands," he said, gesturing to the cloud-covered region. "How many of my tribe have you just killed? How many of my own descendents just died because of your miscalculation?"

Still dazed, Jhoira did not reply. Venser spoke up quickly. "Put her down, Corus."

Corus did not move, did not even flick an eye toward Venser. "Or what?"

Venser paused, but when he spoke his voice was strong and firm. "Or you will have made an enemy for life."

The big lizard hissed. "So be it." He turned at the waist and hurled Jhoira's body high into the air, arcing directly toward the killing cloud.

Venser cried out and took one step forward, but the viashino was far too quick. Venser felt powerful, scaled hands take hold of him, followed by a dizzying rush of motion. Then he too was airborne, hurtling after Jhoira. The last thing he saw before vertigo blurred his vision was Corus's tear-streaked, grief maddened face, the viashino's lips pulled back to expose his needle-sharp teeth.

Vaguely aware of tumbling as he fell, Venser heard Corus cursing Teferi. Then Venser's head broke through the surface of the cloud and the glass storm swallowed him whole.

CHAPTER 2

Jhoira woke to the piercing screech of glass shredding glass. She had the presence of mind to keep her eyes firmly shut as full consciousness returned, but her teeth clenched involuntarily against the awful sound. Her back molars crunched down on grains of sand, which sent sharp needles of pain up through her jaw.

She held perfectly still as she assessed herself. She had landed awkwardly on her shoulders and back, but her spine and skull were intact. Her legs were sore and twisted painfully beneath her. She started to see how deeply she could inhale, but a sharp, shooting pain through her right shoulder stopped her cold. Jhoira tried to flex the fingers on her right hand, noting with some concern that the arm itself was cold and numb. The fingers only twitched at first, but then they curled under her palm. Jhoira said a silent prayer of thanks for the layer of sandy grit that collected beneath her fingernails. Calmly, deliberately, she opened her eyes.

A clear bubble of empty space surrounded her, stretching three feet out from her body in all directions. The air seethed and vibrated as the deadly fragments dashed themselves into ever smaller and sharper pieces. Jhoira saw river-wide currents competing for the right of way and larger, almost tidal, surges of crystalline dust rising high overhead. The glass storm still raged, but she was safe inside this artificial eye, this perfect sphere of stillness and calm.

At least that much of her spell had functioned properly. For

Corus's concerns and in case they themselves needed to break through the barrier she was creating, Jhoira had defined the swarm of sharp-edged crystal as one that would never harm them. The very magic that animated the sand also spared Jhoira, Venser, and Corus from its fury.

Jhoira slowly sat up, scowling at the irony. The safeguards Corus inspired her to include actually saved them from Corus. She gritted her teeth again, sending a new volley of pain through her jaw. Jhoira turned her head and spat to clear the last of the sand from her palate and she struggled to her feet. The clear space around her folded and bubbled as she moved to keep the edge of the storm safely at bay.

The storm's undiminished strength brought on a momentary rush of dread. Teferi had not been part of the ritual and so was not protected from it. His titanic magical capabilities had been fluctuating wildly of late—able to patch a hole in reality one moment but succumbing to a fist-sized rock the next. If Corus threw the planeswalker into the storm cloud after Venser and herself, Jhoira realized her old friend might already be dead.

Damn Teferi anyway. She had to exclude him from the ritual—his ongoing deceptions and omissions, the unpredictable results of his magic, and his current semiconscious state made him ineligible, even dangerous, for most Ghitu rituals. Jhoira had more than enough lives on her conscience from this fiasco, and if Teferi had also been vaporized by flying grit he had no one to blame but himself.

Jhoira paused to get her bearings. She peered into the swirling mass of facets and dust but was unable to tell north from south. Jhoira knelt down on one knee and pressed her palm into the tightly packed sand. Shiv still felt the same to her, unchanged from the moment she set foot on it, despite all that had been done and undone since then. The continent's missing half had returned, restored from three hundred years in a timeless, formless state.

A disruptive tear in time and space had been sealed. Teferi had seemingly exhausted his magical power, and now Jhoira had covered a significant portion of her homeland in a lethal, buzzing shroud. Yet Shiv still felt the same.

Venser spoke of mana here, and Teferi mumbled about surges, yet neither she nor Corus, the native Shivans, sensed any such thing. She knew the world was different from what it had been yesterday because she had seen it change with her own eyes. Shiv had been halved and was now whole. The time rift had been draining the nation's magical energy, and that drain had been plugged.

Why wasn't there any evidence of the change in the land itself? Beyond her memories, where was the proof? Why didn't Shiv's heartbeat grow stronger in her breast, or weaker, or change its endless, rumbling rhythm? Had her innate connection to the land had been stymied, blunted, perhaps even severed?

"Jhoira?" Venser's voice was faint, barely audible over the buzzing and crackling of the glass. Jhoira heard the anxiety in his tone nonetheless.

"Here," she called, her voice still thick from coughing. "Follow the sound of my voice."

She regretted all the young man had endured since they met him, but Venser had been part of the great riddle even before she undertook its solution. So far he had attracted the attentions of two godlike planeswalkers simply by being born and raised in the shadow of a major time rift.

Though Jhoira and Teferi had traveled halfway around the globe they had encountered only two natives of Dominaria who were innately connected to the time rift phenomenon, two beings whose magic was somehow rooted in the underlying structure of the cosmos rather than in the soil of the nations that bore them. The first was Radha, a barbarian warrior from the wilds of Keld. She wielded primal magic from the rift and used it to forge her own unique link to her homeland, becoming a living, functioning part of this world's mana flow. The other such being was Venser, who so far had evidenced no magical ability or interest beyond building his arcane machinery.

"Jhoira? What's going on?" Venser said. "Why isn't the glass cutting me?"

"Follow the sound of my voice," Jhoira said again.

"I will. But you have to keep talking."

Jhoira began to recite the alphabet in her native Ghitu, pronouncing each syllable in the same cadence she had learned as a small girl. Her voice grew louder as her throat cleared and her lungs filled once more to capacity.

Venser had no natural affinity for magic and no spell training, yet he could read the state of Shiv's mana better than she. He had no magic, but he had been seized by an ancient planeswalking dragon and used to open an doorway between worlds. No magic, yet he contributed to the glass storm that went so wildly out of control.

Venser had no magic, but his presence continued to have a clear and undeniable magical impact.

As she continued to recite, Jhoira stood perfectly still and assessed their situation as thoroughly as she had earlier assessed her own body. Their mission was far from over. The Shivan rift was only the first and most pressing of the time fissure phenomena, and sealing it had almost destroyed them all. Thus far they had been following Teferi's lead, but now the planeswalker was injured and exhausted. They were stranded in the middle of Shiv with no means of getting out, and so far the entire desert had proven to be hostile territory. If the heat and the fumes and the volcanic activity didn't kill them, the local goblins, orcs, and viashino seemed more than up to the task.

Jhoira unconsciously raised her hand to cup around her lips and winced as new pain shot through her dislocated shoulder. Hot tears welled up in her eyes, and she growled a withering curse.

"Jhoira?" Venser said. He sounded very close. "Are you all right?"

"I'm fine." She spat the words through clenched teeth. "You're almost here. Keep moving." Jhoira's voice trailed off, but her thoughts continued to address Venser.

Pace yourself, my friend. We've a very long way to go.

* * * * *

Venser woke up from visions of being trapped inside a wide bolt of lightning. The energy surged and crackled all around him, though Venser himself remained fixed in place. He felt the bolt as if it were his body, head in the clouds and feet plunging deep into the ground below.

Once his vision cleared and he saw his predicament, Venser relaxed. Compared to the larger list of painful things that he had recently experienced but didn't understand, this barely registered. He didn't give a second thought to the strange bubble of safety around him. It was currently keeping him alive, so Venser decided not to ponder it too deeply for fear of undoing it.

He paused to consider how much he hated the sights and sounds of the glass storm, especially from his current position. The noise punished his eardrums like a rusty tool, and the flickering edges of innumerable glass flakes tired his eyes. He had an excellent sense of direction, but in this morass he was as lost and adrift as a rudderless ship.

He called out for Jhoira. He took a few steps forward. The bubble seemed to move with him, so he wasn't obliged to stay where he landed. He called again, louder.

On the fifth call, Jhoira responded. Her voice raised both relief and new anxiety, for she was alive but sounded weary, even beaten. As bad as the past few days had been for Venser, he realized they had been even worse for Jhoira. It was her home that had been threatened, and her fellow citizens who had abandoned her and attacked her.

Venser drifted through the glass storm toward the sound of Jhoira's voice. He went astray numerous times until she began ticking off a series of foreign-sounding words in sequence. Venser honed in on the singsong jumble of unfamiliar syllables until it seemed they were coming from only a few feet in front of him.

Then the leading edge of Venser's protective bubble broke the surface of Jhoira's. He almost shouted with joy, but his revelry was ruined by the sight of her. Her landing had been rougher than his—Jhoira's right arm hung awkward and lifeless from her shoulder, and her youngish features were creased with tension and pain. She was half-covered in Shivan grit and half-snarling the words of her song through clenched teeth.

She noticed Venser immediately but kept speaking. Jhoira's face seemed haggard and lifeless as he approached and the glass storm curved around the rounded mass of their shared safety zones.

"Jhoira—" Venser began, but she raised her left hand to silence him.

"I need your help," she said, and Venser quietly thrilled to her words. So far he hadn't been able to offer her anything more than moral support. If she had a task for him to do, he meant to do it quickly and well, if only to repay her for all the times she had saved his life in the past few days.

"Anything," he said.

Jhoira nodded curtly and turned her right side to face Venser. "My shoulder is dislocated," she said, "and there's no wall nearby. I need you to take hold of my wrist and stand firm." She gestured with her right shoulder, which sent a ripple of pain across her face.

Crestfallen, Venser stepped forward and gingerly took hold of Jhoira's wrist. He had hoped to be of more use than as a wall, a second-choice wall at that, but concern for Jhoira's obvious pain quickly blotted out his wounded pride.

"Tighter." Jhoira grimaced as Venser clenched his fist. Then, with a sudden surge of motion, she drove her wounded shoulder hard into Venser's chest.

He was glad she had told him to brace, because otherwise she would have knocked him off his feet. Her shoulder cracked loudly, and Jhoira shouted. Venser reflexively let go of her arm, and the Ghitu woman fell to her knees once more, supporting herself with her stronger left arm.

Deliberately, Jhoira lifted her right arm and flexed each of her fingers in sequence, strumming the air like a master musician. She clenched her fist tight and all of her knuckles popped.

Jhoira refused Venser's offered hand and stood up. "Thank you," she said, though her eyes were still clouded and vacant.

"What is going on here?" Venser said. He waved his arms at the swirling glass that surrounded them. "Why aren't we dead?"

"I made sure the spell could not harm us," she said. She brushed some desert dust from her clothes. "Though I didn't imagine we'd need it this badly."

Venser paused. "Will Corus come after us?"

Jhoira shook her head. "Doubtful. I think he's long gone. He may have stopped to murder Teferi, but I think he dived into the sand and is already halfway back to his tribe by now."

Venser exhaled. "That's good." He blinked. "Can Corus murder Teferi? He's a planeswalker."

"I'm not sure what Teferi is anymore." Jhoira's expression and tone were miserable. "But if a goblin's rock can split Teferi's head open, a fighting-mad viashino can do much worse."

"Fair enough," Venser said. "What about us?" He glanced around at the razor flakes and fragments. "How do we get out of here?"

"We walk," Jhoira said.

"Through the storm?

"Through the storm and the desert beyond. Shiv may have

changed a great deal since I was last here, but there are always huge tracts of open ground to cover." She smiled grimly. "We Ghitu spend our whole lives walking across the desert."

Venser was gratified to see Jhoira smile, but he said, "Where will we go? How will we get out of here? How will I get home?"

"I have a theory."

"But what—" Jhoira raised her left hand again and Venser fell silent.

"The storm has edges," she said. "It's finite. Step one is to get clear of the glass."

Venser nodded but did not speak.

Jhoira's eyes cleared somewhat and she fixed them on Venser. "What do you remember about the storm spell?"

"Not much," he admitted. "I felt your hand and a lot of pressure. There was a surge of energy between us. I thought you wanted me to let go, so I tried, but my fingers didn't work." He shrugged. "Either you pulled free on your own or my numb hand slipped."

Jhoira nodded, but her face was unconvinced. "And you felt Shiv's mana even before I cast the spell."

Venser nodded.

"I didn't let go of your hand," Jhoira said. "It seemed to me that your hand . . . vanished from my grip."

"Vanished?"

She nodded. "Right when I needed it to. You were right, by the way. I did want you to let go."

"What does it all mean?" Venser hated the helpless, confused timbre in his voice, but it was all he had to give.

Jhoira closed her eyes slightly and paused. Venser waited silently, barely breathing, until she opened her eyes again.

"It's just a theory," she said, "but I believe there's something about you that is interacting with the mana here. Maybe it's the fact that you're carrying two powerstones in your pack, but I think it's something else, something internal. It's the same thing that made

Teferi come looking for you in Urborg, and it's probably why Nicol Bolas used you and Radha to break through to this world. But we don't have to know exactly what it is to put it to good use. We just have to be cautious, more cautious than we have been so far."

"I don't have much in common with Radha." Venser said. The barbarian warrior was a wild creature of violent action who wreathed herself in fire and menace. He, on the other hand, was little more than an academic tinkerer from a gloomy swamp.

Jhoira went on as if he hadn't spoken. "Radha had a strong connection to the rift phenomenon. We should assume you do as well, even though it's not as apparent." She interlaced her fingers and stretched her arms out in front of her. "Elder dragons don't take interest in humans without good cause."

Venser experienced a wave of anxiety at the memory. "I see. But how does that help us?"

Jhoira stepped closer to him, so close that he could see the individual grains of sand on her cheek. She smelled sweet and sharp, like the first wafts of smoke from a cooking fire. "Teferi said there were mana surges along the border where the pieces of Shiv came back together. If you can follow that border, you can lead us out of here."

"How? I don't know anything about mana or spells."

"But I do." Jhoira extended her right arm. "Take my hand."

Venser quickly obliged. There was no crackle or surge this time, only the warmth and supple texture of Jhoira's skin. The Ghitu slowly brought her other hand up and whispered softly. Venser heard a sizzling sound just before a foot-high pillar of flame erupted from Jhoira's upturned palm.

"Hold tight," she said. She shuffled her feet through the sand, slowly pivoting in place. Venser stepped with her, circling the Ghitu, his attention split between the fiery column and his friend's intent expression.

Jhoira completed a full circle, then shifted back. Venser noted that the flame expanded and contracted as they turned, flaring up at times and dropping off at others. Jhoira turned back in the opposite direction, stepping left, then right, until she had isolated the point where the flame was brightest.

"Don't let go," Jhoira said. "This spell is supposed to produce a minor spark, little more than a match flame. Something is making it stronger, and it doesn't really matter if it's you or the mana surges. Either way, we can use this as a pathfinder."

Venser started to speak, but the sensations he was feeling pushed all other thoughts out of his head. He did feel something as they completed their circuit, an ambience that intensified in perfect sync with the flame in Jhoira's hand.

"So," she said, "if you're ready, we should go."

"I'm ready," he said. He turned his head back behind them. "Are you sure this is the right direction?"

"No," she said. "But we have a one-in-two chance of being right." She treated him to a dazzling smile. "Are you feeling lucky?"

Venser laughed out loud. "I've never had so much luck," he said. "All bad, of course, but . . . yes. I do feel lucky."

"Then we go." Jhoira stepped out in front of Venser, her arm trailing behind her, her hand locked in his

Together, step by painstaking step, they moved through the swirling cloud of glass behind the flickering beacon in Jhoira's outstretched hand.

* * * * *

Hours later, Venser saw Jhoira's flame break through the outer edge of the storm cloud. From where he stood behind her, Venser had a clear tunnel-view over her shoulder and out into the Shivan wastes. He knew he'd never again be this happy to see an endless expanse of blasted, featureless desert.

They emerged from the glass storm like a bubble surfacing in porridge. The glass still buzzed and whirled around them as they exited, and Venser noted the safe zone around them remained until they were entirely clear.

Jhoira's flame-compass had kept them on a steady heading every step of the way. They had also guessed correctly about the direction and so were now almost precisely back at the spot where they'd left Teferi.

Peering into the bright haze of midmorning, Venser saw the bald planeswalker on a distant dune. Teferi sat cross-legged in the sand with his back to them, but he appeared to be intact and conscious. There was no sign of Corus.

"Venser," Jhoira said, "you can let go now." She turned her head and smiled patiently at him.

"I know," he said. "Do I have to?"

She gave his hand a reassuring squeeze and pulled free. "Stage one," she said, "is complete. Now for the real challenges." Without waiting for Venser to reply, Jhoira strode forward toward Teferi's dune. Venser rushed to catch up and fell into step alongside her.

Teferi made no sign he heard their approach. Venser noted that the wizard's bald head was still bleeding, and it bobbed slightly as Teferi spoke to himself.

"Don't step there," Jhoira said. She gestured to patch of sand near Teferi that had been fused into an irregular sheet of glass. Venser was tempted to step closer and examine it, but Jhoira was making straight for Teferi.

She stopped a few paces short of the dark-skinned wizard and folded her arms. Oblivious, Teferi continued to bob until she said sharply, "Teferi. Get up, old friend. It's time to go back to work."

Teferi's head slowed. He craned his head back over his shoulder and fixed his wide, vacant eyes on the pair.

"Hello," he said. "Where have you two been?"

"Corus attacked us," Jhoira said. "Drove us off. It took time to find our way back."

"Good, good." Teferi turned back toward the sand in front of him. "No harm done, I take it?"

Jhoira's lips curled back over her teeth. "A great deal of harm, actually. Now if you've recovered from your headache, you need to get up and help set it right."

"Recovered?" Teferi rocked forward and almost lost his balance. He made his unsteady way to his feet and turned to face them. "I feel fine, thank you for asking. A bit dizzy, maybe . . . "

"Where is Corus?" Venser said. He kept glancing back at the small pondlike patch of glass, scanning around it for signs of a warrior lurking below the sand.

"Who?" Teferi struck a pose, attempting to lean on a staff that he did not have. He overbalanced and stumbled, but he stayed on his feet.

Jhoira stepped in and peered deeply into Teferi's eyes. "Corus," she said softly, "the last of our retainers. He was in a murderous rage when we left. Did he try to harm you?"

"Hm? Oh, no. I think I heard him shouting about his mana star and something being all my fault. But I didn't hear him clearly." His unfocused eyes wavered. "I assume he left when I didn't reply."

"Jhoira." Venser's curiosity had gotten the best of him, and he now stood on the edge of the glass pond. "You should see this."

He wasn't sure if the irritation in her face was due to the interruption or Teferi's maddening detachment. She paused, apparently considering another rejoinder to the planeswalker but instead came over to Venser.

Venser pointed, unsure how to prepare Jhoira for what she was about to see. The fused chunk of glass wasn't simply a plate on the surface of the sand but a broad chunk of crystal that sank deep into the ground. The view through it was murky and unclear, but Venser could definitely see the broken remains of a mana star embedded in the crystal column.

Corus was suspended inside the crystal just below the mana star. His arms and legs were spread wide, frozen in place, and his powerful jaws were opened in either pain or anger. Half of the viashino's outer scales were missing, exposing the raw muscles and nerves beneath. The rest of his body was charred almost black by unimaginably intense heat.

Venser's hand shot to his belt, to the pouch where he kept his own powerstones. They were inexhaustible batteries but were perfectly safe and reliable as long as they were intact. He inspected his stones daily, searching for cracks and stress fractures that could lead to an explosive release of energy. Venser had only calculated the devastating results of such an event, but Corus seemed to have actually experienced it. If the viashino had vented his fury on the mana star instead of Teferi, if he had cracked the stone in his powerful hands, he had killed himself as surely as if he'd climbed into a dragon's jaws.

Jhoira stood and stared. Except for a slight hitch in her breathing when she first stepped up, she did not react at all to the grisly scene.

"Corus," she said sadly. Then, louder, without turning toward Teferi, she added, "What happened here?"

Teferi started and swooned a bit as he turned toward her. His blank expression was entirely guileless. "What happened where?"

Jhoira huffed angrily through both nostrils, and Venser quickly spoke up before she lashed out. "Corus is dead," Venser said. "He ruptured his mana star and it killed him."

"Oh my." Teferi took a step toward them, staggering slightly. "He shouldn't have done that."

Jhoira stomped her heel down on the surface of the glass chunk, cursing in Ghitu. The fact that the glass did not crack seemed to magnify her rage.

"New plan," she said. She stepped close to Venser, and her voice dropped. "We have no means of getting off Shiv without Teferi's help. So we're going to have to help ourselves."

"Really? How?"

Jhoira's lip curled again. "We're going to build our way out."

Venser felt another small thrill. Building was something he could understand, something he could contribute. "When do we start?"

"Right away." As she spoke Jhoira loosened her outer robes.

"Here?"

"No. We've got more walking to do." Jhoira slipped out of her outfit's outermost layer, stretched it tight between her hands, and tore the square bolt of fabric in half. The Ghitu native offered half of it to Venser, who silently took it.

Jhoira stepped away and wrapped the other section of cloth around Teferi's bald head, shielding his face from the wind and sun. She motioned for Venser to do the same.

"We are two days' hike from Ghitu territory," she said. "If we can avoid being swallowed by the desert or savaged by its creatures, I can take us to safety and find us a place to work." She paused, and her face softened at Venser's clearly dubious expression. "Don't worry," she said. "It may not look like much, but my people know where to find Shiv's resources. All we have to do is find my people."

Venser was not heartened. "And they'll help us?"

"Perhaps," she said. "But even if they don't, they won't attack us. They may even give us a safe place to stay while we plan our next move."

Venser nodded toward Teferi and whispered, "What about him?" Shrouded by Jhoira's cloak, Teferi was a faceless cipher swaying in the sandy breeze.

Jhoira turned back toward her old friend, then faced Venser once more. "We'll bring him along," she said. "When his mind clears—if it clears—I will demand a fuller account of what happened to Corus."

Venser paled. As he tucked the ends of his makeshift turban into his collar, he decided that he never wanted Jhoira to speak of him with the same venom she now employed, with the same expression she now wore when she spoke of Teferi. For Venser hated being thought of as a liar, and, more, he feared the repercussions if his lies caused Jhoira to lose faith in him.

"Let's go," the Ghitu woman said. Venser wasn't sure if she was talking to him, or Teferi, or both of them together.

Without another word, the two men assembled behind Jhoira, and the strange trio marched off into the wasteland.

CHAPTER 3

Venser developed an entirely new level of respect for Jhoira as they hiked. She showed no signs of being affected by the heat. In fact, she repeatedly told him that it was far cooler than normal. She talked about days- and even weeks-long treks through the desert, comparing their current journey to a Ghitu child's aimless wandering. After only a few hours on his feet, Venser believed not only that Shiv was killing him but that it was doing so actively and aggressively, because it hated him and wanted him dead.

The late afternoon sun was not even visible through the hazy ceiling of clouds, but it punished Venser with every step he took. Hot, salty sweat ran into his eyes, which were almost swollen shut. The native cloth Jhoira provided hung limp across his face and the back of his neck, soaked through and crusted with windblown sand. When its corners brushed against his skin, they seared as if they'd been steeped in bleach. The cloth kept most of the larger sand particles away from his breathing passages, but it didn't protect him from the stinging pain as grit blew across his body. Even through his clothes, Venser felt he was being skinned alive one layer at a time.

They had nothing to eat or drink, and his stomach was starting to cramp from hunger. Not that Venser could taste anything anyway—his mouth and throat were coated with dust. As awful as that was, it was actually preferable to breathing the volcanic fumes and stale, hot air that clung to the surface of the sand like a fog bank.

Feverish, his mind began to wander. He had been solitary in the marshes of Urborg for most of his life, yet here in this place and in this company he felt more alone than ever. Except for Jhoira, every native he had met in this alien landscape had tried to kill him. Jhoira, who so far had been kind and patient and communicative, was now completely consumed by determination. She hadn't spoken in hours, and when she had it had been to shush him. "Every time you exhale you lose water," she said. She led them not as a guide, or as a member of the party, but as a stern taskmaster whose every body posture said, "I will leave you behind if you lag."

Teferi, for his part, was still half-besotted from his injury. The planeswalker muttered as he brought up the rear. Venser strained to hear Teferi over the wind but was rewarded only with barely audible, incoherent gibberish.

Jhoira stopped. Venser might have bumped into her if he'd had any strength left in his stride.

"Slag it," she said.

"Who?" Venser croaked. He tried to blink, but his eyes were too dry. He saw Jhoira turn, with both fresh concern and fresh annoyance in her face.

"Stop here," she said. "You're about to black out." She put her hand on Venser's shoulders and eased him seat-first onto the ground. Venser allowed her to position him without complaint or resistance, as pliable as an infant.

"There used to be a spring." Jhoira's breath danced across his ear, tickling slightly, but her voice sounded miles away. "I don't know why I thought it would still be here." She sighed.

Venser fought to open his eyes. The wind eased up, and he heard Jhoira sharply call Teferi's name. Unable to see what mischief the dazed wizard had uncovered, Venser simply stopped trying. His eyes fluttered as they closed, and he felt himself falling.

He never landed. Venser's languorous descent continued long after his face should have hit the sand. Dreaming or dying, he thought, and either is better than another moment in this damnable desert.

"Venser!" Now Jhoira's strident tone was aimed at him. He no longer cared. He would simply continue to fall, to drop out of this world and into the next.

Strong, small hands took hold of his shoulders and shook him until his teeth rattled. The veil that had descended over his eyes did not lift, but he heard Jhoira's voice more clearly than ever.

"Hang on," she barked. "Rest. Stay with us another hour, maybe two. Once the sun starts to set, the heat and the wind will die off. We can look for water then."

"Water," Venser agreed. He would say anything to get those hands to release him, to drift once more. Shiv hated him. Shiv was killing him. You win, he thought. Venser yields to Almighty Shiv. Just let me leave here and never come back.

His wish was partially granted when Jhoira cried out for Teferi once more. Her iron fingers disappeared from Venser's shoulders, and he heard running footsteps in the sand. His moment had passed, however. Jhoira had shaken him out of his lethargy enough to trap him painfully between half-consciousness and complete oblivion.

With an agonizing pop, Venser forced his eyelids to open. He saw Jhoira trying to keep Teferi in a sitting position, but the planeswalker was still struggling to rise. Venser caught glimpses of Teferi's face under the shroudlike cloth he wore and wondered if he looked as desperate and clumsy as the planeswalker.

A few more hours, Jhoira said. They could look for water when the heat leveled off. Until then . . . what? Were they to sit here and bake in the evening sun?

A tiny mote of irritation began to grow in Venser's mind. He was little more than a passenger on this journey, "luggage," as Radha called him. He had followed Teferi, who led them to death, betrayal, and failure at every stop. He had followed Jhoira, who led him to a massacre of broken glass before leading him out into the desert to die. He was tired of following. He was tired of putting his life in others' hands only to be shocked at how carelessly they carried it.

They didn't need him. Teferi was a god . . . or at least had been like a god until he sealed the Shivan rift. Jhoira didn't seem to need anyone, and if Venser's suspicions were correct it was only her benevolent nature that prevented her from abandoning them and making her own way across the wastes. She would certainly have a better chance of survival without two helpless, addle-pated children to look after. Radha was right, Venser realized: he *was* luggage.

And yet . . . Jhoira said there was something special about him, and Teferi had said the same. These two, who lived on a grand scale and shared a purpose no less than the salvation of the entire world, came to him, had sought him out. Could he abandon Jhoira as Radha and the others had? Could he turn on her as savagely as Corus or fail her as utterly as Teferi?

Venser struggled to hold himself upright. The irritation within him grew, expanding from a tiny speck to a towering monument. He could not let this happen. He could not become another disappointment to Jhoira. He would not allow himself to be mere luggage.

Venser coughed, sucked in sand, and coughed again. He forced his eyes to open and shut twice more. He reached out and dug his hand deep into the sand, ignoring the searing sensation that enveloped his fingers. He sank his other hand into the ground and pulled, clawing his way onto his knees. Fresh beads of sweat popped from his forehead, and he paused to catch his breath, his lips mere inches from the surface of the sand.

As he gathered his strength to stand again, Venser heard a subtle hissing. It was hard to pinpoint the sound, but it seemed to be rising from the ground directly beneath his face.

Sleep now, a serpentine whisper said. *Rest.*

A pungent odor rose to his nostrils, and Venser's vision fogged. The voice and the scent seemed reptilian to him, cold-blooded and razor-scaled. He had been beset by serpents too often of late, from Madaran cat-dragons to Nicol Bolas to Shiv's rabid viashino. Snakes, dragons, and lizards were common in the swamps he called home, but they were the norm in this blasted place.

Sleep now. Rest.

Venser started. He was back in Madara, on the shores overlooking the Talon Gates. The dragon Bolas was there, incorporeal but deadlier than an exploding star. Bolas had swayed Venser with magic and sheer force of personality. Bolas had lulled him with honeyed words, then used Venser as both door and doormat, tearing through his body like a boulder through a garden hose without a single thought to the damage being done.

This new sinister, soothing voice did not weaken Venser's resolve or his concentration but sharpened it. He was a native of Urborg, he reminded himself, where black magic was plentiful and mindwalking villains whispered nightly their poison promises in the dreams of the unwary. He had a deep-seated dread of telepathic communication, for in the fens a disembodied voice was more dangerous than an arrow in flight.

Venser opened his eyes. His vision cleared. He was still crouched on all fours, his chin almost touching the ground. Before him, a small, scaled creature rose up from the sand, no longer than Venser's hand. A proud crest of fibrous scales crowned the tiny monster's head, a vivid cockscomb that Venser recognized all too well.

Venser shut his eyes immediately before they met the basilisk's. The creatures were deadly, even at this size. The slightest touch, the briefest glance would mean the end of him. He pitched himself backward, preferring to break his own clumsy neck rather than harden into stone or dissolve into rot where he stood. He was lucky in that he was able to roll away from the creature, turning a backward somersault and kicking up a spray of stinging sand.

"Venser?" Jhoira called. He waved her away and threw himself back again, completing another backward somersault as he shouted, "Stay back! Basilisk!"

"Venser?"

Lightning tore through him, searing his nerves as they radiated out from his spine. Thunder rumbled in his skull, and for a strange, blissful second, the heat and the sand and the stench of Shiv disappeared. Venser felt himself floating once more, only this was a truly physical sensation as well as fatigue-based delirium. Then Venser was back, his knees and palms plowing down into the loose sand.

"Venser!" Jhoira's voice was still distant. But now it was to his left and in front of him rather than behind to his right. His heart pounding, Venser forgot about exhaustion and thirst for the first time in over a day, and he saw Shiv as clearly as if he'd just woken from an afternoon nap. Teferi and Jhoira were now in front of him, both watching him with something like amazement.

"Get away," he said. He jumped up. "Don't even look. There's a basilisk in the sand. It tried to hypnotize me."

But Jhoira was not interested in the basilisk. Her face was fixed on Venser, now many yards away, and her expression was a strange fusion of shock and exhilaration.

"Tell me if it moves," she said. Without turning from Venser, Jhoira carefully unwound a length of her robes. She twisted the end and popped it in her mouth, somehow moistening it with her saliva. Venser experienced a momentary pang of jealousy amid his panic—he didn't have enough spit to dampen a cotton swab—but he held perfectly still and watched the basilisk from the corner of his eye as Jhoira wound the cloth into a tight, needle-sharp spiral.

Still fixed on Venser, Jhoira pricked up her ears, paused, and cracked the twisted piece of cloth like a whip. Venser saw a puff of sand and heard a short, pained hiss. Jhoira instantly jerked her makeshift whip back to her side, casting two tiny scaled legs and a bleeding cockscomb high into the air.

"That was impressive," Teferi said, but as soon as he did his attention drifted off into the sky.

"I tumbled." Venser shrugged at Jhoira helplessly. "Is that how Shivans deal with venomous reptiles?"

The Ghitu beauty smiled, her brilliant white teeth gleaming. "Since I was young," she said. "You learn to strike without looking." She shook out the cloth and redraped it across her shoulders.

"So," she said, her eyes bright. "How did you get way over there?"

Venser started to answer, to tell Jhoira he had no idea, but a shrill call floated over the dunes from the west. It sounded like yet another war cry, an announcement that more hostility was headed their way.

Venser turned. Sure enough, there on the dunes to the west stood a dozen or more Ghitu warriors. They were dressed in brilliant, red cloth and each carried hand-tooled weapons of wood and metal. Their dark skin made them ominous, featureless shadows in the fading sunlight, but Venser could see they each bore goat-skins and clay bottles on their belts.

"Water," he whispered. Momentarily forgotten, the exhaustion and fatigue came back fivefold, and Venser's knees almost buckled.

Jhoira called out in her native language, her joy evident in every syllable. The dour troop did not respond at all to her greeting. Doubt crept across her face, and she glanced at Venser.

A burly Ghitu man stepped forward with a sicklelike blade in his hand. He extended the blade over his head and shouted, and it burst into flame. In response, the entire squadron also drew their weapons. Swords, daggers, batons, all of their tools were raised high and ignited.

The leader growled something to Jhoira. She straightened, fixed him with a withering glare, and replied with a long, eloquent series of words that ended with her own name.

The man hesitated. The others with him muttered. Finally, the leader replied, though less forcefully, and Venser recognized the word "Phyrexian."

Jhoira laughed. "Phyrexian?" she said. She crossed her arms and shook her scolding head. She threw her arm out toward the bald wizard and said something in Ghitu that ended with a specially emphasized word.

"Teferi," she said. Then she crouched, scooped up a half-handful of sand, and held it out so the grains ran through her clenched fist.

"Shiv," she said, and she slipped her free hand under the stream to catch it in her upturned palm. With an exaggerated flourish, Jhoira slipped the handful of sand into her sleeve, then immediately brought her hand out empty.

"Planeswalker." Jhoira drew her empty hand into her sleeve, paused, and brought out a handful of sand.

The Ghitu warriors began to chatter among themselves. Venser didn't think they were impressed by Jhoira's sleight of hand so much as with the story she told. Their leader certainly didn't enjoy being treated like a child, but even he seemed to be weighing the information Jhoira provided.

She turned to Venser. "They thought we were Phyrexian infiltrators." She smiled, expressing all the ease and confidence Venser wished he felt. "I've just told them the war is over."

Jhoira's name was on the warrior's lips, and it quickly spread through their ranks. Her name became a question and an answer, rapidly achieving the rhythm of a chant. They called for her, shouted her name, and howled with the delight of soldiers relieved of duty after a long campaign. The leader scowled at Jhoira, but he raised his weapon, barked out her name, and dropped to one knee.

The rest of his tribe quickly followed so that only Jhoira, Venser, and Teferi remained upright, though Venser wasn't sure how much longer he would remain that way.

"We made it," Jhoira called. She took several steps closer to Venser, scanning his face. "You need water and about five hours of uninterrupted sleep before we can get started."

Venser smiled weakly. "Started on what?"

"Your machine," she said. Her eyes were wide and vibrant. "We Ghitu are builders. And we're going to help you rebuild your ambulator."

* * * * *

Some time later, a second basilisk came across the remains of its cousin, which Jhoira had killed. Familial relations were not warm among these miserable little beasts, and it was more than happy to consume the edible remains of its distant relative.

The ground sizzled under the tiny lizard's claws. It knew it had to keep moving or the sand beneath its feet would liquefy. It skittered across the surface of the dunes, leaving strange scratches in the sand. As it approached the ragged cockscomb and a bit of tail, it lashed at the morsels with its spiky tongue.

The basilisk went rigid as its appendage brushed against its intended meal. A thin veneer of frost raced up its tongue and flowed over the length of its entire body, encasing the monster in a sheathe of frozen dust.

The last thing the basilisk heard was a breathy, almost giddy voice that seemed to vibrate up from the scavenged remains.

Almost, the voice said. *But not enough. No worries, though, eh? We'll try again . . . won't we, my little friends? We'll have to try again. We'll have to try again soon.*

The frozen basilisks remained silent and powder white until morning, when the first rays of sunrise turned the frost straight into steam.

CHAPTER 4

The next few weeks were one of the most productive and rewarding periods in Jhoira's long, storied life. At last she was back among her people and surrounded by the familiar sights, sounds, and practices of an active Ghitu society. She saw whole families, alive and unaffected by either Phyrexian plague or three centuries of desperate subsistence living. She toured working forges and foundries, consulted her elders and peers among the tribe's elite artificers, and dined on the robust food and drink her extended family had wrung from Shiv's hard, unforgiving soil. For the first time since the Phyrexian Invasion, Jhoira allowed herself the luxury of believing she and Teferi had done the right thing. Removing a portion of Shiv to protect it had worked, at least for the Shivans who came with it. The evidence was alive and thriving all around her.

Jhoira did not revel in this partial success but rather let it inspire her to do more. She had not helped preserve this community from one global catastrophe to let it fall to another, more universal one.

The local tribe that took them in were excellent hosts. After centuries in this brutal environment, they had mastered the art of resurrecting the desert's victims. Venser and Teferi were both ministered to by the tribe's healers and shaman, and it only took a few days in bed and a steady diet of a thick, herbal broth to get the rest of her party back on their feet.

Once the immediate danger had passed, Jhoira threw herself into her work. She pushed Venser and the elders to collaborate on the only project that made sense: rebuilding Venser's teleportation device. They had too much ground to cover by any available physical or magical means. With a working ambulator they could continue their survey of the time rift phenomena and execute whatever strategy they came up with.

There was resistance to her idea, both from the elders and Venser. The Ghitu argued about what that strategy would be and if they should have it in place before they committed to the labor. It was also difficult getting the elders to abandon Teferi as an option—the planeswalker still commanded a great deal of respect from the tribe.

Jhoira knew it was her reputation that swayed them as much as as much as the strength of her opinions. The Ghitu valued knowledge and prided themselves on sharing it with each other through their rich oral histories. Jhoira was one of their own, only with a thousand years more experience and learning. She also knew the time-honored histories better than they did and could recite them as perfectly as a master storyteller by a roaring fire. Between Jhoira's arguments and Teferi's continuing detachment and semidazed state, the elders relented, and the project was soon underway.

Venser provided a different kind of challenge. The Urborg artificer was visibly uncomfortable sharing his secrets, which had required decades of trial and error development to unlock. To Venser, who had always worked alone, the Ghitu style of close, personal collaboration was completely alien, even uncomfortable. Jhoira's energy and encouragement quickly overwhelmed his hermetic leanings, however, and she prodded him to expound on his essential design theories at length in front of the stone-faced elder council. Later, after Venser saw the elders' genuine and immediate enthusiasm, he told her she must have translated his theories and presented them far more eloquently than he ever had.

Jhoira put him straight to work, sitting him down with some of the keenest minds and quickest hands the tribe had to offer. They spent a week debating, drafting, and finalizing a blueprint that filtered Venser's machine through the local resources and the Ghitu's long history of elegant design and efficient function. Venser came to her again after this artificers' summit and confessed that his machine had taken huge strides forward just from the collaboration so far. He also admitted he felt like a fraud whenever he issued instructions, a gifted novice in the company of serious, experienced masters.

Next, Jhoira organized a small team of smiths and metalworkers to assist Venser. During these first stages of construction she served as both interpreter and forewoman, communicating Venser's directions and making sure they were executed to his satisfaction. They spent the better part of a week at a combined mine and foundry, the very site the tribe had originally gathered to protect from Phyrexia. Now Ghitu mages put down their weapons and picked up their tools. They focused the heat and pressure of Shiv's violently volcanic roots, then applied them to the exotic ores they had already taken from its rocky foundation.

Jhoira was gratified to see Venser's awe at Ghitu metalcraft. It reflected her own pleasant astonishment at the speed and quality of the smiths' progress. She had spent the first ten years of her life tending her father's forge, and as Venser's team shaped broad, metal plates for the device's foundation she realized she had been away from the fire for far too long.

They spent another two days cooling and tempering the plates with tribal magic. They expertly assembled the ambulator's frame and foundation platform, then built the housing for the all-important powerstones. Less than two weeks after Venser went to work, they had a Ghitu version of his teleportation chair ready for testing.

They had kept Venser's initial design conceit of a chair at the center, as the machine's operator would need to be strapped in and stable during each interspatial journey. Apart from that, the new ambulator was a very different machine. The original had been cobbled together from whatever spare parts Venser could scavenge so that its form scarcely matched its function, but the Ghitu variant had been designed and shaped as a coherent whole.

Where the first ambulator was little more than a square metal seat on a boxlike platform, the new version was more like a throne, complete with a dais and stairs from which the seated king's court could attend him. Instead of the harsh lines and jagged edges of Phyrexian castoffs, the new ambulator curved up gracefully on either side of the operator, arcing up behind and on each side. Instead of a stubby, awkward column and a panel of makeshift knobs and levers, the new controls were housed in the arms of the throne and only required a finger flick to maneuver. Gone were the cumbersome cables and sooty energy exchangers that converted powerstone mana into arcane mechanical energy. They had been replaced with a thin tube of cold, blue light that covered the machine's internal walls like a glowing network of veins and arteries.

Venser's appreciation of Ghitu artifice faltered when Jhoira presented him with the control rig. The device fit over Venser's head and rested on his shoulders like a knight's armored epaulets. It was made of metal but was no heavier than a cold-weather cloak. The rig served multiple purposes, but its primary function was to allow Venser to operate the machine with his fingertips, magically amplifying the strength and clarity of his control over its many complicated functions.

Jhoira took special pride in the device, as she had built it herself and managed to keep it hidden from Venser until the main unit was ready. She had vast experience with reclusive tinkerers, and correctly predicted Venser's objections. He balked at wearing the cumbersome-seeming device, likening it to a ox's yoke.

He complained she was adding yet another set of new controls for him to learn when he already had so much to contend with. He muttered about the wisdom of taxing an already overtaxed pilot when the stakes were so high.

Jhoira eroded his resistance, of course. She did so with the strength of her arguments but more importantly with the rig itself, for she had laced the device with Thran metal, one of the Ghitu's proudest achievements and most closely guarded secrets. No Ghitu artificer could claim the title of master without producing a single, pure ingot of the rare and exotic alloy. It was her people's crowning achievement as metalsmiths.

Thran metal was strong, lightweight, versatile, and possessed of near-mystical qualities. It grew, for one, replacing worn edges and filling in damaged or missing sections. It also behaved differently in different applications, tempering harder and stronger when intended for armor, lighter and more malleable for delicate internal clockwork. To the Ghitu, Thran metal was nothing less than sacrament. To Venser, it was a lure too tempting to resist. He relented and wore the rig—though he always looked uncomfortable in it.

The team was helping him into the rig now for the last in a series of adjustments before the first test jaunt. Jhoira watched Venser scowling as he was jostled by the rig and the Ghitu workers. She hadn't had a single personal conversation with Venser since they arrived. It had been easier than she expected, as they were both so consumed by their work. Now that the work was wrapping up, now that her plan was in place and ready, she would have to sit Venser down and tell him all of it.

When the artificer glanced over and met her eyes, Jhoira smiled encouragingly. Then she turned away. Time and enthusiasm had maintained her momentum thus far, but now she had to dredge up the will to continue. Before she could talk with Venser, she must first talk to Teferi.

Her old friend had scarcely recovered from the events at the Shivan rift. He was still distracted and withdrawn, barely interested in maintaining a conversation. He no longer seemed woozy or dazed, but neither was he lucid. While Venser and the Ghitu built a working ambulator, Teferi had simply sat nearby, always facing away, looking up into the sky. This was how she found him now, sitting quietly on a sandy ridge just outside the Ghitu village.

Teferi's godlike power was also gone, perhaps burned out forever by his all-out effort to seal the Shivan rift. Since then he had shown none of his former magic, and of late he had not even tried to cast a spell or planeswalk from one place to another. His body was not a solid projection of his mind's devising but a gross physical object that was subject to the same threats and consequences as the rest of the mortal beings around him.

It pained Jhoira to see him like this, so diminished and unlike his gregarious self. It pained her that Teferi always intended to abandon her after the Shivan rift was sealed. He planned for her to take up the mantle of saving the universe, and now he was making sure she had no choice but to follow that plan.

Jhoira strode forward, her purpose renewed. Teferi had intended to die in the Shivan rift. He had put them on this course and left her the rudder. He had set this all in motion, and so he would have to accept where it took him.

"Teferi," she said.

Her friend's bald head twitched as he started from a daydream. He looked up at her and smiled, though his eyes were wide and sad. "Jhoira. How fares the venture?"

"We're getting ready to leave," she said. "Two more days, maybe three. I need to know a few things before we go."

Teferi slowly rose to his feet. He dusted off his robes and bowed slightly. "I am at your service."

Ten sharp rejoinders collided in Jhoira's throat, and the logjam prevented any single one from emerging. She regained her composure and said, "What is your condition?"

Teferi cocked his head quizzically. "As you see me," he said.

Jhoira nodded. "Do you remember anything after you closed the Shivan rift?"

The planeswalker shook his head. He shrugged. "There was a rock."

"Yes. You mentioned mana surges. Can you still sense them?"

Teferi paused, concentrating. "No," he said. "I remember what they felt like. . . . I sometimes remember what everything felt like. But I don't anymore."

"You don't what?"

"I don't feel the mana surges." Teferi's tone grew tired and irritable. "I don't feel mana, honestly."

"I see. Do you feel anything?"

"How do you mean?"

"Can you sense the rifts anymore? Can you help us find them? Do you remember anything about them, any thoughts you thought when you were nigh-omniscient and almost omnipotent?"

Teferi chuckled. "No. I don't truly understand the question, but I'm sure the answer is no."

"What did you see when Venser found the basilisk?"

"I'd say it was more like the basilisk found him." Teferi tilted his head back, smiling as he searched for the memory. "Venser teleported, in a sense. Much as his machine did."

"How?"

"I don't know. He's never cast anything before." Teferi was more alert now, more focused. "But, he did build the machine. Maybe building it became a ritual, a kind of spell. He built it so often with his hands that now he can build it in his head and make it real."

"And this new-found magic," Jhoira said, "is connected to the rift?"

Teferi's clear eyes clouded over. "Not sure."

"Very well. Thank you, Teferi." Jhoira took Teferi by the shoulders and held him until he made eye contact. Her voice was low, stern, and ominous. "How much power do you have left?" she said.

Teferi's face was vacant, as usual, but his voice was clear and strong. "I don't know."

Jhoira released him. "I believe you." She let her arms fall but stayed where she was, her face inches from her old friend's. "Are you able to help us seal the remaining rifts?"

Teferi nodded. "I am."

"Are you willing to help us seal the remaining rifts?"

"Of course. Tell me what I can do."

"I would if I knew. If anyone knew." Jhoira stopped herself, exhaled, then continued. "You can listen," she said. "I've come to the conclusion you wanted me to: We must enlist other planeswalkers to help."

Teferi nodded. "Karn?"

Jhoira started, caught off guard by Teferi's prescience. The golem Karn was one of their oldest allies, a highly advanced silver golem who had achieved both independent thought and the ability to planeswalk. Karn had been one of their fellows at the Tolarian Academy. In fact, he had known Jhoira and called her "friend" even longer than Teferi had.

"Karn is not here," she said. "And he's notoriously difficult to reach. The last report we have says he went on an extended tour of the multiverse with another 'walker as his traveling companion. They haven't been seen or heard from in centuries.

"No, I think we have to work with what's here. Two of the rifts we've seen have planeswalkers living nearby. I intend to use Venser's machine to take us back to Urborg, then to Skyshroud. Windgrace is Urborg's protector, so he may be swayed by the threat to his homeland. Freyalise will require more convincing. I'll consider that problem later."

"You sound a bit like I used to." The planeswalker grinned. "It's not so easy to provide answers when you don't have them, eh?"

Jhoira stared at him coldly. "So, to Urborg. Windgrace first, then Freyalise."

"A sound stratagem."

Jhoira watched him carefully. "Unless you can take us there. We've made some crucial changes to the ambulator, but it's still Venser's machine. It didn't work reliably last time we used it."

"I do recall." Teferi nodded. "So I share your concern."

"But you're not up to the challenge."

"No."

Jhoira sighed. "Teferi, we need you. We need your knowledge about the rifts, we need your insight into planar mechanics. Do you have that to offer?"

Teferi swelled up and stood resolute. "I will give whatever I can."

"That's all anyone can ask, or expect. Now," Jhoira said, leaning forward slightly, "what happened to Corus?"

Teferi's scowled slightly. "Corus." He mused, running his tongue over his upper teeth behind closed lips. "Corus ruptured the mana star."

"If that were true, you'd be a cinder. Or frozen ten feet down in a lake of molten quartz. Damaging a powerstone that size releases enough energy to take down a small mountain."

Teferi's features went slack. "Corus ruptured the mana star," he said.

"I believe he did. But I also believe he tried to kill you first."

Teferi did not reply.

"Didn't he?"

The wizard's face twisted in anger and confusion. "He did. But I protected myself. Then he broke the arm off the star. And I protected myself again." Teferi crossed his arms defiantly.

Jhoira regarded him for a few moments. She said, "When Venser tests the machine . . . when we take our first trip on the new ambulator, you will stay behind."

"But I—"

Jhoira held up her hand. "You have to. To limit the variables. If you yourself don't know the state of your own magic, we can't risk it affecting the machine. I do not want a repeat of what happened in Urborg. No more wild cascades across history's greatest cataclysms. I won't risk it. So you stay behind.

"If we make the trip successfully, we will return to collect you. If everything works as planned, you won't be waiting more than a few minutes."

"But Venser can teleport." Now Teferi grabbed Jhoira's shoulder, clamping on tight with his right hand. "All on his own, without study. He's the key to this. He and Radha and the others like them. I can help him. I can teach him how to use it for us—"

Jhoira pried Teferi's hand loose. She held it as she said, "Venser has nothing to learn from you. I would actually prefer that he not learn from you, as you have too many bad habits that he's better off without. And he will help us because he wants to, not because you trick him into it." She released Teferi's hand. "You stay behind. We will return for you."

Teferi's eyes welled up with tears, which he quickly blinked away. "Jhoira," he said, "I want to do more. I still want to make it right."

"Don't," she said. "Do this instead: If you want to help, help. Assist me. Follow my lead." She arched her brow. "Unless you want to stay on this hillside and keep wondering why you're not dead. You're alive, Teferi, and your work is far from over. You left it to me, but I can't do it by myself. We need you. I need you."

Teferi closed his eyes, squeezing two more tears that disappeared into the Shivan sand. He bowed gracefully and said, "Thank you, my friend." He rose, his eyes clear, bright, and dry. "When does the test flight begin? Assuming I'm allowed to observe, that is."

"You are. From a safe distance." Jhoira did not smile. She extended her hand, which Teferi quickly clasped in his own.

"We are partners again?" he said.

"Allies," Jhoira said, "working toward the same goal."

Teferi beamed. "I relish the opportunity."

As Jhoira turned away and Teferi followed, she wondered which of the many Teferis she had seen over the years was scuffling through the sand behind her.

CHAPTER 5

The final tests were complete, and the last-minute preparations were all in place. Every bearing, seal, and joint had been checked and rechecked, tolerances set with razor-keen precision. Venser's twin powerstones were in place, the control rig was resting awkwardly on his shoulders, and he sat ready at the center of his glorious machine.

It was still his ambulator. Jhoira had said so many times during the construction, and Venser knew it was true. His designs had progressed more in the last a few weeks than they had for years back home. He had never imagined collaboration would be so easy or so productive, and he was humbled by the Ghitu's skill and grace in the workshop. Even the damnable rig she saddled him with was proving useful, even preferable to what he was used to. Controlling the machine was now as easy as writing his name, or calculating a column of numbers—he barely needed to concentrate before his practiced fingers were dancing over the controls.

But it was still his ambulator. Jhoira had said so, and he knew it was true.

The Ghitu team she had assembled stood nearby, as did several members of the elder council. Jhoira was on the dais to Venser's right, keeping one eye on the flow of light across the machine's interior surface and the other on Teferi.

Venser did not know what to make of the planeswalker's

nonparticipation in the device's construction any more than he did Teferi's presence at this inaugural jaunt. Teferi was as mysterious as he had ever been, if not more so. Venser was happy to let Jhoira interact with him, except that there was an obvious distance between them now, a coldness that hadn't been there before. Venser accepted the obvious rationale they offered, that Teferi's planeswalking power posed a threat to the machine's central function. He knew there was far more to his friends' complicated relationship, however, and far more to this current disharmony between them.

Not that Jhoira had allowed him much time to reflect on anything but the ambulator. Neither had she given him the chance to ask her about it. The work had gone exceedingly fast, even faster than their best estimations, but every second strengthened the network of time rifts, allowed them to extend and deepen and continue their disruptive effects on the world. The machine had been completed in a dead rush, and now that it was functional they were forced to rush on.

Urborg was the destination of this first journey. It was Venser's home, the place he knew the best and identified with most strongly. All of his life experiences were there, all of his material possessions, so if he was able to teleport anywhere successfully, it would be there.

Urborg was also the site of the Phyrexian Stronghold and the Stronghold's attendant rift. According to Jhoira, this fissure had been created when a dark god's machinery transported the mountain fortress across planar barriers, forcing it from one sphere of existence into another. Such events had happened with alarming frequency in Dominaria's history, and while all of them left some mark on the fabric of the multiverse, only the grandest and most violent created phenomena like the Stronghold rift. Like the one Teferi had closed in Shiv, the Stronghold rift drained the local mana and weakened the fabric of time and space itself.

Even if they managed to seal the rift in Urborg, Venser knew there were at least three more that were large enough and dangerous enough to warrant the direct action of a godlike planeswalker. That such a being was always active in Urborg became another reason to visit Venser's home first. Lord Windgrace had been patron and protector of the swamps for generations, though there was no guarantee the fabled panther-warrior would receive them, or that he would do what Teferi had done.

"Are you ready?" Jhoira said.

"No," Venser muttered. Then, more loudly, "But I'm eager to get home. Let's see what happens."

Jhoira rested her hand on Venser's shoulder, and he again cursed the metal rig, this time for keeping Jhoira's hand from actually touching him. He needed all the reassurance he could get.

"Stand clear," he said. His fingers flew and the ambulator began to hum.

"This will work," Jhoira said, leaning in close to Venser's ear. "I have no doubts because you have earned this success."

Venser smiled weakly. He signaled the Ghitu technicians and they released the last of the couplings that tethered the machine to the ground.

"Good-bye, brothers and sisters," Jhoira called. Venser had picked up quite a bit of the Ghitu language after working so closely with them, and he followed her short farewell address with ease. "We thank you as guests and as peers. You have done a great service to us. You have helped Venser realize his dream. We are going to Urborg"—she raised her hand high—"and we are coming back."

The Ghitu assembly silently returned Jhoira's gesture. As the Shivans all lowered their arms, Jhoira called out to Teferi. "Watch us," she told him. "Observe. If anything goes wrong, learn from our mistake. And carry on." She held her old friend's eyes fiercely, almost challenging him to respond, but the planeswalker simply stared, his face an inscrutable mask.

Now fully annoyed, Jhoira turned back to Venser and said, "Whenever you're ready."

Venser nodded. He gulped. His fingers danced across the panel as blue and yellow lights flashed across his shoulders. The machine whined and revved ever higher.

Rest now . . . .

"What?" Venser did not stop what he was doing, but the soft voice had him distracted. Who was speaking? Why did he feel so cold?

Don't struggle. Rest now. It's so much easier if you rest. . . .

"Do you hear that?" he shouted. The soft, giddy voice was similar to the one he had heard when the basilisk attacked him.

Jhoira shook her head and motioned to her ears. She couldn't hear him, but she seemed to understand what he said. She opened wide and carefully mouthed, "Nothing. What did you hear?"

Venser tried to abort, tried to reverse the ignition process. The machine did not respond, no matter how fast his fingers flew. Panicking, Venser glanced up at Jhoira, then out among the Ghitu, but his eye was quickly drawn to Teferi. The wizard's hands were in motion, his mouth was moving. Was he bidding them farewell? Or was he casting a spell?

"I can't stop it," Venser said.

Yes, that's it. Come to me now. Come to me and rest. Don't struggle. . . .

Jhoira crouched down beside him and shouted back, "Don't try. It's too late."

The ghostly voice dissolved into hysterical giggles, cackling and howling like a rabid harlequin. The sound stopped, and when the voice spoke again it was hungry, cruel, and confident.

Got you.

Then the world went away, vanishing behind a curtain of sizzling energy. The curtain spread and swallowed Jhoira. It rushed out over the ambulator platform, eclipsing the Ghitu and even Teferi Planeswalker himself.

Venser followed them into that flash of yellow-white lightning and fell into an endless void of searing white light. His body was gone, his mind was racing, and all he could feel was a frigid breeze blowing through him as manic laughter rang in his mind.

* * * * *

Karn floated in the Blind Eternities, barely touching the outer edges of Mirrodin. The all-metal plane was a place of his own devising, a test of his abilities and his intentions that had not ended well. Now it was a peaceful place, but Karn always returned to it regularly to make sure that the seeds he planted did not bring forth poison fruit.

Beside him was his planeswalking companion Jeska, once a Pardic barbarian from the continent of Otaria. Jeska had led a strange life both before and after she ascended, and it was Karn's pleasure to serve as her mentor and partner as they explored the widest ranges of the multiverse.

Karn enjoyed the company. He had always been unique among his peers no matter who or what they were. Initially created as a silver golem for Urza's first time travel experiments, Karn was built for independent thought and exploration. His self-determination derived from a Phyrexian heartstone that Urza himself had harvested from the breeding vats in Phyrexia, and Karn had since incorporated some of the most powerful artifacts ever built into his manufactured body. Amalgamated by circumstance and integrated by his own will, Karn's being contained worlds, along with both the power and the mechanisms to move himself and others from plane to plane. He had not ascended to planeswalker status as others did, from an essential innate spark that flared under duress, but he had ascended and was functionally identical to (and perhaps more powerful than) other, more organic godlike beings. He had access to titanic amounts of mana, his body changed to suit his moods and his needs, and he could step from one frame of existence to another as easily as rising from a chair.

Karn's preternaturally clear mind reached out to the world he had created, suffusing Mirrodin with his consciousness and taking its measure. There had not been a major conflict or crisis in Mirrodin for over one hundred years, but something about the place troubled Karn. He felt as a man would upon returning home from a short vacation to find his house and everything in it moved slightly to the left.

Jeska approached him. She was keen-eyed and wore her bushy red hair pinned behind her neck in a heavy iron clip. "What do you see?" she said.

"The same," Karn replied. "Things grow and evolve and change as I anticipated. But there is more at work here."

Jeska fidgeted, her hand teasing the handle of the short sword on her belt. "Are you almost through? I want to get moving again."

"Patience," Karn said, which had become his a mantra when dealing with Jeska. She was quick to act and react, but her alacrity sometimes made her edgy and quarrelsome. If Jeska wasn't doing something that engaged her she usually found someone or something to distract her—and with the power she had, her distractions could quickly turn into disasters.

"I don't even know why you come back here so often. The place hasn't changed in centuries. Whatever you're looking for has either happened already or is never going to happen."

Karn shivered, a cold, electric sensation that drove Jeska's restlessness from his mind. Something flashed in the back of his head, not a voice but a sound that nonetheless conveyed intent and meaning.

"Did you hear something?"

Jeska cocked her head. "No. Should I have?"

"No." The silver golem smiled. "I'm not sure I should have." He lowered his thick, metal arms and crossed them behind his back.

Facing Jeska he said, "I'm finished here for now. Where would you like to go next?"

Jeska's eyes lit up. "Rabiah," she said.

"I don't know if you're ready for Rabiah."

"You mean you aren't ready to take me there."

"Actually, I mean Rabiah isn't ready for you."

"I could go myself. Any time I liked."

"True. That is, if you could find it. But then we would be deprived of each other's company." He turned his back on Mirrodin and considered. "What if I showed you Mercadia? It's a mercantile plane. I have friends there."

Jeska tossed her hair so that the iron clip thumped against her spine. "Then Rabiah?"

"We shall see. Come." Karn extended his hand. "And please keep an ear out for any unusual sounds. I'm sure I heard something. It's best to listen when a strange voice calls your name."

Jeska nodded and shrugged simultaneously. "As you say." She took Karn's hand and they both faded from sight.

* * * * *

Jhoira awoke elsewhere. She knew this wasn't Shiv before her eyes had opened and her brain cast off the waking fog that muddled her thinking. It was cold, very cold. Far colder than Shiv was even in the darkest predawn hours. Colder than Urborg should be, and if her recollection served, colder than it ever had been.

Jhoira sat up. Disoriented, she swung her head left and right, craning for as complete a view as she could manage. It could well be Urborg. There were vast stretches of oil-black swamp and marshland. Picked-clean skeleton bones and metallic limbs sat mired in huge lakes of tarry goo. There were distant copses of spiky, soot-encrusted evergreens, carbonized cypress trees, and toxic pines with grim, ebon needles.

It had to be Urborg. The Stronghold itself hunched menacingly on the horizon, a thick sharp wedge of black rock. The circular Stronghold rift still churned and roiled in the sky over the mountain fortress, illuminating the area below in its eerie purple light.

It was definitely Urborg, she decided. Yet if that was true, why was there snow on the ground? Why were there icicles hanging from the trees? Why could she see her breath roll out of her lungs in thick, white clouds? Why did she shiver, why did her teeth chatter, why had her feet gone numb?

It was impossible for the swamps to be this cold. Urborg was one of the Spice Islands, a volcanic chain situated over one of the most seismically active areas on the globe. Venser's home sat near the center of a tropical weather zone, so Urborg hadn't seen a hard freeze, snow, or even frost for almost six hundred years.

Jhoira got to her feet, now casting around for Venser or the ambulator. Just as this could not be Urborg, the ambulator could not have separated from Jhoira. She was on board, subject to the same magical forces that carried both device and pilot to the intended locale. If the ambulator functioned at all, it had to take her with it.

Jhoira paused and pondered, shuddering at the gloom. Perhaps the ambulator didn't function after all. Maybe Venser's machine was never going to operate as he intended. Jhoira wondered if perhaps it could not.

No, she corrected herself. The device had worked, had functioned exactly as it was designed and developed to function. Venser's genius and the Ghitu tribe's experience had left no room for errors. The machine had worked. It had taken them to their destination.

Jhoira shivered anew and hunched her shoulders. If this was Urborg, then their destination itself had radically changed since they were here only weeks ago.

"Excuse me."

Startled, Jhoira jerked her head toward the unseen man's voice.

He sounded calm and friendly. Jhoira struggled to flex her freezing muscles and prepared for the worst.

"Hello." He came out of the icy mist on foot, a tall man with dark hair and a tall, proud forehead. He was broad-shouldered but lean—his wiry arms were crossed outside his fur overcoat and pulled it tight around his middle. His face was open and his eyes were a deep, penetrating blue. The golden-blond pelt stitched around the overcoat's hood framed the man's face and chin like a thick mane of hair and a lush, thick beard.

"Urza?" Jhoira whispered.

"Hm." The man's eyes twinkled. He pulled the hood back to expose his face and head to the elements. "I'm afraid not. Who I am is someone who thinks you're not really dressed for this weather." Without hesitation, the smiling man stripped off his fur overcoat and held it out to Jhoira. She stared at it for a moment, then looked up at the stranger and shook her head.

"Suit yourself." Undisturbed, the man drew back the fur and tucked it under his arm. He stared at Jhoira, studying her, and said, "Do you have a place to go? You won't last the night if you stay outdoors."

Jhoira shook off another wave of lethargy. She had thrived in colder places than this. She had honed her survival skills in some of the most dangerous terrains across the multiverse, realms of fire and snow alike. The cold here would never kill her. But, she thought, as she glanced down at the bones in the lake of tar, Urborg's predators would almost certainly have an easy time of it.

She faced the stranger and tried to gauge his character. Assuming this was his real face, Jhoira now saw he was not her old headmaster, though he did bear a resemblance. He seemed genuinely human, but then he could be just another Urborg monster in a charming mask. There was something off about him, a discordant note in an otherwise pleasant melody. She couldn't allow herself to trust him until she knew more.

"Forgive my hesitation," she said. "I am newly arrived and lost. In such circumstances I tend toward the overcautious."

"Sound thinking," the man said. "In this place there is no other way."

"Would you help put my fears to rest?"

"Of course. I would like nothing more." He blew on his hands. "Your pardon. I'm not really used to this weather myself." He folded his arms across his chest again so that the fur hung down over his belly. "Now. What can I do to convince you not to let yourself freeze to death?"

"Who are you?"

"I am a traveler." The stranger bowed.

"Not an answer. Are you a planeswalker?"

This raised a half smile. "No. I hate to presume, but I'd say that I am as mortal as you." When he said this, the man's eyes opened wider and bored into Jhoira's. He winked at her.

It then hit Jhoira what it was that made the stranger so unsettling. Though he appeared to be no older than thirty, the man's eyes were profound and fascinating far beyond their vivid color. Like Jhoira herself, the stranger had centuries of experience behind those eyes. Like her, he was older than he looked, far older.

The first glimmers of realization began to form. Jhoira felt a rush of clarity and she said, "What is your name?"

The man raised one eyebrow. "I will answer. But then you must introduce yourself. It's only polite."

"Agreed."

The man bowed again. "Or," he said, glancing up but leaving his torso doubled over, "I could tell you who you are, for I've traveled a long way to be here for the sole purpose of meeting you. Then you may tell who I am, as I'm almost certain you've just worked it out."

Jhoira nodded. "You are Jodah, Archmage Eternal of the Unseen Academy."

"At your service." Jodah bowed lower, then straightened to his full height. "Though that title is woefully out of date. 'Archmage Eternal Emeritus' would be more accurate."

She offered a half-hearted shrug. "It is how you are remembered in the history texts."

"When it comes to history texts," Jodah said. "I find it's usually better not to be remembered at all."

Jhoira wrapped her thin Ghitu robes around her and straightened up. "And you know me, Archmage?"

"Please," he said. "Call me Jodah. And yes, Jhoira of the Ghitu. I know you, or at least of you. You are the eldest elder from Shiv's elite, nomad artificers. You practically invented Thran metal."

"Tch," Jhoira said. "The desert is unkind to flatterers." She bowed lightly. "It is an honor to meet you, Jodah. But why are you here? And how do you know me?"

Jodah's face tightened but his voice remained calm. "I have seen and survived several major catastrophes over the years. Frankly, I'd be a much bigger fool than I am if I didn't see this one coming."

"You know about the rifts?" Jhoira was instantly alert, her voice crisp and strident. "Time and energy phenomena, like the one over the Stronghold?"

Jodah shook his head. "I don't know much of anything for sure. But I do have a feel for things, and I learned a long time ago to follow such feelings wherever they lead me. I have . . . extensive resources at my disposal. So I did my homework, as any good archmage should, and it led me here. It led me to you." He shifted his feet in the snow. "I believe we have a common purpose, Jhoira." His smile grew strained. "I know we have a common enemy."

Jhoira nodded. Her eyes were still sharp and probing. "The rifts threaten everything."

Jodah shook his head. "I don't know anything about rifts."

"Then what did you mean . . ." She paused, remembering the especially frigid temperatures in Radha's home halfway around the world. "The cold, then? The unnatural winter here and in Keld?"

"The cold is everywhere," Jodah said. "Everywhere there's been world-shattering magic. And I believe something very nasty is exploiting it. Our enemy is a person, not a weather condition. I'm not saying the cold is a blessing. It's a threat, a serious one. But it's not the problem I'm most concerned with."

Jhoira felt a familiar knot tighten in her stomach. "Our enemy . . . planeswalker?"

Jodah sighed but his smile remained. "Two things, Jhoira: You must put on this coat right now." He extended the fur once more. "And you have to stop assuming that everyone is a planeswalker."

Jhoira felt her face crinkling in annoyance, but at least the tightness in her gut eased off. "I have a long and checkered history with planeswalkers, sir. If you scratch deep enough where 'world-shattering magic' has happened, you'll usually find one."

"You don't have to tell me," he said breezily. "I've been there."

Jhoira took the coat and said, "Thank you." She wrapped it around her shoulders and instantly realized how truly cold she had been. The archmage emeritus was right, she would not have lasted much longer without shelter.

"Do you have a place to go?" she said. "If the offer still stands, I would like to get out of the weather and hear about this common enemy."

"I do," Jodah said. "And you will. But I think it's best we collect your friend first."

Jhoira's jaw clenched. "What do you know about my friend?"

Jodah blew on his hands again. He sounded slightly amused. "You are an extremely suspicious person, Jhoira of the Ghitu."

"It's how I've lived this long."

He chuckled. "Well, I know nothing about your friend, not really. What I do know is he hurtled through here in a glowing machine. It was a truly spectacular entrance, and I'm surely not the only one who noticed it." Jodah pointed. "He came down somewhere over there. I think he landed very hard. It's extremely cold tonight, and getting colder as we speak. And Lord Windgrace has been enforcing a punishable-by-death artifact ban in the swamps for a hundred years."

Jhoira remembered the gladehunters who had been attacking Venser when she first met him. She was ready to trust Jodah this far, especially if Venser was in danger. But first she smiled wickedly. "See? Windgrace. Planeswalker."

Jodah bowed. "Touché."

She cinched the coat around her waist and stepped forward. "Take me there," she said. "And you go first."

CHAPTER 6

In all of his previous experiments Venser's ambulator either moved him instantaneously from one place to another or it didn't move him at all. He would feel an unsettling internal wrench and his vision would cloud over with golden fog, or he'd feel nothing at all except frustration.

Nothing in his experience prepared him for the Ghitu ambulator's dizzying rush of speed or its cometlike crash landing. The heavy chair and armored rig protected him from serious injury, but Venser had screamed himself hoarse as he plowed into the half-frozen bog. Now he sat dazed and mired up to his knees in the muck, listening to ooze as it filled in the steaming trench behind him.

Venser scanned the swamp around him and exhaled deeply. It worked, he thought. I'm home. It had been the fastest trial ever with the worst landing, but the new ambulator had carried him across a thousand miles of open ocean in a matter of seconds.

Venser blinked. "Jhoira?" He twisted out of the ambulator and stood on the dais. He turned too quickly and almost over-balanced with the metal rig on his shoulders. Muttering angrily, Venser pushed the clumsy device into a more comfortable spot as he rotated his shoulders and rolled his neck to work the kinks out of his muscles.

There was no sign of her. He was disturbed by this but told himself it was most likely she had not made the trip at all. They had designed the machine to carry several people at once, and had ensured that the magical field that surrounded the ambulator also covered everyone on it. He told himself that if the field had failed, it had surely done so at the very start of the trip and not halfway through. If he had lost Jhoira, it happened back in Shiv and not in midair over Urborg.

He shivered. The weather was fouler than usual and much colder. He couldn't remember the last time it had snowed, but now there were several inches of sooty gray already on the ground. The marsh crunched under his feet as he stepped off the dais, a noisy mixture of mud, ice, and frigid water.

Had Jhoira been left behind? He couldn't be sure. He remembered Teferi gesturing as the ambulator departed—had the planeswalker snatched Jhoira away at the last second for some other purpose?

Venser shook his head and fought off a sneeze. He steeled himself and took one last look at the ambulator. It was stuck in the mud but otherwise intact and entirely ready for another jaunt. He considered using it to hop back and forth across Urborg until he found Jhoira but decided it would be just as quick to search the surrounding area on foot. If he didn't find her here, he would take the ambulator back to Shiv and retrace his steps from there.

He hiked in an expanding circular pattern with the ambulator at its center. He didn't call her name, reasoning that she would have answered him by now if she were able. Also, he didn't want to draw any more attention to himself then he had to. If the gladehunters weren't already on the way, there were plenty of nightstalkers and mireshades who would be happy to attend to a lone human.

Venser was fifty yards from the ambulator when he heard the sounds of battle. It was not the sort of battle he was used to, one of feral snarls, slashing claws, and the occasional drawn blade. This sounded more like a full-scale war, complete with explosions and heavy machinery and the awful, moaning sound of seaborne warships scraping against one another.

Venser glanced back at the ambulator, then carefully scaled the muddy hill between him and the noise. Less than a hundred yards away he saw dozens, perhaps hundreds, of combatants rushing back and forth in a wild melee. The noise was atrocious, a cacophony of tearing flesh, shattered metal, and inhuman screams. Venser stared at the chaos for a few moments, his breath condensing on his cheeks as the wind blew it back into his face.

There was no way to tell how long the battle had raged, but the wide expanse of frozen marshland before him was almost covered by strange and terrifying creatures. Two large forces came together in the center of Venser's view, one composed of fell beasts from the wilds of Urborg and the other of machine horrors that surged from the Stronghold mountain's belly. Venser followed the long line of artifact nightmares all the way back to the mountain, and he estimated there were two hundred of them or more, varying in size and shape from humanoid foot soldiers to airborne winged devils to fat, squat war engines that rolled over Urborg's fauna like fast-moving glaciers.

The metal army reminded Venser of the bits and pieces he'd been scavenging for years, but these terrors were whole. They were also active, aggressive, and coordinated in their assault. Unlike the broken Phyrexians Venser was familiar with, these were more steel blue than black and were smooth and polished rather than jagged and sharp. They glowed from within, lurid blue light spilling out at their seams, from their open jaws, and from the brightly glowing stones embedded in their chests.

Urborg's defenders were no less diverse and no less terrifying. Huge tigers and leopards stalked among the machines, savagely tearing off limbs and crushing skulls when they pounced. There were giant insects overhead, wolf-sized wasps and towering mantises that filled the air with buzzing as they skimmed over the icy swamp grass. Endlessly long snakes with spindly double-jointed limbs slithered along the ground and through the trees, their eyes rimmed with red and their fangs spraying poison. Each of the dread menagerie bore the gladehunter mark, a simple, broad-stroke sigil that shined in the darkness. The light from the gladehunter sigils and the Phyrexians' power supply cast green-black and pale blue shadows across the battlefield, illuminating the animal corpses and broken machinery that littered the ground.

Venser considered himself a man of science, not of faith, but in the face of this carnage even he fell back to the childhood oaths that had once buoyed his courage. "Windgrace protect us," he muttered, barely aware that he was speaking aloud.

He was shaken but also mesmerized by the spectacle. The ambulator and Jhoira were both forgotten as Venser stood stock-still and watched the strange battle unfold. Both sides were focused and well-organized, and neither had a clear martial advantage. The Phyrexians were precise as they advanced but quickly fell into rabid, uncontrolled action as soon as they were engaged by the gladehunters. Urborg's forces were not as coherent as a group, but they were ruthlessly efficient once single combat was joined.

No wonder the gladehunters hadn't come for him yet. Lord Windgrace must have marshaled all of his forces to meet the invaders, sending every last artifact-hating member of his legion into battle against the machine horde. The war raged on and Venser was reminded of the massive sheer cliffs of Shiv and the towering waves that dashed against them—though in this case he could not say which was which. The Phyrexians surged forward, were repelled by the gladehunters, and withdrew. The gladehunters pursued but were met with fierce resistance from Phyrexian reinforcements and pulled back. This ebb and flow played out four times as Venser stood amazed. It became more like two oceans coming together at each one's high tide, their strongest storm surges meeting, testing each other, then pulling back, all without any regard for the landmasses underneath.

A small knot of combatants split off from the main body and thrashed its way toward him. Venser retreated several steps back down the rise so that only his head was visible from the field. He had never seen live Phyrexians before and had certainly never seen them in action, but neither had he seen the gladehunters rampant. This was the first time he had encountered the fearsome beasts when they weren't out for his blood, and he took this opportunity to marvel at their dreadful killing power. He was oddly thrilled, not only because they were ignoring him but also because they were killing and dying to protect their shared homeland.

A red and black striped night tiger seized a Phyrexian foot soldier by the chest, its massive jaws almost completely engulfing the artifact warrior's torso. The feline brute crunched down, sending a fountain of blue sparks up into the air, then savagely twisted its head left and right. The foot soldier's hips and legs flew in one direction, its mangled upper body flew in another. The big cat coughed and spat a dying blue crystal into the half-frozen muck.

The tiger was then immediately skewered by a gleaming silver-black lance that erupted from the front of a Phyrexian war wagon. The square machine was bigger than an oxcart, and it rolled inexorably forward on twin metal treads. The articulated lance lifted the tiger's massive body high into the air as the wagon rumbled on. It rolled over the lower half of a gladehunter mantis, crushing it flat, and the machine sent a lethal jolt of electricity through the tiger's body. The big cat let out one final, defiant roar as its eyes boiled and its tongue curled to black ash.

A dozen gladehunter wasps quickly descended on the war wagon, each bearing a foot-long stinger and vivid yellow stripes. They settled on the machine, covering its front end with their bodies, well clear of the lance and the treads. The wasps stung the war wagon repeatedly, each blow punching through the thick metal armor. Venser saw the caustic venom dripping from those stingers each time they withdrew, and he saw it dissolving metal everywhere it touched. It was dripping freely from the wounds they made, running like an open sore, and Venser wondered how much of the toxic poison had been pumped into the blocky machine's innards.

The war wagon slowed. The wasps departed as quickly as they had come, rising into the air as one on hard, translucent wings. Venser heard the familiar grinding sound of cogs and gears gone astray, and the Phyrexian wagon shuddered. Instinctively, Venser dropped down behind the hill just as a powerful internal explosion ripped the mechanical monster in half.

Venser peeked up over the rise. The war wagon was dead, silent and smoking in the snow. Overhead, two Phyrexian harpies with scythe hands dived straight into the swarm of gladehunter wasps, cutting two vicious paths through the center. The flying devils screeched as they banked, turned, and plowed through the swarm again on their way back up. Foul, green goo splattered on the field below and random pieces of wing and stinger landed nearby.

Just as Venser began to fear this battle would never end, the gladehunters stopped. Each of the fell menagerie ceased to advance, ceased to engage the enemy, and held its ground. Responding to some unseen signal, Urborg's defenders then retreated, withdrawing without turning their backs or exposing themselves to Phyrexian attack. Indeed, more than one metallic invader lost limbs or life when they tried to strike at the retreating horde.

The Phyrexians did not hesitate once the field was clear. They surged in, filling the space, jostling each other as they crammed the marsh to overflowing. Venser did not know why they were staging themselves thusly and not pursuing the enemy, but they were somehow more terrifying in this confused, chaotic state then they were in organized ranks.

Venser looked more closely. It was not that the Phyrexians weren't pursuing the gladehunters but that they couldn't. Some invisible force was holding them in place, blocking their exit and herding them back into one another. If he peered intently at the edges of the Phyrexian horde, he could see the fog and the smoke baffling off a clearly outlined perimeter, a rounded bubble of impassable space.

The noise and clamor disappeared without warning, though the abominations were all scrabbling over one another and scratching at the barrier. Silence reigned and Venser felt a chill that had nothing do to with the weather. The entire force of gladehunters stood just beyond the edge of the imprisoned Phyrexians, stacked five and six deep with hungry eyes fixed on the enemy.

The silence was shattered by a panther's growl so loud it pained Venser's ears. He crouched down again, fearful, but he also kept close watch on the Phyrexians.

A big cat roared, but the sound came from everywhere, around Venser, below him, behind him, and from inside him. The terrifying bellow eclipsed everything else—his fear, his interest, his sense of self-preservation—and Venser found himself filled with almost uncontrollable bloodlust and . . . pride?

The roar came again, and the entire Phyrexian force rose into the air. They formed a disharmonious mass of metal blades and sharp-edged jaws, each straining to be free, but all they did was damage each other. Soon the ball of invaders was floating twenty feet over the surface of the marsh. Venser watched carefully, noting the small black shoots that sprang from the frozen ground below it.

Something between a scream and a roar rolled over the field. The shoots responded by leaping up into the mass of Phyrexians above, each becoming a sturdy, sinuous vine cane as it crawled inside a machine body. The metal horrors screeched and flailed, but they were soon so clogged with vines that they lost what little mobility they had. Fat black thorns popped from the surface of the ever-swelling vines, starting at ground level and rising up each cane like bubbles in a boiling pot.

The thorns met the seams of the lowest Phyrexians in the mass, and Venser heard more metallic grinding from within the invaders when the surge proceeded inside. An awful series of sharp pops and mournful groans rang out as the Phyrexians' insides were punctured, sundered, and shredded. Thinner thorn canes crawled up the outer surface of the Phyrexian assembly, marring their polished blue-steel exteriors with deeply etched scars and thin curls of metal.

The artifact invaders stiffened and struggled, dripping gold-tinted oil and venting hot clouds of toxic steam. The outer vines contracted as the inner thorns tripled in size. One last shudder ran through the compacted mass of Phyrexian horrors, and the marsh fell silent once more.

All over. Rest now. Safe at last. Rest. . . .

Venser caught a flicker of a thin, armored human figure standing just outside his peripheral vision. He jerked his head and ducked down further, but the phantom in the dull gray helmet and tattered rags was gone, his presence barely registered on Venser's consciousness.

But he had been there. Venser had seen him, had seen pale, human skin on the helmed figure's bare arms. Were there Urborg collaborators among the Phyrexians?

Rest, little fly. Your work is done, your burdens lifted. Lie down and rest. . . .

The high, manic voice faded as the ball of thorns and metal began to contract. Its progress was slow, deliberate at first, but then with a sudden, brutal sound the entire mass collapsed, crushing the Phyrexians inside into a compacted mass half its original size. Metal crunched and shattered as the vines continued to surge up across its surface. They curled around and back across themselves, covering the mass in multiple layers of thick black thorns until the ball's own weight made it sag on its woody foundations. The invaders were all silent and still, broken into their component parts and suspended among the thorns. The battle was over.

Venser quickly crept back down the hill toward his ambulator. He was not sure what had just happened, but he had an educated guess. It was time for him to go. Without the Phyrexians to occupy them, the battle-maddened gladehunters would almost certainly turn on him, and he was determined not to be here when that happened.

The ambulator was now in sight. He didn't think he could pry it out of the swamp on his own, but he might be able to activate it, to have it carry him instead. Barring that, he would backtrack the trench his landing had created and continue to search for Jhoira. He knew this particular area well, so it would not take him long to search or make it back to the safety of his workshop.

The air shimmered in front of him and Venser plowed face first into a wall of luxurious fur and rock-hard muscle. Sheer terror ran through him as he realized with whom he had just collided.

Lord Windgrace stared down as Venser stepped back. Urborg's panther-god protector was enormous, towering on his hind legs, his arms, shoulders, and chest broad and heavily muscled. He wore a simple armored tunic that left his massive arms bare. His black fur shined in the gloom, and his eyes were a paralyzing shade of yellowish green. His lips curled back over his sharp white teeth, and he puffed steam from his triangular nose.

"You there," Windgrace said. "You're the maggot who builds machines." His voice rumbled out of his expansive chest, so low and foreboding that Venser's spine quivered.

He tried to drop to his knees. He tried to plead for forbearance. He tried to apologize for a lifetime of antagonizing the gladehunters and insulting their patron. Instead, Venser simply stared up at the awesome figure with his mouth hanging open and clouds of white fog rolling from his lips.

Windgrace's eyebrow rose. Venser felt himself floating helplessly into the air until he was eye-to-eye with the panther-man.

"I would have words with you," Windgrace said. "Before I decide what to do with you."

Venser tried once more to talk, but all he produced was a sad strangling sound.

Windgrace ignored him, looking past Venser to the feral assembly of beasts and monsters waiting nearby. "My children," he said, "you fought well tonight. But the war is far from over.

"In the meantime," he said, focusing his dreadful gaze back on Venser, "we have this. It may be Phyrexia's. It may be the Weaver King's. It may be nothing at all.

"But whatever it is, I shall determine. I will know what it knows. And either Urborg will have a new convert . . . or you will have a new toy." Windgrace flicked an eye toward the thorn ball and said, "Do not let this monument to Phyrexia's failure stand for long. You know your duty. Strip them down, pick them clean, and scatter them across the swamps."

An unsettling series of hisses and growls signaled the menagerie's assent. Windgrace did not linger but snorted again and turned away. Almost as an afterthought, Windgrace beckoned with his index finger.

Venser's body responded, floated past Windgrace and on toward the ambulator. The panther-god padded alongside his captive, his long strides elegant and unhurried.

"Come, maggot," Windgrace said. "Urborg needs you. One way or the other, you shall serve that need."

CHAPTER 7

Windgrace ferried Venser across the marsh with the artificer hovering beside him like some strange, floating dog. They began their journey alone, just the two of them, but as Windgrace strode across the crunching mud Venser saw and heard the fell and monstrous denizens of Urborg assemble behind him and join in the march.

The creatures from the battlefield were first. They assembled behind their lord and master, a narrow parade of beasts and nightstalkers. As Windgrace led them across the half-frozen flats, more of Urborg's residents joined the ranks.

They came alone, in pairs, and in small groups. Venser saw creatures both familiar and unknown, commonplace horrors like the mantises and legged serpents moving side by side with shambling, indescribable things with blood-matted hair and bright, jagged fangs. Urborg's small but diverse human population was also represented, exotic, dark-skinned warriors with bushy, knotted hair and black metal blades. Beside them walked pale, fair-haired mages in gilt silver robes and simple peasants armed with farm tools. Venser recognized two major lich lords, ashen-faced necromancers who brought small contingents of zombified men, reanimated beasts, and undead monsters. The air over the procession was thick with buzzing wasps, gruesome skirges, and carrion birds. Shades and other flickering phantasms appeared and disappeared at the edges of the parade, careful to avoid staying in plain sight but willing soldiers in Windgrace's dark army.

The panther-man grew less bulky as he walked, his thick muscles tightening around his bones. Where he had been broad and bulging, he became lean and lithe, supple and graceful as his ancient race had been long ago in Urborg's past. There had not been whole tribes of panther folk in Venser's home for centuries, but Windgrace single-handedly kept their memory and quasimystical prestige alive. His people had ruled the swamps for generations, and though they were now all but extinct, the panther folk still ruled through their last surviving member.

They soon came to a heavily wooded area that was bounded on three sides by steep hills. The hills protected the area from the worst of the wind and helped keep the filthy snow from drifting in. The disturbing procession of creatures stopped at the entrance to the moonlit hollow, eerily patient as they stood and watched their master. Windgrace glanced toward two thick trees that were growing a few feet apart. Venser floated toward these trees, following the planeswalker's gaze.

Venser hovered between the trees as four serpentine figures slithered up the roots and curled themselves around the trunks. Two stretched out and encircled his ankles while the others crawled higher and took hold of his wrists. The legged snakes tightened around Venser's limbs, then pulled back, hanging him spread-eagle and facing his host.

Windgrace paid Venser no mind as he padded over to a foot-high ridge that rose over the sharp marsh grasses. Supremely confident, effortlessly supple, the panther-man lowered himself onto the ridge with his legs folded under him and his elbows lightly balanced on his knees.

"Tinkerer," the glossy-black figure said, "if you lie I will know it, and this interview will end." He bared his fangs and ran his rough tongue over his lips. "Very suddenly. Tell me your name."

Venser paused to find his voice, and he said, "Venser, my lord."

"You are one of my charges then. A native of Urborg."

"I am."

"And yet you build Phyrexian machines."

Venser felt the danger rising as anger crept into Windgrace's powerful voice. He struggled to remember how to deal with godlike planeswalkers, feverishly working through his memories of Jhoira, Teferi, Radha, and Nicol Bolas.

"With respect, my lord," he said, "I build my own machines. From Phyrexian parts."

The panther-god growled. "As you will. You build your own machines, in direct and repeated violation of my decrees."

Venser swallowed hard. He was terrified by the awesome figure before him, but terror and awe were not avenues he could afford to pursue. "I only used pieces," he said. "I broke them down into their component parts and cannibalized them for my needs. My machine was only ever Phyrexian in terms of raw materials. If there was any life in all that metal and wire, I made sure to strip it out before I repurposed it."

The panther's ears flattened. "So you 'repurposed' the abominations."

"Yes, my lord."

"And you have no connection to Phyrexia at all."

"No, my lord."

Windgrace's eyes glittered. He held his long arm out with his hand cupped and waited. Within seconds two skirges swooped down, cawing raucously, and deposited two glowing objects in the panther-man's broad palm. Venser's body went cold, and sweat broke out across his forehead.

"These stones," Windgrace said, lowering his hand and holding the ambulator's power source for Venser to see, "are Phyrexian. Your machine"— he nodded back toward the spot Venser had landed—"is made from Phyrexians. And the last time you used it, just weeks ago, Phyrexians stirred within the Stronghold. They started slowly but increased as the temperature dropped. Now they come in a steady flow from that thrice-damned pool of energy that sits overhead.

The snakes squeezed tighter around his arms and legs. Windgrace stood glaring, and Venser was unable to hold his eyes.

"Child of Urborg," Windgrace said, "did you think you were exempt? Did you think I arbitrarily decided to root out and destroy every last artifact in the swamp? That I spent the past three hundred years organizing my gladehunters on a whim?"

Venser did not reply, could not for fear of further angering the planeswalker.

Windgrace continued. "Did you consider even for a moment that your machine could call out to the other machines I've had dismantled and buried? Did you dream that its vitality would revive the most dangerous invaders Urborg has ever known?"

"I beg your pardon, my lord. I did not believe that my small efforts would have any impact on your realm."

"Not my realm," Windgrace said. "Our home. You invited these oil-blooded bastards into our home. You all but held the door for them." He snorted angrily through his nose. "I scarcely believe what I'm hearing, tinkerer. Are you corrupt, co-opted, or simply confused?"

"Confused, my lord."

Windgrace narrowed his eyes and flattened his ears once more. "Continue."

Venser inhaled deeply. "I am neither powerful nor wise. I saw only the task at hand, not the larger impact it would have."

"And that is supposed to earn you amnesty?"

"No, Lord Windgrace. I am guilty. I have repeatedly and willfully violated your laws. But I did so to achieve something, to reach a goal that I had set for myself. I only wanted to become wise and skilled, and to use my wisdom and skills on Urborg's behalf."

"So you did. And that is one of the only reasons you are still alive to have this conversation." Windgrace clasped his hands behind his back and began pacing. He crossed to the far end of the hollow, then returned. He considered Venser with an appraising eye. "What are you?" he said at last. "What are you really?"

"I am a builder." Venser spoke with the strength of certainty and with the resolve of a man who has accepted his own impending death. "A traveler. If I am not these things, then I am nothing."

Windgrace's fur bristled. "As you may yet be, little tinkerer. But for now I think you are more than that, even more than you suspect. It is not just your machine that opens the hole above the Stronghold. It is you yourself. Why are you here? Why do you use the machine to mimic your own magic?"

"I don't have any magic, my lord. I can't cast spells. I am just as you see me, finite and mortal. I never thought my ambulator could pose a threat to you and our home."

"As you say. But 'finite' and 'mortal' do not negate 'unpredictable' and 'dangerous.' I have battled finite, mortal enemies for three centuries. I spent the first hundred years scouring away the living remnants of the Invasion. I spent the next two hundred destroying their seeds, burning their roots, and cutting them down wherever they appeared. You and your machine undid my work, brought us back to full-scale conflict in a matter of weeks. Don't speak to me of 'mortal' and 'finite' as if they are shortcomings. With all my power—my infinite, immortal power—I have barely kept the enemy from overrunning Urborg."

Venser's face fell. "I'm sorry."

"Don't be," Windgrace said. "Be useful. Stand beside your fellows, stand with me and help us stop the slide you started."

Venser looked up. "If you will allow me," he said, "I will do whatever I can to fix the damage I've done."

"I might allow it. First tell me what you know about Phyrexia, about these new metal demons that seem connected to the cold."

"I can't. I don't know anything about Phyrexia or the cold."

Windgrace nodded as if expecting Venser's answer. "And the Weaver King?"

Venser blinked. "That name means nothing to me, my lord."

That's it, play dumb. Together we can get past him. . . .

Panic raced through Venser and he squirmed against his bonds. Every muscle in Windgrace's body tensed. He approached Venser, coming within arm's length, and his eyes glowed lurid green. "And yet," the planeswalker said, "you commune with him even now."

"What? No." Venser struggled hard against the snakes holding him, but they hissed and squeezed even tighter. The voice in my head has a name, he thought. A name known to the panther-god, a name that Windgrace speaks with hatred.

"He keeps his thoughts hidden from me," Windgrace said. "But I can feel him here, within you. What is he telling you?"

Play dumb. Say nothing. Together we can fool him. . . .

"I hear a voice," Venser said slowly. "It tells me to avoid your questions."

The panther-man's eyes glowed brighter. "What else?"

Venser's voice gained strength. "He tells me to rest. To stop struggling. To lie down and do nothing."

"As the spider tells the fly trapped in its web," Windgrace said. "How strong is the voice? Have you heard it often?"

"Not strong," Venser said. "Barely a whisper. And I have only heard it three or four times."

"Starting when?"

Venser considered. "Weeks ago," he said. "In Shiv."

This confused the planeswalker. Windgrace's tail swished through the frigid air, and his claws slid out of their sheaths.

"Call out to him," Windgrace said. "Respond to his commands."

"But I—"

"Do it now."

Venser's eyes snapped shut, and he concentrated. *I'm here,* he thought. *I need your help. What must I do?*

A full minute ticked by before the disembodied voice replied.

Naughty, naughty, it said. It giggled. *Whose side are you on?*

Windgrace pounced, hurling himself at Venser with his jaws open wide and his claws extended. Venser yelped, and he heard the mad-harlequin voice echo his own. The planeswalker's shadow engulfed him, but before the massive panther-man tore him to shreds Windgrace's body transformed into an ethereal image of sparkling fog.

The ghostly image of Windgrace disappeared into Venser's skull. Pain shot through Venser's body, and he involuntarily thrashed so hard that he actually pulled his right hand a clear foot away from the tree, drawing the serpent's body with it.

The Weaver King was screaming now, his high-pitched shriek as delirious and disturbing as his laughter had been. Venser felt something pull free from him, like peeling a tight, woolen cap from his head after a long, sweaty trek. As the giddy voice withdrew, Venser heard it speak to him one last time.

Rest now, it said. *Don't struggle. We'll be together soon.* Then it dissolved into manic giggles that slowly faded into silence.

Panting heavily, Venser tried to recover his wits and his wind. Lord Windgrace did not return, but the snakes holding Venser retracted, drawing his arms and legs out straight once more. His muscles were cramped and his joints were starting to ache, but at least he was alive.

He cracked open his eyelids and scanned the small army that had followed them to Windgrace's hollow. Alive for now, Venser thought, but for how much longer?

The gladehunter beasts and warriors of Urborg made no move toward him, however. They only sat and watched, either unable to enter the area without Windgrace's leave or unwilling to risk the panther-god's ire.

Something familiar flickered in the corner of Venser's eye. He turned his head and saw the same ragged figure he had seen earlier, the scarecrow with the gray metal helmet. This time the thin, gangly man did not vanish from view but stared at Venser with mute curiosity. Venser took the opportunity to stare back and memorize as many details as he could.

The reedy figure stood perfectly still in the distance, his white eyes gleaming from the shadows of his helm. He was dressed in rags and tatters that seemed to flow around him like smoke. The conical metal shell on his head reached down to cover his entire face but for a darkened gap around the eyes, and even that gap was split by a thick, metal nose guard. A curved blade sprouted from the top of the helm, jutting forward with its pointed tip preceding the warrior like a lance tip. His nose and chin were muffled under a loosely tied rag and, he carried a dull-gray scabbard and blade on his hip.

Venser glanced back to his fellow denizens of Urborg, who made no move toward the new arrival. Then Venser called out, "Who are you?"

The scarecrowlike man cocked his head slightly. Venser heard a sinister rustling pass by him, a whisper of wind and malice. The helmed warrior pulled a round throwing spike from the back of his belt, twirled it expertly in his hand, and drew back his arm.

No, Dinne. I have special plans for this one. The Weaver King's voice was quiet, almost unnoticeable, but Venser heard it. So did Dinne the helmed scarecrow, apparently, for he smoothly sheathed his spike, bobbed his head toward Venser, and flickered out of sight.

Venser waited for the Weaver King's taunting laughter to return, but it never came. Instead, the same sparkling fog that had preceded Windgrace's departure appeared, heralding his return.

Lord Windgrace's body collected itself from the mist, growing darker and more solid as Venser watched. The planeswalker's body froze in place for a moment before converting fully to flesh and blood, his luxurious fur glistening in the moonlight as the cold wind touched it.

Windgrace materialized with his eyes on Venser. He stood staring until a dark-skinned man in leather armor emerged from the nearby throng. He was a native of Urborg, and his ceremonial war paint marked him as warrior-chief. He wore his thick hair bound tightly behind his head and a necklace of sharp, triangular teeth. The chief carried a polished wooden club with a sharp, metal blade embedded in its heavy end.

Windgrace nodded. The man came forward, bowed, and spoke to the panther-god in hushed tones.

"You've done well," Windgrace said. He extended his huge hand and placed it on the chief's shoulder. The man stood up straighter. His shoulders broadened. His hair burst out of its metal rings and fluttered around his head as if he were standing in a high wind.

"Go now," Windgrace said. The chief bowed again. He turned and, spotting Venser's wide-eyed interest, bared an enormous grin full of sharp, serrated sharks' teeth. With a feral growl, the chief winked hungrily at Venser and bounded back into the assembly.

Windgrace stood silently for a few seconds as he stared at Venser. "I like this new machine of yours much better," he said. "There's hardly any Phyrexia in it."

He considered the artificer for a few more seconds, then grunted and turned away. The serpents holding Venser's limbs released him, dropping him clumsily into the half-frozen mud and frosty grass.

Venser's arms and legs would not respond, so he had to lie there, helpless and ignoble, as Windgrace padded over. Venser felt the planeswalker's shadow like a solid thing, and it weighed on him until the artificer tilted his face up.

The panther-god stood with his massive paw extended. "Rise, Child of Urborg," he said. "We have much to do."

Numbly, Venser raised his hand. Windgrace engulfed it in his own, and Venser felt a surge of healing magic flow through him. Suddenly spry and limber as if he'd just awakened from a good night's sleep, Venser got to his feet.

As soon as he was upright, Venser dropped to one knee before Windgrace. "My lord," he said, "I am at your service."

"Rise," Windgrace said again, a touch of irritation in his throaty growl. He reached down and caught Venser by the scruff of the neck. He stretched the artificer out to his full height and deposited Venser on his own two feet.

"You are neither my friend nor my enemy," Windgrace said, "nor servant, nor victim. I don't know what you are, but I do know you are not Phyrexian. And now I know you are not the Weaver King's creature."

He turned toward the other natives of Urborg still waiting patiently at the hollow's edge. "Guard his machine," Windgrace said. "No one is to touch it for any reason." He held his hand open for Venser to see, closed it, and opened it again to reveal the twin powerstones.

"You are with me now, tinkerer," Windgrace said. He tossed the stones to Venser. "You are in this up to your neck. You and your machine work for me." He growled softly, deep in his chest. "Or you don't work at all."

Venser nodded, his breath hot against his teeth. "Thank you, my lord."

Windgrace scowled. "Don't thank me," he said. "I may ask you to give more than you care to before this is over."

"Yes, my lord." As he spoke, Venser was thinking of Jhoira and how she would have shared his reaction. "You wouldn't be the first, my lord."

CHAPTER 8

The Weaver King darted across the Stronghold's interior, skating on thin, silver lines of magical force. Each gossamer thread in the complicated web connected the Weaver King to one of his subjects, a direct link between his mind and theirs. His skein was very large these days, a tangled network that he skittered across like a mad, dancing spider.

Many of his vassals were scarcely aware he existed, as his mind was a flighty thing that never lingered long in one place. His thoughts frequented the strange and wild places most thoughts never went and dwelled where most minds never visit. In truth he had more subjects than he could keep track of at one time, and there were many he had never visited personally.

Venser was one of his newest favorites. The mangy cat-god had severed his link with the artificer and driven the Weaver King off, but that was no worry. He had plenty of other amusements for the short term. He also had several more connections to Venser already in place, so it would be a small thing to breeze by for a visit at a later time of his choosing.

He had been Oleg il-Dal when the Phyrexians brought their Stronghold to Urborg. In the years before the Invasion he had been a leader of prominence in the wilds of Rath. Oleg was a born warrior, tall and strong with a wild mass of orange-red braids that hung down to his waist. His beard was likewise braided and long, giving him a fearsome appearance on the battlefield. More than a few of the evincar's dog soldiers had last seen Oleg's wild mane before falling to his sharp blade and strong arm.

But Rath had been created as a testing ground, and Oleg's followers were tested beyond their endurance. His band of Dal nomads was slowly whittled down to just over a dozen by the myriad dangers that preyed on those who lived outside of the Stronghold's protection. Between hostile tribes, swarms of slivers, lava-spewing laccoliths, and the endless flood of flowstone, each moment of each day was potentially lethal. After his people began to sicken and die from some unknown malady, Oleg led them to the Stronghold. He negotiated their entry and saw to their care, choosing to accept a life of servitude to the Evincar Volrath over no life at all. If his tribemates disagreed with his choice, they had every chance to say so or strike out on their own. None of them did.

Instead, they were installed in the Stronghold's City of Traitors, a permanent village constructed in the lowest regions of the hollow mountain's belly, and put to work. The Dal were nomadic, but they were good at construction and strong enough to work all day. Oleg and the others gave up the ways of hunter-gatherers and became carpenters, masons, and machinists.

That is, some of the Dal found work in the City of Traitors. Oleg and most of the rest were called upon to serve in other ways, in the evincar's notorious laboratories. Volrath, himself a shapeshifter, was fascinated by the changes that could be wrought on the human form. He started by twisting and combining existing bodies, improving them, making them larger, stronger, more monstrous. He soon mastered this art to the point of boredom and moved on to greater challenges—namely, breeding his own creatures from recycled flesh and bone and imbuing them with dark, magical power.

Volrath first placed Oleg in an oubliette for several months. No jailers, no physical torture, just an endless series of stone corridors.

He survived by eating lichen and vermin, and by drinking the foul water that collected in the maze's corners.

Then the true experiment began. His body continued to starve, but his mind was aggressively destroyed, shredded, sifted through, and reassembled by the evincar's sustained mental abuse. Oleg was shown images from his past, memories more real than the nightmare around him, only to have them whisked away as he staggered close. Volrath played loud, discordant sounds for days without respite. He released strange animals into the maze that Oleg never saw but could always hear as they slavered and snarled ever closer. The evincar projected colorful lights onto Oleg's face, penetrating his private thoughts and dreams no matter how hard he closed his eyes or how hard he slammed his head into the wall. The lights burned his face at first, singeing the tips of his long hair and beard, but he soon developed a tolerance. With the resistance came the realization that he needed the lights now, that he was weak and wretched without them. He sought them out to bathe in, to soak them up like a thirsty plant in spring's first rain.

After two more months of this Volrath threw a new twist into the game. The evincar placed a Dal woman and her child in the maze, two innocents who had come begging to the City of Traitors for asylum. They could have been members of his own tribe, so similar were their situations. Instinctively Oleg reached out to them with his hands, called to them with his voice, and for the first time sent a thin, silver filament directly from his psyche to theirs.

The child died instantly, weeping tears of blood. The woman survived, albeit as a mindless husk, and Oleg realized that while she could no longer control her thoughts or actions, he could. She did what he said, only what he said, when he said it. His new-found skill quickly grew stronger with practice, and she began to act on his every whim even if he didn't issue a direct command. She would sing, or dance, or stand on her head, and all he had to do was think.

The Dal woman lasted a week in the oubliette before she suc-
cumbed to lack of food and water. During that week, Oleg *il*-Dal
died at last, and the Weaver King was born.

For the next several months Volrath fed him a steady diet of
increasingly strong minds and bodies. At the end of that time the
Weaver King had spun himself a thick, comfortable web of puppet
strings on which to take his entertainment.

But Volrath fell in the end, replaced by a far more bloodthirsty
evincar who had no interest in his predecessor's breeding pits.
Abandoned and forgotten, the Weaver King stayed where he was,
obliviously capering his days away below the City of Traitors until the
Invasion began and the Stronghold shifted from Rath to Urborg.

Changes begun by Volrath were completed by that planar over-
lay. As Oleg, he had heard the dire rumors of living things that
fell through the cracks in reality. "Shadow creatures," they were
called, trapped in a hellish limbo between existence and nonex-
istence, barely present in the physical world, unable to truly die.
As the Weaver King, he experienced it for himself.

When the planeshift happened and the Stronghold broke
through to Dominaria, not all of the beings inside completed the
journey. Oh, the evincar's soldiers made it, and the legions of Phyrexian machines, and the endless swarms of slivers. But the Weaver
King stayed behind, forgotten in his dungeon. He became a shadow
thing, a phantom, an ageless, insubstantial wraith with nothing to
do but look out onto a world that he would never again touch.

At least, that is what he thought at first. He had nothing to
do but think when he first became insubstantial. Eventually his
thoughts dried up and he drifted. He had no sense of how long
he stayed like that, a blank man in a blank world, but he recalled
everything once he saw the light.

He heard a disembodied voice whispering in his ear as a distant, glowing purple circle slowly took shape among the haze. Its
light was dim but powerful, and with the half-heard voice urging

him on, the light soon penetrated the fog that surrounded him. Focusing on the light brought him back to himself. Moving toward it awakened his hunger. The voice vanished as he drew close, its satisfaction evident.

The voice and the light led him here, back into the world of flesh, bone, and blood. He found that his abilities were not hampered at all by his shadow state. It was also invigoratingly easy to find new subjects among the people of Urborg, to follow the scent of their hidden urges and suggest things they'd never allow themselves to think on their own. He never failed to relish the sensation they felt when they realized his words were no longer suggestions but dictates. He wasn't just a voice in their heads or some private bogeyman; he was lord and master. He was their king.

For years the Weaver King's snare lines and probes wormed their way into dreams and whispers all across Urborg. Every mind he touched opened up a new book of delicious memories and delightful experiences and, most importantly, a host of new acquaintances to visit. He traveled along the thoughts of mother for son, daughter for father, lover for lover, always leaving a trail of silver mind-silk so he could come and go as he pleased. He leaped from mind to mind this way for decades, his skein stretching far and doubling back on itself, forking left and right until he could skate across the surface of his web for weeks without ever taking the same strand twice. Volrath was dead. The Stronghold was dead. Long live the Weaver King.

He came out of himself and inspected the network of silver filaments. Dinne the Dart had very nearly put a damper on his master's fun with the artificer. He couldn't visit Venser again if Venser had a spike in his head. Perhaps it was time for the Weaver King to admonish his strong right hand.

Dinne, he called, *attend me.* His singsong voice sparkled in his own ears, and the joy it raised sent excited tremors along the tightly stretched silver web.

Dinne faded into view immediately. He was a good and loyal subject, faithful to his king at all times—except when his bloodlust got the better of him. Dinne had been a warrior of the Vec tribe back in Rath, but he had burned out after one too many campaigns in the Rootwater Forest. The Weaver King knew Dinne had been first injured by a poison-toothed merman and further abused by a self-righteous Kor shaman. When he stumbled back to his garrison in the Stronghold, Dinne il-Vec was no longer fit for military duty. Surviving his ordeal made him faster and deadlier than ever with his throwing spikes, but it also left him near-catatonic and unable to follow orders.

Volrath gave Dinne to the Weaver King partially to see what would happen but also because the evincar had a sadistic streak of frugality in him. Dinne had no other use than as fodder, so Volrath tossed the broken man into the oubliette knowing that Dinne would either be redeemed or consumed. Either result would be to Volrath's gain, but the evincar never saw the result of this particular trial. Volrath fell, and the Weaver King played with Dinne until they were both swept into the shadow realm.

Welcome home, dart tosser, the Weaver King said, his tone affectionate and playful. *I've been watching you.* Dinne's mind had long ago betrayed the fact that in life, he had detested anyone calling weaponry "darts." During their time together, the Weaver King had seen to it that the Vec warrior maintained that strong feeling but was unable to act on it.

Now the raider stood silent as he awaited his master's voice. His taciturn ways were an aspect of Dinne's personality that even the Weaver King couldn't break. Dinne rarely spoke, not by voice or thought, not even to his king. Not that such a thing ever stopped the Weaver King from interacting with Dinne. In fact, all it really meant was the he got to indulge in his favorite form of conversation, the monologue.

As gratifying as it was to make Dinne interact, the hard, brittle things in his mind were almost too sharp to play with and required plenty of softening before the Weaver King could freely scuttle across them. Unless he planned to make a day of it, it was better to keep Dinne focused elsewhere, their connection superficial.

Don't kill the special ones, the Weaver King reminded him. The silent Vec nodded, his white eyes smoldering within his helmet.

I'd like you to stay close to my new friend. Venser, the artificer. Keep an eye on him especially, but also look at his friends. I'd like to see if they can be my friends too. Some of them are just as interesting as he is. Wouldn't you agree?

Dinne's helm nodded again, but the warrior was otherwise completely still.

Though not as useful. The Weaver King giggled. *Be ready to bite when I whistle for you. It'll be glorious. It's ever so much easier to meet people when they're fighting you and not putting up walls or barriers to new acquaintances.*

The helm tilted once more.

But do keep clear of the panther. That one is special too, in a way that I haven't sussed out yet.

Dinne stood unmoving, neither defiant nor compliant.

Right, then. Off you go.

Dinne flickered away into the aether. It took a serious frame of mind and a vicious disposition for a shadow creature to injure someone in the real world. Under the Weaver King's tutelage, Dinne could do it at will, shifting between physical and ephemeral in rapid succession. The Weaver King prided himself on helping his subjects achieve their full potential. He had started small, forcing frogs to jump so high that their leg muscles burst and their bones shattered when they left the ground. Where Dinne had been a competent warrior in life, as the Weaver King's creature he had slaughtered a castle full of well-armed men in a single evening.

Ah, the Weaver King thought, his mind turning, *a distraction.* One of his subjects to the south, a narcotic-addled mercenary, had just drawn his sword while robbing an Urborg merchant family in their home. The rookie bandit had not originally intended to harm anyone. But now that the father, mother, and two children were abject and weeping at his feet, he was thrilled to be weighing the value of death over life. He was rampant with joy at the power of making the judgment himself and yet hesitant to make his joy manifest.

Do it, the Weaver King told him. *Because you can.*

Distant screams soon reached the Weaver King's ears, vibrating along his silver threads. Laughing, he let himself go and soared across the surface of his web once more, delighting in the simple pleasures his fascinating life afforded him.

* * * * *

"He's a devil," Jodah said. "A psychic vampire. He's mad, he's playful, and he's hungry."

Jhoira nodded. "And he's after you." They had come up against an impassable toxic bog that wasn't quite frozen enough to support them. They had agreed that falling into the sulfur-smelling waste was not worth the risk and were walking the edge of the bog until they found another, more solid path to Venser's crash site.

Jodah had been talking about the Weaver King while they walked. He had been thrilled with Jhoira's extensive knowledge about Rath and its shadow creatures in general, but he was visibly troubled by this one in particular.

"He's after us," Jodah said. "Both of us and everyone like us. Our minds are more interesting to him simply by virtue of how much is in there. We've been alive for a long time, Jhoira. We have more memories, more thoughts than most people."

"Hm. And he told you this?"

"No. Not exactly." Jodah sighed. "I know a great deal about mind control and manipulation. My best friend was possessed by my worst enemy once, and I didn't notice. Since then I've made sure to protect myself, to educate myself on that sort of thing. The Weaver King got to me but not without revealing himself in the process."

"So you backed down a psychic vampire?"

"No." Jodah was sounding more exasperated with each new exchange. "I just didn't give him what he wanted." The archmage seemed to argue with himself silently as he walked. "All right, I shammed senility until he got bored. Happy now? I threw out a few spells on the sly to fool him. Mostly on myself. Eventually he moved on but not before I got a good sense of what he was like and what he was after."

"And what's that?" Jhoira stopped and waited for Jodah to face her. "And you don't have to be ashamed of tricking your way out of danger."

Jodah nodded gratefully. "I wasn't ashamed until I had to tell you. You seem like more of a dealing-with-things-head-on sort of person."

"Perhaps. But the important thing is that your strategy worked. You learned something about our enemy."

"Thank you," Jodah said.

"So what did you learn? What is he like and what is he after?"

"He's a devil," Jodah said again. "He's like a cruel, spiteful child. And he's after as much painful fun as he can inflict."

"I see. And how does this threaten me?"

Jodah slipped his hands into his pockets. He looked miserable and cold. "I made him aware of you."

Jhoira stood and drank this in. She jerked her head to one side and strode past Jodah. "Keep walking," she said. "And talking."

Jodah stepped up beside her and kept pace. "He was in my dreams. He kept flattering me with how special I was, how much he wanted to get to know me better. He . . . he showed me Jaya, that friend I was telling you about earlier. Just as I remembered her."

"You were fooled," Jhoira said gently.

Jodah's dry laugh echoed off the trees. "Not a banner day for the archmage emeritus." He wiped his brow, took a few steps without speaking, and said, "The dream-Jaya got me thinking about other long-lived creatures. Lich lords and nature spirits, primal avatars, the lucid undead. People who have seen and done enough spectacular things to hold the Weaver King's interest. I believe he was trying to get some value out of all his hard work in binding me, as I had proved so disappointing." Jodah lowered his eyes. "Forgive me, Jhoira. Your name came up."

Jhoira paused as she fought to pull her foot free from a grasping nettle vine. "I'm mostly surprised that you've even heard of me."

"Your name comes up a lot, actually. I have access to a wonderful library, one that Commodore Guff himself considered an annex to his own. You've been party to some of the most important things that ever happened."

"Guff is dead," Jhoira said flatly. "He died with a book in his hands. And like you, Jodah, I vastly prefer not to be mentioned in history texts at all."

Jodah's face tilted down once more. "I am sorry." The archmage straightened up and said, "Would it help if I mentioned how that attitude is one of the many things we have in common?"

Jhoira kept walking, but she smiled slightly. "You don't need to help the situation. Just let it go."

"For example," Jodah said. "I dived into the Fountain of Youth four thousand years ago. It's why I'm still here."

Jhoira continued to smile, though she did not show her face to Jodah. "*The* Fountain of Youth," she said. "Or *a* fountain of youth?"

"It's *the* Fountain of Youth to me," Jodah said. "I never needed another. And you, you drank the slow-time water of Tolaria."

"Twelve hundred years ago," Jhoira said. Now she did turn and smile at Jodah. "Drank it by the gallon. And now that you mention it, this the first time in a long time that I've met someone far older than me who wasn't trying to kill me or change the world."

Jodah beamed back at her. "Fountain of Youth." He tapped his own chest. "Slow-time water." He gestured at Jhoira. "It's good to be us, isn't it?"

Jhoira surprised herself by laughing out loud. "Yes," she said. "Sometimes, yes. I suppose it is."

"Then we agree. I do prefer being agreeable."

"Here's more good news we can agree on," Jhoira said. "We've arrived." She pointed to the frozen trench that had been carved into the marsh ahead.

"So we have," Jodah said. "But there's no machine."

"And no Venser."

"Ah, but neither is there a body. Or wreckage. Maybe he got back in and took it somewhere else. Wait. . . ." Jodah's voice trailed off as he peered into the mist surrounding the marsh.

A pale man emerged from the woods. Jhoira didn't recognize Venser at first he seemed thinner but somehow stronger than he had before. He also bore a small green symbol on his left cheekbone, just below his eye.

"Hello," Venser said. His voice was stiff, and it rustled against the freezing air.

"Venser," Jhoira said. She presented Jodah and said, "This is Jodah. He's a friend."

Venser nodded. He stepped closer and nervously cleared his throat. "Lord Windgrace requests the pleasure of your company."

"Well met, Venser," Jodah said. "But I understood you to be an artificer. Is that a gladehunter mark on your face?"

Venser's eyes darted back and forth between the new arrivals. "It is. Please come with me now."

"But how did—" Jhoira's question was interrupted by a loud, rumbling roar that echoed in from every direction.

"Too late," Venser said.

Jodah let out a pained cry beside Jhoira. The archmage shot into the air, stiff as a stone, floating there. The predawn sky over Jodah shimmered, coalescing into a huge panther's head. The image lunged forward with its jaws open wide. It distorted itself as it streamed into Jodah's eyes, nose, and mouth.

The archmage screamed. Jhoira shot a look at Venser, but the artificer's expression was as miserable and helpless as her own.

CHAPTER 9

"He'll be fine," Venser said, though he didn't feel or sound hopeful.

"What's going on?" Jhoira said. Over their heads, Jodah was still hanging rigid in the air.

"Windgrace," Venser said. "It's what he did to me when he sounded me out. There's a . . . mind spy at work here. Windgrace needs to know if your friend can be trusted. If so, he'll be fine. If not . . . Windgrace will fix him." Privately, Venser added, "Like he did me."

He didn't know Jodah, but he knew Windgrace would not tolerate anyone's agents but his own. All Venser and Jhoira could do now was trust in the panther-god to save Jodah without killing him.

Jhoira stepped in close to Venser. "Are you all right?" she said. "Are you yourself?"

"I'm intact," Venser said. "And a little overwhelmed." He reached out and touched her shoulder to make sure she was real. "I'm glad you're alive. I'm glad you're here."

She glanced up at Jodah before asking, "What happened to the ambulator?"

"Windgrace has it. Something went wrong when Teferi—when I panicked during the launch. I lost sight of you in transit. I got distracted from the controls." He sighed. "I just wanted you to be safe. Not to drag you down with me."

Jhoira's face hardened. "What about Teferi?"

"He—Look out!"

Jodah was straining against his paralysis and had succeeded in moving his arms. Venser knew this was a sign Lord Windgrace was almost through, and he pulled Jhoira aside. The archmage fell several feet to the ground, but he landed solidly and kept his footing.

"Ouch," Jodah said. He shook his head clear. "That wasn't a good thing, was it?"

"We don't know yet," Venser said. Jhoira shot him another look, a pained one.

Then Windgrace appeared, thick-muscled and feral, his eyes wild. "You have been touched by the Weaver King," Windgrace said. "But he left almost no marks on you."

Jodah stood to his full height and dusted off his robes. "That information was there for the asking," he said. "You didn't have to sit on my head."

"Mind your tone, Archmage."

Jodah's shoulders sagged. "You know me too?"

"I do now. Your enemy is mine, and hers, and his. I will put you to work on it."

Jhoira stepped between Jodah and the planeswalker. "No, Lord Windgrace. You will not. We have even more important work to do here."

The panther-man's eyes flickered like green candles. "You are one of Urza's protégées," he growled. "Teferi's consort. The ageless Ghitu."

"Jhoira," she said. "But I am no one's consort."

"Ageless?" Venser said.

Windgrace's fur bristled. "You and the Zhalfir whelp broke and ran during the Invasion while the rest of us bled defending our homeland," he said. "What is your business here?"

"Our common enemies," Jodah said. "The Weaver King. The

unnatural cold. The Phyrexian hordes."

"And the hole in the sky that enables them all." Jhoira and Jodah stood side by side, both unwavering under the panther-god's fearsome glare. Venser envied their resolve.

Lord Windgrace paused. His breath rumbled in his throat, not quite a growl. He turned to Venser and said, "These things are all related?"

Venser nodded. "I suspect so. And if Jhoira believes it, so do I."

Windgrace addressed Jhoira. "Where is Teferi Planeswalker?"

"In Shiv," Jhoira said. "Though he is planeswalker no more."

"Interesting. How did that happen?"

Jhoira paused to glance at Venser, then at Jodah. "He used up his power sealing the rift over my homeland." She gestured up to the crackling disc on the horizon. "A phenomenon closely related to that. He saved Shiv but was greatly diminished."

"So he lives?"

"He does. His mind has been dampened along with his magic, but he lives."

"I will speak with this diminished planeswalker," Windgrace said. "Venser, attend me."

"What?" Venser gulped as Windgrace's tail twitched menacingly. "I mean to say—yes, my lord. But why are we—"

"Lord Windgrace," Jhoira said. "I have much to tell Teferi, much to ask him. I have also known him for a very long time, and in his current addled state, I may be the only one who can make sense of what he says."

Windgrace huffed. "And your point?"

"If you allow me to accompany you," she said, "if you bring Jodah and me with you, we may all find the answers we seek."

"A worthy suggestion." Lord Windgrace swiveled his massive head around the clearing. Venser stood ready beside him, praying that the panther-god would forget about him. Jodah and

Jhoira stood shoulder to shoulder, looking up at the planeswalker expectantly.

"No," Windgrace said. Venser did not have time to draw breath before he felt himself vanishing, slipping away from Urborg and into the nothingness of the void. He couldn't speak but he tried to send his thoughts directly to Jhoira, to beam them from his brain to hers.

Help me, he thought. *The only thing I can do is make things worse.*

* * * * *

Jhoira and Jodah stood alone by the trench.

"Arrogant bastard, isn't he?" Jodah shook his head. "I thought for a second there we had convinced him."

"We did," Jhoira said. "But he doesn't trust us."

"He trusted your friend easily enough."

"Venser was suitably awed," Jhoira said. "He's a native and he grew up hearing the legend of Windgrace."

Jodah nodded. "So what do we do?"

Jhoira tightened the fur coat around her waist. "We follow." She walked past the end of the trench and up a small rise.

Jodah was right beside her. "How do we do that?"

"With Venser's machine."

"Oh? I thought it didn't work."

"It works fine."

"It dropped you off in the middle of a frozen swamp and half-buried itself in the mire."

"It works fine without Venser. My theory is that Venser's untapped potential interferes with the ambulator's function. I made sure to build this one to accommodate that interference."

"But it didn't work."

"No. But I think I know why. And how to fix it."

"That would be ideal." They hiked along for a few moments. Jodah said, "Do you know where to find it?"

"No. That's why we have to start looking now."

"I see. And have you a method for getting past Windgrace's gladehunters?"

Jhoira's pace slowed. "No."

"Because I strongly doubt that he left it unguarded. Venser said 'Windgrace has it,' not 'Windgrace wrecked it.' If the planeswalker kept the machine intact, he must have a use for it."

"And if he has a use for it, he values it. And he will make sure to protect that value." She stopped walking. "I see your point."

Jodah shrugged. "I'm just thinking out loud."

"Keep thinking then. Do you have any ideas?"

"On how to recover the machine without being eaten by those from Urborg? No, I can't say that I do."

Jhoira paused, her jaws working furiously as she considered her options.

"What I do have," Jodah said, "is an alternate means of transport." He waited for her to absorb this before adding, "It's not like planeswalking. It's more like a series of tunnels that I use from time to time."

"Can it get us to Shiv?"

"Almost certainly. It takes some effort to set up the passageway, and I can only take us to preexisting, suitable places. I can't make us appear exactly where we want to be, but it works by following ley lines and mana channels. If our destination has magic . . ."

"It does. Not in abundance, but it exists."

"Capital." Jodah nodded. "If there's mana, we can go there. Shall I begin?"

"Please. And if you don't need my help, I will scout the area for signs of Venser's machine."

"And Urborgian monsters." Jodah bobbed his head and waved

his hand magnanimously. "By all means, scout away. I love having a solid fallback plan."

Jhoira nodded, treating the archmage to a confident smile. "Let's get started."

* * * * *

Windgrace was rough and impatient, but Venser had no quarrel with the planeswalker's power. The artificer had endured more than his share of teleportation magic over the past years, and especially in the last few weeks, but his journeys had never been as smooth or efficient as this.

They were gone from Urborg and standing in Shiv faster than it takes a stiff wind to extinguish a candle. There was none of the stomach-churning discomfort or vertiginous falling sensation that he expected. Guided by a master like Windgrace, Venser completed the trip as easily as closing and reopening his eyes.

Venser's memory must have had something to do with their landing site, for they appeared in the exact same place from which the ambulator had departed. The Ghitu elders and craftspeople were no longer assembled there, but a single figure stood patiently waiting as the hot wind fluttered the sleeves of his robe.

Venser was not surprised to see Teferi standing there. He began to understand Jhoira's recurring sharpness with the planeswalker— Teferi pretended that he knew more than he did as often as he pretended not to, and it was maddening to have to keep track of his playacting.

"Welcome back," Teferi said. He bowed to Lord Windgrace. "And welcome to you, Protector of Urborg."

"So it's true," Windgrace said. "You have changed since we last met."

"Have we met, my lord? I cannot deny that you are familiar, but much of my own mind is still opaque to me."

"Spare me your babbling. We are in haste. What goes on here?"

Teferi arched his brow innocently. "Here, my lord? Nothing. What needed to be done was done. That which still needs to be done has led Venser and Jhoira to your homeland."

Windgrace turned to Venser, who quickly spoke up. "Lord Windgrace is asking about the rifts, Teferi. Jhoira thinks the one over the Stronghold is . . . growing more unstable."

"How is Jhoira?"

"Willful," Windgrace said. "Short of patience. And possessed of an inflated opinion regarding her opinions."

Teferi smiled. "So unchanged then?"

Windgrace snarled. "I have no time for this. There are oddly evolved Phyrexians marching out of the Stronghold by the score. Winter has come unseasonably early and shows no signs of ending. I know these things are connected. Your Jhoira says the rift is also involved." He sprang forward and landed lightly on his feet, his nose mere inches from Teferi. To his credit, the erstwhile planeswalker never flinched.

"There is time magic at work," Windgrace said, "which has always been the province of Tolarians. I believe you may have useful information. Share it with me. Now."

"Any information I have is gone," Teferi said. "All my insights were lost along with my planeswalking. I am a shell of myself, Lord Windgrace, a hollow man. I can't help you."

The panther-man clenched his sharp teeth. "Won't. You won't help."

"It's not a question of desire but of ability."

"I can compel you," Windgrace said. "I can command your desire and your abilities."

"Of course you can," Teferi said. "You are still a planeswalker."

"And you are still a child." He turned to Venser. "This is pointless. Do you have anything to add?"

Venser watched Teferi's guileless face. "No, my lord."

"Then we are done here."

"If I may," Teferi said. His voice was distant and vague, but Windgrace's ears swiveled eagerly toward the sound. "The Stronghold rift is the result of Phyrexian activity. It does not surprise me that you are finding Phyrexians inside."

"These are not the same. These are not the Invasion Phyrexians from which you ran and hid," Windgrace said.

"Oh? How so?"

"These are more refined. They are smaller and more autonomous. And they have been built and bred to fight in the cold."

"Yet the dark god who created them and spurred them on is long dead. Or has that changed too?"

Windgrace stiffened. "The Lord of the Wastes is no more. I am certain. But these new minions act very much like his old legions did."

"So we have Phyrexians that don't fit and an enduring cold that doesn't fit." Teferi turned to Venser. "Does anything you've seen so far explain this riddle?"

Venser paused, carefully considering Teferi's words. "We saw both history and alternate realities through the Stronghold rift. Some showed landscapes dominated by machines and refineries. If one of those alternatives, one of the potential worlds inside the rift, was frozen as well as overrun with artifact monsters . . . maybe it is spilling out into this world."

"Excellent," Teferi said. He grinned at Windgrace. "He's very smart, you know."

Windgrace huffed impatiently. "If these are invaders from another reality, how do we seal ours off from theirs? How do we keep them out?"

"I could guess," Teferi said. "But it would just be a guess. Venser?"

"Why are you asking me? You're the one who shut the Shivan

rift. Go ahead and guess how you did that if you really want to help."

Teferi straightened, his half smile fixed. "With every last shred of magical power I had. Even if I could do it twice, it might not work again. Not with the a time distortion to contend with."

"So we need a planeswalker," Venser said.

Teferi nodded. "Or a timewalker, someone skilled at moving against the temporal flow."

"You?"

Teferi gracefully bore Windgrace's scorn. "No, my lord. I can stop time temporarily or remove things from its progression." He shrugged. "Rather, I used to be able to do those things. But even at my peak I've never been able to take myself or anyone else out of the present, not into the past or the future."

"Then you are useless to me." Windgrace backed away from Teferi, but his angry eye lingered on the bald wizard.

"I almost certainly am," Teferi said. "But there are others who may be of service."

"Stop playing games. Who do you mean?"

"Freyalise," Teferi said. "The rift above her Skyshroud Forest is similar to the one over Urborg, as it was also created by Phyrexians during the Invasion. She may be having troubles of her own that mimic yours. And unlike me, she is still whole, her power complete." Teferi smiled brightly. "You two should collaborate. Two planeswalker heroes of the Invasion united to stop another Phyrexian horde. It has a symmetry that appeals to me."

Windgrace glowered. "I would sooner murder an infant in its cradle than I would disturb Freyalise on your say-so."

"Is her privacy more important that Urborg's existence?" Teferi made a quizzical face. Venser expected Windgrace to bristle at Teferi's words, but if anything the panther-man grew calmer, more serious and still.

"You are truly Urza's heir," Windgrace said.

Teferi bowed. "Thank you."

"It is no compliment." The planeswalker spoke to Venser. "Come. We will consult with Freyalise."

"Good-bye, then," Teferi said. "I'm glad I was able to help in the end."

Windgrace's ears flattened. "You're coming too, Tolarian."

"What?" For the first time since they arrived, Venser thought Windgrace had Teferi's full attention.

"Say no more," Windgrace said. "I would take it as a grave personal insult if you expected your ploy to work as intended. I am not your dupe."

"But I am—"

"You are playing games. We are not. If you will not work with us willingly, we will pry what we need from you by force."

"Freyalise dislikes me," Teferi said. "She detests me, in fact. If you bring me to her she may well consider you her enemy."

"Then I will not bring you to her, nor her to you. We will meet on neutral ground."

"How will we do that? Freyalise will not leave Skyshroud."

"It is truly pitiful how far you have fallen," Windgrace said. "I have no need to explain myself. Make ready, both of you. We're leaving."

Teferi tried to say something else, but Venser knew better. Before the first breath had even entered Teferi's body, the Ghitu launch platform was full of blinding light.

* * * * *

Jhoira sat watching Jodah as the archmage prepared his transport tunnel. It was not a flashy affair. In fact, it was little more than an existing hole in the ground with a shimmering skin of liquid rippling over it. Jodah had spent most of his time finding the hole. The magic was almost an afterthought.

The longer it took the more Jhoira worried that they'd arrive too late. Windgrace was not likely to stay in Shiv for long, and it would be just her luck to pass by him as he was planeswalking Venser back to Urborg. She had no idea how much longer Jodah's preparations would take, but she was starting to think they'd be better served simply to sit and wait.

She had found no trace of the ambulator. There were strange tracks that told her it had been dragged from the trench and moved into the deep woods, but she was unable to follow the trail past the tree line. It was encouraging that the gladehunters hadn't simply pulverized the machine where it fell, but the fact that it still existed was small comfort when she didn't know where it was.

The layer of liquid over Jodah's tunnel undulated and the archmage yelped. "Stand back," he said. "Something's headed here."

"Planeswalker?"

Jodah paused, scolding Jhoira with his eyes. But he said, "Yes. This time you are correct."

Windgrace, Venser, and Teferi shimmered into view opposite Jodah and the tunnel. Jhoira regarded the trio with different levels of concern—Venser seemed about to drop from exhaustion, Teferi looked as chastened as she'd ever seen him, and Windgrace was larger, wilder, and more agitated than ever.

"You there," Windgrace said to Jodah. "You are a longtime ally of Freyalise."

Jodah glanced at Jhoira. "Actually, no," he said.

"Nonsense. You were instrumental in her casting of the World Spell."

Jodah shrugged. "I have had extensive dealings with Freyalise in the past. But I would not call us allies and neither would she."

Windgrace grew slightly larger and a great deal more imposing. "But you are on cordial terms?"

"No, not at all."

Windgrace looked from Jodah to Jhoira to Teferi and said, "Why is everything so difficult with you people?" He closed his eyes and clenched his fists. "Venser."

"Yes, my lord."

"Does Freyalise hate you?"

"No, my lord. I've never had any dealings with her at all."

"That's something. All of you stand ready."

"But Lord Windgrace," Jodah said, "Freyalise does hate me."

"And me," Teferi said.

Jodah nodded. "Perhaps it would be best to leave us out of it?"

Windgrace's eyes narrowed. "No," he said. "At the very least I can hand you two over to her and enjoy it as she chastises you. Think of yourselves as a peace offering."

Jhoira stepped forward. "And me?"

"I know of you," Windgrace said. He pointed to Teferi. "And I know you're in league with this one and so probably know as much as he does. If Freyalise kills him, we may need you to provide our answers." The panther flexed his muscles and shook himself angrily. "And I have no more interest in debating this."

Jodah had sidled up to Venser, and Jhoira heard him mutter, "I don't want to go to Skyshroud."

Venser nodded sympathetically. "It's probably no consolation," he said, "but we're not going to Skyshroud."

"Oh." Jodah considered. "Is there any chance—"

The archmage never finished his thought. Windgrace didn't simply 'walk them away this time, he stretched out his arms and encircled them all in a sparkling stream of glittering, green-white pine needles. Outside the ring, Urborg faded away and was replaced by a strange, endless void. Distant stars and planets twinkled against a black sky that was dotted with vast clouds of dust and flashes of fire.

"Freyalise," Windgrace said. "I would speak with you."

Jodah looked miserable. Venser looked miserable. Only Teferi seemed sanguine, his face open and alert. Even so, from his expression Jhoira knew that Teferi did not fully appreciate the gravity of the situation—or at least he pretended not to.

The cosmos continued to spin around them. All was silent for several long, ponderous moments. Then a woman's clipped voice replied.

"Well met, Windgrace. Stand where you are. I will come to you."

CHAPTER 10

The shadow raider who had been Dinne *il*-Vec watched silently as the strange people vanished from sight. Despite his mute ways and his shattered psyche, Dinne was extremely lucid. He understood everything they said and held it in his thoughts for the Weaver King to access later on.

He didn't understand their appeal to his master, however. None of them but the panther had shown the slightest sign of battlefield skills or magical power. Dinne believed he could kill all four of them before they realized they were under attack. If not for Windgrace—no, if not for the Weaver King's dictates to avoid Windgrace—Dinne would have tested his theory and gotten a few of his spikes wet.

Instead he simply observed as they quibbled and argued and made wry asides. Clearheaded as he was, Dinne did not waste his thoughts on unraveling their strange ways or following their labyrinthine exchanges. He did note with some interest when they disappeared, especially as he could still see their afterimages lingering among the needles suspended in the fog.

As he watched and waited, Dinne spotted a familiar figure moving through the swamp. The dark-skinned man had a mouthful of serrated teeth and carried an Urborg war club. His face paint told Dinne the man was a chief, but he knew that already, having seen the man lead others into battle and lay low his opponents with his terrible weapon.

He glanced back at the flickering ghosts of Windgrace and the others. They had gone some place he could not follow. There was nothing to do but wait, so his skills were wasted here. For all the good he was doing the Weaver King, Dinne might as well be killing the Urborg chief.

Absent as a sleepwalker tossing back the bedclothes, Dinne drew one of his round throwing spikes. He didn't understand the true nature of his shadow state, had never even considered it very deeply, but he knew that these weapons were as solid to him as they were to his victims. He had been wearing the spikes when he was cast into the void between planes, and every one he threw always found its way back to him. He didn't know or care if they drew their substance from his own or if they sought him out like love-starved pets. It was enough that he'd never run out, that there would always be something heavy and sharp to curl his hand around when the killing time came.

It was coming now. He could feel it. The Urborg chief drew Dinne's eye, pulling it as surely as if tethered to it by wire. The chief was a warrior too. He didn't spend his time bickering. Such a man deserved a warrior's death.

He moved over the swamp toward his target, his legs taking steps though his feet never touched the ground. He could move like lightning once his blades were drawn, flickering behind and in front of his quarry, stabbing them at will. This kill would be face-to-face, however, as he planned to indulge himself.

He slid in front of the chief and willed himself solid. The target saw him, something the Weaver King always encouraged. Dinne did nothing as the chief snarled and bared his sharp teeth. The Urborg brute brandished his war club.

Dinne drew a spike. He held it out carelessly, rolling it back and forth between his fingers for the chief to see.

"Come on then," the dark-skinned warrior said. "Come at me."

Dinne made no offensive or defensive motion but simply continued to roll the spike. The chief lunged forward, his club raised high with the metal blade's tip facing Dinne. The Vec raider held his ground as the tip hurtled down toward his face and at the last moment shifted to his phantom state.

The club passed through him without resistance. Off balance and overextended, the chief also stumbled through Dinne's ghostly body, almost sprawling face-first into the frosty grass.

The chief struck again from this awkward position, exhibiting inhuman agility that almost impressed Dinne. Almost. The club passed through him again, and this time the chief maintained his footing.

"Coward," he spat. He planted his feet and lowered his weapon. "Urborg is full of ghosts. I can tilt at them any day of the week if I choose to." He brought the curved club-blade close to his own face and ran his red tongue over the edge. "You don't even taste like anything," he said. "Come out and fight or let me be on my way."

Dinne could see the chief plotting as he spoke. The man had more magic in him than his speed and his sharp teeth. Dinne was curious to see what it was.

He didn't have to wait for long. The Urborg chief extended his club in both hands, holding it horizontally across his chest. Brackish, purple smoke drifted from the blade and circled around the handle until the entire weapon was coated in bruise-colored fog. Was the smoke venomous, Dinne wondered, perhaps caustic?

Dinne faded from sight as the chief brought the club up for another swing. The warrior paused, momentarily stymied by the loss of his target, then swung anyway, correctly guessing that Dinne had simply turned invisible and stayed in the same spot.

The fog-shrouded blade stung and burned Dinne as it sliced through his shadow body. He paused to relish the sensation, one of the few he was still able to feel. After a lifetime of the Weaver

King's choking off most of his mind and body, Dinne savored any physical experience, even painful ones. The club had injured him, yes, but at least he felt the injury as real.

The chief was swinging wildly now, filling the frigid air with vile curses. Dinne endured a few more swipes of the tainted blade before stepping around behind the raving warrior. He stood inches away from the back of the chief's head as he waited for the man to grow tired. When that happened and the chief stopped swinging entirely, Dinne turned his back and paced off thirty steps.

There, Dinne turned and planted his feet. He became solid once more, a spike ready in each hand. Long ago, he might have called out, taunted his enemy before striking. Now, he only brought the two spikes together and tapped their ends to produce a metallic clang.

The chief whirled in place. Dinne waited until that half rotation was complete, then drew back both spikes and let them fly.

His aim was perfect. The chief screamed and dropped his club. His hands shot to his eyes but were baffled by the presence of a Vec throwing spike embedded in each socket. Howling, the chief fell to his knees, clawing at the shadow weapons and doing even more damage to his punctured eyes.

Dinne smiled under his helm. He had not thrown the spikes to kill but to blind. The weapons vanished from the chief's skull, and Dinne stood waiting until they reappeared in his belt. The raider drew four more spikes and hurled them in quick succession, driving them deep into the Urborg man's knees and shoulders. The chief staggered back as each sharp weapon landed. His arms and legs useless, the man fell heavily to the ground, melting the half-frozen mud with his own warm blood.

The Urborg chief was blind and crippled, but his tongue was still strong. In all his years as a soldier and the Weaver King's cutthroat, Dinne had never heard such invective. Once more he was almost impressed by the chief.

Dinne glanced back at the place where Windgrace and the others had vanished. The memory of them still lingered there, transparent statues in a perpetual argument. He still had no idea where they were, how they had gone, or when they would return.

He made himself solid again. The Weaver King never punished him if he did as he was told. He was always praised, even rewarded, as long as he was loyal and obedient and saw his missions through.

Dinne drew a single spike and rolled it between his fingers. His current mission was to watch, and he was doing that to the best of his ability. Anything else that happened, well, that was entirely up to him.

He moved forward toward the screaming, blood-soaked chief. Dinne nodded. He had plenty of time for this diversion, even if he did have to keep one eye on the Weaver King's prospective playthings.

* * * * *

Jhoira had been to the Blind Eternities many times before but never under Lord Windgrace's care. When Teferi had brought her here in the past they had moved with the flow of the great void, in concert with its arcane rhythms. They were always careful not to disrupt the powerful currents of energy and magic, as they helped comprise the foundation of the entire multiverse.

Windgrace was not so restrained nor so concerned with leaving things as they were. He created semisolid platform of mana, an immovable rock amid the gently swirling chaos, and set them down on it. Jhoira heard the substance of the Blind Eternities object, howling in impotent frustration at this outrage. The others heard it too, but only Windgrace seemed unconcerned. He had planted his feet here, and here he would stay until he got what he came for.

Jodah looked especially forlorn over their volatile position—or perhaps he was thinking forward to his reunion with Freyalise—but Venser and Teferi seemed genuinely pained. Despite the circumstances and the fact that none of them had the slightest bit of control over their immediate fates, Jhoira was consumed by curiosity. What did Venser and Teferi share that made their reaction so much more severe? Why did so many powerful entities keep zeroing in on Venser as if he were a novelty to be dissected?

She felt she knew the answer, or a small piece of it. Venser was a planeswalker. They always recognized one of their own kind, recognized that special spark that made them unique. Between the attentions Venser garnered from Teferi and Nicol Bolas and now Windgrace, there was no other explanation.

The only detail that didn't fit was the fact that he wasn't a planeswalker. He was not as Freyalise or Windgrace, not godlike or possessed of infinite mana or able to traverse the planes. He in fact had no magic of his own to speak of, save that he had teleported a few yards, once, and under duress.

But he had done it. When confronted by a Shivan basilisk, Venser moved without his machine, without any spell training. Somehow he had accomplished a feat that only one in ten thousand could manage.

She wondered if Venser realized he was still wearing the ambulator's control rig. Under different circumstances, she might poke a little fun at his earlier hesitation, point out to him that she had been right about its weight being bearable. Right now, all she could think about was the special functions she had built into the rig without Venser's knowledge. They would never get a better chance to employ it, not unless Teferi's planeswalking power returned. Or Venser's developed. Or they found the ambulator.

A surge of heat tinged with the scent of pine rushed past them. Jhoira prepared herself for Freyalise's arrival, wondering if the presence of a second planeswalker (or third if she counted Venser, or fourth if she also counted Teferi) on Windgrace's platform would split it asunder or stretch the Blind Eternities beyond the breaking point.

But Freyalise arrived as delicately as a butterfly, appearing whole and proud before them as the last of the hot, forest wind went past. The patron of Skyshroud was slight and severe, almost comically small compared to Lord Windgrace. One look into Freyalise's sharp features and penetrating eyes left no doubt as to her power, however. She was as feared as she was mysterious, a self-styled goddess who had twice taken great efforts to preserve Dominaria as a whole simply to protect the parts she actually cared about.

She was dressed in her preferred garb of an elf woman. Her fine green and white gown left her shoulders bare and her arms exposed to the elbow, where long leather gloves extended down to her fingertips. Her bushy hair stood out from her head, cropped to neck length, and she wore the traditional Llanowar eye patch of brass-colored metal and a single glittering gemstone. Her skin was soft and fair, but its color changed with her mood, evolving from milk white to sunset red as her anger mounted.

"Windgrace," she said. The panther-man nodded respectfully.

Freyalise saw Teferi. She sneered at him and said to Windgrace, "You travel in strange company, my lord."

"Only as dictated by circumstance. You recall I once traveled with you."

"If I had forgotten, I wouldn't be here now," Freyalise said. "But I am here. I have answered your call. Now, before you tell me what you want, tell me why he is here."

"The time rifts," Teferi said. "They're getting worse. Just as I said they would."

Freyalise silenced him with a withering glare. "My question was to you, Lord Windgrace."

"Teferi speaks true. Phyrexians have come again to Urborg.

They are not as we fought them long ago. They are cold-weather machines, designed to kill in arctic conditions. They spew from the fissure the Stronghold made when it cracked the sky. I—We have come to see if Skyshroud has experienced something similar."

Jodah stepped forward with his hands folded firmly into his sleeves. "Hello, Freyalise," he said. "I just want to confirm that you are ignoring me rather than overlooking me." He met Jhoira's puzzled eyes and said to her, "I don't want to surprise her. She lashes out."

"You are no longer capable of surprising me," Freyalise said. "You wore out that option fifteen hundred years ago."

Venser had crept up beside Jhoira. He whispered, "Am I the only one here who isn't ancient or ageless?"

Jhoira turned and held his eyes. "Yes," she said.

"The cold," Jodah said. He turned to face Windgrace. "Tell her about the cold."

Freyalise did not look at Jodah, but she said, "Keld has been cold since before I planted there."

"It will soon get colder." Windgrace folded his arms. "Urborg is in the grip of a magical winter that is also tied to the rift. Or so say the Tolarians."

Freyalise hesitated. She said, "How severe is it?"

"Very," Windgrace said. "And getting worse with every passing day."

"It's not as cold as the Ice Age you and I ended," Jodah said. "Not yet."

Venser whispered, "Why is he antagonizing her?"

"An excellent question." Jhoira motioned for him to be quiet. "Let's listen and we'll all find out together."

Freyalise swiveled her head around the platform, magically shoving everyone but Windgrace to the edges. When the two planeswalkers were alone at its center, she said, "Keld is also suffering through an unnatural cold," she said. "I had thought it a symptom of the mana-draining effect the rift has. I thank you for this new information."

Windgrace nodded. "And the Phyrexians?"

The small woman shifted uncomfortably. "They have come," she said, "but only recently and not in great numbers."

"Not yet," Jodah called.

"If you speak to me again"—Freyalise's tone was savage, and she left an ominous pause between her thoughts—"I will extract your tongue and hang you with it."

Jodah nodded, truculent as a mischievous child, but he kept silent.

Windgrace spoke. "Is this happening anywhere else?"

Freyalise shrugged. "I don't look past Skyshroud's borders any more than you look beyond Urborg's."

"Then this is our problem for now," Windgrace said. He nodded. "Perhaps it's time we worked in concert once more."

"Reform Urza's team of planeswalkers?" Freyalise tossed her head dismissively. "No thank you. With seven dead in our last outing, we'd have too much work to do filling out the roster." She turned and gave Teferi and Venser a critical look. "And I'm not interested in running down new recruits."

"No teams, Freyalise. No nine. Just you and I. We are the ones who accomplished our mission during the Invasion. I still trust you and your abilities."

"As I do you and yours. But I am older now, Windgrace. I am less inclined to hitch my fortunes so closely to another's."

Windgrace nodded. "So you will not help."

"Oh, I'll help. Just not as you suggest."

The panther's ears swiveled. "What do you propose?"

"We both know our own homes. We know our own minds and inclinations. We know what we are capable of. Let's not fool ourselves. We both work best alone, but I propose that we work in unison."

Windgrace's keen eyes blazed. "Together," he said, "but separate."

"Yes. If the time rifts are connected, our efforts will complement each other. Pursue your strategy in Urborg while I pursue mine in Skyshroud. If either one of us has any success, we can share and mutually profit from it."

"Agreed. But Freyalise . . . have you a strategy to pursue?"

"I would never presume to advise you, sir, not in the art of war or in magic. I expect the same courtesy."

"And so you have it." Windgrace smiled. "It is good to rely on you again, Freyalise, even in this fashion. Good hunting, Patron of Skyshroud."

"Yes, good hunting." Freyalise turned and nodded toward Venser at the far end of the platform. "I must presume upon you, my lord. There is a member of your party I would have to assist me."

"Take any but the artificer. He is from Urborg, so he is mine."

"Of course. My plans are for another. With your permission . . ."

"By all means."

Freyalise smiled coldly. She glanced at Teferi and Jodah. To Jhoira's surprise, Freyalise turned fully around to face her. "Come with me, Ghitu elder."

"Me?"

Teferi, Jodah, and Venser all reacted at once. Jhoira could not distinguish who said what, but the overall mood was concern bordering on panic.

"Silence," Freyalise said. Each of her friends was pressed back again, the air squeezed from their lungs as they teetered dangerously on the edge of Windgrace's platform.

Jhoira found she could move, so she stepped forward. "I cannot refuse you, Freyalise."

"No."

"But I can ask you why."

"Indeed. And do you also delude yourself that I must answer?"

Jhoira thought for a moment. "No."

"Smart girl." Freyalise faced Windgrace and bowed deeply. "Thank you, my lord. Call me when your battle is won."

Windgrace's eyes sparkled. "I will."

Freyalise's lips curled into a cruel smile. "Or if you need my help." With that, the patron of Skyshroud waved her arms and faded into nothingness.

With Freyalise gone, the others were also free to move. Jhoira felt her own body thinning, leeching into the void around them. Jodah stepped up beside her and whispered, "Don't do this."

"I don't think I have any choice."

"Then be very careful. Freyalise is unpredictable. Selfish. And quick to anger."

Teferi had not come forward, but he also spoke, calling out, "Also, she will not hesitate to sacrifice you if it will serve Skyshroud."

"I am open to practical suggestions. What should I do?"

"Stay alive," Jodah said. "I will come for you."

Jhoira's body and voice were almost gone. "Thank you, my friends. Farewell."

Before she slipped away entirely, Jhoira cast her eyes toward Venser. The artificer was still shock-silent, his expression slack and beaten. Except for the glint of anger in his eyes when he looked at Windgrace, Venser was the picture of a man whose burden had just exceeded his strength.

Good. Anger was just what Venser needed. Anger overruled fear, anger sparked action. At this stage Venser had to draw on whatever fortifying emotions he could dredge up.

"Hold on to that," she tried to say, but by then she had nothing left with which to speak.

CHAPTER 11

Jodah tried to avoid traveling by planeswalker whenever possible. He preferred to stay on Dominaria, in touch with the mana that he knew and could shape into spells without hesitation. Besides, the sensation of slipping from here to there and from existence to nothingness and back always unsettled him.

Windgrace brought Jodah, Venser, and Teferi back to Urborg, to the same spot in the marsh. Jodah suffered a rush of vertigo as his legs became solid enough to bear his weight. He stumbled forward slightly, his feet sinking into the crunchy mud.

An unseen force lifted him several inches into the air and pushed him back away from Windgrace and Venser. Teferi was likewise shunted aside, he and Jodah coming to rest twenty yards away from the planeswalker.

"We are quit," Windgrace said. "Amuse yourselves as you can, or be consumed by the fen. All I require is you stay out of my way."

"My lord," Teferi said, "if you would have me I would serve as your advisor in the coming trials."

"I need no advice from a cowardly academic. Return to your time labs and ruin someone else's home."

"Is that an insult to me, my lord? Or to your new ward?" Teferi nodded at Venser.

Windgrace paused, his feline features curled into a smirk.

"You'd like him for yourself, wouldn't you? You have sensed what I have, that he is something new. You can't wait to get him alone and sift through his essence until you figure out how to put him to use."

Teferi's voice grew harder. "Perhaps. But how is that different from your plans?"

"The difference, you Tolarian maggot, is that I have rightful claim. Whether he knew it or not, Venser benefited from my protection all his life. The fact that he used that life to spit in the face of everything I tried to build here only adds to the debt he owes. Without me, Urborg would be little more than a killing ground where the prey has long since been hunted to extinction and the predators feed on each other for sustenance. Only the strongest and most savage would survive." He turned to Venser. "Would you count yourself among that esteemed group?"

Venser did not bow, and his voice was vague and unfocused. "No, my lord." Jodah noticed the artificer's mood and saw an opportunity.

Windgrace's chest rumbled like thunder. "No indeed. Go your own way, Teferi, and leave us to my work."

Windgrace and Teferi locked eyes. To the bald wizard's credit, he did not blink or flinch in the face of a hostile and fully powered planeswalker.

Jodah made a small hand signal that caught Venser's eye. He twitched his head slightly, over his shoulder toward the transport tunnel he had constructed with Jhoira. Venser stared at him and Jodah was relieved to see the artificer's brain working behind his glazed expression.

Venser nodded back, almost imperceptibly.

"My lord," Jodah said. Teferi turned first, breaking the stare down, but Windgrace also cast his eyes toward the archmage. "If you are done with me as well and I am truly free to go . . . I would go. There is nothing to keep me here."

"Be off," Windgrace said. "I have no quarrel with you, Jodah of the Unseen Academy, but Freyalise's slight regard is enough for me. I would sooner see the back of you than develop a dislike of my own."

"Agreed." Jodah bowed. "With your permission . . . I have my own method of leaving Urborg."

Windgrace nodded. "Employ it."

"I shall. As Jhoira bid us, I bid you: Farewell."

"Farewell, Jodah."

He glanced at Teferi and Venser. "The same to both of you. If the world survives, I hope that we will meet again."

"As do I," Teferi said. "I look forward to it."

Venser nodded slightly but kept his eyes leveled at Jodah. "Count on it."

Jodah nodded back. Without further preamble, he turned and slipped off into the thick, marsh grass and the frozen black evergreens.

* * * * *

Venser watched Jodah go with a mixture of relief and sadness. Relief that at least someone would emerge from this fiasco alive, sadness that he had to face the rest of it alone.

And he felt very alone indeed. He didn't consider Windgrace a colleague, and he didn't consider Teferi at all. In fact, all he truly thought about was how to get off Urborg and back to Jhoira's side.

He was not prone to deluding himself and accepted there was more than a practical element to his interest. If he understood half of the dizzying conversations he'd been a party to, Jhoira was infinitely older than he'd thought, which only made her more impressive to him. Her experience had not made her aloof or callous like the other immortals he'd met. If anything Jhoira was warmer, more patient, and more human than anyone on the short list of people he knew.

Venser watched the path Jodah's feet had made in the snowy dust and tried to factor the archmage into all this. Jodah had signaled him, tried to impart some secret while the planeswalkers were occupied, and Venser had responded. But he was uncertain what that nonverbal exchange signified. He was certain that Jodah had no intention of leaving Urborg unless it was to go after Jhoira. Venser himself would like nothing more than to join him, but there was the very real obstacle of Lord Windgrace.

The panther-god spoke up, pulling Venser from his reverie.

"Time is shorter than my patience, Teferi. Do I need to remove you from this equation?"

Teferi shook his head. "Leave me as I am. I have insight and information that you may yet need."

"Doubtful."

"All the same, I will be standing by to answer your call."

Windgrace bared his fangs in a feral grimace. "And in the meantime you may well be crushed and swallowed by an Urborg anaconda. Do us all a favor, Tolarian: close your eyes and hold your breath while you wait."

The bald man turned away, speaking to Venser as his voice trailed off. "Stay alert, my friend. You might just get the chance to return to your workshop and your life's work when this is all over."

Windgrace waved his hand. "From now on, Venser's work is to assist me."

Teferi did not reply, and Venser stared after him as the wizard withdrew. Then Windgrace's power flowed and Venser was gone.

* * * * *

Jodah easily found his transport tunnel and set to work. This particular spell functioned on very little mana, which was fortunate because mana was increasingly hard to come by. He was well versed in every aspect of Dominaria's magical resources, so he could tell how thin Urborg's supposedly powerful swamp magic had become. Swamp mana was rarely his first choice in any case, so he was just as well served by drawing other colors from more distant landscapes. The memories alone of his long tenure in Teresiare provided all the mana his tunnel required. All he currently lacked was an endpoint, a destination to compete the connection between where he was and where he needed to be.

Skyshroud, to be exact. The thought of Jhoira with Freyalise troubled Jodah deeply. The planeswalker was ruthless and driven when it came to protecting her territory, and he knew she considered every non-elf creature expendable. Jhoira was perhaps safe from the Weaver King's interest while she was in Skyshroud, but she was not safe from Freyalise's monomania, the great personality flaw that eventually claimed all planeswalkers.

The liquid that spanned his tunnel's entranceway shimmered and glinted back to life as Jodah infused it with fresh mana. It was also fortunate that Windgrace had marshaled most of Urborg's dangerous denizens to his cause. Jodah knew he was little more than a meal to the locals, and while he was eminently capable of defending himself he preferred not to expend the effort. Between the rifts that consumed Jhoira's attention and the Weaver King's whims, he had far more important matters to contend with than his immediate surroundings.

Jodah heard footsteps approaching and reluctantly tore his attention away from the tunnel. He readied two spells, a defensive shroud of concealment and an aggressive bolt of blistering force. He held them ready, eldritch power throbbing in his arms until his hands glowed.

Teferi stepped out of the mist. The oddly subdued planeswalker now carried a strange staff that Jodah hadn't seen before, a brass stick that was segmented and curved like a spine.

"Greetings, Archmage." Teferi bowed, and as he straightened he planted the end of his staff in the frozen mud.

"Greetings, Teferi of Zhalfir. What is your purpose here?"

"Same as yours, I imagine. I would see Jhoira returned, removed from Freyalise's tender mercies."

"Then leave me to my work." Jodah turned back to his tunnel but kept the spells he had at the ready.

"I shall. But before you also push me aside, hear what I have to say."

"Only if you can say it quickly," Jodah said.

"Jhoira needs the ambulator," Teferi said. "She is cleverer by far than anyone when it comes to design. She took an active hand in building this version of Venser's machine, and she made sure to include aspects that will aid us greatly in sealing the rifts."

Jodah did not turn. "She told you this?"

"I saw it myself. When the machine was first used, I stole a deeper glance at its innards. It not only moves through the world, it collects information about the journey. In transit, it also acts as a signal beacon."

Jodah stopped. "A beacon for whom?"

"Planeswalkers," Teferi said, "one in particular. She kept this from Venser and from me, but I have seen it. I think she no longer trusts me." He spoke with a subtle pride that rankled Jodah. "But she has accepted my approach to the problem. The rifts must be sealed by a planeswalker's power, all of it, directed toward the phenomenon with a tightly focused will toward eradicating it."

At last Jodah looked up. "Is this how you came to your present condition?"

"It is. Shiv is whole once more, and the whole only stands intact because I dedicated myself wholly to its preservation."

"I see. Forgive me, Teferi, but I will not follow your advice. I don't need the ambulator. I can reach Jhoira on my own."

"She needs it," Teferi said.

"She will have to say so herself. Rest assured I will ask when I see her."

Teferi shook his head sadly. "Venser is the key," he said. "He can pilot the machine. He must pilot the machine in order for it to help Jhoira."

"So you say. But Venser is currently on Windgrace's leash."

"He is craftier than you suspect. Perhaps more than even he suspects. Properly motivated, he will slip the tether upon him. You need his help."

"And what do you need?" Jodah stepped forward. "You have a planeswalker's tendencies even if you don't have one's power. You dole out scraps of information and only those that suit your larger purpose."

"My larger purpose," Teferi said, "has remained unchanged from the start. I wish to save the world, all worlds. Surely, as a witness to the unimaginable consequences of a planeswalker's actions, you can appreciate how devastating a single wrong decision can be. I only endeavor to restore what I have damaged. To return some of the order and stability that my work has undone."

"Then you are unique among your kind. And you are correct, I have seen firsthand what your kind can do. I cannot follow your lead, Teferi. I will not put more innocent lives in your hands."

"But who among us is innocent?" Teferi smiled at him. Jodah felt another surge of anger at that bald man's insouciance, at his deliberate and calculated charm.

"I am." Venser's voice preceded the artificer, who came out of the marsh exactly behind Teferi. "I may have sinned against Windgrace and Urborg, but as far as changing the world I am so far blameless."

"Ah," Teferi said, "we are assembled at last. I trust Lord Windgrace is not on your heels?"

Venser started to speak but waited. Then the artificer said, "He sent me back to his lair while he reconnoitered the Stronghold. There have been no Phyrexian incursions for two days, and he feels they are massing for a major attack."

"Then you are left to your own devices?" Teferi seemed delighted by his clever choice of words. "Splendid."

Venser was visibly unamused. "Jodah," he said, looking past Teferi. "What were you trying to tell me back there?"

"You know," Jodah said, "because you are here. I wanted to offer you the chance to come with me when I go after Jhoira."

"He cannot," Teferi said. "Windgrace would surely notice if he left Urborg."

Venser gave Teferi an exasperated look and strode past him to Jodah. "He's right, damn him," Venser said. "If I go, Windgrace will eventually follow to punish me and anyone with me."

Jodah paused. "Damn him indeed." He was considering Teferi's words and hating himself for it. As shifty and unreliable as the muddled planeswalker was, Teferi did have a unique perspective on the task before them. Jodah pointed to the wizard and said to Venser, "He says Jhoira needs your ambulator. Is that possible?"

Confusion crossed Venser's face. "I suppose so," he said. "But I can't get to it. Windgrace has it under guard with orders to destroy it before they allow anyone near."

"But it might help?"

"It might. It would at least give her a means of escape if Freyalise acts against her."

"Then she should have it. It is Teferi's gambit, but I don't think we should let our dislike of him color the facts."

Venser shuffled his feet. "There is another problem," he said.

"Tell."

"I can't pilot the ambulator to Skyshroud. I've never been

there. I have no connection to the place. I could go back and forth across every inch of Urborg—well, every inch I'm familiar with—but taking it to Skyshroud would involve a great deal of trial and error."

"How much?" Jodah said. "How long?"

"Days," Venser said. "Perhaps weeks."

An idea occurred to Jodah. He paused, letting his mind examine the notion for flaws. Finding none, he said, "I may be able to cut that down considerably. If you had a target in Skyshroud, a signpost, would you be able to go straight to it?"

"Of course. But how would I acquire—"

"I can set it up for you. My conveyance," he gestured to the liquid-capped tunnel, "is all but ready to go. I can go to Skyshroud. Freyalise herself will be my signpost. Then all I need is a beacon for you to hone in on, a signal fire so you can follow from here." He nodded, his conviction growing. "I'll be the scout. Then you can bring the machine to Jhoira. Or if it becomes necessary, take her to safety in it."

"Windgrace will still come." Venser's concern was quickly overwhelmed by his growing enthusiasm. "But if we move quickly he may not be able to spare the attention. Also, the ambulator is at least as fast as a planeswalker. We can stay ahead of him."

"Are you willing to try?"

Anger flickered across Venser's face. "My workshop is a short walk from here," he said. "There are devices there I can use. I spent a year and a half setting up tracking and relay stations for the chair to follow. If I don't have something ready-made, I can adapt what I do have."

"Get busy then. Meet me back here as soon it's ready."

"Where will you be?"

"Skyshroud. I mean to contact Jhoira without alerting Freyalise and tell her what we have planned. Once I'm sure everything works and is in place, I'll come back."

Venser paused. "Then we both go to Skyshroud."

Jodah nodded.

"Then we have a plan."

"By your leave," Teferi said to Venser, "I will accompany you to your workshop."

"No," Venser and Jodah said together.

A pained expression crossed Teferi's features. "I can help," he said.

"We don't need it," Jodah said. "Your kind only ever helps themselves,"

"I am the only one who has successfully closed a time rift," Teferi said. "If you won't have my input, what would you have me do?"

"Advise Windgrace," Jodah said. "Share your input with him if it's so valuable. Or do as he bid you and hold your breath." Jodah faced Venser. "Get started, builder. Be ready when I return."

Venser nodded. "I'll be waiting." He retraced his steps and vanished into the misty bog.

Left alone with Teferi, Jodah raised his hands. Light and heat bloomed from them and circled back up his arm like a coiling snake. "Don't interfere," he said. "Don't try to follow me. The tunnel will not work for you."

Teferi bowed. Without another word, he tugged his staff free of the mud and shuffled away.

Jodah watched until he could no longer see the planeswalker's once-gleaming white and blue robes. He turned and busied himself with the mouth of the tunnel, his keen mind already sorting through the steps he'd need to take to reach Skyshroud. He closed his eyes and extended his hands, drawing upon his memories of home and the evaporating mana supply those memories afforded him. Concentrating, he pushed the magical force into the liquid over the tunnel's entrance, extending the passageway out and west toward Keld.

He had lived long enough to see crises come and go. He had learned one thing for sure in his four thousand-plus years: people were the important thing, the living and vibrant part that gave life real value. If one planned to save the world, one must not lose sight of the individuals who made it worth saving.

Then Jodah stepped into the tunnel, the liquid cap shimmering like a thing alive.

CHAPTER 12

It was midnight over Skyshroud when Jhoira arrived. The moon hid its face behind a cloud, but Freyalise was surrounded by a green eldritch glow that illuminated the forest's edge.

Skyshroud itself had not changed since Jhoira was last in Keld, but the surrounding areas were very different indeed. Just weeks ago a huge saproling thicket encircled Freyalise's home and carpeted the forest floor. Now that thick, green tangle of grasping vines and half-sentient bodies was dry and brittle, dying in the cold. The desiccated remnants of the lush, green undergrowth were now little more than tinder waiting for a spark.

Freyalise marched to the edge of the forest and extended her arms. Jhoira followed, so as not to be left in the dark, but she stopped shy of the planeswalker. She had no desire to be caught in the backlash of whatever magic the patron of Skyshroud was casting.

Jhoira saw movement deep inside the forest among the wasted, broken trees. She peered closer, not ready to believe her eyes. She would never have imagined Freyalise tolerating the slivers, let alone summoning them to her side. Just the same, the woods were teeming with the insectlike monsters, thousands or perhaps tens of thousands strong.

She took an involuntary step back in the face of the slivers' incessant chattering and clicking. The smallest was no bigger than a songbird, and the largest was as tall and broad as a bear. They had been bred by Volrath in the harsh proving grounds of Rath, where they had developed a highly coordinated hive-mind that went far beyond simple cooperation, beyond even symbiosis.

They had been designed to display a wide range of magical abilities within a single hive. Over the course of a hundred forced generations of abuse they had acquired the power to share those abilities. Anything a single sliver could do was instantly transmitted to every other sliver nearby. A fire sliver sitting next to an armored sliver magically yielded two armored fire slivers. If there were a dozen or a hundred, all acquired the same combination of powers. The biggest slivers shared their strength, the lightest ones their speed, and the deadliest ones their lethality.

"Stand still, Ghitu." Freyalise did not turn when she spoke. "I am not yet in complete control of the swarm."

Jhoira watched as Freyalise gestured dramatically with her arms, guiding the innumerable masses of sharp-bodied vermin like an orchestra conductor. When Freyalise raised her arms, the slivers mounded high on top of each other. When she spread her hands wide, they dispersed among the trees. When she pointed, they swirled toward her target like the thin end of a cyclone.

Freyalise held her position, arms gracefully extended until the clicking and chattering had faded to a dull, muted drone. Then Jhoira stepped forward. "My name is Jhoira, Lady." She spoke calmly. "How shall I address you?"

Freyalise exhaled and lowered her arms. She slowly turned, half-facing Jhoira, and said, "I already like you more than your mentor. You have far better manners.

"You may call me Freyalise, Jhoira. I have brought you here to assist me, but you are not my slave. I need your ingenuity, your confidence, and your personality—and for that you must be free to speak and act as you see fit."

Jhoira bowed her head. "My purpose has always been to seal the rifts. At Shiv, at Skyshroud, at the Stronghold, and wherever else they are. If that is your purpose I will aid you however I can."

"My purpose is to save this place. The elves here are my children, and without Skyshroud they have nothing."

"Skyshroud will not be safe until the rift is sealed."

"I accept that. But I am weaker now than I have been for a long, long time. I am barely able to keep the slivers focused on these cold-weather Phyrexians. Had I begun years ago, by now I might have been able to act as their queen instead of their handler."

The planeswalker's shoulders slumped slightly, and she seemed for the first time like an ordinary mortal, and a weary one at that. Jhoira felt a surge of sympathy for the stern woman, but she pushed it aside and said, "What must I do?"

Freyalise did not answer immediately. She stared vacantly out into the depths of the forest for a few moments. When she did speak, her lips barely moved. "Later," she said. "Right now you must move out of harm's way."

The planeswalker tossed her head. Jhoira rose gently but swiftly into the air, climbing as high as the tallest trees in a matter of seconds. Under other circumstances it would have been a pleasant sensation, but Freyalise's melancholy troubled Jhoira even beyond the other considerably weighty matters that burdened her.

The moon emerged, its eerie silver light revealing a good deal more of the forest below. Jhoira gasped: along with thousands of slivers, the forest was crawling with Phyrexians.

The sleek, steel machines were smaller and more refined than the ones she knew, but they were unmistakably forged in Phyrexia. The moonlight glinted off their silver-blue bodies, and Jhoira smelled the unmistakable odor of the glittering oil that was their fuel and life's blood.

The sights, sounds, and smells of the merciless invaders filled Jhoira with sudden rage. She had spent the first half of her long life either preparing for them to invade Dominaria or battling to keep them at bay. She had captained warships against them, designed and built special weapons to destroy them, taken up sword and spell against them on the battlefield. She had even tried ignoring them, avoiding them in order to protect what was most precious to her at the time.

It never mattered, none of it. Her careful planning and diligent work, useless. Her defensive postures and offensive actions, all of it as fruitless and thankless as trying to scoop out the ocean with a spoon. No matter how thorough their preparations, how firm their resolve, or how complete their victory, Phyrexia always returned. The Lord of the Wastes had been gutted, broken, and bled dry during the Invasion. Yawgmoth was dead, yet here his presence was felt in this throng of mechanical nightmares that could not and should not exist, his will as malicious and destructive as ever.

For perhaps the first time since Teferi had started them on this complicated path of universal salvation, Jhoira forgot about the larger dangers and focused on the conflict in front of her. Maybe she hadn't ever made a difference when it came to protecting her home, but by the Nine Hells, she would watch and relish the spectacle of Freyalise defending hers.

The planeswalker appeared below, halfway between Jhoira and the ground. She was still gesturing at the slivers and wordlessly moving her lips. The green light around Freyalise intensified, adding to the moonlight and making the forest as bright as a struggling sunrise on a cloudy morning.

Jhoira could see the largest of the slivers from her vantage point and so was able to extrapolate the entire swarm's appearance. Though they shared abilities they tended not to change their original form, so the smallest ones were every bit as tough and strong as their larger hivemates. They were all sharp-nosed and angular, with hard exoskeletons and two supple tails. Each of the shelled monsters was shaped like an arrowhead and moved swiftly on multiple sets of legs. They charged across the forest floor and up the sides of Skyshroud trees, and some even soared through the air. Freyalise must have instructed them to cover high and low ground together, else the entire swarm would have been airborne.

The patron of Skyshroud danced below Jhoira, swinging her arms to direct her voracious army. The slivers streamed toward the Phyrexians, curling around the trees as they closed on their enemy.

The Phyrexians showed no fear when the first wave of slivers burst through the thinning underbrush, not even as the slivers plowed straight through their first line of defense. Jhoira heard the sickening crack of living shells mix with the awful shrieks of shearing metal as insect and artifact shattered against each other. The Phyrexians did not withdraw; the slivers did not relent.

The mad rush continued, scores of slivers bursting and dying as they dashed themselves against their foes. Phyrexian armor was proving more durable than the slivers' chitinous outer covering, so it required five or even ten slivers to seriously damage one invader. Jhoira did not see head-on conflict as a winning strategy, but Freyalise's forces outnumbered the Phyrexians twenty or thirty to one, and the planeswalker clearly felt her losses paid for themselves in damage done.

The swarm abruptly changed tactics and direction, veering off from the phalanx of metal monstrosities on each side to cordon off any escape. Three huge slivers lumbered out to meet the invaders, one with spikes along its shell, one with huge, rounded hammerhands, and one with the long, sharp horns of a prize bull. As Jhoira watched these three changed shape, melting and morphing into ghastly amalgamations of all their physical attributes.

A humanoid Phyrexian and a spider-legged war engine rushed out to meet them and were promptly speared by horns and battered to pieces. The fallen invaders gushed blue-white foam and black oil tinged with gold. An earsplitting shriek rose up from the spider engine as it died and the Phyrexian assembly responded, surging forward and burying the large sliver trio under blue-steel bodies and sharp, razor teeth.

Freyalise cast her arms wide and brought her hands together in a thunderous clap. The smaller slivers around the perimeter all swelled at once, doubling in size and splitting their shells to reveal whole new ones below, each glistening wet and crimson-colored. The mucouslike slime bubbled and steamed away as the horde closed the circle and rushed in on the Phyrexians there. Metal joints and servo-powered limbs struck back, but Freyalise's swarm was too big and had too much momentum. They crushed the Phyrexians against each other, mashing themselves against the invaders without respite.

Freyalise whistled and pointed with her index finger. Four small slivers soared down from the treetops, each with three hollow horns across their wedgelike faces. The open-ended horns left drops of a smoking orange substance in their wake, each drop igniting when it hit the forest floor. The triple-horned slivers flew into the tangled mass of invaders and defenders, striking the melee precisely the same distance from each other.

The thin, orange gel splattered across the red slivers' bodies. There was a sizzle as the saplike substance ate through sliver shells and an implosive *whump* as the entire assembly ignited.

The Phyrexians were caught in the middle of a hundred exploding bodies and a deluge of sticky, flammable goo. Freyalise crowed in triumph as she watched the Phyrexians stagger, soften, and fall. The planeswalker's howl echoed Jhoira's exultation—the slivers and Phyrexian invaders were both spawned by the Lord of the Wastes, yet she had never seen two tools of Phyrexia's malice used so efficiently against each other.

Freyalise did not celebrate long. Her skin shifted to the bright red of a salamander as she dropped down to less than twenty feet above the flaming pyre. The patron of Skyshroud clapped again. To Jhoira's total surprise, the larger-horned, spiked, hammer-handed slivers pushed their way free of the burning Phyrexians piled on top of them. They lurched through the intense flames, almost totally ignoring the inferno, and with each step Freyalise's face became a deeper and angrier red.

At the perimeter of the battle, the trihorned red slivers also rose again, regenerating amid the ovenlike heat that popped Phyrexian chassis like chestnuts. Even those insects that had been splintered and broken in the initial assault were recovering, their split shells spontaneously mending and their broken limbs reattaching themselves.

Jhoira began to see the beauty of Freyalise's plan. So long as one sliver maintained the ability to restore itself after lethal injury, Skyshroud had an inexhaustible supply of feral warriors to battle the invaders. No matter how many slivers were killed or how brutally, every one could be restored to rejoin the battle over and over again.

The initial force of Phyrexians now had less than half its original number standing, and many of those that remained were badly damaged. The swarm changed tactics again, dropping to the ground behind the three largest and charging in on foot. It was jarring to watch a bug-thing no larger than a fox topple a ponderous, bottom-heavy Phyrexian scuta, but it was stupefying to watch the same bug shatter the shield bearer's thick carapace as if it were made of glass.

It was also exhilarating. The smallest sliver was no less physically powerful than the largest, and Freyalise had turned that to her advantage too. The Phyrexians' cold machine logic dictated that they kill the biggest threats first, and by concentrating on the three massive slivers they left themselves wide open to destruction by the more numerous small ones.

Freyalise rose higher into the night sky. Jhoira leaned forward as much as she could from her airy perch and watched, riveted, as Freyalise began to spin.

Skyshroud's patron quickly disappeared in a swirl of rushing air and magic, her body surrounded by a solid wall of wind and clouds like the eye of a hurricane. Jhoira heard a clear, strong voice ring out over the vortex as Freyalise sang. Fiery red sparks lit up the whirlwind's exterior as they were carried around and around by its momentum.

The slivers in the forest below ran rampant, pushing in on the Phyrexians from all sides. Jhoira gaped as the insect monsters mutated once more, shape, size, color, and physical attributes all shifting so quickly that she could scarcely track the changes.

The end result was quite clear, however. The enraged mass of flying, exploding, regenerating, flame-spewing, hammer-handed, trihorned slivers covered the invaders five deep in a seething pile. The slivers clicked and hissed and chattered, forcing themselves ever downward until they were all spread out evenly on the surface of the ground. They had either consumed the Phyrexians or pulverized them down to a flat pile of debris and slag.

Freyalise paused, then crossed her arms. She turned up and smiled savagely at Jhoira, sharing her victory with the Ghitu observer. The planeswalker extended her gloved hand and waved, bringing Jhoira instantly down to the ground. Seconds later, Freyalise herself appeared next to Jhoira, her skin still vivid red, her arms still crossed, and her teeth still clenched in grin of well-won victory.

"Magnificent," Jhoira said. She bowed. "I congratulate you, Freyalise. I am awed."

Freyalise's voice came with a sharp edge. "When you see Radha," she said, "tell her about the battle she missed."

Then Freyalise's exposed eye rolled up in her head. As Jhoira cried out and rushed forward, the patron of Skyshroud toppled backward onto the ground and landed heavily in the brittle, brown-gray remains of the saproling thicket.

* * * * *

Freyalise awoke near sunrise. Jhoira was sitting next to her when the planeswalker opened her eyes, watching over Freyalise as she rested and recovered her strength.

The patron of Skyshroud's metal-and-gemstone eye patch flickered a few seconds before her eyelid did. The fair-skinned woman looked at Jhoira without recognition for a few moments, then Freyalise shimmered away into a cloud of green-gold dust. She reappeared moments later, upright but unsteady on her feet. She stared at Jhoira silently for a long time as the sky grew lighter. Eventually, she spoke.

"I am almost done, Jhoira. I cannot continue this indefinitely," she said.

Jhoira nodded, hesitant to reply. Freyalise's pride was both her strongest asset and her most dangerous shortcoming. It was not wise to challenge her even if the planeswalker herself had opened the door to such talk.

"You were brilliant just now," Jhoira said. "They won't be back soon. If you could reserve your strength until then . . ."

Skyshroud's patron shook her head. "Preserving this place for so long has left me almost completely bereft of strength. Between the Gathans, the cold, the Phyrexians, and the rift, I cannot sustain myself much longer . . . nor my home, nor the slivers."

"Are they still a danger without your guidance?"

Freyalise shrugged wearily. "Who can say? They are almost mindless. They respond to anyone with the magic and the will to command them."

The planeswalker's final words before she fell came back to Jhoira. "You need Radha."

Freyalise's jaw tightened at the mention of the Keldon elf. "She was to be my champion. She had the magic, and she definitely had the will. But that will also made her useless to me, causing her to follow her own path of blood and carnage."

"Can you reach her? Can you convince her that this fight is as much hers, as much Keld's as it is Skyshroud's?"

"No one has ever convinced Radha of anything Radha didn't want to believe," Freyalise said. "Except you. I watched with keen interest and no small amazement when you shut her down and brought her to heel."

Jhoira coughed uncomfortably. "I don't know that I accomplished any such thing. All I did was distract her."

"You are too modest," Freyalise said, and her tone was not approving. "You impressed Radha and got her attention, and you did so with sharp words and a thimbleful of fire magic. Once I had enough fire mana to boil an ocean, but Radha never accepted me as her leader, much less as her goddess."

"Where is Radha now?"

Freyalise face reddened. "She has gone to Parma. When it became clear that Keld was freezing, and the early winter went beyond even a berserker's tolerance, she led her warhost to north into the frozen wastes."

"Why?"

"To attack Keld's ancestral enemy. Her devotion to her grandfather's people is complete, as is her will to eclipse every Keldon warlord that ever lived. She reasoned—wrongly—that if she could defeat the frost giants and ice monsters in Parma, it would end this killing cold."

"So she has abandoned Keld as well as Skyshroud."

The crimson tint faded from Freyalise's cheeks. "Not entirely. Behold." The planeswalker waved her hand dismissively. A surge of scintillating vapor curled out from her fingers and lit up the nearby trees as it spread.

Freyalise's magic and the rising sun revealed something that Jhoira had not seen in the inky darkness, not even when the slivers were alight. The Ghitu's stomach churned. Each tree that bordered the forest from where Jhoira stood to the far end of the horizon had a sallow-skinned Gathan raider nailed to it.

The barbarians were all dead, scores of lifeless bodies pinned to the trunks by thick wooden spikes driven deep into their hands and feet. Many were burned. Most bore lethal slashes and stab wounds on their torsos and throats. All had rough Keldon symbols carved into their faces.

"Radha returned here once more before she headed north. Her greatest enemy was dead, but many of his underlings still sought to level Skyshroud to build their long ships. So Radha and her 'host spent a few hours decorating my forest before she struck out for Parma."

Jhoira nodded. Her voice was grim. "At least she still gives some thought to her first home."

"Nonsense." Freyalise darkened once more. "Yes, the lumber raids ceased. But this obscenity was not a warning intended to protect the forest. Radha did this for her own amusement and to strengthen the powerful dread her name evokes among her enemies. She is a true Keldon now. Killing is not enough, victory is not enough. She yearns for total dominance, so she wrought this desecration of both the Gathan brutes and my forest."

"Surely she wouldn't—"

"Insult me? Spit on the forest that raised and sustained her? Of course she would, and did. She would rather have her name spoken in fearful whispers than hear it praised. She scoured as much of Keld as she could before the cold called her to Parma, she and the reptile and the eight-fingered demoness from your tribe."

Jhoira choked back a wave of guilt and horror. Skive and Dassene had been members of Jhoira's honor guard, but they had joined Radha of their own free will. Now they were Radha's, and if Freyalise spoke true they were like Radha, bloodthirsty and cruel.

"They say she travels with the ghost of a blind boy she killed. He bears a wound that spells 'target' across his face in High Keld. He never speaks. He kills without warning, without a sound, without hesitation. He bears those thrice-damned knives that Radha herself cuts from the blades of her fallen foes." Freyalise spat, and the ground sizzled. "This is my champion, Jhoira. This is Skyshroud's ablest daughter."

"Freyalise," Jhoira said gently, "did you take me to bring Radha back to you?"

The planeswalker's eyes were wet, but her voice was clear. "There is no one else. I am almost spent. If Radha does not take control of the sliver swarm it will turn and prey on Skyshroud once more. The Phyrexians will overwhelm us, and the slivers will eat the remains. And I will have failed utterly as patron and protector of my children."

Jhoira weighed her next words carefully. "I would take up the mantle you wanted for Radha, Freyalise. But I do not have the power."

The planeswalker shook her head. "I never intended you to. I only want you to find Radha and tell her when I am dead. She has to fight for Skyshroud or the forest will surely die."

Jhoira held her tongue, unable to speak the truth. She had no more sway over Radha than Freyalise did, especially not since the barbarian elf had bonded with the cold, hard landscape of Keld.

"Jhoira," Freyalise said, "will you do this for me? For Skyshroud?"

The Ghitu held Freyalise's desperate eyes for a moment. She said, "I will do what I can, Freyalise."

"Do more. Bring my people the help they need." Freyalise's eyes flashed fire. "Swear it."

Jhoira straightened. "I swear," she said, "that I will bring help."

Freyalise swayed. She closed her eyes and inhaled deeply. "Thank you."

Jhoira stood waiting for Freyalise to speak again, to open her eyes. As she waited, she wondered how she would ever live up to the promise she had just made.

CHAPTER 13

The Weaver King moved across Urborg like a malignant cloud. He was frustrated and angry. Far too many of his subjects had been ignoring him of late. He had made a comfortable home here in this dark country of swamps and monsters, but the very aspects that made this place and these people so suitable were also the cause of his current irritation. Urborg was Urborg, after all, and when Windgrace spoke, Urborg listened.

The panther-god had taken almost all of the sentient beings away from their natural cycle of hunting and killing. Now they convened in large groups, docile and obedient to their furry master, heedless of the fact that they would normally be at each other's throats. The Weaver King was almost beside himself. This simply would not do.

At least Dinne was still his to command. The Vec raider had no connection to Urborg, had no life of his own beyond the Weaver King's wishes. There was only so much Dinne could do on his own, however, only so many throats he could cut. Each loss closed not only the doorway to one mind but to all the minds that victim knew. Each subject Windgrace took diminished his pool of playthings. The more blood Dinne spilled, the less robust the Weaver King's kingdom.

He still had tethers attached to his two favorites, the artificer and the archmage. Jodah had been a disappointment on his own, but he had led the Weaver King to a host of other fascinating alternatives. Venser was currently unavailable, as Windgrace himself had staked claim to the artificer's mind, but that didn't mean he was permanently out of reach. As soon as the Weaver King devised a way to get around the panther-god—better still, a method of killing or claiming a planeswalker—he could resume his full-fledged indulgence. With the situation deteriorating as it was, the Weaver King decided to concentrate on a solution to this Windgrace problem.

The Weaver King skated along the silver thread that led to Jodah. He was pleased to find the archmage hard at work, his mind focused elsewhere. Industriousness had its own special flavor, one that the Weaver King savored. Staying with Jodah, the Weaver King felt along the connection between himself and Venser. Oddly enough, Venser was preoccupied as well, also toiling away at some task or another that the artificer found completely absorbing. A panther's growl drifted into the Weaver King's consciousness, and he quickly withdrew.

Soon, he told himself, careful to keep his thoughts from vibrating along the thread to Venser's mind. Soon I will split the panther's psyche into pieces and grind them to pulp between my teeth.

He was so consumed with ire that he almost missed Jodah's disappearance. If he hadn't been right on top of the archmage, the Weaver King might not have noticed at all. But he was, and he did. Jodah vanished right out from under him for a split second, then reappeared far, far away.

Now this was truly interesting, the Weaver King told himself, and not just because there was nothing else of interest afoot. Jodah had somehow instantly traveled halfway around the world in the blink of an eye. Even better, the archmage relaxed upon completing the journey, allowing the Weaver King to sift through more of his deepest thoughts and most closely guarded secrets.

Skyshroud, the Weaver King thought, savoring the unfamiliar

word. It was a dying place, slowly inching its way toward oblivion, but it was still packed with hundreds of potential subjects. Jodah's further thoughts on his new locale almost brought the Weaver King to tears of delight.

Jhoira. Jodah was thinking about the Ghitu immortal, the one he had offered up in his own stead, the one who had also journeyed to this strange new place. She was there when Jodah arrived, and the Weaver King now had both motive and opportunity to follow. He hesitated only because of his fondness for Urborg and his appreciation of the residents of his adopted home.

The Weaver King maintained his surreptitious watch on Jodah as he reached out and twanged the thread that led to Dinne. If he were clever and sly, the Weaver King might be able to influence two places at once. If Dinne's shadow existence could follow the same paths that the Weaver King did, Jodah and Jhoira might have a new playmate to hunt them through the stunted trees of Skyshroud.

The Weaver King concentrated, calming his wild thoughts and bringing all his psychic vigor to bear on his still-forming plan.

Let Windgrace close the Weaver King's every route in Urborg. He would blaze a new trail to Skyshroud, where the fruit was less numerous but far more succulent.

* * * * *

Jodah stepped out of his tunnel's egress onto the frozen rocks of Keld. He emerged from under the exposed roots of a massive tree that had been burned and broken off halfway up its length.

Upon seeing Skyshroud the archmage felt wistful and forlorn. He had suspected Freyalise was out of sorts when he saw her in the Blind Eternities. Now that he was here and he saw the state of the place, he knew the planeswalker was even worse off than she looked. It was unimaginable that the elf goddess would allow her people to scratch out an existence in this meager, exhausted place. He wondered how well-off it would be without Freyalise's blessings and quickly concluded that it would not be at all.

Jodah moved into the woods, grimly noting the crucified warriors overhead. Now that he was here the clock was ticking against him, each second a chance for Freyalise to notice and come for him. He was further disadvantaged by the fact that he had to build the transport tunnel toward Freyalise in the first place, when he'd vastly prefer to be as far from her as possible for as long as possible. He needed to find Jhoira, or at least her current location, before he could return to Urborg.

He picked his way past a broad, burned-out circle, unwilling to cross it and expose himself to plain view. Freyalise must be nearby. This still-smoking battlefield had her fingerprints all over it. He had no love for Phyrexia, but he half-hoped some of the mechanical soldiers were still active in the area to keep the planeswalker's attention off him.

"Jodah." Jhoira's voice came softly from the deep woods to his right, but Jodah did not reply until he saw the Ghitu herself. It was too easy for magic to mimic the sound he most wanted to hear.

But it was Jhoira. She approached him openly, without fear or suspicion. She seemed both glad to see him and worried that he had come.

"Hello again," he said. "I've come to help."

Jhoira shook her head. "It's not safe here."

"Not for any of us. Venser is standing by with his ambulator. Teferi said you might need it, but he's too slippery for me to trust. I thought I should ask you myself."

Jhoira's face soured at the name. "Teferi is following his own path. I am no longer sure mine aligns with his."

"Fair enough. But we need to hurry. Freyalise will be coming any second now."

"She knows you are here," Jhoira said, "and she does not care.

She is conserving her strength for the coming trials." She shrugged. "She sent me to shoo you away."

Jodah felt a twinge of despair at Jhoira's concern for the elf goddess. Freyalise could inspire as well as intimidate, but the end result was usually the same for her mortal allies. "Can you use Venser's machine?"

"I can." Jodah saw that it did not please her to agree with Teferi. "How?"

Thunder rumbled from the far side of the forest. A column of orange fire speared up into the sky.

"It's starting again," Jhoira said. "If you can leave, do so now."

"Not until you agree to meet us here. Venser and I."

"I agree. If I'm able, I will return here in a few hours' time."

Jodah smiled. "Why wait? Stay here for the next ten minutes. If I'm not back by then, we'll come looking for you." Before she could argue or gainsay, Jodah turned and sprinted back toward his transport tunnel. He ran straight across the circle of scorched earth and burst through the decaying remnants of a thick hedge row. He paused to get his bearings in the bright morning haze, then dashed for the hole under the large, broken tree that housed his gateway.

Without pausing, Jodah took a running leap and plunged into the thin layer of liquid stretched over his tunnel. He floated momentarily, his momentum seemingly lost, then burst through another liquid cap and rolled onto his feet in the icy swamps of Urborg.

Teferi was there, casually leaning on his staff. He waved a hand at Jodah and said, "I can take you to Venser."

"Where is he?"

"In his workshop. I followed him there so that I could act as your guide. You have to let me help you, Jodah. Please."

Jodah silently prepared another spell in case he needed it. Then, to Teferi, he said, "All right. Lead on."

The bald planeswalker moved quickly for one so seemingly distracted. Jodah hustled after him, weaving between patches of quicksand and vast pools of tarry oil. Faster, Jodah thought. I've only got ten minutes.

Soon they came to a patch of rockier ground. Beyond that was a small hillside with a metal door built into its side.

"He's in there," Teferi said.

Jodah calculated how much time it had taken them to get here. He doubled the time to allow for the return trip and realized he was not going to make it.

"Stay here." Jodah pushed past Teferi and navigated the rocky field, bounding from stone to broken stone until he was at Venser's door.

"Hoy," Jodah called, his voice low and tight. "I've found her. Do you have the device?"

Footsteps approached the door. The heavy metal slab creaked on its hinges, revealing Venser with dark half-circles under his eyes.

"Do you have it?" Jodah asked.

Venser held out a fist-sized metal box with a blinking dot on each of its faces.

Jodah accepted the box and turned it over in his hands. "This is all you need to follow me?"

"That will do it."

Jodah looked up. "And you've found the machine? You can get it past Windgrace's guards?"

Venser hesitated, giving Jodah his answer. "Come on," the archmage said. "We might as well do this together so I'm not stranded in Skyshroud waiting for something that never comes."

The artificer relaxed a little. "Thank you," he said. "I'm at something of a loss when it comes to Lord Windgrace."

"I have the same trouble with Freyalise," Jodah said. "It's maddening to anticipate the whims of a god. We either work for them, fall to them, or we stand aside."

Venser nodded gratefully. "It's this mark," he said, pointing to the inch-high symbol on his cheek. "I don't know if it really has any power or if I'm just too frightened of what it represents. I feel like Windgrace is with me always, spying on my thoughts."

Alarmed, Jodah said, "Do you hear his voice?"

"No."

"Do you hear any voices?"

Venser smiled, producing a ghastly effect on his drawn-out face. "You mean, do I hear a giddy, demented voice that tells me to rest and let things happen? No. I haven't heard the Weaver King since Windgrace chased him off."

Jodah sighed. "That's good. Nor I. Now. Where is this machine of yours?"

Venser shook his head. "I don't know."

"But you have some idea."

"Yes, actually. There are only a few places he could have hauled it to if he planned to keep an eye on it."

"Let's start at the closest one," Jodah said. "And we'll work through them all until we find it."

Venser took several tools off a table by the door and stuffed them into his belt. Jodah spotted two yellow stones in Venser's belt-pouch, but the artificer was quick to turn away.

"Your machine's power source?" He gestured to the pouch.

Venser's face flushed. "Yes," he said. "I try to keep them out of sight because they're so valuable."

"If they help us reach Jhoira, I'll personally get you a full set of twelve." He stepped back and held open the door. "Teferi's out here, by the way. Don't let him distract you."

Venser grimaced. "I wish he'd just go away. I don't trust him."

"That's because you're smart. Now let's go," he said. "I don't like to keep a lady waiting."

* * * * *

Teferi stood quietly as Jodah and Venser conversed. Not surprisingly, they paired up and headed for the center of Windgrace's territory. Both men nodded at him, but neither hailed him or invited him to come along.

Teferi didn't mind. In the short term, nothing Venser or Jodah did would change what needed to be done, what only Windgrace and Freyalise could do. After the planeswalkers had decided their own fates, it would be up to Teferi and Jhoira to decide the multiverse's. With Venser's help, of course.

He glanced over to Venser's workshop door, which the artificer had made sure to bar before he left. There was nothing worth stealing inside, not to an ordinary thief or Teferi. Besides, he had more important things to do.

Teferi started out after Venser and Jodah, but he turned away from their path within fifty yards. They were trying not to be seen by Lord Windgrace, whereas he was hoping to speak with the panther-god in person.

He was slowly coming to accept the truth: almost if not all of his transcendent magic had deserted him when he closed the Shivan rift. He experienced brief flashes of his former glorified state, bits and pieces of a half-remembered waking dream—but these were fleeting and only served to deepen his confusion.

The last clear thoughts he could remember were of vying with the rift phenomenon. Though it was not a living thing he recalled struggling against it and feeling it struggle against him. It had wanted to consume him, as a bucket of ice water wants to draw the heat out of a hand dipped in it.

As a planeswalker Teferi was limited only by his power and his force of will. The rift's appetite far outstripped his power, but his will had conquered it. Just as that hand in a bucket of water could punch its fingers through the bottom of the pail to let the water out,

Teferi had changed the rules of his contest with the rift, letting it feed on his near-omnipotence as he unmade it, as he turned it aside and back upon itself at its most basic, elemental levels.

It had not been easy, but he had done it. There was strength in the pride he took from this, confidence he could stand on. It would not be easy to bring other planeswalkers into his plan, but he had every intention of doing that too. He'd already set Freyalise and Windgrace to doing what was necessary, a subtle push here and there until logic and their own reasons led them to finish the job.

Freyalise was growing more desperate. She would have probably done the right thing on her own by now if she wasn't so dedicated to the future of her elves. With Jhoira by her side, there was no way Freyalise could avoid coming to the only conclusion that made sense, the only path open to her. If Skyshroud was to be saved, Freyalise would have to make the ultimate sacrifice and abandon her power as Teferi had.

Windgrace was another matter. He was just as proud as Freyalise but far more vigorous. The panther-man might waste weeks or even months destroying the endless waves of cold-weather Phyrexians that emerged from the rift. Teferi had to make sure Windgrace acted in unison with Freyalise, or in close enough concert so that their efforts would be sufficient. By Teferi's reasoning, sealing two rifts more or less simultaneously would have an exponentially larger positive effect than doing them in sequence. Closing the Shivan phenomenon had slowed the entire rift network's chaotic effects on Dominaria for a time. Unhappily, the disruptive effect had already gone too far. It had its own momentum. An ever-growing weight of entropy could not be reversed by attacking it piecemeal.

The encroachment of this icy alternate reality was just one example of the worsening situation. Teferi's power was almost spent, but he still had a strange, almost intuitive relationship with the rifts that he attributed to his interaction with the one in Shiv. However that perception survived, it was still his and it allowed him to sense where the rifts were and to some extent how dangerous.

For lack of a more accurate term, it also let him gauge each rift's attitude. Just as each region and landmass in Dominaria produced different stripes of mana, each rift was partially defined by its surroundings. Shiv's fissure was hard, hotly defiant, and unyielding as stone. Urborg's was predatory and hostile, and gave rise to monsters. Skyshroud's was proud and indomitable, partially isolated from its fellows as it sank its roots deep into the foundation of the multiverse while simultaneously stretching toward its upper limit. This instinctive grip on the rift phenomena was not as useful as limitless magic when it came to traveling the globe or clearing his path of obstacles, but it was invaluable for locating and prioritizing the rifts as he puzzled out the riddles they presented.

Whatever the Stronghold rift's character, it had allowed Phyrexians from another place to bleed through the network into this world. Windgrace had to be convinced that the only way to stop the Ice Age Phyrexians from overwhelming Dominaria was to seal off their access.

Teferi's mind wandered as he walked, his thoughts gently bouncing from notion to notion. He remembered Corus attacking him in Shiv but not how he had escaped. He recalled the secrets Jhoira built into the Ghitu ambulator but not the construction of the device itself. He knew Venser, Jodah, and Jhoira seemed angry with him but had no good idea why.

Teferi slowed as he approached the campsite. He spotted human sentries ahead with the gladehunter mark on their faces. He tried to gather his thoughts for what promised to be a very difficult discussion, but Jhoira's name and face kept appearing to him, distracting him.

Teferi wanted more than anything to sit and talk through his confusion with her. He desperately wanted to know what had happened between them, but he also dreaded the answer.

Teferi pushed aside his thoughts and proudly stuck his staff in the mud. "Warriors of Urborg," he said, "I have come to parley with your lord and master."

The two sentries were alert and instantly drew steel as they approached him. Teferi didn't worry. Things had gone pretty far astray so far, but his plan was still viable. By his lights, things could certainly be a good deal worse.

CHAPTER 14

Venser led Jodah through the tangled swamps of Urborg. Though he was fraught with worries about Jhoira, Windgrace, the rifts, and Teferi, he was also pleased to be back in his element. Here in Urborg, working with his beloved machines, he was useful again.

They soon came to a boggy hollow between two icy ridges. A huge willow cast a curtain of its whiplike branches over the deeper recesses of the dank place, and three men of Urborg stood sentry, their gladehunter brands glowing and their thick knots of hair waving in the breeze. Venser waved Jodah down and raised a finger to his lips. The two peered through the mist and watched.

A heavy, bristle-furred shambler came around the eastern ridge, its broad feed scraping through the icy mud. The burly, bearlike creature was mottled brown, and its eyes glowed red over the gladehunter mark on its cheek. The stationary sentries barely acknowledged the beast as it patrolled by. Sniffing the air and growling, the shambler muddled off around the western ridge.

Less than a minute later another monster slithered in from the east. It had a broad, square head like a lion's, but its hind end trailed off into a snaky tail. It hauled itself forward on short, stubby forelimbs and flicked its tongue in and out like a serpent. Venser heard Jodah stifle a gasp when the archmage saw that the beast's bulbous tongue had a human face on it, a wizened, skull-like visage that was twisted and drawn into a miser's sneer.

That horror moved along, and soon a third patrolling beast crossed in front of the hollow. This one was a long-legged insect with compound eyes along the length of its spine and veins of lurid purple inscribed on its transparent wings. A sharp spike jutted out of its soft, horn-shaped mouth, and it was accompanied by a cloud of ghastly yellow gnats.

They waited and watched until the shambler returned. Confident that these were the only guardians patrolling the area, Venser signaled Jodah so that the archmage would lean in close.

"It's here," Venser whispered. "The ambulator. This is the place."

"Are you sure?"

Venser nodded. He had only stretched the truth a little when he told Jodah there were few places Windgrace could have stored the Ghitu ambulator. There were actually hundreds of caves and deadfalls and hidey-holes the planeswalker could have used, but Venser knew where his machine was as surely as he knew he had two hands and ten fingers.

Things had changed, he had changed since completing the journey from Shiv. The machine had dominated his thoughts for the last two decades and had always been a part of him figuratively. Since Jhoira helped him rebuild it and it carried them across great distances, he now felt connected to it. Even shut off and stowed, the ambulator tugged at him, called out and buzzed in his brain like an inspired idea that he had yet to articulate, demanding that he pay attention.

The stones in his pouch also resonated with the machine. They were no brighter or hotter than normal, but Venser felt them yearning for the back of the hollow as iron filings toward a magnet. He and the stones and the ambulator felt like part of the same larger machine, one that insisted on being complete.

Venser also felt a familiar pall, the cold, frustrating sense of reaching one's limit. He sipped a long lungful of air and said, "This is where I need your help."

Jodah smiled. "You got us here," he said, "but it's up to me to get us in?"

Venser colored. "Something like that."

"Do you have any suggestions? Any spells to recommend?"

"I have no magic," Venser said. "I'm a builder."

"I see. Well, no matter. Rest easy, my friend. I may have just the thing."

Venser stiffened at Jodah's choice of words. The Weaver King kept admonishing him to rest easy, and Windgrace had singled Jodah out as one of the Weaver King's toys. Venser forced himself to relax. Jodah had proved himself reliable so far. Jhoira trusted him. Besides, the archmage was visible, and he wasn't prone to fits of insane giggling.

"Which of those creatures is the fastest on its feet?"

Venser blinked. "The shambler," he said. "Though I can't be sure."

"That was my thinking as well. And we don't need to be sure. We just need to agree."

"Can you do it alone?" Venser said. When Jodah raised an eyebrow, Venser pointed to the gladehunter mark on his own cheek and said, "I'm afraid of this betraying us to Windgrace."

Jodah relaxed. He patted Venser on the shoulder and said, "On the contrary. That is going to get us close enough for my plan to work."

The archmage stood up, towering over Venser. He reached down and helped Venser up. "Produce your beacon box," he said. "And grab me by the scruff of the neck. It's time to steal back your machine."

The sentries completed two more cycles as Jodah outlined his plan and Venser worked up his nerve. Finally, Venser stepped out into plain view. He was sweating slightly in the cold but maintained a firm grip on Jodah's robe. The taller man allowed Venser to half-drag him along as they approached the hollow.

"Brothers," Venser said. He cast Jodah down into the muck and raised the beacon high in his clenched fist. "See what I have found in the swamps."

The three knot-haired sentries reacted instantly, forming a line across the entrance to the hollow. Two drew short swords and the third a stout-handled morningstar.

The box blinked and hummed overhead. Venser gestured at Jodah and said, "This man was once my partner. He built this device to work in concert with mine. As a show of loyalty to our lord, I give him and his abominable machine to you."

"Go back where you came from," said the gladehunter with the morningstar. None of the sentries had moved, each resolute at his post. "Or you'll be gutted same as him."

The shambler loped into view, and Venser hesitated. The vaguely manlike brute slavered when he saw the box. He opened his six-fingered fists and flexed his long, sharp claws

"Go on," Jodah hissed.

"I will go," Venser said. "But I would leave this, and him, here with you."

"Steady," the gladehunter with the morningstar told the shambler, who was preparing to pounce. To Venser he said, "We don't want it. Or him. Take them both out into the swamp and bury them."

Venser swallowed. "Now?"

"Now." Jodah sprang to his feet with glittering, green smoke swirling from his fingertips.

The shambler was almost fast enough. It leaped forward before Jodah had reached his full height, its heavy body moving as swiftly and gracefully as a bird's. If not for the smoke that floated between it and Jodah, it would have surely finished its short flight, crushed the archmage to the ground, and torn him apart.

As it was, the smoke flowed up into the monster's face, and it froze in midair. It floated for a split second as two of the human gladehunters charged forward. The third, their leader with the morningstar, turned and shouted back into the hollow.

"Destroy it! Break the machine now!"

Whatever he spoke to had no time to act. Wreathed in emerald smoke, the shambler dropped down into the muck, bounded back toward the hollow, and took hold of an Urborg sentry in each clawed hand. Roaring, the monster thundered on, casting the full-grown men at their leader as if they were skipping stones.

Jodah was right behind the shambler with another spell already blossoming from his hands. Twin streams of blue-white liquid surged out over the shambler's shoulders and slammed into the lead gladehunter, covering him in a translucent mound of foam. The man's morningstar fell from his hand and splashed into the bog as the shambler and his two fellows all crashed into him where he stood.

Venser dashed forward, hoping to reach the ambulator before something acted on the leader's command to wreck it. He quickly passed Jodah, who was still pouring gummy magic onto the struggling pile of gladehunters.

The other patrolling sentries quickly closed on the hollow, but Jodah now controlled the encounter. He kept one hand aimed at the shambler and the three humans while the other swiveled out to greet the insect-winged horror. It screeched like a demon as Jodah's spell mired its limbs in foam. The last sentry tried to slither under the archmage's magic, but he caught it before it came close enough to strike. Stepping back, Jodah continued to enshroud the sentries, working his hands back and forth until the sentries were all struggling under the same seething mound.

"Go," Jodah said. "I don't know how long this will hold them."

Venser crossed into the darker recesses of the hollow. He stopped, quickly scanning for signs of any hidden guardians. Satisfied, he held the beacon box out so its blinking lights illuminated the area. He caught a brief glimpse of copper-colored metal before something thin, strong, and sharp encircled his neck.

Venser coughed and choked as he was jerked roughly into the air. He felt woody vines digging into his flesh and felt sharp-edged leaves tearing through his clothes. He cursed himself for overlooking the obvious, though he was also impressed by Windgrace's forethought. With so many formidable monsters guarding the hollow, who would suspect that the most dangerous sentry was the willow tree?

The tree keened and hissed as it wrapped its countless tendrils around Venser. His ankles, wrists, and throat were noosed and yanked tight. His face, torso, and thighs were scraped and squeezed by innumerable whip-thin vines. The switches burned where they touched his skin, and though he could barely breathe, Venser smelled a sickly, acid scent as his skin sizzled and melted under the tree's caustic touch.

He tried to call out for Jodah, but he had no breath. He tried to shake his arms free, but he had no leverage. He tried to suck air through his constricted throat, but he had no strength.

The tree bore him up higher, drawing his body into the larger mass of squirming tendrils overhead. Over the pounding of his pulse and the sound of his eardrums about to burst, Venser heard Jodah calling. The archmage was bringing his magic to bear on this new threat, but his foam-trap was next to useless against such a large creature with so many limbs. Venser watched through red-rimmed eyes, helplessly observing the black, rustlike coating Jodah sent shooting up the tendrils holding the artificer in place.

Venser's world went white. He stiffened and shuddered in the throes of a seizure, his own heartbeat eclipsed by a dull, buzzing drone. The cutting, burning pressure around his throat disappeared, and he coughed up something wet and painful. His arms and legs came loose, and he felt himself alternately floating and falling, though he couldn't see anything.

Then Venser landed on the hard ground. He dug his fingers into the mud and pried his face free, wracked by spasmodic coughing. He was only bleeding slightly, but he felt seared and half-skinned by the cruel, clutching vines. Instinctively, he tried to roll away from the tree, but his movements were slow and clumsy.

Venser completed another awkward revolution before Jodah's strong hand found his shoulder. "Easy," the archmage said. "It's all over."

Venser slumped faceup on the ground. He wrapped his arms around his midsection and doubled over, drawing in huge gulps of air and coughing. He wrestled himself into a sitting position and struggled to see Jodah clearly through the haze of pain.

"What did you do?" Jodah asked. He seemed quite calm, almost tranquil. If there was a lingering danger from the willow tree, the archmage didn't give it much thought.

"Me?" Venser sputtered. He waited for another wave of coughing to subside.

"You got yourself loose," Jodah said. "I did some damage, but I don't think I even got its attention."

"What . . ." Venser managed. "What did you see?"

"It had a hold of you," Jodah said. "Then it didn't. I couldn't tell if it just let go, or if you somehow wriggled clear."

"Had me," Venser said. "It had me tight."

"Well," Jodah observed. "It's quiescent now. Look." He gestured upward, and Venser followed his hand. The tree was still alive, but it was now placid and still, its seething tangle of vines slack and sluggish.

Jodah reached down and helped Venser to his feet. He was careful not to crush the beacon box still held tight in the artificer's fist. "Has this happened before?" the archmage said.

Venser waited for his head to stop swimming. He cleared his throat and breathed deeply. "Once," he said. "In Shiv."

"I see. And I imagine this was of great interest to Jhoira? Perhaps Teferi as well?"

Venser eyed Jodah suspiciously. He did not like the probing, penetrating tilt to the archmage's questions. "It was," he said. "Though we didn't have time to linger on it."

"Just like now," Jodah said. He hooked a thumb over his shoulder, pointing to the blue-white mass of Urborg sentries and monsters. "They're good for another few minutes. If our leafy friend here is content to let us pass, I hope you can get your machine working before they break loose."

Venser started. He swiveled his head and fixed on the darkest part of the hollow. His ambulator was there, the machine complete and intact. Best of all, Venser saw the way its network of blue lights flashed and realized it must still be in perfect working order.

"It'll take no time at all," Venser said. He opened his fist, checked the beacon box, and clenched it tight again. "Follow me," he said.

* * * * *

How very rude, thought the Weaver King. He had taken special pains to aid one of his subjects in need, and the wretch didn't even acknowledge the effort.

The Weaver King gleefully skated across the skein he had stretched across Urborg, exhilarated and giddy. What a rare treasure Venser was, a rare opportunity. So much potential to develop, so many urges to nurture.

He quickly forgave Venser for overlooking the Weaver King's aid in quieting the willow sentry. To be fair, it was very unlikely Venser could have spotted the Weaver King's subtle hand at work. Since Windgrace had marked the artificer's mind off limits, the Weaver King had been forced to weave his most subtle webs, to forge connections so delicate and refined they were like whispers on the wind. Windgrace himself had overlooked the Weaver King's continued presence in Venser's mind, and he consoled himself that Venser was far less keen than the panther-god.

However keen his mind, Venser had other strong points that stirred the Weaver King's interest. In his panicked state, the artificer had somehow moved himself out of the willow's clutches, vanishing then reappearing as effectively as any shadow creature— yet Venser was wholly flesh and blood. Venser was not ephemeral like the Weaver King or Dinne, but neither did he have the unassailable presence of a Windgrace. If Venser wasn't insubstantial or omnipotent, how did he do what he had done?

The Weaver King slowed his flight and focused on those strands that connected him to Venser and Jodah. The archmage was also partially protected by Windgrace's lingering presence but just as vulnerable to the Weaver King's finer efforts. He made a mental note to look more deeply into Jodah when the chance occurred. The crafty four-thousand-year-old archwizard had kept many secrets hidden when the Weaver King first met him, but now, like Venser, his true value was becoming clear.

Venser and Jodah, Jodah and Venser. The Weaver King slid back and forth on the silver threads he had spun between his two new favorites. Joy and desire burned brightly in the Weaver King's jagged mind. There was so much to play with here. So many things they could do, so many things he could make them do if they'd only take the time to listen.

He knew he didn't dare speak much louder for fear of rousing the panther. It was a kind of exquisite torture, this self-denial. The Weaver King had rarely even contemplated restraint before, but for once he took his pleasure in the waiting, in the consideration of what he wanted versus the price he'd pay for getting it. He felt wise and virtuous simply for searching for alternatives to his usual fervid rush toward his amusements.

He was soon rewarded for his patience. As he hung back and simply observed the two, he noted how deeply Venser focused on his beloved machine. When he was like this there was almost nothing the Weaver King could say or suggest that would appeal to the artificer. Venser's will and desire were united when he worked, the machine creating and filling needs to consume Venser's mind completely.

Then Jodah spoke. "Will it work?"

The Weaver King struggled to contain himself. There, he thought. That's all I need.

The thing about Jodah and Venser, Venser and Jodah, was that they had so much in common. Beyond their hidden talents and their bookish tendencies, both had a healthy interest in the same compelling woman.

Just now Jodah had broken Venser's communion with his machine. Venser came out of that communion reluctantly, almost angrily, and his anger took on a sharp new flavor when it saw the archmage emeritus. Jodah, who like Jhoira had been alive for millennia. Jodah, who like Jhoira was a powerful wizard and confident adventurer. Jodah, who had so much in common with Jhoira, who could stand as peer and equal to Jhoira, who was clearly smitten with Jhoira. Jodah, with whom Jhoira was in turn clearly smitten.

The Weaver King let go, surging across random sections of his extended web as laughter hissed from his mind like steam. Venser respected Jodah. Venser was coming to trust Jodah, even admire him. But on a deep, primal, instinctive level, Venser resented Jodah. He rankled at the archmage's ease with the Ghitu woman and how she responded to it.

On that level, Venser hated Jodah. Just a little. It was all the Weaver King needed.

He sent his multifaceted mind out across the length and breadth of his web, giving almost all of his subjects a simultaneous moment of pure dread that started in their brains and sent crippling shudders down through their spines.

* * * * *

Venser had been staring at the machine's inner workings for too long without speaking. "Will it work?" Jodah said.

The artificer scowled briefly as he turned. "It's ready," Venser said, and Jodah noticed the strain in his voice.

"Are you all right?"

"I'm fine." Venser stood. He inspected the seat of the ambulator's chair. His shoulders sagged momentarily before he turned. "Take this." He held out the beacon to Jodah. "I can take you back to your tunnel any time."

"Now is good," Jodah said. He pocketed the beacon in his robe and cast his eyes back to the mound of imprisoned sentries. He glanced at the machine over Venser's shoulder and said, "How does it work?"

"It's complicated," Venser said. "I'll handle the controls, but, if you must know, it creates a magical field that—"

"Easy, friend," Jodah said. "I just want to know where I should stand."

Venser flashed him a weary smile. "Sorry," he said. "Once I'm in the chair, you can stand anywhere on the dais."

Jodah nodded thoughtfully. "And you're sure it won't crash like last time?"

"I'm almost certain." The artificer's humor seemed to improve at Jodah's anxious expression. "I was careless last time, distracted. I was worried about Jhoira."

"Well, don't worry this time. We'll get her back together."

Venser nodded. "We should go."

Jodah wondered if Venser had always been so distracted by his own device. As soon as he laid hands on the ambulator, the artificer all but disappeared into it. It drew his eye and his attention to the exclusion of almost everything else.

The archmage shrugged. Perhaps Venser was more worried about the device functioning properly than he let on. If it took them to Jodah's tunnel and on to Skyshroud, it would be well worth all the gloom that had spread across Venser's face and slowed his quick mind's inner workings.

Venser adjusted the metal rig on his shoulders. He breathed deep and seated himself in the chair. Jodah stepped onto the solid, metal platform as Venser's fingers flew over the internal controls.

The ambulator hummed and disappeared, taking Jodah and Venser away.

CHAPTER 15

Teferi strolled into the Urborg encampment like a visiting dignitary. He held his spine straight and his head high, employing his metal staff as a walking stick.

"Hail," he called to the sentries. "Teferi of Zhalfir to see Lord Windgrace."

A half dozen gladehunters stood before him, two humans and a small collection of marsh monsters. All wore Windgrace's mark. None of them responded to his greeting.

"May I pass?" he asked.

"We were told you might come." The gladehunter who spoke was a six-foot-tall mantis with a triangular purple hood concealing its face. Its words came through a series of harsh clicks and whistles.

Teferi smiled. "And am I welcome?"

You are not. Windgrace's powerful growl came out of the air itself. *You were warned to stay out of this affair.*

"I cannot, my lord. You have the power, but only I have the knowledge. You may break my body and burn my mind, but before you do . . . at least take what I have for you. Use it. I know things you do not, and what I know can help you."

We shall see.

Teferi felt the air churn around him, and a tingling sensation settled over his entire body. His vision dimmed for a moment, and he found himself standing in the bottom of a huge, hollow chamber. He sensed the crackling disk overhead, the confluence of energies arcane and temporal, and he knew where Windgrace had taken him even before the panther-god spoke.

Welcome to the Stronghold, Windgrace said. Then the planes-walker appeared, towering over Teferi, his muscles rippling and his tail slashing the air. With Windgrace came light, and Teferi now saw the inside of the mountain fortress clearly.

Despite the presence of Windgrace, Teferi was almost consumed by the view. It was not as he expected, not at all. There were supposed to be entire cities within the mountain's hollow center and vast expanses of machinery. What he saw was merely a cavern, an empty hole with thick, stone walls.

"Do you feel it?" Windgrace said.

"The rift? Yes, I do."

"I was referring to the taint of madness. This is the lair of the Weaver King, though I have never found him at home."

Teferi bowed. "It must frustrate you, my lord, to be aware of this malign presence yet unable to root it out."

"It does," Windgrace said. "It does indeed." He floated down so that he was directly in front of Teferi. "Can you hear the echoes of his mania?"

Teferi concentrated, half-closing his eyes. He only heard water dripping from the rocks and the creaking of the cavern walls as they shifted and settled. There was something else, a faint, merry, wild sound that could have been laughter. "I hear something, my lord. Again, I sympathize with your inability to find its origin."

"Very well." Windgrace crossed his massive arms and puffed through his nostrils. "But I have not brought you here to commiserate. You are here to be tested."

"Tested? How so?" Teferi spoke gently, playfully. "How shall I prepare?'

"You have already passed," Windgrace said. "I half-suspected you were in the Weaver King's thrall. I see now that is not the case."

"Good news," Teferi said. "Though I confess I am not familiar with the name."

"Be glad of that ignorance," Windgrace said. "Be glad that without your power you are of no interest to him."

"I am glad, my lord. Glad to have one less distraction from my purpose. The Weaver King is your quarry," Teferi said. "The time rifts are mine."

Windgrace scowled. "Then it is your contention that there is no connection between the two?"

"I could not say. I am increasingly sure there is a link between the rift and your cold-weather Phyrexians."

Green fire flared from Windgrace's eyes. "You vex me, Tolarian. I do not believe you are as weak as you pretend, so I cannot simply ignore you. I do believe you know more and intend to do more than you are willing to say, so I cannot simply kill you. Yet neither will I simply let you run loose to continue your intrusive tampering and your ham-handed attempts to influence events. So I put it to you: What other course is open to me?"

"Examine my thoughts," Teferi said. "See for yourself what I know and intend."

The panther's ears flattened. "Your thoughts are . . . closed to me for some reason. Either because you conceal them—"

"Or because they are likewise closed to me," Teferi said. "I have lost a great part of myself, Windgrace. Almost everything I had and was is gone. You have called me a coward, accused me of running and hiding when the Phyrexians invaded. I will not argue that point. But, it is also true that I risked everything to correct my mistakes. I did spend every last drop of my power in Shiv, and Shiv is now saved. Having done so, I cannot save Urborg, or Skyshroud. I don't have the ability . . . but *you* do. Together, you and Freyalise can push the boundaries of chaos back much farther than I did alone. And if you let me I will tell you how."

Windgrace simply stared. "You vex me, Tolarian."

Teferi bowed. "I seek only to make things better. To make Urborg and Skyshroud safe."

"In aid of some larger goal."

"I make no secret of that. There is still dolorous and difficult work ahead that may well consume those who do it."

"And having been consumed, you would see us act as your agents. Freyalise and me."

"Not agents. Fellows. This is not a threat to one place or one entity. If we—you, Freyalise, Jhoira, Venser, and anyone else we can gather to our cause—if we do not stop the time rifts and reverse the damage they have done, nothing will survive. No one. Not the most powerful planeswalker on the most distant plane."

"So you still claim some special understanding of these cracks in the sky."

"I do."

"And you wish to share this understanding."

"Absolutely."

Windgrace shook his head. "I will not hear it."

"Why?"

"Because I don't have the luxury of an academic. Long-term thinking will not remedy Urborg. It may already be too late. There are Phyrexians on my doorstep. There is a mind-vampire marauding unchecked. There is a new kind of planeswalker who does not have the transcendent spark." Windgrace's dark fur bristled, and he lowered his heavy head down into Teferi's face. "And there is a Tolarian meddler trying to push me into repeating his own ill-considered act even as he pretends to know less than he does and to be less powerful than he is."

"My power is spent," Teferi said. "I have no more mana, no stronger spells than a half-talented hedge wizard. But if you listen to what I have to say—"

"No." Windgrace stood tall. "Behold, student of Tolaria. Here is your new classroom, your new laboratory. If you would set your keen mind and perceptions against the foundation of all our problems, this is the place. The rift is here. The Weaver King is here. The Phyrexians will soon be here again." The panther-god bared his sharp fangs in a predator's smile. "Observe and take copious notes. If you survive to learn more that will be 'of use,' you will have earned the right to share it with me."

Teferi paused, trying to maintain his calm demeanor as well a modicum of control over the conversation. "You mean to strand me here?"

"If you can be stranded. I half-expect you to teleport out as soon as I turn my back."

"I cannot. I cannot leave this place."

"Of course you can. If you start climbing now, you should be outside in less than a week."

Teferi tightened his grip on his staff, struggling for words.

"Alternately," Windgrace said. "You could rest and recover your strength. If you were more like your old self, you would be of extreme interest to the Weaver King. And what you two would do to each other is of passing interest to me."

"My lord, I must protest," Teferi said tightly. "Abandon me if you must, but do not stake me out like a goat for the tiger." He tilted his head back and spoke proudly, defiantly. "I deserve better."

"Then make it better." Windgrace stretched out his arms and rose into the air. "Be worthy of it. While you are here, focus on the rift above. Study the tangle of psychic energy that covers this place like a net. If you are not as weak or addled as you pretend, the Weaver King will be hard-pressed to treat you as roughly as he treats my citizens. Be strong and sure so that the rift will reveal more of its secrets to your keen mind and probing eye. Who can say? You may yet learn something that will stop the rift apart from feeding me to it."

Teferi sadly lowered his head. "And if I am that weak? If I am that addled?"

Windgrace rose higher. "Then you will die here as ingloriously as you deserve."

The panther-god soared higher and vanished through the upper reaches of the hollow mountain. Teferi watched the ceiling for several long minutes, then lowered his head. Muttering a curse, he threw his staff down with an angry clatter.

Teferi gracefully lowered himself into a cross-legged position. He saw something flicker near the corner of his eye, a ghostly afterimage that put him in mind of a gaunt, armored figure. The half-seen apparition made Teferi's spine go cold, and he concentrated, bringing up fond memories of the Zhalfirin tide surging in to cover the broad, flat rocks of his private beach, the one that had been gifted to him by royal decree.

Teferi eyed his staff. The brass stick twitched. Teferi focused harder, willing the stick to rise, and it slowly floated up from the rocks and drifted over to his waiting hand.

The bald man smiled, savoring this small step forward. He laid the staff across his lap and took deep, measured breaths. There was still hope. As long as he was alive and aware, he could still make something good of the disasters that seemed to follow him like carrion birds.

Pushing aside the phantasmal image and the faint echoes of strange laughter, Teferi steepled his fingers in front of his face, closed his eyes, and began to chant.

* * * * *

The ambulator worked perfectly. Venser and Jodah completed their short hop across Urborg as smoothly and quickly as if Windgrace himself were ferrying them.

They arrived a few yards from Jodah's transport tunnel. As the machine powered down, its soft, high-pitched hum slowly faded. Steam rose from the ambulator's metal skin and from the rig on Venser's shoulders, but the equipment was only slightly warm to the touch.

Jodah blinked. "Impressive," he said.

"Thank you." Venser quickly checked the machine for signs of wear or loss of function. Once he was satisfied there was no damage, he nodded to Jodah, and the archmage leaped down to the flattened patch of marsh grass near the shimmering pool.

"To review," Jodah said, "I'm going through the tunnel. When I emerge in Skyshroud, I click this gem on top of the beacon." He held up the blinking box, displaying its top face to Venser. "Then I wait for you to materialize in the ambulator."

Venser nodded. "It should take no more than a minute for the chair to find the signal. I'll plot a course and come to you directly."

"One minute," Jodah said. "Maybe two. I'll be waiting." The archmage waved a jovial farewell, but his eyes were firm and serious. "Thank you for your help."

Venser said, "Farewell, Archmage," as he busied himself with the control rig. He glanced up and saw Jodah waiting. Venser simply nodded.

Jodah nodded back. He clutched the beacon box in both hands and stepped into the tunnel entrance.

Venser watched Jodah fade away on the other side of the liquid screen. He exhaled and slumped back into the ambulator's chair, letting his head fall into his hand. He massaged the bridge of his nose between two long, callused fingers as he tried to organize his thoughts.

The gladehunter mark did not stand out from the rest of his face, but Venser still felt it there. It didn't burn or seethe or throb, and it wasn't raised like a wart or mole, but its presence was still undeniable as a fresh wound.

He had lived most of his life expecting to be caught and punished for the work he did, but the feeling was far more acute now. Windgrace had given him the chance to atone, and he had used it to sin against the panther-god once more. He had attacked Windgrace's soldiers, stolen the machine, used it, and now he was preparing to use it again to escape his duty to his homeland. He wondered if he would truly make it out of Urborg before Windgrace came for him. He wondered if he'd ever be allowed to return.

A soft buzzing sound and a blinking light came from the right armrest control. Jodah's signal had come. Venser sat up and extended his hands, lightly flicking switches and turning dials. The signal was strong and Venser easily isolated it. From there it was a simple matter to calibrate the chair's guidance mechanisms on this new destination.

As he did so Venser smiled slightly. Now he had three places he could travel to: Urborg, Shiv, and Skyshroud. Each had been converted into energy patterns the machine could re-create on command, their unique coordinates laid out in specific relation to each other. With each trip the machine added more magical-spatial data to its matrix. Venser quickly calculated figures as he worked. If he had a week to do nothing but jaunt around Dominaria, he could map the entire globe and thereafter go anywhere he liked at any time.

Jodah's signal stopped, yanking Venser out of his private thoughts. He moaned softly, only half aware he had made the sound. His fingers flew faster over the controls, but the machine only confirmed his initial fears.

He wasn't finished. The machine was still several seconds away from recording all of the signal data, and without complete information Venser could not reliably go to Skyshroud. He might wind up alongside Jodah and Jhoira, but he just as easily might land in the middle of the ocean or on top of an erupting volcano.

His hands continued to dance, confirming and reconfirming what he already knew.

He had to do something. He couldn't just sit here waiting for Windgrace or the gladehunters to track him down. If he tried to reach Skyshroud now, there was no telling where he'd end up. If he didn't try now, he would lose the best chance he had of reaching Jhoira before some new catastrophe happened.

Rest now. Don't try. Stay and rest awhile. . . .

The Weaver King's voice was a snake's whisper, low and sinuous. Venser felt all the things he always felt, the panic from recognizing another's voice in his thoughts, the fear from wondering what secrets had already been betrayed. He also felt the powerful dread of the Weaver King himself and the shame of allowing Windgrace's enemy in without offering the least bit of resistance.

This time Venser also felt anger. Fear and dread shriveled like paper in fire as Venser's outrage swelled. The Weaver King had erred in pushing him at this particular moment, for Venser had reached his limit. There were too many people making too many demands on him. Planeswalkers and archmages aside, Venser's own sense of duty and the guilt from shirking that duty were more than enough to spur him to action. The Weaver King's exhortations appealed to his weakness, that childish desire that told him to hide his head and wait for the danger to pass. It was a compelling notion no matter how irrational, but Venser would no longer be compelled. Windgrace would never succumb to such a ploy, nor Jodah, nor Radha, and Jhoira least of all.

Venser gritted his teeth and stabbed his fingers in deliberate, measured motion. The ambulator whirred to life under his fingers. A film of yellow energy crawled up the dais and over the arms of the chair, slowly covering Venser in a gleaming skin of crackling light.

Stay. Do not leave. I forbid it. Rest. . . .

"I will not rest," Venser said, "until my work is done." Resolute and full of purpose, Venser flipped the last switch. The ambulator shuddered and faded into a curtain of golden yellow sparks.

The marsh was quiet for a moment or two. Then a high, manic giggle broke the silence and the Weaver King said, *Well, I guess you showed me.*

CHAPTER 16

Confusion and fatigue momentarily overwhelmed Venser, so it took him several seconds to recognize that the ambulator had stopped midjourney. It took several more to realize where he was.

He recognized the Blind Eternities from his previous planes-walks with Teferi and Windgrace, but then he had been a passenger, protected. Now he was alone, and his ambulator floated aimlessly through the colorful void, pitching and rolling like a cork on a lazy river. There was no sense of motion, however, none of the stress that would normally accompany an end-over-end tumble through empty space.

The irrational calm and stability he felt began to worry him. This was unlike any other ambulator trip he had taken before. Of course, he had to acknowledge that every ambulator trip he had taken so far had been unique and unpredictable, but this one still troubled him. It felt different. It was deeper, stronger, and far more profound than a simple hop across the ocean.

The ambulator was meant to carry him through space without resistance, but this time he felt the multiverse pulling at him, drawing him along like a submerged riptide. This trip wasn't a simple matter of disappearing from point A and effortlessly reappearing in point B. It was more like closing his eyes and struggling up a steep hill against a strong, driving rain. Each incremental advance was a struggle that required sustained effort from him.

Was this the result of a half-completed trip on the ambulator? Or was it more proof that he himself was the variable, the supposed powers he had yet to manifest somehow affecting the machine's proper function?

He tentatively ran his hands over the controls, confirming that the ambulator was still responsive. Perhaps this was not as dire a trial as it seemed. He could return to Urborg if he chose. He would not, of course, as he was unwilling to give the Weaver King or Windgrace another chance to bring him to heel, but he was not trapped here.

Venser looked out into the abyss, across the vast expanse of potential matter and newborn energy. His strength and focus began to return and he struggled to relax and clear his mind. At least the environment here wasn't toxic, or even worse, hostile. It was desolate, but also beautiful in its fashion.

The more he looked, the more he saw. This was not a trick of the eye or a flight of fancy. Details about the void came into sharper view when he concentrated on them. Recognizable shapes emerged from the chaos as they did from clouds beheld by a child. There was a globe of fire, a sphere-shaped world dense with red and orange flames. There was a city as big as a moon, every inch of its surface covered in towering architecture through which streamed multitudes of humans and monsters. There was a world that mirrored itself, its shape formed by two symmetrical parts that fitted together to form a perfect circle. And there was a world of silver and black metal, a vast and complicated crucible of alloy and oil.

This last sphere lingered before Venser, the ambulator's glittering lights reflecting back off the plane's metallic surface. The chair drifted toward it, perhaps responding to Venser's desire to see it more closely. He had created a metal world of his own in a sense, a small one that was as expansive as his imagination but bounded by his workshop's walls. Whomever had created the larger clockwork world had resources and vision far beyond Venser's.

Something flashed on the metal plane's outer edge. The ambulator righted itself so that Venser could see the new development clearly, but even as he squinted through the brackish void a strange figure materialized in front of him. It was man-shaped, square and massive, and it gleamed like silver in the sun. He actually seemed to be made of silver, or some magical silver metal that flexed and breathed like a rhino's hide. The metal man had broad shoulders, and his round head sat nestled inside a high collar that rose up to his ears and covered the back of his skull. His torso was plated, and he had a majestic golden symbol inscribed across his chest.

"Oh," the silver man said. His voice was slow and deliberate, and he spoke with the gravity of a serious, learned man. "Now it starts to make sense."

Fearful for reasons he would never identify, Venser raised a trembling hand and said, "Hello."

The silver man stared with wide, soulful eyes. He extended a four-fingered hand toward Venser in the ambulator and said, "Interesting. You don't need that, do you?"

Unnerved, Venser felt his hands stiffen on the controls. The silver man's tranquil interest was disturbingly familiar. He had endured similar appraisals by Nicol Bolas, Windgrace, and Teferi, and now Venser prepared to encounter yet another planeswalker. He remained outwardly still and agape as he surreptitiously prepared the ambulator in case he needed to escape. "What do you mean?"

The silver man paused, distracted by a sound behind him that Venser did not hear. He let his eyes drift from the top of the ambulator to its dais floor. He raised his hand in an unfamiliar gesture and said, "I would speak with you at length. And soon. But I must excuse myself for the moment."

Venser watched the silver statue fade. The strange apparition stared as he went, his heavy features uncannily expressive, and he regarded Venser with a complex blend of guarded curiosity, genuine concern, and profound sadness.

The silver man's body rippled before it completely vanished, creating a visual distortion that clouded Venser's eyes. He blinked them clear and saw that the silver man was growing more solid. His appearance was practically unchanged, but Venser noticed a slight decrease in his bulky body's size—the silver man had become leaner and more flexible, his movements a shade more lively. The shine from his body struck long, silver lines in the void around him that stretched ever outward like the first rays of sunlight across the morning sky.

"Upon deeper consideration," the man said, "I could never let you proceed, burdened as you are. It will only make it more difficult for us to meet again." He floated in close with his arms crossed. He nodded respectfully and reached out with his thumb and index finger.

Venser wanted to speak, but his tongue felt like stone. He only managed to blink and sweat slightly as the silver man brushed his fingers across the artificer's cheek.

"You really don't need this," he said. His voice seemed higher-pitched, more excited. The man lightly moved his index finger across Venser's face back and forth until he found some sort of purchase.

"You are a remarkable young man," he said. "You shouldn't go tagged like the family pet."

Through his paralysis Venser felt something sticky separate from his face. He stared at the silver man's oddly intense expression as the stranger peeled off Venser's gladehunter mark like the skin from a grape. The silver man held the green symbol in front of Venser and closed it in his broad fist.

"You have so much to offer," he told Venser. "So much unrealized potential. So many great things yet undone. When next we meet, you and I will get to know each other much, much better." The silver man winked and smiled, then he flickered out of sight.

For several moments Venser could only sit and stare out into the void. The strange worlds he had glimpsed before were gone, the planes of fire and metal and city lost in the endless clouds of empty space and dust.

The mark was gone. Venser reached up and rubbed the empty spot on his cheek. He no longer felt Windgrace's hold on him. The cold fog of the panther-god's displeasure had lifted and Venser savored a moment of buoyant relief. Was quitting Lord Windgrace's service truly this easy? Was the gladehunter mark something to be shucked and discarded like corn silk?

The artificer forced his leaden limbs to move. He still had a job to do. All he needed was to employ the tools he'd brought along to help him do it.

Venser's hopes for a reliable ambulator were shrinking fast after this last misstep. The machine functioned, its mechanisms operating perfectly. He could see the strength and quality of the design and craft. There were no flaws or errors that could account for the troubles he had, but the fact remained: Except for the short skip across Urborg with Jodah, the machine had gone disastrously wrong every time he used it. The chair had separated him from Jhoira due to causes unknown and beyond his control, and now he was stalled in the Blind Extremities.

Then Venser remembered Skyshroud, and his paralysis broke. Jhoira needed his help there. Jodah was waiting there. If the box hadn't simply malfunctioned, the sudden interruption of the archmage's signal could be dire news indeed for all of them.

The ambulator spun, taking away the view of the void that had housed the metal plane. Venser's fingers came alive on the control panels as he extrapolated the rest of his trip's course. Jodah's incomplete signal gave him direction but not distance, so he would have to go very slowly. He could still make it to Skyshroud if he was careful and reached the forest without overshooting it.

Venser cleared his mind, shoving aside everything but his destination. Skyshroud was where he needed to be. Skyshroud was where he must go.

The ambulator whirred and blinked. Venser felt heat, pressure, and a galvanic tingling all over his body as a sheen of yellow light enveloped the chair. Venser focused his thoughts, energy crackled around him, and the Blind Eternities were soon empty and uninhabited once more.

*   *   *   *   *

Jodah scrambled out from under the exposed roots that framed his tunnel. Freyalise was waiting for him.

"Hello," he said. His fingers closed around the beacon box inside his sleeve, and he pressed down on it until he heard a click. "By your leave, I've come to talk with you."

The planeswalker waved angrily and bore Jodah up into the air. Pure force slammed into him from all directions, battering his body and forcing the air from his lungs. "You are not welcome here," Freyalise said. From bitter experience, Jodah recognized both the cold, patrician tone and the dangerous mood that produced it.

The pressure around him eased, leaving Jodah to float freely inside a faintly glittering, emerald cloud. Freyalise waved her arm again and sent him hurtling toward the wasted trees of Skyshroud. She pointed to this tree and that, and with each gesture Jodah followed her finger. He shouted and cursed as she dashed him from trunk to trunk, slamming him into the tough wood hard enough to bruise him without breaking him. The beacon box was crushed between his arm and his chest on the second impact, and he left a small cloud of metal bits in his wake.

Freyalise beckoned, and Jodah's limp body sailed toward the ground. She stopped him several feet in front of her and righted him with a contemptuous shrug. Through pain-slitted eyes Jodah saw Jhoira standing behind the planeswalker. The Ghitu's body was rigid, her fine features pale with concern.

He forced his swollen, blood-slick lips to form words. "Jhoira," he said. "Brought help."

"Help?" Freyalise let out a half-snarled laugh.

Jodah fought to stay conscious. "I have powerful friends," he said. Experience had told him Freyalise responded best to brevity and respect. It had also told him she could be distracted, even rattled, by a seemingly defeated enemy's bravado. She never seemed quite sure how to handle anything except a coward's groveling or a valiant's grudging respect.

This time the planeswalker was not distracted. She said, "So you do. And I can imagine the sort, planeswalkers in name only. Which of these will come to your rescue, Archmage? Karn? Teferi? Jaya Ballard? Which of them still cares and is capable—the construct, burned-out academic, or the child-woman taskmage?"

Jodah's eyes snapped wide open. He coughed, spit a tooth to the side, and stared Freyalise full in the face. "Jaya's gone," he said quietly.

The planeswalker faltered for a moment. "As you must also go," she said. "Jhoira has agreed to perform a service for me. She is unavailable until she has completed it."

"Freyalise," Jhoira said, "I have given you my promise, and I will see it through. Is there any purpose in killing Jodah now? More, is there any purpose in my witnessing his death?"

Freyalise glanced back at the Ghitu. "His death, if I kill him, will not be on your conscience. Simply because he called out to you does not make him your responsibility."

"My responsibility is to find Radha," Jhoira said. "Yours is to protect Skyshroud. Are either of those advanced by Jodah's murder?"

"Keep quiet," Freyalise said. "This one will be of use to me or he will not be at all." She turned to Jodah. "Your life is yours.

You may keep it, Archmage, or you may throw it away. But it will be you who gives me a reason to spare you—or to slay you and be about my business."

Jodah nodded, maintaining as much of his dignity as he could. Struggling to move his sore arm through the thick, green cloud, the archmage reached inside his robe.

"The cold is returning," he told Freyalise. "What you and I dread most is happening: a new Ice Age begins. You know what will happen, what has to happen next. You know the scale of the World Spell you will inevitably cast. We both do."

Freyalise's face flushed red. "Do not speak to me as an equal."

"To save Skyshroud you'll have to destroy it," Jodah said. "Unless you use this." He pulled out a small hand mirror. The glass and the elegant silver handle had survived his rough journey without the slightest crack or scratch. The mirror gleamed brightly in the gloom, casting back more light than it received.

"Is that the original?" Freyalise said. "Or a decoy?" She opened her hand, and the mirror sprang from Jodah's grasp to hers.

"It functions as it always has," Jodah said. The mirror was his trump card, a powerful artifact that had been a crucial element in his previous dealings with Freyalise. It acted as both repository and filter for the highest forms of magic. Spells cast into it could be refracted back out with incredible precision and to more profound effect.

Freyalise inspected the mirror in the air. She called it to her hand, examined it up close, and tucked it into the sash of her elegant dress. "As always," she said, "you presume too much. Were I willing to cast another World Spell, this trinket would be of no use at all."

Jhoira spoke up, "If that is true, why keep it?"

"Freyalise." Jodah stretched his neck forward. "I've come to help you. I brought you the mirror so that the sheer magnitude of your effort to save Skyshroud doesn't raze the forest to the ground and burn alive every elf in it. If you refuse this help, I will question whether you are unwilling to do what needs be done," Jodah said, "or simply unable."

The planeswalker's face soured. She glanced over to Jhoira before she muttered, "You may question any thrice-damned thing you like, and the world will keep turning." Then, louder, she said, "Able, Archmage? I am able. Barely, I'll admit. And the fact that I am barely able obviates the need for your mirror. To channel and redirect my power through it would diminish the spell to the point of uselessness. What I gained in control I would lose in strength tenfold. No, whatever I do must be done directly with an effort unrestrained."

"So," Jodah said, "you're going to follow Teferi's advice after all?"

"Certainly not," Freyalise said. "Have you gone mad? Why would you entertain such a thought?"

"Because you are already following Teferi's example," Jhoira said.

The patron of Skyshroud turned, her face flooding crimson. "Explain yourself."

"He, too, mapped out his strategy far in advance. He kept it to himself and hid it from others, because it was too terrible to contemplate openly. He created a situation for himself that only he could address and only with gargantuan sacrifice on his part."

Freyalise glowered. "I did not create this," she said. "And do not speak of sacrifice to me, Ghitu. There is nothing I would not do to ensure the survival of my people."

"Then ensure it," Jodah said. "Do something."

"I have done. I am doing. I will do more."

Jodah met Jhoira's eyes. The Ghitu nodded, and they both said, "Let us help you."

The scarlet tint of Freyalise's face paled. Weary, she shrugged and made a slapping gesture with her hand. The cloud around Jodah dissipated, and the archmage landed awkwardly on his feet.

"Most of my elves are already gone," she said. She turned her back on Jodah and spoke to Jhoira. "He would be a good companion for your journey north. If you will have him, I will send him with you."

Relief lit up Jhoira's face. "Yes," she said. "Please allow him to accompany me."

Freyalise turned her head toward the archmage. She narrowed her eye, and her metal patch started to glow. "I regret my bad temper," she said. Freyalise nodded and a new surge of greenish mist rose up around Jodah. He braced himself to be hurled about again, but instead of lifting him this spell settled over him like dew.

Jodah felt a rush of strength. His entire body tingled. The soreness in his arms vanished, and he felt his swollen features returning to normal. In a matter of seconds he was restored. Shortly after that, he felt better off physically than he had in years.

"Go with Jhoira," Freyalise said. "Send word to my champion." Freyalise turned away. "Then come no more to Skyshroud." The planeswalker rose into the air.

She had risen only a few yards when the gold-yellow sphere appeared. Freyalise stopped where she was, aggressive fire mana sparking from her hands, but Jodah guessed this was no new danger. He had given up on Venser when the beacon box shattered, but it seemed the Urborg artificer had come through after all.

The ambulator took shape inside the sphere of energy. Jodah saw Venser's lanky form seated in the device's control seat. He stole a glance at Jhoira, noting the effect Venser's arrival had on her mood and posture. The archmage took some small satisfaction from the knowledge he had done the right thing—Jhoira might not have needed the ambulator to complete her task in Skyshroud, but she definitely needed to see Venser intact and in front of her before she pressed on.

Jodah dimly registered that Freyalise did not share their joy at seeing Venser. The planeswalker still had her spells ready to cast, and she stared angrily at the artificer as if she expected him to attack.

The golden glow rolled back to reveal Venser at the center of his steaming machine. He quickly stood and stepped down onto the ambulator's dais, careful to keep a watchful eye on Freyalise.

The planeswalker spoke sternly, her voice strong. "What is that?"

"That's the artificer from Urborg," Jodah said. "You saw him last at Windgrace's side."

Freyalise spat. "Not the boy," she said. "That."

Venser hesitated in his confusion. He opened his mouth to speak, but instead of sound, a gauzy, silver stream emerged, a development that shocked no one more than Venser himself. The stream continued until the tail end of the phantasm cleared the artificer's jaw. The ectoplasmic apparition briefly took on a humanoid shape, becoming a long, sinewy figure with a great wild tangle of bushy, orange braids. Then the delirious laughter began, and Jodah's stomach fell. To his right, Freyalise's skin turned red, as thunder clapped above her.

Hello, hello, hello! the Weaver King cried. He maintained his human outline inside the smoky, silver substance, and he tossed his head gaily as he spoke, facing them all in turn. *I'm so pleased you invited me to see you at home. So many things to see, so many people to meet. It's cold here, too, isn't it? I like the cold. It's bracing and it helps me think clearly.*

Freyalise unleashed a blast of fire at the Weaver King. He laughed as it passed cleanly through him, but Venser lost some hair to the flames before he was able to dive clear.

The Weaver King's mirth stopped short. His ghostly form still wore a smile, but his eyes were cold, hard, and empty. *You're like him,* he said, *like Windgrace. You don't want me to have any fun.*

"There is no joy for you here, parasite." Freyalise clenched two fists of fire and prepared to strike again.

Oh, but there is. The bugs here are fascinating. We have some in Urborg, of course, but yours are so much more . . . diverse. The Weaver King's body had started to drift apart, wafting away in the evening breeze.

"Stay and fight," Freyalise said. "You will suffer if I have to hunt you down."

Suffering is good for the soul. At least, that's what I always tell people. A roaring wave of sound rose up from the trees. Jodah stepped back, tilting his head to follow the thick stream of wedge-shaped monsters swirling up from the forest.

"Stop." Freyalise's anguish was in her voice and in the renewed blast of fire magic she unleashed on the Weaver King. Neither worked to good effect on the sliver swarm or the Weaver King's raucous laughter.

Rest now, the Weaver King said. *I'll need some time to get acquainted with my new army . . . but I'll be back soon.*

Shrieks of laughter mixed with the high-pitched keen of a thousand frenzied slivers. The smoke that housed the Weaver King's form dissipated, but Jodah could see his malign presence surging among the tide of insect monsters. The slivers quickly burrowed into the deeper woods, leaving Jhoira, Jodah, Venser, and Freyalise at the forest's edge.

Freyalise's entire body was tense, clenched like a fist. She turned to Jhoira and said, "What was that?" The planeswalker turned to Venser. "And why did you bring it here?"

"That was the Weaver King," Jodah said, eager to cut in before Freyalise began brutalizing Venser. "A mind raider and puppet maker. He escaped from the Stronghold in Urborg a short time ago. Now it seems he has followed Venser here."

Freyalise rose up, her feet several feet off the ground. She rotated slowly, casting her dire eyes on the other three.

"Urborg's problem is now Skyshroud's," she said. "And if this petty king has taken control of my slivers, there may be no hope for my children at all."

CHAPTER 17

The Weaver King was ecstatic. He had never had subjects like the Skyshroud slivers, never had so many oddly powerful creatures so fully under his control. He didn't know or care if they were naturally hive-minded, if their insect brains responded to his commands more naturally than animal ones, or if the slivers were simply too primitive to offer resistance. Whatever the reason, he allowed himself to run rampant on the backs of the chittering horde.

They streamed through the forest by the thousand, whittling the tallest trees off at the base with their pointed feet and sharp-edged shells. Their roars and screeches filled the woods with the ravening sound of scavengers gorging themselves on fresh carrion. They were innumerable, indistinguishable as individuals, and yet this was not a burden to him. In fact, their numbers somehow made them easier to command and more susceptible to his direct control.

He congratulated himself on discovering a wholly new type of stimulation. In his dealings with higher animals, he preferred to nudge their own darker inclinations and let the subject provide the entertainment. It was completely different with these alien insects, more like controlling one huge body with a thousand responsive parts.

The Weaver King cackled. He had not fully inhabited a physical body for quite some time, but they were his body now, a vast and complicated body capable of truly wonderful feats. He felt their abilities move and mingle amid the swarm, expanding and extending across the whole like shared body heat. Sending a flight of slivers into the air was akin to raising his arm in a friendly greeting. Igniting two or three dozen to leave flash fires in their path was no more challenging than brushing his long hair out of his eyes had been back on Rath. His swarm rippled and changed as they coursed through Skyshroud, horns and wings and poison-tipped spikes emerging from their hard backs only to soften and merge back into the shells that spawned them.

The swarm poured into a clearing, and a galvanic thrill ran through the Weaver King. Four elf warriors (rangers, their thoughts told him, Freyalise's Skyshroud rangers) stood rooted and wide-eyed in shock as an avalanche of skittering bodies covered them. It was over quickly, almost too quickly, but the Weaver King was too deep in his private joy to quibble over such details. In the past he had enjoyed the process of sending four or six or eight of his subjects against one another in a grand free-for-all, but this was far more engaging. This was his will enacted on a large scale, a veritable army that moved, killed, and feasted in immediate response to his slightest passing fancy.

The slivers moved on, leaving a pile of slick elf bones scattered in the dirty snow. Had there been more victims for the swarm ,the Weaver King might have spent hours running them down. The forest was almost empty, however, and though the slivers showed no signs of fatigue, the Weaver King's own energy soon began to ebb.

He kept them moving even as he considered his next diversion. He could reverse their course and descend upon the others at the forest edge. He was unwilling to risk losing Venser in the melee, however, and he wanted to spend a lot more time with Jhoira and Jodah before he finished with them.

Freyalise was also a problem. Like Windgrace, she was too

formidable to attack directly, her mind proof against his magic. The forest witch was also steeped in the same limitless power Windgrace had, making a face-to-face confrontation dangerous. If there was to be unpredictability in his daily routine, he preferred to be the source of it. There was too much about Freyalise he didn't know, too much she could do if he troubled her. Better to wait, to strengthen his hold on the slivers and master their natural arsenal. Freyalise would fall to a coordinated sliver swarm, or her heart would break when she was forced to destroy them. Either option appealed to him, and he spurred his horde on to another mad rush through the trees. I will put my new body through its paces, he thought, before I send it against a planeswalker.

The leading edge of the sliver mass broke out into another small clearing. This one was also occupied, but not by Skyshroud elves. The Weaver King recognized cold, steel Phyrexians from the same force that emerged from the Stronghold and was invading Urborg. This unit numbered but a dozen, perhaps a scouting party for a larger phalanx.

The Phyrexians did not attack but circled themselves facing outward to beat back the slivers if they came too close. On a hunch, the Weaver King sent his minions circling around the metallic warriors, keeping the bugs a safe distance from the Phyrexians' keen-edged limbs and their toxic ranged weaponry. Controlling the slivers was so effortless that he had the attention to spare on the Phyrexians, and so it was that the Weaver King realized something wonderful.

Collectively, the cold Phyrexians were remarkably similar to the slivers. They were essentially drones, lethally powerful drones who had been created to follow a dominant leader. There were no more heroes in the Phyrexian band than there were in the sliver horde, no charismatic leaders or gifted tacticians that stood out from the crowd. A brilliant battlefield general like Windgrace would always defeat them, as their only method seemed to be charging at the enemy head-on. They were all simply cannon fodder, grunt soldiers who either lacked the capacity for strong thinking or had seen that capacity beaten out of them. They were followers in dire need of a leader—and the Weaver King was ready to lead.

He sent a strong, straight thread directly into the mind of the largest Phyrexian. The monster's psyche was stunted and half-complete, filled with thoughts and passions that he could not decode. It was a living mind, however, capable of accepting rudimentary commands and making basic decisions within the limits of a large-scale bloodbath. The Weaver King was pleased.

The Phyrexian's mind was also rife with dark passions and violent impulses, and this was a language the Weaver King spoke fluently. The mechanical man was totally loyal and subservient to his Machine God, that half-glimpsed and completely misunderstood creator who had woven himself through every fiber of the Phyrexian soldier's being. That entity had foolishly never bothered to personally imprint on such lowly members of his army. Perhaps his forces were too numerous, or such advanced treatment was not available to the infantry that rolled off his assembly lines. Whatever the case, whatever the cause, these cold-weather horrors were designed to follow orders and destroy the enemy without the capacity for questioning who gave those orders or against whom they fought.

The Weaver King had appeared to Venser as that strange, silver planeswalker to break Windgrace's hold on the artificer. Now he attempted to appear to the Phyrexians as the voice of their lord and master, the ineffable demon who had given them life and charged their oily blood with magic and bloodlust.

The Phyrexian's head clicked and whirred. It rotated its face to where the Weaver King hovered, invisible and intangible. The Weaver King sent another thread into the Phyrexian's clockwork mind, then another.

Bow, he told it. *Bow before your master.*

The Phyrexian continued to stare through hollow, metal sockets. Then the monstrosity lowered itself to one knee and tilted its head down almost to the ground.

The Weaver King stifled his glee. He cast threads onto the rest of the Phyrexians here, sending, *The rest of you as well. Bow down and worship me, for I have come to lead you to victory. Follow me and your purpose will be fulfilled.*

Twelve Phyrexian nightmares all dutifully bent and touched their heads to the soil. The slivers clicked, mewed, and clattered all around them. The Weaver King sent out a single command to his insect horde, and they all fell silent, their staccato movements gradually giving way to complete and utter stillness.

The Weaver King surveyed the clearing, drinking in the endless patchwork of killing machines both natural and manufactured.

Now this is an army, he thought. He caressed the thread that connected him to Dinne and plucked it like a violin string.

Dart tosser, he said. Dinne did not respond, but the Weaver King knew he had the raider's full attention. *Stop wasting time with that afterthought. Go out and find me the largest concentration of Phyrexians in Urborg. Keep them in sight and wait for my signal.* The Weaver King stifled another giggle, knowing that if he started it would be hours before he stopped.

I'll be back soon. Don't tell Windgrace, though, as I want him to be surprised.

The slivers began to chatter and moan. The Phyrexians rose to the sound of servo motors revving high. The Weaver King let himself go, the manic sounds of his joy echoed in the throats of his newly assembled regiment.

* * * * *

Teferi sat facing the silent armored figure. He was still cross-legged on the floor of the Stronghold's hollow interior, his staff propped up on his knees and glowing softly at the tip.

The warrior flickered in and out like a ghost, balefully watching Teferi without ever speaking. Teferi could not place the man's tribe, but he was almost certainly a refugee from Rath. Teferi knew a little about shadow creatures and had even encountered two or three in person, and while this creature was far more dangerous than they, he was also clearly of their ilk.

It had been hours, and so far the warrior had made no hostile act. He was well armed and Teferi could see his body had been trained and tempered to the rigors of soldiering. He cut an odd, unsettling figure, somehow dire and ominous yet melancholy at the same time. Teferi had tried speaking to him, but the armored man was prone to vanishing and reappearing by way of a reply. He didn't seem skittish or nervous but rather annoyed that he had been observed, a snake who has to reposition himself for a lethal strike because his prey has spotted him.

Teferi had briefly entertained the notion that Windgrace had sent the warrior to task him, but that theory did not pan out. The man had no gladehunter mark, for one, and if he were here to test Teferi he had yet to demonstrate how. Though he did not let his guard down, Teferi had long since turned his thoughts to larger issues—the cold, the Phyrexians, and the Stronghold rift.

Windgrace had treated him unfairly, but Teferi's time in the Stronghold was well spent. He was close enough to the rift to maintain a clear surveillance of it, the kind of slow, methodical examination that he had not enjoyed in Shiv. The Stronghold rift contained a full slate of titanic forces, magical, spatial, and temporal. The combination of these forces facilitated the appearance of these alternate-reality Phyrexians, though Teferi knew there were other root causes at work. A planar intrusion of this magnitude would require several rift-scale phenomena all responding to the same magical stimulus, and this unnatural cold snap was caused by far more than another breach in the foundations of the multiverse.

These creatures were out of time as well as place and they bore the signs of extremely potent and unstable magic.

Teferi blinked and scanned the cavern until he spotted his silent observer. The armored man had withdrawn to the west end of the mountain, half-concealed by a stalagmite. Teferi was loath to draw more attention to himself, but he could wait no longer. It was time to try his magic again.

Stripped of his planeswalker potential, Teferi had been forced to relearn the painstaking process of drawing mana as mortal wizards did: from the local surroundings and his memories of home. A thousand years of practice made this process familiar to him, but he likened it to swimming across an ocean. The fact that he could easily grasp the task at hand did nothing to make it easier.

As a godlike being, he knew mana was his for the taking. As a formerly godlike being he was continually frustrated by how long it took to marshal his strength. Zhalfir would still be out of his reach if he hadn't spent more time there than anywhere else, both as mortal and planeswalker. Without his long-term residence in Zhalfir and its environs, and without the experience of channeling mana on a gigantic scale, he would have been lost. He suspected that he might still be without access to Zhalfirin mana if he hadn't been the one who created the spells that removed it and used them to send his homeland into phase.

He was ready now. He had collected the mana and stored it in his staff, where he could access it more quickly. He could not planeswalk, but he could cast a simple levitation spell that would lift him out of the bowels of the mountain. There was a good chance Windgrace would pounce on him the moment the spell took shape, but Teferi had to take that chance. There was nothing for him to do and precious little more to learn here. He had to get out.

His hands tightened around his staff, and Teferi floated off the cavern floor. He rose only a few inches, but he was thrilled by this initial success and strived to keep his mind focused. Dropping several inches onto his backside would be embarrassing and painful. Falling from the middle of the mountain to the frozen swamps below would surely kill him, so he had every intention of being careful.

The armored man started when Teferi moved as if shaken from a restless sleep. His featureless, white eyes shone from under his helmet as he craned his head to track the wizard's progress. Teferi pushed the observer from his mind, concentrating on keeping the flow of mana intact between his staff and his body.

The armored man stepped out from behind the rocks. His hand went to his belt, and he drew a thick, round spike. He expertly twirled it between his fingers and cocked his arm behind him, ready to throw.

Teferi dropped several inches but managed to stay aloft. He didn't want to start over from the floor, but neither did he want to receive a sharp throwing weapon in midflight. The flight spell was simple and familiar, yet it took all of his concentration and all the magic he could assemble. Did he dare spend that mana on a defensive spell? Could he afford not to? And on a more practical level, what could he cast that was simpler and more familiar than this first-year-student's trick?

The memories of his home crowded his brain, but now a different recollection rose above the others. He had been in a similar situation recently, seated and preoccupied as a dangerous opponent stalked ever closer. Corus had been consumed by rage and grief when he attacked, and Teferi had been helpless. Yet Corus was dead now, and Teferi was still here. If he could only remember how he bested the viashino, he could perhaps use the same strategy against the silent, armored scarecrow.

The warrior let his spike fly. Teferi watched it tumbling through the air toward him and resigned himself to abandoning his flight. There were simpler spells than levitation, spellcraft that was more familiar to him and easier to cast. For purely defensive measures, there was nothing cleaner or quicker than phasing.

He had invented this branch of blue magic himself, testing its use and drilling himself until it was second nature to him. At the peak of his powers Teferi could teach the lowliest apprentice to phase in less time than it took to eat lunch. It seemed grand and impressive to utterly remove a threat from existence with the wave of a hand, even if it was only for a short time. Decades of pains-taking research made it deceptively easy in practice, especially once Teferi perfected the method.

He borrowed just a taste of mana from his flight spell and focused it on the incoming spike. He didn't need to be faster than the darts or more accurate than their caster. He simply needed to be still.

The spike's gleaming tip touched the edge of the spell bubble around Teferi. The spike disappeared in a minor puff of blue dust.

Teferi exhaled. He would be safe now. Anything that came close enough to touch him would simply cease to exist for a short time, and he had enough mana in his staff to power the shield for hours.

The armored man remained silent, but his posture betrayed his confusion. He didn't seem anxious or frightened, nor even angry. He drew a spike in each hand and quickly cast them at Teferi, watching intently as they too vanished inches from their target.

"You can't hurt me," Teferi said. His voice echoed back and forth across the cavern.

The warrior remained unconvinced. He vanished from sight, reappearing at four different places around Teferi and hurling a dagger each time he flickered back in. Teferi smiled patiently through the barrage and waited for the white-eyed phantom to give up.

The armored figure faded into view ten yards directly in front of Teferi. His hand stole back to his belt, and his whole body stiffened. He clutched madly around his waist, searching the empty loops for something to throw. He glared at Teferi from under his helmet. Defiantly, he extended his empty hand and waited as if he expected it to fill itself.

A spike phased back, robbed of its momentum but still pointed toward Teferi. It hung in the air for a moment and fell noisily to the floor. The other spikes quickly followed, returning to the world in sequence as they filled the cavern with the sound of ghostly metal on stone.

To Teferi's mild surprise, the warrior's hand did fill itself—the first spike he'd thrown evaporated on the floor and reappeared in its master's grip. Curious, the wizard thought. Whoever this warrior was, he must have worked very hard to become this dangerous. It must have taken inhuman discipline to master this sort of control over his shadow existence.

The armored phantom drew back his weapon once more. "Are you just going to keep trying to stab me all night and day?" Teferi said.

Dart tosser.

Teferi's warming interest died in the cold dread of that disembodied voice. It was a sharp, brittle, jagged sound, full of joy and malice. He was too familiar with such voices and did not relish listening to another.

But the speaker wasn't interested in Teferi, only the armored would-be killer. The white-eyed wraith had lowered his weapon when the voice first spoke and was standing almost at attention, a soldier awaiting orders.

The orders soon came. *Stop wasting time with that afterthought,* the voice said, and Teferi stifled a harrumph when he realized that meant him. *Go out and find me the largest concentration of Phyrexians in Urborg. Keep them in sight and wait for my signal.* The mad voice paused, then added, *I'll be back soon. Don't tell Windgrace, though, as I want him to be surprised.*

The warrior obeyed without hesitation, sheathing his spike and disappearing into the stone wall without so much as a glance for Teferi. Just as well, Teferi thought. He still had to get out from under this mountain, and he couldn't do that if someone kept throwing sharp objects at him. There was ample mana left in his staff, and he was more than ready to fly again. He had almost certainly just met Windgrace's Weaver King, and Teferi wanted to be well clear of here when that brittle-voiced madman next returned home.

He sat once more and touched his index fingers together in front of his nose. His staff glowed, and Teferi rose into the air once more.

CHAPTER 18

Venser's relief at finally catching up to Jhoira was quickly overwhelmed by Freyalise's mounting anger. She stared fiercely at him as her face slowly turned crimson. Fear and regret mingled in his mind, and Venser despaired when he couldn't decide which was worse: the fact that he had ferried the Weaver King to Skyshroud and so deserved whatever ire Freyalise had, or the fact that he'd been totally unaware of the Weaver King's presence and so deserved it more.

"I'm sorry," he said, hating the feeble sound of his own voice and the negative effect it had on Freyalise's mood.

"Yes, you are." The planeswalker's lips curled back, exposing her clenched teeth. "I expected Windgrace to have better control of his pets," she said and half-closed her exposed eye to inspect Venser's face, "though I see you are no longer affiliated with the gladehunters. How did you manage that?"

Venser did not answer, unsure of the truth and fearing her reaction to his best guess. Freyalise's eye glowed, and heat rose around Venser, stalking him like a hungry wolf.

"I asked you a question," Freyalise said.

"The Weaver King is a subtle creature," Jodah said. He stepped forward and positioned himself between Venser and Freyalise. "Windgrace himself cleared both Venser and me after he drove the Weaver King from our minds. Or so he thought."

Freyalise did not look at the archmage but remained focused on Venser. "So the fault is not yours," she said, "even though you slipped out from under Windgrace's protection by your own choosing."

Venser moved so that he stood next to Jodah in full view of the planeswalker. "I escaped on my own," he said. "But the mark was taken from me in transit."

"Taken? By whom?"

Venser noticed Jodah and Jhoira both leaned forward to hear the answer.

"A planeswalker," he said. "A man. He was big and silver."

"You saw Karn?" Jhoira said. Jodah flinched when she spoke, and Venser shared his concern. Freyalise looked mad enough to incinerate them all without being interrupted.

"He never said his name," Venser said. "But if Karn is powerfully built and made of metal, it was probably him."

"Tall, broad, heavy. Speaks in a deliberate voice." Heedless of Freyalise, Jhoira came toward Venser with her hands circling directly in front of her chest. "He has a golden symbol here, his name spelled out in the ancient language of the Thran."

Venser nodded. "I don't read Thran," he said. "But that is exactly the creature I saw."

Now Jhoira came forward, placing herself in front of the others. "This changes everything," she said. "Karn has come because I called out to him."

"And if I cared," Freyalise said, "I would ask where he is, for I do not see him."

"He is a traveler," Jhoira said, "exploring the far edges of the multiverse for decades, perhaps centuries. It may take time for him to reach us, but the fact that he answered my call is the best news we could have."

"I disagree." Freyalise planted her gloved fists on her hips. "The best news I could have is to hear that thing"—she pointed to the ambulator—"can take you to Radha."

Venser blinked. He opened his mouth but wisely shut it without voicing his objections as Jhoira and Freyalise fixed him with their own unique warning glances.

The planeswalker spoke, her voice rising as if she addressed multitudes. "Hear this, maker from Urborg. You can repair the damage you've already done by taking these two north and collecting my champion."

"But I—"

"Else," Freyalise's color shifted to a deeper, dustier brick red, "you are useless to me. And there is nothing to prevent my exacting fair recompense for what you have already cost me."

"Freyalise," Jhoira said, "I must ask you to release me from my vow. Temporarily. Allow me to seek out Karn and guide him here. He can do ten times the good Radha can."

The patron of Skyshroud's face was as cold and still as a porcelain mask. "By what measure?"

"By all measures. He is a planeswalker. He has intimate knowledge of the multiverse's structure, form, and function. And"—she locked eyes with the angry forest goddess—"he will help us willingly. He would not come this far otherwise."

"But he has not come," Freyalise said. "And now I cannot afford to wait."

"Yes you can," Jodah said. "The Weaver King said he would need time to master the slivers."

"And you believe him?"

"I believe he is a braggart. He sometimes tells his victims the truth because he enjoys the fear it raises in them. He likes few things more than to make a threat and carry it out on his own terms."

Now it was Freyalise who opened her mouth but reconsidered before she spoke. She seemed distracted by something behind her, deep in the forest. Her threatening color shifted back toward her normal, fair-skinned appearance, and the angry light faded from her eyes.

"Your Weaver King," she said, "has just added the Phyrexians to his growing horde."

Venser felt a new surge of regret, but Jhoira said, "All the more reason to bring Karn here as quickly as possible."

Freyalise closed her eyes, the glittering gem on her eye patch growing dim. She stood silently for a few seconds, breathing deeply. "Go," she said at last. "I will do what needs to be done, alone as always."

"Not always," Jodah said. "Listen to us, Freyalise. We can help you."

"So you say, Archmage." Freyalise opened her eyes, and her body began to fade behind a curtain of green and gold light. "But I have been disappointed too often of late. Radha, Windgrace, and now Jhoira . . . all of you failed me, abandoned me when I counted on you. I will protect my people as I always have done. I need no one else."

"Wait," Jodah said, but the planeswalker paid no heed. She vanished, leaving a cold wind that barely stirred the dead leaves on the ground.

As Jodah stared solemnly at the space Freyalise had just occupied, Venser and Jhoira turned to each other and spoke simultaneously.

"Are you all right?" he said.

"Tell me about Karn," she said.

Venser paused, realizing that Jhoira's energy and interest had already answered his question. "He was distant," he said.

"Physically or mentally?"

"Both." Venser recalled his strange interlude in the Blind Eternities. "He seemed to recognize me. Said that 'everything made sense now.' He promised to return soon."

"I see. Why did he remove Windgrace's mark?"

"I'm not sure. He said I didn't need it. Or the ambulator. Do you know what that means?"

Jhoira stiffened. "I have a theory."

Venser didn't like Jhoira's evasive tone. "What did you mean when you said you called him?"

Jhoira shrugged. "I added an extra function to the ambulator," she said. "Specifically, to the control rig. If the machine worked it sent a summons to Karn. A cry for help, really. It's the same principle that we use when studying the weather. You have to take your instruments high above the clouds to avoid interference."

Venser nodded, his throat tightening. "And you kept this a secret." His mind raced, wondering how much Jhoira's extra functionality had contributed to the ambulator's unpredictability.

"I did." Jhoira's wise eyes grew sad. "I'm sorry."

"I forgive you," Venser said instantly, "though I would like to know what other secrets are built into this metal yoke."

"It does what I told you," she said. "It gives you precise control. It collects information from the chair and the chair's surroundings, information that we can use to fine-tune the ambulator's function."

Venser waited for her to continue, certain there was more. "And?" he said.

"It collects information from you," Jhoira said. Her eyes cleared, and her resolve returned. "Karn was right, Venser. You don't need the ambulator. In fact, my theory is that your nascent powers are the main reason the chair never functions as you intend."

A thousand thoughts collided on their way to Venser's tongue. The only one that managed to emerge was, "What powers?"

"You can planeswalk," she said. "Without the machine. I'm almost positive."

Venser's mind flashed once more to the godlike beings who kept taking an interest in him. To compare himself to them seemed laughable. "But I can't do magic."

"You've already teleported twice," she said. "I've seen it."

"I'm mortal," Venser said. "I sleep and eat and bleed."

Jhoira nodded. "I don't have all the answers," she said. "Perhaps I have none at all. My theory is incomplete but evolving."

Venser went light-headed. He shuffled back a few steps and fell heavily into the ambulator's seat. "I don't understand any of this," he said.

"You do," Jhoira said. "You just can't process it, can't articulate it. Think of this as an unusual machine that you've happened across. You don't know what it is, but you can make educated guesses. Function follows form, but in this case you already understand the function. All we have to do is puzzle out the form of your unique planeswalking spark."

Venser bowed his head to collect his thoughts. "How do we do that?"

"We don't. At least, not right now." Jhoira stepped up onto the dais. "Give me the rig," she said. "Karn is close. Calling him again will help him find us as quickly as possible."

Venser lifted his face. "You can operate the ambulator?"

"I can," she said. "Now that you have. Machines have memories, Venser, and over the years you taught yours how to teleport. It remembers those lessons, even in this new incarnation.

"I made the control rig to learn still more. I designed it so you could be its template, so you could teach it how to planeswalk. Now that you have, the rig can share that knowledge with the chair, and anyone who knows how to use the chair."

Venser clutched both arms of the ambulator. "That's a fine line, Jhoira. I'm not seeing a big difference between teleporting and planeswalking. Is it possible you've mistaken my teleportation device for something grander?" But even as he said it, he remembered how different it had felt.

"No one teleports to the Blind Eternities," Jhoira said. "And you were there. Only planeswalkers can do that."

Venser tilted his head and propped it up with his elbow on the ambulator's armrest. "All right," he said. "I yield to your extensive experience. What should I do?"

"Move quickly," she said. "It will only take a few seconds for me to signal Karn."

Venser sighed. "And you think he'll come this time?"

"I hope so. If he does, we will be in a much stronger position with much better options."

"Only if Karn is completely unlike the rest of the planeswalkers we've encountered."

"He is. He has changed much since I last saw him, but he is still entirely unique. He cannot be judged by standards set by Freyalise or Windgrace."

"Or Teferi." Venser stood up. He stared down at Jhoira, sighed again, and hooked his fingers under the control rig. He wrestled it over his head, noting once more how light it was. Jhoira had been right about that, right about so many things. He could do much worse than to trust her judgment now.

Venser handed the metal yoke to Jhoira. "Don't leave me alone here too long," he said. "You may think I can planeswalk on my own, but I don't want to rely on that if Freyalise or Windgrace come looking for me."

Jhoira took the rig and gracefully slipped into it. It looked odd on her shoulders but not uncomfortable. "I won't be long," she said. "And you won't be alone. Jodah can . . ."

The Ghitu's voice trailed off as she glanced past Venser. He turned to follow her eyes, surveying the otherwise empty valley. The archmage was gone.

The look of confusion and concern on Jhoira's face pained Venser. "Go," he said. "Bring the silver man here."

Jhoira stared at Venser from the dais. "Are you sure?"

"The sooner you go, the sooner you can return," he said.

"What about Freyalise? And Windgrace? And the Weaver King?"

Venser stepped off of the ambulator. He folded his arms behind his back and planted his feet. "Windgrace has Urborg to worry about," he said. "And I'm ready for the Weaver King. He can't surprise me when I know he's coming. Besides, he has already antagonized Freyalise. They should both be fully occupied with stalking each other for the foreseeable future." Venser thought of the planeswalker-mortal pairings he had seen and experienced over the past month. "And if Jodah has gone after her as I think he has, punishing me will be the last thing on her mind."

He thought Jhoira might argue, might correct him on the finer points of Jodah's aims and Freyalise's reactions. Instead, the Ghitu nodded and settled into the chair.

Envious and impressed, Venser watched as Jhoira operated the controls as quickly as he ever had but with far more efficiency. It was in Venser's nature to be meticulous, to flip every switch and move every lever several times to make sure he had left no room for error. Jhoira did everything once, with a delicate touch, and she did not repeat herself.

The ambulator began to whine, and the familiar yellow glow scintillated across its metal surfaces. She turned to face him, and just as the envelope of energy extended over her, she mouthed the words, "Thank you."

Then Jhoira disappeared, leaving Venser alone with the rotting corpses of Gathan brutes and the skeletal remains of Skyshroud's trees.

* * * * *

Jodah moved through the forest. It was dark, and the terrain was unfamiliar, but his past experience with Freyalise and his affinity for strong magic guided his steps. Thunder roared nearby, and Jodah felt the ground shake. Bright flames lit up the dim skies to the east, and he heard the excited clicks and screeches of a thousand frenzied slivers. Freyalise had clearly decided not to allow the Weaver King an extended opportunity to strengthen his hold on his newly assembled legions.

Jodah moved toward the sounds of battle. It was in fact far easier to track the patron of Skyshroud's whereabouts than it had been to leave Jhoira and Venser behind. He had thrown in with them because of his role in bringing the Weaver King into their lives and because he believed in the threat of the time rifts, but he could not let Freyalise follow her own purposes without trying to dissuade her.

As he expected when dealing with planeswalkers, circumstances had spiraled spectacularly out of a mere mortal's control. The godlike beings were magnets for chaos, gathering the most powerful and disruptive influences to them no matter what their intent. They were titans whose power made the impossible happen, but they were also flawed, and their shortcomings were likewise amplified to fantastic degrees. Teferi's childishness and love of mystery made him reckless and manipulative in his efforts to solve them. Windgrace's uncompromising tenacity manifested as near-tyranny among the people of Urborg. Jaya's impetuousness made her careless and eventually cost her her life. And Freyalise . . . Freyalise's maternal rigor blinded her to the welfare of anyone beyond her extended family.

Freyalise was not above making huge sacrifices to achieve her ends, especially if the martyrs were not of elf blood. She saved the world once, long ago, but she did so for her elves and without regard to the impact on others. Jodah himself had helped steer her World Spell toward a safer, less destructive effect, and now that she was heading down that road once more he was determined to minimize the damage she'd invariably do.

Another peal of thunder and another gout of flame rocked the forest. He stumbled as the ground shifted beneath him, but he pressed on. At least she had the mirror, he thought. Freyalise was stubborn and proud, but even she would not hesitate to use a tool that increased her control over transcendent magic, as a similar artifact had done with the World Spell.

He approached a stand of smoking, charred trees. Jodah steeled himself and climbed a slight rise. He was greeted by the sight of a newly cleared acre of forest, a broad, flat circle of fallen timber and shattered metal.

Freyalise was marching inexorably toward the center of the forest. The small-seeming woman pushed back the seething mound of slivers and Phyrexians as effectively as a seawall during high tide, containing them but also driving them deeper into Skyshroud with each hard-fought step. The horde had piled itself high before her, its own weight crushing those at the bottom of the heap. The uppermost members of the Weaver King's puppet army bounded high overhead, hurling themselves forward like fleas from a bear's back, but none of them ever came close to the planeswalker. The best they could do was slam to a sudden stop twenty yards overhead before Freyalise's magic cast them back onto the mobile mountain of insects and metal.

Jodah was awed by the sight. Freyalise was glorious, her power surging around her like a bright, hot wind. She seemed so small, so brittle compared to her enemy, yet it was they who were giving ground. The archmage stood stock-still, his impetus withering as he considered his contribution to Skyshroud's defense. He knew spells that would help, that would add force to Freyalise's cause and allow her to conserve more of her strength. He dared not use any of them for fear of disrupting the planeswalker's strategy but also because he did not wish to anger her further. At this stage, even a beneficial act could cause Freyalise to turn and destroy him for interfering.

Follow your instincts, Archmage. Freyalise's thoughts slashed through his mind like a scythe, though the planeswalker did not take her eyes or her power off the horde. *Stand where you are until I have finished.*

Which is what I am trying to avoid, Jodah thought, but his words stayed inside his own skull. He did not have the ability to project his thoughts, and Freyalise had clearly chosen not to hear them.

Instead, the patron of Skyshroud raised her fists and screamed. It was an ugly, grating sound, the roar of a feral beast that came seasoned with equal measures of pain and fury. The mound of slivers and Phyrexians exploded, or rather the leading edge of the mound exploded, driving the rest back like leaves in a hurricane wind.

Jodah was blown back against a tree trunk, and he slumped, dazed, to the forest floor. His first thought was that Freyalise had done what he feared most and given her ultimate effort without employing the mirror.

Freyalise's detonation only the ended this battle. Jodah's ears stopped ringing and his vision cleared, allowing him to follow the glowing cloud of red-hot metal parts and flaming dismembered limbs that rose over Skyshroud. The survivors and the wounded were hurled along with the dead, all descending and disappearing together among the trees on the far side of the woods.

As Jodah rose, Freyalise fell to her knees. Her arms hung straight down so that her knuckles scraped across the charred ground, and her head slumped forward. Jodah ran toward her, wobbling as he came, but he was neither fast enough nor welcome to provide any assistance.

Freyalise straightened her head as Jodah came close. He slowed to a walk as the patron of Skyshroud planted her palms in the layer of soot and oil, drew her legs up under her, and struggled to her feet.

She turned to face him. She looked weary, weaker and more careworn than he had ever imagined.

"Freyalise," he said, "can we speak?"

The planeswalker's head lolled to one side, but she shook off her drowsiness, and her eyes gleamed, clear and full of purpose once more.

"I do not know," she said. "Can we? So far all you've offered is a steady stream of infantile needling."

Jodah nodded. "And I apologize," he said. "I reacted to your shortness with me, to the hostility that I feared and you have so eloquently expressed."

"Answer your own question," she said.

"Can we speak?" Jodah glanced left and right. "I hope so. There's no one else here, no audience for you to bluster before."

"Or for you to use as a shield. I would have killed you a hundred times over by now if doing so didn't mean I was stung by the taunts of an insect." She regally folded her arms. "We can speak, Archmage, but choose your words carefully."

"I want to help you," he said. "I want you to save Skyshroud without destroying something else in the process."

"Always the voice of reason." Freyalise tossed her head to one side, away from Jodah. "You can do nothing here, Archmage. My course is set."

"It doesn't have to be," he said. "You don't have to do this alone. And I say you shouldn't."

"Is that all you have to contribute?"

"Not all. I've already given you the mirror."

"Ah, yes." Freyalise turned back and raised an eyebrow. She extended her arm out and the silver-handled mirror floated from her belt to her hand. "The trinket. You have truly exceeded your mentor, Archmage. This is a masterpiece, every bit as powerful as Voska's mirror was. More so."

Freyalise's praise worried Jodah more than her threats. He cleared his throat and mumbled, "It has its uses." Louder, he said, "And I wish that you would use it when the proper time comes."

"You know my mind, then?" Freyalise smiled at him, for once without malice or scorn. "You know what I intend, and when?

After all this time you still try to anticipate my actions. You think you understand me, that you can shame me or push me toward your goals."

"I want to live," Jodah said. "I want Skyshroud and all of Dominaria to live. I want you to live, Freyalise."

"Then you are a glutton," Freyalise said calmly. "For you only wish for more of what you already have in abundance."

"As you say. But to me the greater sin is not valuing the life you have. You have given too much of yourself. If you attempt another World Spell it will consume you utterly." He leaned forward so that their faces were only inches apart. "And it won't work."

"As you say." The planeswalker's pale, sharp features softened. Scorn returned to her face, but her voice remained level. "You do not know everything, Jodah. No one does."

"That would include you, Patron of Skyshroud."

"True." Freyalise tucked the mirror back into her belt. "But I know my own mind. I know in my heart what needs to be done. And as much as you frustrate me, as maddening as your insolence is . . . I would see you far from here when I do it."

Jodah felt an unseen force slither between his feet and the ground. Freyalise's eyes sparkled as her magic lifted Jodah up and carried him back toward the edge of the burned-out clearing.

"Freyalise, wait."

"Good-bye." The planeswalker reached up and covered her metal eye patch with her hand. She closed her fingers around the device, twisted it, and pulled it free. Her irises were mismatched, ice-blue on the left and ruby-red on the right. "I am sorry about Jaya, Archmage." Freyalise rested her fists on her hips, and she smiled. "And thank you for the mirror."

Jodah called her name again, but the speed of his departure only increased. He stared at the small, elegant figure as she disappeared behind the rise, and he fought to fix that image in his mind as he floated away.

He had failed. All his words and best efforts had been for nothing. He had the numb, disquieting feeling that this would be the last time he ever saw Freyalise. As such, he wanted to remember her as she was now, her beautiful face wholly visible for the first time in centuries. She was as he remembered her, as he always wanted to remember her: confident, focused, and relentless.

"Good-bye," he whispered, but he was already planning to resume his pursuit and find her again as soon as his feet touched the ground.

CHAPTER 19

Jhoira could have gone anywhere in the ambulator. Venser's machine was limited by the places its pilot knew intimately, but she had studied or visited all of Dominaria's rich and diverse landscapes. She had also visited other worlds, planes so numerous that even her well-ordered mind lost track of a few. As Teferi's companion and the former captain of a plane-spanning ship, Jhoira had seen more than her share of the multiverse's marvels.

The irony of going nowhere was not lost on her. The Blind Eternities were both more and less than nowhere, but she had been there too, so it was but a small challenge to return. The trackless void always looked different, but it was always the same place to her.

It was also mildly amusing that her first solo planeswalk (albeit assisted by Venser's artifice) was intended to be so short. She allowed herself the luxury of lingering a few moments longer, both in the hopes of seeing Karn and to gather her thoughts in the blessed silence.

As she expected, the Ghitu version of Venser's machine worked perfectly without Venser, perhaps even better without him. He was not a planeswalker as she understood it, but he was something very much like a planeswalker. Sitting him down in a teleportation machine was akin to tethering an eagle to a long-tailed kite—even if the bird were able to steer the device, its own streamlined body and wings would affect the air currents that kept the kite aloft. Takeoffs and landings would be exponentially more difficult and dangerous.

Jhoira, my dear. How splendid to see you at last.

Something flashed in the distance, and Jhoira leaned forward in the chair. Her heart began to race as a heavy-limbed figure materialized from a vast, pinkish cloud of dust. It was Karn, and he was as silver and solemn as the day she first saw him.

Jhoira had not spoken with her friend since he ascended over three centuries ago. He presented himself slightly leaner than she recalled, but she had grown quite used to planeswalkers altering their appearance even if they were not aware of the changes. He still bore his name proudly across his chest, "karn" being the Old Thran word for strength. She had given him that name because of his physical size and strength but also for his determination.

Karn was a true stalwart, enduring indignity and atrocity alike without ever wavering in the slightest. Urza gave him sentience and rudimentary emotions but treated him like a disposable tool. After killing an enemy in battle, Karn spent twenty years in mourning, practicing his own peculiar brand of pacifism that prevented him from harming anyone or anything no matter what the provocation. And though he never spoke of it directly, she knew he had braved the dangers of time travel for her, back when she was actually as young as she looked. As an alumnus of the Tolarian Academy, Jhoira had a terrifyingly clear notion of the risks such a journey demanded, both for the traveler and the world around him—and Karn had faced those risks and endured the agonies of temporal displacement simply to save her young life.

He came to her now, his wide features bent into a happy smile. He was alone, without the planeswalking apprentice Jhoira had only heard about, and this made her glad. She knew very little about Jeska, but what she did know made her wary. Beyond the private joy of friends reunited, in the short term Jhoira preferred to avoid wild-tempered barbarians with histories of attempted world conquest.

"Jhoira," he said. He spread his arms wide and moved forward as if to hug her where she sat. She hesitated, both because of their awkward position and because of the strange, glassy sheen to his eyes. Karn's artificial orbs had always been dark and somewhat mournful, but they had always been alive with intelligence. She looked into his face as he floated there, arms outstretched and a strained half smile on his lips. These eyes were black and lifeless, cold chips of stone with no warmth or animation.

"Do not fear," he said. "Step off your conveyance and embrace me, old friend. I will protect you."

"You're not Karn," she said. The figure before her shifted slightly, his outline undulating, and she felt something move in her mind.

"Of course I am, my dear. Don't you recognize me?"

"I believe I do. You are the Weaver King, and you've taken this shape from my memories. How did you get inside my head?"

The figure of Karn grinned, exposing teeth that the real silver golem never had. "It wasn't easy," he said. His voice became more excited, more animated as he spoke. "Your mind is sealed off tighter than a monarch's tomb. But every fortress has its weak spots. Yours are named Jodah and Venser."

The false Karn changed then, rippling and melting like a candle in the summer sun. He giggled as long, thick tendrils stretched out from his head like serpents. His body withered, and for a moment Jhoira stood facing a leering, emaciated human male with hip-length braids. Then the Weaver King faded away.

I had hoped to get to know you better, Jhoira of the Ghitu. But there will be time for that later. Plenty of time. Right now I have to return to Skyshroud and finish killing the forest witch. Shouldn't be too hard, should it? Not if your doubts about her abilities are anywhere near the mark.

Jhoira tightened her jaw. Her fingers stabbed down into the ambulator's controls, unhurried and deliberate.

My, my. You are a tough nut to crack, aren't you? Take it from me, my dear, because I should know: One doesn't shut me out so effectively without lots and lots of practice. I wonder now . . . have you ever let anyone in?

"If you were as fearsome as you like to pretend," she said, "you'd know already."

Well put. But as I said, I have plenty of time to get to know you better.

Jhoira finished with the controls and folded her hands into her sleeves.

You're just going to leave? You're not even going to threaten me? You're hardly any fun at all.

Jhoira did not reply. Instead she listened to the awful sound of the Weaver King's grating laughter as the ambulator's magical field enveloped her. One day, she would make certain to hear a very different sound come out of him, one inspired by Ghitu fire.

* * * * *

Venser passed the time while Jhoira was away by tossing stones into Jodah's transport tunnel. He wasn't sure if the thing was still active, but the thought of random Skyshroud stones splashing into the bogs of Urborg was as close to an amusement as he could manage.

She's a cold one, isn't she?

Venser dropped a handful of rocks and sprang to his feet.

And here I thought that Shivans were hot-tempered, hot-blooded, full of hot air, at least. . . .

The artificer whirled around, searching for a visible sign to shout at. "You stay away from her."

The Weaver King laughed merrily. *Can't do that. Well, won't, that is to say. But I am a merciful king, and I hate to see my subjects downtrodden by anyone but me.*

She'll never be yours, Venser. She'll never pine for anyone who isn't a thousand-year-old archmage or a Phyrexian impostor.

"Shut your filthy mouth," Venser said.

Has she told you that story? She wouldn't tell me. Not directly. But I'm sure I picked it up somewhere—

"I'll kill you," Venser said. It was the first time he had said such a thing, and he was gratified to find that he absolutely meant it.

That's good, that's lovely. I can use that.

"Then use it, you gibbering coward. I'm standing right here."

Yes, you are. And you'll be there when I finish with Freyalise.

"You should kill me now," Venser said. He meant that, too, for if Jhoira was alive he wanted to keep the Weaver King away from her, and if she was dead he wanted to personally drag the Weaver King kicking and screaming into the afterlife.

The Weaver King laughed. *Or what? You'll build a machine to punish me? Your machines don't work, boy. Jhoira knows it. Teferi knows it. Hells, half the Ghitu in Shiv know it by now.*

"Shut up," Venser said. "It does work. If it doesn't—"

Oh, it doesn't. The machine doesn't work, Venser. You work. Without you sitting in it, your ambulator is just an ugly chair that isn't even comfortable.

Venser regained his temper. "If it doesn't work," he said, "where did Jhoira go?"

With a chuckle, the Weaver King said, *To the same place you went. Remember when the ambulator "didn't work" and you wound up stuck in the void? That's where she is now. That's where she'll stay.*

The artificer swallowed another retort. The monster was probably lying again, but there was nothing for it but to wait until Jhoira and the ambulator returned. Sure enough, a gold-yellow glow collected around the spot where the device had been.

Oops, the Weaver King said, his tone mockingly concerned. *It seems I've been caught in a fib. Such is life, full of small victories and minor setbacks. Carry on, Venser. I will come for you directly.*

Venser clenched his fists. "I'll be ready."

No you won't. But it's funny to me that you said so.

The malign presence rustled off into the woods. Nearby, the ambulator emerged from its characteristic hazy glow with Jhoira at the controls. Venser breathed a sigh of relief.

Jhoira bolted from the chair and ran up to Venser. He thought she was going to embrace him, but she grabbed his shoulders tightly and kept him at arm's length.

"Did you really see Karn," she said, "or just that foaming-mad beast?"

They exchanged descriptions of their encounters with the disguised Weaver King. Jhoira made him review every detail of his experience, especially the differences between the Karn who had first approached him and the one who had scraped off the gladehunter mark.

His tale seemed to mollify Jhoira. After he told it to her the second time she even released his shoulders. Pins and needles continued to bubble through his joints as she recounted her own tale.

"So there's still hope," she said. "The first Karn you saw sounds like the real thing."

Venser said, "You think he's coming?"

"I do. I just hope he hurries. Things are more dire by the minute." She was staring over Venser's head, apparently lost in thought as she spoke.

Venser cleared his throat. "While we're waiting," he said, "would you tell me about Karn? I only met him once, maybe, but he seems like an interesting creature."

"You'll find him fascinating before I'm through," Jhoira said.

She made eye contact with Venser and smiled warmly. "He's a living artifact, you know. As close to a real manmade man as there can be. Although technically he was made by a planeswalker—and became one himself—so I guess you could say he's a planeswalker-made planeswalker."

Jhoira laughed lightly at his uncomfortable expression and said, "I'm sorry, Venser. I'm just a little rattled by some of the things that animal said to me. But rest easy, my mind is my own."

Venser nodded. For the first time since he escaped Urborg, he longed to see Lord Windgrace. The panther-god might have failed to excise all of the Weaver King's presence from Venser's mind, but he had driven him off for a short while. It was more than anyone else had been able to do. "So," he said. "Karn?"

Jhoira nodded. "Might as well. If he comes, he's sure to come here first." She found a comfortable tree to sit against and started talking, her voice as smooth and practiced as an expert teacher.

"Urza had been at war with Phyrexia for thousands of years before they invaded Dominaria. He and the Lord of the Wastes took each other's mettle and tested each other countless times before it came to all-out war. Early on, Urza tried to take the fight to Phyrexia, but that ended in disaster. It usually did with Urza. But this disaster had its benefits too. Urza discovered that some sentient Phyrexians contained a device he called a heartstone, an artifact that allowed them to grow and generate independent thoughts. Urza . . . brought a heartstone back with him." Jhoira's brow furrowed, but she kept talking. "The whole story is much longer, but let's leave it at that. He brought a heartstone back, and he incorporated it into the designs for his new silver golem. . . ."

* * * * *

The Weaver King marshaled his forces at the western edge of Skyshroud. More Phyrexians appeared with each passing hour, and each was quickly impressed into service. The sliver hives pumped out more subjects for him by the score, all born to follow a single leader. He had only taken control of the horde a short while ago, and it had already doubled in size.

With all these fascinating followers in this strange new place, he thought, why am I so bored? The larger his army became, the less fun he had. Perhaps it was the fact that there was almost no one to send his soldiers against. Apart from his horde, the forest was almost completely deserted, elves, animals, and magical monsters alike few and far between.

The place itself was a bit of a disappointment as well, dismal, dry, and without compelling flavor. Windgrace dominated Urborg and united its dangerous, disagreeable denizens through over-whelming force of personality, suffusing the rocks and mud and forcing the natives to toe his line. Fear of the panther-god generated a strong feeling of resentment and suppressed the locals' selfish tendencies. The Weaver King knew better than anyone that such tendencies were not easily dismissed, and keeping them in check only served to heighten and clarify them as they waited for release. Urborg was a violent place, a greedy, sullen place that offered fertile ground for his amusements. Here in Skyshroud, Freyalise's follow-ers worshipped her. Many of them wouldn't take a single step if they thought their patron would object, and that servile obedience permeated Skyshroud like a sickly, noisome fog.

He decided that ultimately, conquering Skyshroud was too easy and too hard. The near-mindless marauders in his army were no challenge at all, yet Freyalise was beyond his reach and a real danger to him. A being of his considerable talents should not be wasting his time here but should be striving for something truly epic.

He turned his attention to his legions halfway across the forest, who had been sent to scour the area for new recruits and fresh meat. Freyalise was there, turning back his foragers like dust before the broom. Jodah was at the scene, but between the archmage's strong, focused mind and the presence of a planeswalker, the Weaver King could not access Jodah's thoughts without drawing attention to himself.

Even more irritating was Dinne's disappearance. The Vec raider could not disobey the Weaver King's orders, but he had grown quite obstinate and less pliable recently. Commanded to locate Phyrexians in Urborg, Dinne would have to follow through, but the Weaver King had not specified when. Like a truculent child, Dinne did what he was told at his own pace and in his own way, skirting the very edge of disobedience without actually opening himself up to rebuke. He might take days to find the metal monsters and days more to report that he'd found them, and he could justify it all by claiming to have followed his orders to the best of his abilities.

A dark thread of anger wove its way through the Weaver King's thoughts. Dinne required correction, and if he didn't recover his former alacrity and reliability it would be a most violent and memorable correction.

A massive explosion rocked the forest. Through his web of silver mind-threads, the Weaver King felt most of his foraging horde vanish, shredded or incinerated out of existence. The remainder were hurled high into the air toward the west, apparently intended to rejoin the main mass of his army here.

He sighed in his mind. These almighty planeswalkers thwarted him at every turn. If not for Windgrace, he'd have Venser dancing on a string by now. If not for Freyalise, he'd have free run of Skyshroud and have Jodah and Jhoira battling to the death for his amusement. It seemed that he'd never have the free hand he craved as long as these godlike squelchers kept stifling his fun. But how could he, a mere king, contend with gods?

You don't need to contend with them directly. The voice was quite like his own, giddy with a touch of real menace. It was older somehow, richer and more confident, and it came not from within his own mind but from everywhere, from the rocks, trees, and air around him.

The Weaver King's wild ardor cooled, and he became afraid. *Who's there? Who are you?*

I am here. I am everywhere. I am he who called you out of the shadows and into Urborg. It suited my purposes to turn you loose in the swamps, little mind spider. It does not suit them to have you brooding here, weighted down by ennui.

The Weaver King thought back to the voice he had heard just before he escaped the void. He knew better than to take such claims at face value, for he himself had swayed too many beings over the years by pretending to be something that was personally awesome to them. This voice was no sham, however, the speaker no charlatan. The being who addressed him now was pure power, perhaps even more so than Windgrace, and the blackness behind it made the Weaver King tremble. *Are you a planeswalker?* he said.

Oh yes. I 'walk. I traverse the multiverse at my leisure. But the fact is I prefer to walk the night. Famous for it, really.

The Weaver King hesitated, and when he did reply his tone was that of a confused child. *Am I your subject, then?*

By no means. You are my trusted retainer, free to do as you wish. But you must do something, little spider. Your progress in Urborg was satisfactory, but you have stumbled badly here in Skyshroud. Any petty warlord can assemble an army. I want you to infect Dominaria.

The Weaver King discovered he did not like being criticized, but he was neither mad nor foolish enough to make an issue of it now. *As do I,* he said. *But Windgrace and Freyalise—*

Are more powerful than you, yes. But I sought you out precisely because you attack the mind, which is a planeswalker's greatest weakness. We can be distracted, enraged, or grief-stricken as easily as a lesser being if you have the skill. If you have the spine. If you are ready to strike when the right time comes. That is all I require.

The Weaver King felt calm wash over him. He recognized this dynamic even if he was not accustomed to being on the this end of it. *What would you have me do?*

Do as you will.

When?

Now.

But—

You control one army here, the voice said. *And you can quickly build another in Urborg, where the slivers are less abundant but the Phyrexians come in ever-increasing waves. If you are truly a king, send them against both your planeswalker enemies at the same time. Give them a real enemy to fight, a physical threat to satisfy their heroic tendencies.*

And this is how I should serve you?

Everyone serves me at this point. No matter what they do, whether they know it or not. Like you, I am a subtle creature, and the uncertainty of chaos intrigues me. Teferi and his ilk seek to close the time rifts plaguing this world. It is one to me if they succeed or fail. I simply want the experience to be as detrimental to them as possible. And I want to observe.

A notion occurred to the Weaver King, a way to obey the darkling voice and establish a means to escape it. The Weaver King dampened his innermost thoughts to keep them hidden even from the exalted mind that now confronted him.

Observe, then, the Weaver King said. He delighted in the boldness of his tone, in the crackling edge of delirious joy that crept in as he went on. *I will bedevil the planeswalkers and create such a spectacle that you will be unable to turn away.*

Superb. This is the Weaver King I cherish. Carry on.

The ominous presence fluttered away. The Weaver King waited, then he summoned all of his Skyshroud horde to him. It would take some time for them all to assemble, so he turned his thoughts toward Dinne and sent a stinging jolt of pain along the threads that connected them.

Dart tosser, the Weaver King said, *I am waiting.*

Moments passed without reply. Then images came back up the threads between the Weaver King and Dinne, a clear view through the silent raider's eyes. Dinne was standing on the edge of a frozen-solid swamp that bordered the Stronghold. The marsh stretched out over several acres, but none of its natural features were visible.

Instead, the entire area was packed tight with Phyrexians. Metal monsters of every size and shape huddled together, their limbs scraping sparks against each other. Dinne did not use words, but his mind and memories spoke of Windgrace's terrible counter-offensives that had destroyed hundreds of the artifact invaders and driven the rest into this isolated spot.

The Weaver King giggled. The panther-god had done Dinne's work for him, herding the Phyrexians together for one final, all-out encounter. But it was hopeless. As he watched through his servant, the Weaver King saw more Phyrexians march out of the hollow mountain and drop from the crackling purple circle in the sky, and these new arrivals went straight to the already crowded swamp.

Windgrace was a fool fighting a fool's war. So long as the rift remained open there would be no end to the steady flow of Phyrexians, no end to the cold weather that accompanied them.

Good soldier, the Weaver King said. Carefully, almost tenderly, he stretched a thin, sharp line out to the Phyrexian nearest Dinne, bending the machine brute to his will as easily as toppling a child's tower of wooden blocks. His influence flitted from mind to mechanical mind, darting and hovering like a hummingbird around the perimeter of the frozen swamp. Once he had completely encircled them all in a ring of converts, the Weaver King's dread power surged in toward the center of the assembly, spreading like contagion until the entire invading force was his to command. As each Phyrexian was subsumed, they fell silent and still. Soon the swamp was filled with a gallery of terrifying statues that glowed at the seams and vented oil-scented smoke.

Here in Skyshroud, the slivers and Phyrexians moved as one, rearing up on their hind legs or raising their servo-powered arms high. In far-off Urborg, the gallery of statues broke its paralysis and turned outward, each facing whatever attack Windgrace chose to launch.

Seek the rift, he told them all. *Seek out the planeswalker who protects it. Give no quarter. Hold nothing in reserve. This is your final battle, and the only options are victory or death.*

As one, both armies let out a terrifying shriek that was part war cry and part madman's laughter. The hordes rushed out into the woods and into the marsh. The Weaver King smiled.

Then he turned his attention back to the whisper-thin strands he had attached to Venser, Jodah, and Jhoira. *One of you will be my salvation,* he thought, though he already suspected which. *And the others will be my pleasure.*

CHAPTER 20

Teferi hovered over the Stronghold, midway between the mountain's peak and the circular rift in the sky. He watched as Phyrexians fell from it like rain, grimly assessing the foul creatures as they hit the ground and immediately charged out into Urborg proper, rabid as wolves. They were no longer aimless rabble but an army, guided and directed by a steady hand.

He was not so concerned about the danger they posed as the danger they represented. The rifts were all unstable, but the one above the Stronghold was aboil, crackling with volatile energies that licked out in vivid jags of purple lightning. It shifted and surged more violently as the number of Phyrexians increased and the biting, unnatural cold deepened. They could not allow things to degenerate much more without facing permanent catastrophic results.

Windgrace's rumbling voice rolled into Teferi's head. *So, Tolarian,* the panther-god said, *what have you learned?*

"My lord," Teferi said, "we are approaching a crisis point."

Windgrace appeared before him, a bladed staff in his hand and his tail waving angrily. "Is that all?" he said. "That much has been true for weeks now."

"True." Teferi nodded. "But the wound over Urborg has become infected. Soon it will burst and shower your home with poison."

"Poison can be endured," Windgrace said. "Infected wounds can be cauterized."

Teferi bowed his head. "Then you have reconsidered my suggestion?"

"No," Windgrace said. "I have taken the measure of these creatures. It will not require all my power to scour them from the swamps."

"The creatures, no. But what about the rift that spawns them?"

The panther-god showed his teeth. "That was your obligation, Teferi. Your riddle to solve. If you have nothing else to offer on that score, I might as well put you back inside the mountain."

"I am at your service," Teferi said. "But I can do much more for you by your side."

"Then do so. You are at my side now, and all I hear is more of your academic prattling."

Teferi straightened. "The rifts are not merely physical. Nor magical. They are a mixture of concrete and abstract forces. One of those forces is time."

"As you have said. Does this repeated revelation offer any insight, or am I missing something?"

"You are missing the scope of the problem. The rift network is now permeated by time paradoxes that grow more dangerous with each passing moment. These Phyrexians should not exist. This cold weather should not exist. The rift makes both possible. The rift is the heart of the matter. Deal with the rift first, or Urborg will not survive." Teferi held his head high, proud and confident. "Nothing will."

Windgrace growled. "Time is your province, your playground. I am not surprised you found time at the center of this phenomenon."

"I will not apologize for my expertise. Temporal energy is my special interest, and there is plenty of it here."

The panther-god shifted in the sky, swinging around so that he floated alongside Teferi. When he spoke, Windgrace's voice was low and tight. "I am a warrior, Teferi. Time stretches on the battlefield, or compresses, or sometimes stops entirely. Mine is the way of tooth and claw, and it is not subtle. I have no interest or facility in the esoterica of chronal disturbance."

"Yet I do," Teferi said. "And you dismiss my opinion time and again."

"Because I do not trust you." Windgrace kept his face toward the rift. "You are a subtle creature, slippery and indirect. I would rather suffer the consequences of overexamining your advice than those that come from following it blindly."

"I am what I am," Teferi said. "What can I do to convince you?"

"Nothing." Windgrace drifted up but cast his eyes down on the antlike colonies of Phyrexians that were marching through his marshy home. "I destroyed a thousand Phyrexians today. There are thousands more. It is difficult work but well within my abilities. I am not so drained as Freyalise: I can beat them back indefinitely."

"The rift will not last indefinitely," Teferi said. "It is critical now and will rupture soon."

Windgrace fixed Teferi with his gleaming, green eyes. "And the result?"

"Desolation. If it doesn't hurl the entire rift network into explosive chaos, it will definitely open a permanent pathway between here and whatever alternate reality the Phyrexians came from. The winter will become permanent, as will your war to keep Urborg free of artifact invaders."

Windgrace hesitated, his gaze traveling back and forth between the rift and the Phyrexians on the ground. "I would consult with Freyalise," he muttered.

"Please do. I imagine Skyshroud is as put-upon as Urborg by now. The sooner you both accept the truth of what I say, the sooner you can stop the destruction of your homes."

Windgrace's muscles tensed. He clutched his bladed staff so tightly that his hands shook. "Very well," he said. "But Freyalise is not easily swayed. It may take more than my voice to convince her."

"Are you convinced, my lord?"

"I am convinced of your brazen recklessness. It will take more than your voice to turn me to your methods."

"Call out to Freyalise," Teferi said. "Perhaps hers is the voice that will sway you and yours the one to sway her."

Windgrace growled again, his anger palpable. "Presumptuous cur," he muttered. Then he called with his mind, *Freyalise. I would speak with you.*

Teferi tried to calm his thoughts as he waited. Just as it seemed the patron of Skyshroud would never answer, Freyalise's voice came clear and sharp through the frosty air.

And I with you. Hail, Windgrace. Be patient a while longer. If I fall, or fail, I will need you to take up my cause.

What do you mean?

Watch, she said. *And you will see.*

* * * * *

The world went mad just as Jhoira reached the point in Karn's story where the planeswalking golem regained control over his all-metal plane.

Everything happened at once. Jodah came shooting out of the woods, propelled against his will by unseen magic. A distant roar rose up from the west side of the forest, the ghastly sound of the Weaver King's army running rampant. The ground shuddered, and the sky was split by red lightning. The Skyshroud rift emerged from the gloom, an eerie canyon with foglike walls that soared high into the night sky.

Jhoira leaped up when she saw Jodah but stopped dead when

the cacophony of noise hit her. Venser rose and stood beside her, knowing that Karn's further adventures would have to wait for another day.

They glanced at each other, nodded, and ran toward Jodah. He was moving faster than they could run, but his course was clear and they raced him to its endpoint. Venser could only guess at how long the archmage had been carried this way, but judging from Jodah's angry expression and tightly crossed arms, he guessed it had been a considerable journey.

Jodah noticed them coming, and his demeanor improved. He shouted and waved his hands as the last of the impelling force around him petered out. Jodah dropped stiffly onto his feet and stumbled back a step just as Venser and Jhoira reached him.

"What's going on?" Jhoira said. "Where did you go?"

Jodah gestured wildly with both hands. "Freyalise is about to do something rash," he said. "You have to get away from here."

"Rash?" Venser said. "Be more specific."

"Explosive," Jodah said. "Devastating. She means to cast another World Spell or its equivalent. Half of Keld could go up in flames."

Venser stifled his immediate reaction, that Keld would welcome the fire. Jodah was clearly distraught, and his agitation was already affecting Jhoira. To her, Venser said, "Will that close the rift?"

"I don't know." The Ghitu watched Jodah as she answered. "The only practical experience we have is Teferi's, and he cast no spell. Freyalise's best effort may be enough to ruin Skyshroud without sealing the rift."

"Theories and conjecture." Jodah spoke angrily. "But it serves my point. We have to stop Freyalise from putting herself at risk for no possible benefit." He turned and pointed to the ambulator. "Can that thing take me back across the forest?"

Venser paused, afraid of the reaction an honest answer would draw.

"It can," Jhoira said. "But unless you know exactly where she is, it can't take you to Freyalise."

"Actually," Venser said, "it can't take you anywhere else in Skyshroud. This is the only place I've seen."

"I've seen more," Jhoira said. She placed a hand on Jodah's shoulder. "I can't guarantee success, but we can search for her if you think it will help."

Jodah looked at her hand, then into Jhoira's face. "Never mind," he said. "The two of you should take the chair back to Urborg."

"What about you?" Venser said.

"I'm not through here." He turned back toward his transport tunnel. "I can modify that to take me straight to Freyalise. It won't take but a few minutes."

Jhoira's grip on Jodah's shoulder tightened. "To what end?"

"Ow." Jodah smiled sadly and placed his hand over Jhoira's. He gently pried her fingers loose and said, "She needs me. She needs someone. A goddess without supplicants is a tragedy. A planes-walker without companions is a disaster waiting to happen." He smiled at Jhoira. "You know that already, don't you?"

"For a thousand years," Jhoira said. "But I think you're mis-taken. Freyalise will not be deterred by your voice or any other. She's desperate."

"I've managed it before," Jodah said. "I have to try again." He turned partially away from Jhoira and bowed to them both. "Go. I'll be all right. It was a great pleasure meeting you both."

The ground shook once more, and sheets of crimson electricity cascaded across the sky. Venser instinctively took Jhoira's hand and took a step toward the ambulator, pulling her with him. To his genuine surprise, she did not resist.

"Stay alive, Archmage," she said. "Don't die here. I will come for you."

Jodah nodded. "Count on it." He looked over Jhoira's head to

Venser and said, "Thank you, my friend. Now get your machine humming and get out."

Venser paused. "Farewell, Jodah."

"And you."

Isn't this precious?

Tension knotted Venser's stomach muscles. Not now, he thought. With everything else they had to contend with . . .

Now is the perfect time, said the Weaver King. *And I can't have you leaving before the party's over. Jhoira, maybe. But you, Venser. I want you by my side forever and ever and ever.*

Venser saw both Jodah and Jhoira staring at him. He still held Jhoira's hand and stood in midstride, but he hadn't moved since the Weaver King spoke.

"What's wrong?" Jhoira asked.

"It's the Weaver King," Jodah said.

"I don't feel him."

"Nor I. But I recognize that look on Venser's face." He stepped forward and snapped his fingers in front of Venser's eyes. "Hoy! Builder! Are you yourself?"

Venser's pupils darted back and forth in his eye sockets. All of his other muscles were paralyzed, his legs and tongue alike.

"He's beguiled," Jodah said. "The Weaver King still has his hooks in."

Clever Archmage. Venser heard the voice, but neither Jodah nor Jhoira reacted to it. *I'm going to miss him if he doesn't live through this. And I'm going to punish him if he does.*

Jodah said to Jhoira, "Can you carry him?"

"Not quickly. Not on my own. But the two of us together could."

No you can't. Now they did hear the high, mocking voice, and Venser saw the chills running through both his friends.

Stand ready, Venser. I am expert at expanding my subjects' horizons. You may not know what you can do or how to do it . . .

but I'm willing to try. What's the worst that could happen? To me, that is.

The artificer moaned softly through his nose. Help me, he tried to say. Or at least kill me.

Mana flared around Jodah's fist, but he had no target for his spell. He jerked his head around, trying to find some trace of the Weaver King to attack. "Let's just grab him," he said to Jhoira. "Stuff him in the ambulator and turn it on."

"Right." Jhoira stepped forward and slipped her hands under Venser's arms. "It's almost that easy, you know."

No, my child. Nothing is easy. Not even this.

Venser moaned again as his body began to tingle. It was a similar sensation to traveling in the ambulator, an icy-hot shower of needles all over his body.

Jhoira's hand slipped out from under his arm. Or rather, her hand passed through his arm as his entire body dissolved into intangibility. Venser could see their expressions, but he knew that their shock was far less than his own. What was happening to him?

Come now, the Weaver King said to him. *We have things to see and gods to murder.*

Jhoira cried out as Venser disappeared. He took some small comfort from her concern, then was gone.

* * * * *

"He'll be back," Jodah said.

Jhoira stood in the spot Venser had recently occupied, her fists clenched tight. "Venser?" she said. "Or the Weaver King?"

A flicker of embarrassment crossed Jodah's face. "I meant the Weaver King. I don't know where he's taken Venser, but I don't imagine it'll be healthy." He stepped forward and placed his hand on Jhoira's shoulder she had done to him. "You still have to go," he said. "It's not safe here."

"Not for any of us," she said. "And I can't leave Venser any more than you can Freyalise."

"You have to," Jodah said. "You're the only one who can keep this going."

"Keep what going? Nothing I've done has made any difference at all."

"Then now's the time to start. Go back to Urborg."

"No. Not without Venser. Not without you."

Jodah smiled sadly. "It's good to be us sometimes, isn't it?"

Jhoira nodded. "Sometimes."

"And sometimes it isn't. Sometimes . . . because we know things no one else knows . . . we have to do things we hate."

"What can I do in Urborg that I can't do here? Die? Be swallowed up by a time rift?"

"You can share what you know. Teferi's a basket case, but with your input he might still come up with the answer you've been chasing. And Windgrace might listen to you even if you're only repeating what Teferi says."

The Ghitu shook her head. "No. Venser is here, and Karn is coming. There's still hope."

"Who is Karn?"

"An old friend. He can help."

Jodah frowned suspiciously. "Planeswalker?"

"Yes. And you really must stop assuming that about everyone I know."

He started, unsure if Jhoira had intended to be humorous. She smiled slightly, and he shook his head. "How do you know he's coming?"

"I summoned him with the ambulator. He'll be drawn to it."

"Then he'll be drawn to Urborg when you take it there. Don't argue any more, Jhoira. Skyshroud is going to burn, and if you survive that and the Phyrexians and the slivers, you still have to deal with the Weaver King."

Jhoira hesitated. "I don't want to leave."

"And I want you to stay. I'm sure Venser does too. But you need to go."

Jhoira was torn, her body vacillating between the ambulator and the forest. "Venser?" she said.

"I'll find him," Jodah said. "If there's a place for him to be and he's still alive there, I'll find him and bring him back to you."

Jhoira stopped moving and stared hard at Jodah. "But Freyalise comes first."

"She has to. If I can stop her then all of our chances for survival increase."

"All right," she said. Jhoira lunged forward, wrapped her arms around Jodah's neck, and kissed him deeply.

She broke off, leaving him dazed, and said again, "Stay alive, Archmage." Then Jhoira turned and ran to the ambulator without looking back.

CHAPTER 21

Venser awoke nestled in the boughs of a stunted Skyshroud tree. He blinked, trying to clear his head and determine exactly where he had landed. Carefully, he shifted his weight and turned his head.

Venser choked and sputtered, almost dislodging himself from the tree. A dead berserker's face sat inches from his own, the warrior's livid scars connected to form a jagged symbol. Venser glanced down, both to gauge how far he had almost fallen and to look at something besides the dead man.

Past the berserker's burly form and the thick, wooden spikes that held him in place, Venser estimated it was thirty feet to the ground. It was a considerable drop, and dangerous, but Venser counted on the thick layer of ash and mulch below him to cushion his landing. He also decided to risk a broken ankle rather than crawl down across the mutilated corpse, which would require him to use the wooden spikes and handholds and footholds.

Venser drew his long legs under him and took a firm hold on the tree branch. The Weaver King's hold on him was gone, and that gave him some relief. It was likely that the mind raider had gotten what he needed from Venser and turned him loose to focus on his other distractions, but Venser was still heartened. He was growing increasingly fearful of the Weaver King's presence and the control he had over Venser's mind and body.

Prepared to let himself fall, Venser stopped. What had the Weaver King really done to him? He had never consciously teleported (or planeswalked, if Jhoira's theory was to be believed) without his ambulator, never cast the most basic of spells. Yet he had vanished from the edge of Skyshroud and reappeared high in the trees with no other explanation than powerful magic.

Was that magic truly his? Could he achieve of his own volition what the Weaver King had forced on him? He was tired of being pushed and pulled and chased from one place to another, and he did not look forward to the long drop. Perhaps it was time to try.

He stared at the ground for a few moments, etching the sight of his destination in his brain. Then Venser closed his eyes and tried to picture himself on the ground, upright and safe. He concentrated, willing himself to appear on the spot in his mind's eye.

Nothing happened. Venser opened his eyes, inhaled deeply, and tried again. Nothing.

It was supposed to be easy. According to Jhoira, he had done it several times before without thinking. He had seen how effortless it was for Windgrace, Teferi, and Freyalise. Then again, he was not like Windgrace, Teferi, and Freyalise. Perhaps his method of teleportation was unique and involved more than willpower alone.

Venser scooted up with his back against the tree trunk. He closed his eyes again and imagined himself in the ambulator's seat, its Ghitu controls under his fingers. Breathing deeply, he extended his arms halfway and visualized the commands that would make the device go. Feeling utterly foolish, Venser pantomimed pressing the right switches and levers in the proper sequence, following Jhoira's example of quick, efficient, and nonrepetitive motion.

He completed the launch sequence. He was still in the tree. Grumbling in exasperation, Venser repeated the process, tapping his fingers over phantom control panels and listening for the characteristic hum of the ambulator's power source.

His stomach lurched, and for a vertiginous moment he thought he had fallen. Eyes closed, he felt something solid beneath his feet. His leg muscles tensed as they bore his weight again, and Venser smelled charred wood and burning leaves.

He opened his eyes to find himself on the forest floor. He shut his eyes tight, rubbed them with his fists, and opened them wide.

He had done it. Unable to control himself, Venser shook his fists in triumph and shouted, "I did it!"

But what had he done? Was he now a mage? Did he have oceans of mana at his disposal? He would have to find a mentor and learn some sort of spellcraft. Venser the Wizard, he thought, amusing himself to the point of laughter.

Then, unbidden, a small, selfish, and stupid thought occurred. He no longer needed the ambulator. He had wasted his life, spent twenty years on high-level design, dangerous scavenger hunts through the swamp, and painstaking trial and error for a result that he could have achieved by closing his eyes and playacting. He was not a wizard, nor a planeswalker, but an idiot. Venser the Fool.

Logic and rational thought quickly pushed aside his absurd fit of pique. He had learned the finer points of teleportation by building his machine. Without that experience, he might never have accessed his hidden talent for teleportation, with or without the Weaver King's influence.

There were also far more pressing matters on his docket: the fate of his friends, the intentions of his dangerous enemies, and the fate of the entire world. Venser did not want to die at all, least of all as a forgotten pawn in a cosmic-scale game of titans. Jodah had chosen to stay and help Freyalise, but Venser was more than willing to take the archmage's advice and escape before the patron of Skyshroud brought the forest down around his ears.

As for Jhoira . . . she was either with Jodah or she had taken the ambulator to Urborg. Venser wondered if he should dare to take such a long journey under his own power, then realized he might have no choice. He decided to let pragmatism guide his actions. He would teleport himself back to where he had left Jodah and Jhoira. If they were still there, he would tell them what he had discovered about himself. If they were not, he would try to make it home.

Red electricity spiked and jagged across the sky, lighting up the forest below. Heavy thunder boomed, and the ground churned beneath his feet. Venser quickly settled back against the tree, picturing the last place he had been. He didn't think he'd have to go far—if "far" was a concept that mattered—as the other crucified corpses he had seen were all along the forest's edge. Since he was among them, he reasoned that all he had to do was follow the outer rim of the woods and eventually he'd return to his starting point.

Venser closed his eyes. He reached out and moved his fingers in a perfect re-creation of the motions that triggered the ambulator's main function.

Lightning flashed overhead again, and before it flickered away and left Skyshroud in darkness once more, Venser was gone.

He appeared again as the thunder from that same lightning strike boomed down, almost a half mile behind him. Venser blinked, disoriented, and when his vision cleared he realized he was standing directly behind Jodah.

The archmage was still adjusting his transport tunnel with short, sharp gestures and a flowing trail of blue mana. Venser called out, "Jodah."

The archmage whirled with a spell at the ready. He seemed surprised to see Venser. He also seemed disconcerted that he hadn't heard the artificer coming.

"Venser," he said, "are you . . . you?"

"The Weaver King is gone for now," Venser said. "I'm not sure why he released me." He cocked his head at Jodah's alarmed expression, then realized what it meant. Venser said, "I share your concern. Is there any way to tell if he's still waiting in my head?"

"None that I know of," Jodah said. "But I suppose it won't matter if we move quickly enough." He stopped moving his hands across the liquid surface of the tunnel entrance. "But I don't mean to speak for you. Will you accompany me to Freyalise, or do you prefer to stay here?"

"Hm," Venser said. "About that . . ." The artificer's voice trailed off as he stared at Jodah's transport. Venser hoped his expression wasn't betraying his thoughts. Jodah was quick-witted, and he would probably stop Venser if he knew what the artificer had in mind.

"Is this thing safe?" Venser said.

"Absolutely." Jodah stood and stepped back, presenting the tunnel to Venser with a wave. "I've used it for thousands of years, and it's never failed me. Simple but reliable."

Venser nodded. "And does it lead to Freyalise?"

"Not yet. Right now it's still part of the circuit between here and Urborg." He blinked. "Say," he said, "you have a third choice, now that I think about it. You can use this tunnel to go after Jhoira."

The Ghitu's name raised a strange set of conflicting emotions. Venser said, "She took the ambulator?"

"She did. At my urging, mind you. She wanted to stay and look for you, but since I was staying anyway I convinced her to let me do it." He grinned. "Thanks for making my job so easy."

"I would prefer to go back home," Venser said. He cleared his throat and added, "I'd prefer it if you came too."

"Sorry," Jodah said. "I've made up my mind. But don't worry about me. I haven't lived this long without learning a few tricks." Jodah stepped back to the tunnel and extended his hands. Warm, blue light sparkled across the liquid surface and sparked to his palms.

"Still works," he said. "And it's ready for you. Good luck, my friend. Give my regards to Jhoira. And Windgrace. I hope to see you all again someday."

"Count on it," Venser said. The artificer lunged forward with both hands, stiff-arming Jodah backward into his own tunnel.

"Hey!" Jodah said, but his voice melted away as the tunnel's magic took hold and whisked him out of sight.

Venser scanned his surroundings, knowing he had to work quickly. Jodah's tunnel was practically instantaneous, and he didn't want the archmage to simply leap back in on the Urborg side and return here.

The ground was littered with rocks of all shapes and sizes. Venser recognized some as possessing metallic ores, and while he was not familiar with the geology of Keld he did know something about magical transport and the energy it required. He seized a wide, flat stone with sharp edges, raised it over his head, and brought it down on the roots that surrounded Jodah's tunnel.

It only took three swings to sever the dry, wasted root. Venser went to work on another, and another, until he had broken the entire upper framework of Jodah's spell conveyance. Venser threw the jagged stone in, then bent and shoveled more stones in with both hands. He cut all of his fingers and almost crushed his thumb in the process, but within seconds he had piled rocks high enough to fill the lower half of the entrance.

Panting, he watched with satisfaction as the liquid suspended across the tunnel collapsed, drenching the pile of stones in a clear, syrupy substance. The glow within the liquid fizzled out like a match immersed in water. Jodah would not thank him for it, but Venser had saved the archmage as the archmage had saved Jhoira.

The ground shook once more, so violently that Venser fell to one knee. A second tremor shook several trees loose from the ground and sent them toppling against their neighbors. Venser flashed back to Shiv, moments before Teferi had gone out to seal the rift there, and realized that Skyshroud was in a similar state. The air here tingled and pressed in on him from all sides. Lightning and thunder came almost continuously now. It was way past time to go.

Struggling to keep his movements calm and measured, Venser sat with his back against the pile of stones. He pictured his workshop in Urborg, the place where he had worked, slept, eaten, and dreamed for almost a decade. He knew this place better than any other. If he was to test his power over long distances, he'd never find a better destination.

Venser's fingers danced, though he kept his eyes wide open. He saw a flash of light in his peripheral vision that quickly crawled across his irises. Then he disappeared.

* * * * *

Freyalise marched alone into the precise center of Skyshroud. The forest's mana was almost spent, and her own resources were approaching their limit. There were countless slivers and dozens of Phyrexians clamoring to get close to her, to engulf her like a wave and tear her to pieces.

She sneered at them. "Too late," she said. And it was. She had arrived.

The planeswalker looked up into through the middle of the Skyshroud rift. Its sheer fog walls soared up on each side of her, and she knew they also penetrated deep into the Keldon bedrock below. Phyrexian machine magic had created this rip in the multiverse's fundamental structure, but it was her efforts that had diverted Skyshroud here from its intended destination. The rift was as much her fault as it was Yawgmoth's.

Perhaps things would have been different if she hadn't interfered. She could have become Skyshroud's patron no matter where the forest landed, but both practicality and pride had led her to put it here.

Practically speaking, Keld was ideal. There were no elves here, or goblins, or ogres. There was virtually no competition for space from anyone but the Keldons, and since they had no interest in forest dwelling and her people had no interest in leaving, it had proved to be a near-perfect arrangement. Once she had established her own boundaries and come to terms with the Keldon Council, the elves of Skyshroud were free to live and prosper. Good relations with the council also meant the elves were free from the threat of hostile outsiders, for in all its long history, Keld had never been successfully invaded. It was hardly worth the effort, for one thing, as no rival nation would ever fight for a frozen chunk of stone that was without resources beyond tough wood and fiery mana. For another, the Keldons thrived by making war on other countries, and it was the height of foolishness to antagonize them. It was safer to offer your throat to a hungry lion. She had heard tales of how the stone-gray berserkers made examples of unwelcome visitors, sending foreign merchant and warships alike back to their home ports burned and blackened and weighted down with corpses.

Freyalise spat a curse at the Weaver King's horde, her magic pressing them farther back. As for pride . . . she wanted to establish an elf kingdom here, far enough from Llanowar to be independent but close enough for her two fiefdoms to support each other in times of trial. It had never come to pass as she intended, and Skyshroud and Llanowar remained separate and distinct. But she knew that she had done right by her people, always making sure that they grew strong enough to weather whatever storms blew in without abandoning them completely. She never coddled them, never provided more than the bare necessities to ensure their survival, yet they had always prospered. Of that she was unreservedly proud.

The slivers and Phyrexians pressed in once more, their noise and fury souring Freyalise's reverie. The rift was a consequence of Skyshroud's appearance here, a part of it, yet it was destined to destroy the forest. The rift had depleted the local mana until Freyalise herself had to make up the shortfall. The rift brought the Gathans, who did not respect the ancient Keldon pact between

beserker and elf and made bloody war upon her people. The Gathans enraged Radha, who abandoned Skyshroud to punish them for
their crimes and claim her half-Keldon heritage. Radha's defec-
tion caused Freyalise herself to take command of the sliver horde,
which had been turned against the planeswalker so easily that she
despaired ever relying on the symbiotic little beasts.

Which brought her to this. Skyshroud had fallen, not in battle
or to overwhelming magic, but to the slow, steady depletion of its
vital force. She thought she could sustain it indefinitely, but now
it was overrun by metal Phyrexian war beasts and the twisted,
abhorrent results of Phyrexian science on living flesh. Her elves
had been forced to flee their home and endure the horrors of an
unnaturally cold Keldon winter. She reckoned that less than half
would survive the first year, but half was better than none. When
she was through, every living thing in Skyshroud would be but
ashes and memories.

Glaring hatefully at the horde, Freyalise slowly and deliberately
peeled off her long leather gloves. She cast the accessories aside
and lowered herself to her knees. The patron of Skyshroud pressed
her hands into the soil and opened her eyes wide, seeing all of the
Weaver King's army and beyond to the edges of the forest itself.

This was her place, her kingdom. If it was going to die, she
would deliver the death blow and make sure to take as many of
its despoilers as she could.

Freyalise cupped her hands to form a small mound of dirt
between them. She stared hard at the tiny pile and felt the strength
of forest mana flowing through her. It had been so long since she
used Nature's energy for anything but the continued existence of
this garden among the frozen peaks, but now she reclaimed it. The
verdant force that sustained this place leeched from it now and
flowed back into its source, the planeswalker Freyalise.

All around her, trees shriveled and blackened as if surrounded
by fire. Most of the forest was dead or half-dead already, but

without her blessings the plants could not even maintain their natural shapes. In seconds the Skyshroud forest withered away to almost nothing, as fallow as a forgotten field.

A small, green shoot sprang up between Freyalise's hands. She focused on the tiny, green tendril, shutting out the sights and sounds of the nearby horde. She whispered softly to it, coaxing it up from the dirt and encouraging its growth with the ancient language of Gaea, the living spirit of this world.

The shoot responded, swelling fat and green as it reached up past Freyalise's head. Broad, flat leaves sprouted from the first vine as a second tendril broke through the surface of the dirt. Freyalise spread her hands wider to accommodate the vines, which twisted and braided themselves together as they climbed to form the last living Skyshroud tree.

The surge of growth continued. Satisfied, Freyalise stood and took several steps back. The braided vine continued to expand outward and upward as she fed more mana to it. When the tough, woody column was taller than she was and ten yards wide, Freyalise gracefully leaped to the top. She stood firm as the vines seethed and slithered below her, riding them high above the forest floor, high above the ravening mob of the Weaver King's puppets.

As she fed mana to the burgeoning tree, it in turn fed her. She felt clearheaded and joyous, stronger than she had in decades. Reclaiming the power she had lent Skyshroud meant the forest was truly lost, but it also meant she could deal with the challenges that faced her as she saw fit.

Freyalise rose higher, bounded on each side by the walls of the canyonlike rift. The base of her column was now one hundred yards across, almost to the edge of the force barrier that kept the Weaver King's army at bay.

Higher, she thought. *Wider.*

The column responded, stretching up and swelling out until it smashed through the magical barrier. The Phyrexians and slivers did not hesitate. They scrambled up the woody tower, and though dozens of them were crushed to paste by its thick, undulating vines, hundreds more came shrieking up the sides, trampling each other in their zeal to reach Freyalise.

Freyalise watched them come. She felt nothing but the desire to see them all die for their effrontery, and beyond that a peculiar calm. Unhurried, Freyalise reached behind her and took Jodah's mirror into her hand. She examined it as the wooden column continued to carry her up, as the horde continued to close the gap between them and the planeswalker at its peak.

It was a marvelous mirror, she thought. Jodah had smashed the original, but his replacement was even better—more elegant, more subtle, and more powerful. It was a shame it was useless to her. With a careless flick of her wrist, Freyalise tossed the silver-handled mirror away, casually watching it from the corner of her eye as it tumbled.

Freyalise. I would speak with you.

Windgrace's words irritated her, as she did not want to be distracted. Still, she respected the panther-god and could sympathize with the strain in his voice.

And I with you. Hail, Windgrace. Be patient a while longer. If I fall, or fail, I will need you to take up my cause.

What do you mean?

Watch, she said. *And you will see.*

Windgrace's presence dwindled. She heard the buzzing click of Phyrexian voices and the rasping sound of slivers taking flight. They would be upon her soon.

Freyalise crossed her arms, gathered strength from the tower of vines beneath her, and waited for the end.

CHAPTER 22

Teferi and Windgrace waited silently as they bathed in the spectral light from the hole in the sky. The meaning of Freyalise's last sending was unclear to Teferi, her actions closed to his perception. What he could perceive was his intuitive bond with the Skyshroud rift. Both phenomena were now seething in unison, one waxing and the other waning as the energy within them pulsed back and forth. For him, there were no other fissures, no larger network. The tumultuous exchange between these two was all he knew, as this mismatched pair of Phyrexian-born rifts threatened to tear the entire multiverse wide open.

He felt fresh waves of alien cold flow down from the disk of crackling light, driving the unnatural winter's roots deeper into Urborg. He saw shining new armies of cold-weather Phyrexian footsoldiers tumbling through the night air and materializing at the foot of the mountain. By the hundreds they came, those that dropped disappearing under the icy crust that had formed over Urborg and bursting free to prowl the marsh and prey on its inhabitants.

Teferi fought the urge to ask Windgrace for details. He would know Freyalise's fate soon enough, and perhaps his own. Either the patron of Skyshroud would seal the rift, which Teferi would sense as it happened, or she would not . . . in which case he would see the explosive effects of her failure close-up.

Windgrace's ears twitched. "Your Ghitu partner has returned."

"Jhoira? Where?"

"She is at Venser's workshop." Windgrace's chest rumbled, and a soft growl crept up his throat. "She came by way of Venser's machine."

"Is Venser with her? Or Jodah?"

"No."

"Can you bring her here?"

"Easily." Windgrace's tail lashed.

Teferi waited, then said, "Will you?"

"No. Now be silent." The panther's pupils narrowed to vertical, black slashes. "Freyalise has begun in earnest."

"Please help her, my lord."

"She has not asked for help."

"Then help yourself." Teferi gestured to the rift above, to the frigid air and metal monsters pouring down. "Close that doorway once and for all."

Windgrace said nothing, though his fur bristled in the wind.

*　　*　　*　　*　　*

Jhoira was on her feet and partway out of the control rig before the ambulator's yellow glow fully receded. She was not willing to bring the machine so close to the rift, but now she was faced with a far more mundane problem: She didn't know where to go. She needed to find Windgrace, or at least Teferi, if she was to do any good. The ambulator could take her to the edge of the Stronghold rift, but that was all. She had neither the knowledge nor the power to change what was happening on her own.

She stepped back from Venser's door to get a clear view of the disk. The black wedge that was the Stronghold gleamed along its edges in the arcane glow. Jhoira looked higher, then shielded her eyes to cut back on the glare. Two familiar figures floated between the mountain and the rift, stiff and anxious as if awaiting bad news.

Jhoira turned back to the ambulator. It was not designed to fly or hover, but it could take her to where the two planeswalkers were. Once there she would either have to rely on their power to keep the chair aloft or ambulate back to the ground as soon as she started falling. She paused only to calculate how much time she'd have, then dashed back up the steps that led to the dais.

"Jhoira, my friend. I've missed you."

The voice was familiar, but she had heard it mimicked too recently to trust her ears. She turned toward Venser's hut, not wanting to believe her eyes, expecting another trick or diversion to make her drop her guard.

Karn stood between her and the door to Venser's workshop, his hands clasped behind his back. The finely engraved Thran character on his chest shone in the dim light. His heavy features were open and joyful as best they could be. He seemed solid and relaxed.

"I heard you calling me," Karn said. "I am sorry I did not answer sooner." He glanced up past the mountain's peak. "Is that what you're dealing with?"

"I was recently attacked by a Karn impostor," Jhoira said, "a mind reader who used my own recollections to fool me. I need to know you are who you appear to be."

Karn brought his arms around and stroked his broad chin. "Easy enough," he said. "Though I suppose any proof I offer will immediately be nullified by your suspicion that I found it in your thoughts."

"You can see the quandary." Jhoira stepped closer to the edge of the dais, well within reach of the chair and its controls. He certainly had Karn's bearing.

The heavy, silver figure shimmered and appeared beside Jhoira on the dais. He reached out his powerful arms and swept her up to his breast, her toes three feet from the ground. The golem swiveled his face down so that his nose and Jhoira's almost touched.

"I would never harm you, Jhoira." The iron grip around her eased, and Karn set her gently on the platform. "If you don't believe that, you may run. Even better, stand where you are. I will take my leave." He stepped past her, planting one massive foot on the soil of Urborg, and Jhoira said, "Stop."

The silver man paused. He twisted at the waist and smiled up to her.

Jhoira exhaled. "It's good to see you, Karn."

Karn nodded. "It's been far too long. But there'll be time for reunions later." He gestured up to the rift. "What is that?"

A familiar sense of comfort settled over Jhoira. Karn was Karn, practical, focused, ready and willing to help.

"I don't know exactly," Jhoira said. "But they are scattered all over the globe."

Karn stared unblinking into the disk. "This one's very unstable. Is that Teferi I see?"

"Yes. And Lord Windgrace. Can you take us there?"

"Of course." Karn extended his arm, inviting Jhoira to step closer. As she did, the silver man flinched and jerked his head to the west. "Wait," he said. "Something terrible is happening."

"Where?" Jhoira said.

Karn spoke without moving his head. "Keld," he said. "Sky-shroud Forest."

* * * * *

Freyalise laughed, exultant in her restored power. Her woody tower was now as tall as Keld's mightiest peak and one hundred yards at the base. The vines had stopped their furious growth and hardened, wrapping so tightly together that they became indistinguishable from a single massive tree.

If it existed, Freyalise still could not see the upper edge of the Skyshroud rift, not even from this lofty perch. On her way up she had exercised her regained strength by blasting wave after wave of slivers and Phyrexians into cinders and slag. Her flames were green and fat with mana, which flowed back into the tree and up to be reused at Freyalise's pleasure.

Dear lady, came the Weaver King's familiar voice. *I cannot imagine what you intended, but I have to say, 'well done.' You've converted an entire forest into a single tree. It will be a fitting monument under which to bury you.*

"Begone, filth." Freyalise stared up at the endless walls of fog on either side of her.

But I have so much to say before I go—

Begone. Freyalise's thoughts lashed out like a barbed whip. She registered the rewarding sound of the Weaver King yelping in pain. *Now.*

I will go, leaf witch. The mad harlequin's voice was gone, leaving a dark and ragged whisper. *But I will not stop, will never stop. The slivers will breed, the Phyrexians will build, and I will make sure every last one of them comes screaming for your blood.*

Spurred by their master's anger, the horde screeched and roared as they redoubled their efforts to reach the top of Freyalise's tree. The patron of Skyshroud drew breath to send another scalding threat directly to the Weaver King's mind, but the malign presence skittered off into the mass of seething monsters below.

"Irritant." Freyalise paused to proof her mind against any further thought-to-thought contact. She was through with distractions, through with counsel, through with the endless chatter that barraged her everywhere she went. The next person who came to deter her from her path would have to do it in person, and wade through a swarm of slivers to do it.

Freyalise felt the presence of the madman's horde climbing ever closer. She focused on the mana she had, the mana in the tree, and her eyes flashed. A sickening sound rose up in a circle around the platform on which she stood, and she imagined the countless bodies now impaled on the long, wooden thorns that had just erupted along the tree's upper third. She raised her clenched fist and tightened it, igniting the thorns in an extended series of colorful explosions.

The planeswalker swooned for a moment, overtaken by a surge of weakness. No, she thought. Not so soon. I was just starting to enjoy myself.

Freyalise shrugged, shaking off her selfish impulses. As gratifying as it would be to savage each and every one of the beasts that the Weaver King promised to send for her blood, it was a joy she had to forbear. For there was another reason she had closed herself off to the outside world, that she could not bear to think of what Teferi would say when she followed his example.

She had watched him in Shiv, so she knew what he had done. His effort shamed her, and not only because it was successful. His vast experience with temporal forces gave him information and insight that she didn't have and didn't begrudge. No, it wasn't Teferi's superior grasp of the situation that shamed her. It was his bravery. He had gone into the Shivan rift prepared to die, intending to do so to accomplish his goals, and it was that boldness and dedication that put the lie to her own. She had thought she was willing to do whatever it took to preserve Skyshroud, had gone so far as to chose it over her own tribe in Fyndhorn and her beloved favorites in Llanowar. She felt more responsible for Skyshroud and its strangely evolved culture because neither had existed on Dominaria before she brought them here. The elves of Fyndhorn and Llanowar had been an uninterrupted part of Dominaria since the dawn of history. They had strong roots, so reluctantly she had left them to fend for themselves as she tended to her newest and most tentative bloom.

As she watched Teferi spend every drop of his power, she realized that she had been wrong. She was not willing to die for

Skyshroud, not even willing to diminish herself for it. Her love of the natural order caused her to allow hardship and misery to be heaped upon her transplanted children, and it had almost caused her to allow their destruction.

Freyalise recovered her balance and stood up straight. She saw it clearly now. None of this was natural, not the first arrival of Skyshroud or the doom that now threatened it. She had been trying to combat the danger through vital means, by encouraging strength, tenacity, and magical ability in her followers. Such a course could never hope to succeed against these rifts and the capricious horrors they unleashed.

Temporal manipulation had always been anathema to Freyalise, and she needed no other confirmation than what she had seen in this valley. The elves of Skyshroud could not be expected to thrive under such a burden. No one could. It fell to their patron to protect them, and now, at long last, she would.

Freyalise's body shifted from pale, fair skin to a swirling, kaleidoscopic glow of green and red shapes. Her eyes vanished behind a curtain of stars that cascaded from her lashes with each blink like glittering dust from a moth's wings. Her gown shriveled in the heat and Freyalise floated off the circular, wooden platform, her naked body sheathed in a skin-tight cocoon of raw eldritch fury.

Windgrace, she called. *I cannot hear you, but listen to me: The Tolarians are correct. We are the only ones who can save our people and only according to their methods. Skyshroud is gone but for a single tree. I will do what I can to see that the rift and the Phyrexians and the winter claim no more victims here. I am honored to have fought by your side. Fare well, Master of Urborg.*

The sides of the Skyshroud rift grew thicker and more opaque as Freyalise's body changed. Her face and head remained as they were, a sculptor's study in feminine beauty wrapped in a seething skin of primal force, but her body shifted and merged into a flat, whiplike cone. The cone shot up into her skull, and Freyalise's head threw off white light bright enough to singe the wood below her.

Her mind was all that remained, her unconquerable will and all the incalculable power she could muster. On the tree a new surge of slivers and Phyrexians had reached the summit, but they could only screech and wail and cover their smoking eyes, helpless in the bright fury that was Freyalise.

Up, she thought. She was a creature of the soil, but she would not lower herself to digging in it. She would go out and find the upper reaches of the rift. She would attack it at its summit and drag it down upon itself, pulling it inside out as she had her gloves. She would stuff it into itself until it was more manageable, open wide, and swallow the damned thing whole.

Now. Freyalise struck skyward, the last Skyshroud tree dwindling to a pinprick below. Her head was a comet, her body the tail. She cut a glittering path through the angry, darkened clouds, boiling away the smoke and filthy moisture around her to create a circular canal of clean, clear air between herself and the ground.

There. The sheer, smoky walls softened and diffused into nothing several miles above Dominaria. There was no edge for her to latch on to, no seam that she could grasp, but she knew her upward journey had come to an end. She felt the rift clutching for her like a thing alive, like a hungry baby bird snapping for the worm in its mother's beak.

I know you, she said. *I've known you all my life. You're what happens when magic is turned against Gaea, against life in all its myriad forms and in contravention of the roles they were meant to play. Today I am life's champion. I abhor you. I will destroy you.*

Freyalise arced up over the rift's bounding walls, curved back down without losing momentum, and slammed into the top of the western wall. The ghost-gray fog received her, contained her, gathered and thickened around her. Then the rift swelled like a blister and burst as Freyalise tore free. She continued on to the opposite wall and plunged in again. It churned for a moment, then expanded and broke open.

Freyalise continued to zigzag from one end of the rift to the other, blowing holes in its substance as she descended and weakening its structure. Each time she emerged, the fury around her dimmed. Each time she plunged in it took her longer to fight her way out.

The comet with Freyalise's face wavered as it crossed the distance between the rift walls. Was it enough? Had she damaged it sufficiently to see things through? She hoped so. She had reached the limit of what she could do in this realm.

Hanging in midair for a moment, Freyalise drew in the last of the mana she had reclaimed from Skyshroud. She had no more regrets. She had no more hesitation. She had no long list of memories to catalogue, no peers to bid farewell. She was Freyalise and she had always walked alone.

The comet opened its eyes and mouth wide. Freyalise sang as she slammed into the rift one final time, a single, clear, sustained note that would always haunt the minds of those who heard it and survived.

She released all of her power in a single, explosive burst, choking the rift, overwhelming it with a feast far too rich and complicated for such a low and bestial appetite. The half-solid walls of the Skyshroud rift bulged outward, then toppled back in upon themselves. A green ring of flames blew outward from the planeswalker's location, uncannily silent. The world groaned as its terrible wound was healed.

Far below, the Skyshroud tree stood covered in countless skittering bodies. The tightly braided wood shifted, creaking so loudly it shattered several Phyrexian heads. Then it too erupted in a powerful blast of silent, emerald fire.

Debris rained down on the remains of Skyshroud. The tunnel Freyalise had carved through the clouds remained, their sooty gray billowing respectfully around the column of clear air. Starlight shone straight down to the forest floor, unimpeded by bough or fog, and it glinted off the surface of a small, silver hand mirror lying among the shreds of bone, wood, and metal.

Freyalise was gone. The rift was gone. And the valley that once housed Skyshroud now sat empty, silent, and still.

CHAPTER 23

Teferi silently cheered when he felt the Skyshroud rift implode, but he paled when the Stronghold phenomenon almost doubled in size and ferocity. His apprehension grew as Windgrace turned on him in a fury.

"Freyalise is dead," he said. "She followed your path and paid an even higher price."

"Dead," Teferi said. He neither felt surprise nor tried to feign it. "As I thought I would be." He blinked. "But now is the time for you to act as well, my lord. The Skyshroud rift is sealed. You can compound that success by sealing this one, and quickly."

Windgrace stubbornly crossed his arms.

"My lord," Teferi said. "What more evidence do you need? Freyalise was successful—"

"You've a strange definition of success," Windgrace snarled.

"Then deny the evidence before you." Teferi pointed to the rift. "See how it roils? The rifts are a network, Windgrace. They are connected. Especially yours and Freyalise's. Closing one does not disperse the energy it contained but only redirects it to the rest of the network. Don't you understand? Everything that was there is coming here." Teferi threw his arms wide. "Everything."

Windgrace opened his mouth to speak, but another voice interrupted him.

"It's true, my lord. Forgive my sudden intrusion. My name is Karn."

Teferi's eyes widened, and he struggled to turn quickly, hampered by his levitation spell's slow, lazy speed. Karn was there, every gorgeous, massive, silver inch of him. Jhoira was with him, floating safely in a bubble of Karn's magic.

"Shovelhead," Teferi said. He beamed in spite of himself, in spite of the dire circumstances. It was always good to see a friend.

Karn nodded to him. "Teferi. We have much to discuss."

"In time," Windgrace said. He rushed through the air, his arms folded and his spine stiff, until he was directly in between Karn and Teferi. "First you will talk to me."

"I am at your service, my lord. But our time is short."

"Then it will have to stretch. What are you?"

"I am planeswalker. Though I daresay I am exceptional even in this exalted company."

"And why do you have the air of Phyrexia about you?"

Karn shrugged. "For the same reason you have fur and fangs, I imagine. I was a construct before I ascended. Some of my components were Phyrexian."

Windgrace sniffed the air suspiciously. "And you are ready to throw in with this one?" He jabbed his thumb back over his shoulder toward Teferi, who was still trying to make eye contact with Jhoira.

"I am. Jhoira has been describing the rift phenomena to me. I must concur with Teferi's assessment. The rifts are unnatural, and they feed on whatever magical essence they come across. Only beings like us can provide the power it takes to satiate them. Only we have the force of will necessary to destroy them."

"I see. And what prevents you from exercising your power and your force of will?"

"As I said, I am exceptional. If we truly intend to seal the rifts, it takes a planeswalker. If we seek to end their temporal distortions, it requires me."

"That doesn't answer my question, construct."

"According to Jhoira," Karn said, "there are major rifts yet to be closed. Zhalfir, Otaria, Yavimaya, and Madara. But like me, there is one rift that is unique. The disaster at Tolaria was fueled by temporal flux. I must reserve myself for it."

"You Tolarians and your time magic," Windgrace spat. "Why are you so suited to that particular spot?"

"Because I was there when it happened. And more importantly, I am the only living thing that has ever traveled through time, and that is what must happen if the Tolarian rift is to be sealed."

"You make no sense to me."

Karn turned to Jhoira and gestured encouragingly. She fired an angry glare at Teferi before she said, "The rifts' time distortion has its roots in Tolaria. There was a double disaster there. The time-machine fiasco followed millennia later by a world-class destructive spell. The Tolarian rift has been funneling temporal chaos into the rifts for who knows how long. It will be next to impossible to seal it now. If Karn goes back to a time before the second disaster, there is a chance he can fix the damage before it becomes irreparable."

"Which at this point," Karn said, "it is."

Teferi floated up beside Windgrace. "Magnificent, Jhoira," he said. "You have exceeded my already high opinion of you. But we linger over what has yet to be done at the expense of what must be done immediately. "Windgrace," he said, "my powers are depleted, but I retain some small residue. I tell you that," he pointed to the disk, "will soon split, and when it does there will be no hope"

Windgrace's ears twitched. His vertical pupils contracted to thin slits, and he said, "Venser has returned." The panther-god bared his wicked fangs. "And sometime recently he has taken the first step toward his grand destiny. That is hope, Tolarian. A new kind of planeswalker."

"Venser has 'walked?" Teferi grinned like a small boy. "That is good news, make no mistake. But Venser does not have what we need."

"No? Why don't we go see for ourselves?"

"What do"—Teferi said, pausing through a wave of nausea and a fogging of the brain—"you mean? Oh." Teferi and Windgrace now stood outside Venser's workshop, where Venser and his ambulator both stood waiting. "This is most inappropriate, my lord. We should be planning strategy with Karn and Jhoira."

"Hold your tongue." Windgrace hunched down, his shadow completely enveloping Venser. "Son of Urborg," he said, "where is your mark?"

Venser swallowed but answered in a strong, clear voice. "I lost it in the Blind Eternities, my lord. The Weaver King took it from me."

Windgrace bristled. "He still pursues you? I see no trace of him."

"He was here." Venser tapped his temple. "And may still be."

Windgrace dismissed the Weaver King with a wave of his massive hand. He was staring intently at Venser. "You're a planeswalker," he said.

"I suppose so. I don't fully understand it all, but, yes, I went to the Blind Eternities once. Mostly, I just teleport from place to place."

"And from plane to plane?"

"Yes. Though I have not done so yet."

"Something else I wish I had the chance to teach you." To Teferi, he said, "And what do you say will happen if Venser teleports into the time rift?"

"Perhaps nothing," Teferi said. "He doesn't have the kind of power it takes to affect the rift's internal energy."

"I see. So once again no one can do what you say needs to be done except for people outside your party. Venser is not capable. Karn is too important. It falls to Freyalise and me to die for your cause."

"I did it too, my lord, and did it first. And I did not die."

"By your own admission, the rift you sealed was less than the ones here and in Skyshroud. Freyalise is gone. And you would have me walk into the center of that storm and let it consume me."

"No," Teferi's sharp tone surprised his own ears. "You must fight it, Lord Windgrace. This is a battle, warrior, a contest like no other. You must strive against the rift, snarl and snap and tear at it while it tries to drain your life's essence. It is a fight you can win, a fight you can survive, but only if you have the stomach to try."

The panther-god's body rippled as his muscles tensed. He puffed black smoke from his nostrils and growled.

Windgrace. The Weaver King sounded heavier, more serious than before. *I have returned to take Urborg from you. My army is already assembled. If you dare, bring your swamp rabble and meet me on the battlefield.*

"He's learned how to take control of the Phyrexians," Venser said. "How many are there?"

Windgrace glared from Venser to Teferi. It was rare when Teferi could not think of something to say, but this was one of those times. "I'm leaving you here," Windgrace said. "Both of you."

"Don't take the bait, my lord." Teferi looked pleadingly at the panther-god. "Go up to the rift and seal it. An hour longer and Freyalise's sacrifice will have been in vain."

"I am still considering," Windgrace said. "And while I ponder, I will tear that phantom's spine out and strangle him with it."

"My lord," Venser said, "please. Tell me where Jhoira is."

"Up there," Windgrace said. "With her planeswalker construct. I expect they'll come to you once they realize where you are." His ears twitched again, and Windgrace smiled cruelly. "The archmage draws near," he said. "Bend his ear with your chatter. Or not. I no longer care." He began to shimmer and fade. "Good-bye, Tolarian, and good fortune to you, Venser of Urborg. I shall not return for either of you."

Venser watched Windgrace vanish with an odd mix of relief and anxiety on his face. He seemed glad to escape the panther-god's anger but at the same time less than sanguine about their collective future. Then he noticed Teferi inspecting his ambulator, and quiet anger eclipsed all else.

"Remarkable," Teferi said. "Do you think you could teach me to use it?"

Venser gritted his teeth, but before he could speak Jodah came over the edge of the swamp. The tall man was red-faced, and his hair was tousled.

"Jodah," Teferi said, "much has happened. Let me give you—"

Jodah ignored Teferi entirely. He stormed up to Venser and knocked the artificer flat on his back with a strong right fist.

"You stupid, impudent child." Jodah's voice was a low, menacing hiss. "Do you have any idea what you've done?"

"I saved you," Venser said. He cradled his bleeding lip and pulled himself to his feet. "There was no hope in Skyshroud, and you knew it."

Jodah hit him again, a short, sharp blow on the opposite side of Venser's face. The artificer went down again, sprawling into the icy mud.

"Jodah," Teferi said. "Freyalise chose her own path. There was nothing you could have done to change it, least of all punching Venser after the fact."

For a moment Teferi thought he might be the next recipient of Jodah's angry blows, but the rage seemed to drain from the archmage. "This is madness," he said. He looked down at Venser.

"I'm sorry, but I can't stay here. I am through." Jodah turned and strode back into the swamp the way he had come.

Teferi went to Venser and gave the young man a hand up. "Do you know where he's going?"

Venser spat blood and wiped his swelling lip. "He's got a tunnel he uses. I assume he's going back wherever he came from."

"Can you take me there?"

Venser's astonishment blended with his injuries to produce a wholly unintentional comic effect. "You can't be serious."

"I am. The archmage is a powerful wizard. As we need all the help we can get, we certainly need him."

"I'm not going anywhere near him," Venser said. "Not until he's calmed down."

Teferi tried to contain his enthusiasm. "Well, then," he said, "would you show me how to use the ambulator so that I can go after him?"

Venser eyed him suspiciously and said, "No. No, if it's that important to you I'll take you there myself. But I'm staying out of arm's reach."

"Fair enough. Thank you, Venser."

"Don't thank me yet," the artificer grumbled. "And don't look to me when he knocks you down. Come closer."

Teferi obligingly sidled up beside Venser. To his bemusement, the young man sat down in the mud and extended his arms. He moved his fingers over two invisible stringed instruments and took deep, measured breaths.

"What are you doing?" Teferi asked.

"Shut up," Venser said. "I'm teleporting."

This time Teferi felt a gentle breeze and a slight tingle between here and there. The trip was over before he fully realized it had begun, and now he and Venser were on the edge of a small copse of trees. Jodah was there as well, making sharp gestures at a pool of liquid suspended over a hole in the ground.

"He's all yours," Venser said. "I will come no closer."

Teferi went out alone. He called, "Jodah," from a safe distance in case the archmage lashed out again.

But Jodah barely responded to the sound. Instead he kept working with his tunnel transport and kept his back to Teferi.

"Jodah," he said, "we need to talk."

"No we don't." The archmage did not turn.

"There are trials ahead that you could help see us through. We need you."

"No you don't."

"We do. I need you, Venser needs you . . . Jhoira needs you."

Jodah did turn now, and Teferi was grateful he had kept his distance. "You astound me," Jodah said, rage steaming from his words. "How low will you go?"

Teferi smiled blankly. "What do you mean?"

"I mean you are as manipulative a creature as I've ever met. Everything you say is designed to produce an effect, but worse, it's also designed to conceal the effect you're after. You're a liar who lies about his lies to himself."

Teferi drew himself up to his full height. "I'm sorry," he said. "I thought you were the kind who didn't shrink from hard work when it was worth doing."

Jodah stopped. He didn't turn, seeming to argue with himself, and said softly, "Urza."

"What?"

Jodah stood and faced Teferi. "I said 'Urza.' I am descended from the Brothers. Did you know that? I am descended from Urza's family, the one he had before he ascended."

"I had heard that about you, but it never seemed important enough to mention."

"I'm mentioning it, you pompous fool. Because I may have the blood, but you are heir to Urza's mantle in ways I will never be. You are exactly like him, Teferi, a glib, patrician, elitist, all-knowing and all-powerful high muckety-muck who thinks everyone should simply get in line and follow his lead. You believe that yours are the only answers that work, that your plans are the only ones worth following. But Urza was often wrong, and people always suffered for it. You are often wrong, and people around you suffer for it."

"I only asked for your help."

"That's all you ever ask for, and it's never all you mean. You don't want my help. You want my total dedication. You want me to do what you can't because you believe it needs to be done."

"That may be," Teferi said. "But in this case, I'm right."

"And it doesn't matter. Don't you get that?"

"No," Teferi admitted. "No I don't."

"Then try harder." Jodah turned back and waved his hand over the tunnel one last time. He stepped back and walked past Teferi toward Venser until the artificer started to withdraw.

"I'm sorry I hit you," Jodah said.

"You seemed angry," Venser mumbled, his swollen lips distorting his words. "But I'll get over it. I'm sorry I pushed you into the tunnel."

"So am I. I know that you're right, there was nothing I could have done except die alongside Freyalise. But it was my decision. You should have let me see it through."

Venser's looked pained. "Freyalise died?"

Jodah laughed, shaking his head in amazement. "You didn't even know, did you? It's all so absurd."

Venser did not reply, and Jodah did not wait. He turned back, marched past Teferi, and stepped into the tunnel.

"Is there a message you would like to send to Jhoira?"

Jodah regarded him with open contempt. "I've said all I have to say, to her and to you." With one final nod toward Venser, Jodah completed his step and melted into the curtain of thick liquid.

* * * * *

Karn wanted to stay and examine the Stronghold rift, so he sent Jhoira back down to Venser's workshop. The ambulator was still there, but Venser, Teferi, and Windgrace were nowhere in sight. Uncertain of what to do, Jhoira ascended the dais and inspected Venser's machine. To her surprise, the twin powerstones that powered it had been removed.

She smiled wryly. Venser must have been here, and his habit of keeping the stones with him was a hard one to break.

The air shimmered in front of Venser's door. Venser and Teferi appeared, Teferi standing upright and Venser sitting down with his arms half-extended. The artificer was bleeding slightly from a split lip, but otherwise he seemed his normal, preoccupied self.

"Venser," she said and was rewarded by a warm but weary smile.

"Freyalise is dead," he said.

"I know. I'm glad you're not. Is Jodah . . ."

"The archmage lives," Teferi said. "But he has gone back to his home. I offered to bring you his message, but he demurred."

Jhoira looked at Teferi, then back to Venser. The artificer nodded. "He was angry about Freyalise. And because I wouldn't let him stay to help her."

"And I'm wondering," Teferi continued, "if you will continue to ignore me no matter what company we're in."

"We'll talk later," Jhoira said, "in private, when this is all over."

"Optimistic," Teferi said, "yet somehow dire. I can wait, Jhoira. I only hope we'll both be available when this is all over."

"Where do things stand?" she said.

"Unchanged. Windgrace has gone out to rout the Weaver King, but he still must seal the Stronghold rift—in the next hour, if we are to take any benefit from it. After that . . . let me first say that I support your theory. Karn must attack the Tolarian rift before it became so unstable. If we are to stop the spread of Phyrexians and frigid weather, we must remove time from the equation. How did you intend to send Karn back?"

Jhoira wrestled with her frustration, stamping it down for the time being. "He has an idea. I thought your expertise would be valuable before we made the attempt."

Teferi bowed. "I'm flattered," he said.

"Don't be. Be useful instead."

"I shall endeavor to be nothing less."

"I will signal Karn."

Venser stood, slightly shamefaced. "Do you need to use the ambulator?"

"No." Jhoira shook her head, her eyes kind. "He's close enough now to hear my thoughts."

"Oh," Venser said. "Good." He glanced at Teferi, then back at Jhoira. "Can we wait inside? I haven't eaten for days."

"Certainly. Go on inside and fix yourself something. I'll be in directly."

"May I join you?" Teferi scampered after Venser. He opened the door and went inside as Teferi went on. "I'm out practice when it comes to eating, but it's a hobby I'm eager to resume." He patted his belly. "The sooner the better."

Venser was already inside, but he left the door open for Teferi to follow. Jhoira watched the bald man slip into the workshop. She climbed up the ambulator and settled into the chair.

Karn, she thought. *We're almost ready to begin.*

Thank you, came the immediate reply. *I have one last survey to make. Then I will join you.*

Hurry, she thought. *Please hurry.*

CHAPTER 24

Lord Windgrace looked down upon the Phyrexian horde below. They were as numerous as grains of sand on the beach, all tightly packed into a single, rock-hard mass. They were waiting for something, and he was certain he was that something.

His hackles rose, and his fury mounted. The Weaver King had challenged him to a full-scale war, a clash of armies. He was done with armies, however, done with sending his own people to battle the Phyrexians' latest invasion. The Weaver King was an insect, an insignificant pest who didn't deserve to spill any more of Urborg's blood. Now, Windgrace thought, I will show you how a planeswalker makes war.

He spread his mighty arms and descended, dropping faster than a falling star. He gathered his mana to him, his power surging in his chest like a roar waiting to erupt. Then he did roar, a thundering, explosive sound that drew the attention of every Phyrexian in sight.

Windgrace exploded into the center of the assembly like a giant black powder bomb, liquefying the metal brutes close by and shredding those in the distance. He rose from the smoking crater he'd made and conjured his bladed staff to his open hand.

"Hoy, clockwork demons," he bellowed. "I have swamps full of your predecessors' bones. Come and die to enrich the soil of Urborg."

They closed upon him immediately, without fear, without mercy. The panther-god swung his staff, slashing through the first row of artifact devils like a reaper among the wheat. Those that weren't cut in two soon toppled anyway as a bubbling, black infection foamed up in the wounds, dissolving their blue-steel bodies in its wake. The rot spread back to those that hadn't been touched by Windgrace's blade, and it gave the planeswalker a savage thrill to melt so many of these icy horrors without the slightest measure of heat.

Something huge and ponderous with crushing claw-hands seized him from behind. It exerted enough pressure to crush a long ship's hull and sent surges of electric agony coursing through Windgrace's body.

Windgrace grunted. He flexed the muscles in his burly arms and shoulders, shattering the metal claws into shrapnel. He whirled in place, dropped his staff, and brought his hands together with the clawed creature's head between them. The Phyrexian's upper body collapsed, squashed flat and mangled by the brute force of Windgrace's blow. The panther-god kicked out with his foot, splitting the armless, headless invader up the middle.

Windgrace abandoned himself to the slaughter. There were Phyrexians everywhere, each in dire need of his dark ministrations, and he did his best not to leave any of them waiting. He charged forward into their ranks, scattering them like frightened birds. His bladed staff became a solid circular blur, a sawmill's blade that left necrotic black foam on every invader it touched. Those so afflicted dissolved, along with any others that were splashed in their collapse.

He increased his size, swelling to over twenty feet tall. He pounced among the enemy's thickest concentration, breaking them with his teeth and savage blows from his silky black forehead. Time and again they swarmed over him, ants engaging an angry bear, and each time he cast them off with massive sweeps of his arms, flinging them free with such force that they splattered against the trees or crushed themselves against their fellows.

"Weaver!" he rumbled. "This ends here!"

For you, maybe. But I have other plans.

Windgrace tried to isolate the source of the taunting harlequin voice, but even his keen ears were stymied by the racket the Phyrexians made as they fought and died. No matter, he thought. I'll simply kill every last one of them until he and I are the only ones left.

A bolt of sickly yellow slammed into him, burning his back and blinding him with pain. He shrank back to his former size, his fur smoking. Windgrace turned to face the pair of heavy warwagons rattling toward him on metal treads. Each bore a cannon that was trained directly on him, and he could see and feel the energy gathering within for another blast.

Enraged, Windgrace flew forward, dodging the cannon beams as he came. He latched onto each long barrel, one in each hand, and his arm muscles bulged. The wagons rose off the ground for a moment, still spinning their treads, then their own weight hauled them down to the ground, bending each cannon into sharp right angles. Windgrace held on as he pivoted and strained. The cannons and their rotating turrets tore free, and Windgrace spun in place, flailing the next wave of Phyrexians with the remains of their most powerful weapons. After enough revolutions to clear a wide circle around him, Windgrace angled his shoulders and cast the mangled turrets high into the air. They landed among the multitude and exploded, leaving only charred and smoking slag inside the blast radius.

The Phyrexians held their distance, menacing him with their limbs and their weaponry but well clear of his reach.

"Lord Windgrace?"

He recognized the voice and didn't bother to turn. "What do you want?"

Karn stepped up behind his fellow planeswalker. "I have come to urge you to address the Stronghold rift."

"Then consider your errand complete. You have urged me, and I have refused. Again. Begone, or I will forget that you were only Phyrexian in a past life."

"With respect . . . is this the most constructive use of your power?"

Windgrace lashed out with his claws, slicing a Phyrexian scuta into roughly equal parts. "It'll do," he said.

"Then if you'll allow me . . ."

Windgrace stopped and faced Karn. "Allow you to what? Nine Hells, you Tolarians are exasperating."

Karn bowed lightly. "I was made to battle these creatures, my lord—well, not these creatures precisely, but ones much like them. Please," he said, "let me clear the field."

Windgrace coughed angrily. He prepared to lash out at the construct, to send him to the far edge of the world, but the metal man had already begun to shine. Karn lifted his arms out straight and floated into the air. He began to spin, picking up speed as he twirled, and the light coming off him grew stronger and more intense. Intrigued, Windgrace watched carefully as Karn became a whirling mass of white-hot energy.

You should withdraw, my lord, the construct said, *or at least take cover.*

The panther-god snorted disdainfully, but he raised bubble of solid mana around him. He shifted his visual range to allow him to see through his own barrier just as Karn released an omni-directional wave of force.

The wave spread over the entire battlefield, disintegrating the Phyrexians as if they had never been. There was no wreckage, no debris, no pools of glistening oil. Even the invaders Windgrace had already dispatched vanished in that killing surge of burning white.

Karn slowed his rotation, and the light around him dimmed. Windgrace lowered his shield and appraised the scene. There were no Phyrexians left in the immediate area.

"Impressive," he growled, "for a construct."

The horde was far from vanquished, but the closest invader was now a solid ten minutes away even at a dead run. Karn had bought them time and breathing room, but he had not won the day.

"I thought we might take this chance to talk," the metal man said.

"About what?"

"About the future. Your future, mine, and Urborg's."

"I've already had this conversation today."

"Then it bears repeating. Your duty is here. Mine is far away, halfway around the globe and three hundred years past. I cannot act until you do, or my efforts will be utterly wasted."

"Like your time on this field," Windgrace said. "Leave me to my work."

"I am trying to make your work easier, my lord."

"I fail to see how."

"By defeating your enemy. The Phyrexians are not the disease. They are a symptom. You wouldn't cure a sore foot by chopping it off, would you?"

"That depends on whose foot it is."

"For the sake of discussion, let's say it's yours."

"Discussion?" Windgrace did not try to restrain his astonishment. "Why are you having discussions with me now? Your power is impressive. Your assistance is grudgingly appreciated. But I am through with discussions and talk."

"Why? Surely a handful of words with me will not derail your evening's carnage."

"For the sake of discussion," Windgrace said darkly, "let's assume that I'm a coward. I have become so enamored of my immortality, so greedy for it, that I would prefer to let Urborg die in my place. Would that satisfy your machine curiosity?"

"It would if it were true. But you are no coward, my lord. And the rift may not even take your life."

"It took Freyalise's life. And Teferi's power."

"So it would seem. But Freyalise was weaker than she had ever been. And Teferi was only diminished to what he was before he ascended. What were you before you ascended, my lord?"

Windgrace glared, and his tail slashed the air.

"I was a construct," Karn said, "an amalgamation of parts and magic designed for a specific purpose. When that purpose was fulfilled, I was put aside. But I would still choose that over knowing I had not done all I could to protect the ones I love."

"I was a hero," Windgrace said. "In ages past, the panther tribes ruled Urborg. I was their warrior chief, a man to be respected and feared."

"And you can be that again. If you are truly Urborg's protector and you wish to remain so, you must risk what you have. To save your home from these horrors one minute only to lose it the next when the rift erupts would be a poor tribute to the panther tribes of old."

Windgrace tossed his bladed staff aside. He stalked up to Karn and glared. "Can you lie, construct?"

"If necessary. But I find the truth is far more reliable."

"Your Tolarian masters lie. They have lied to me at every turn. I cannot and will not do what you ask unless I am given certain assurances. Urborg must be provided for."

"I give you my word," Karn said. "It will be."

"Ha! Yet you yourself are bound for Tolaria to seal the time rift there. Who says you will be able to return, that you'll survive long enough to keep your word?"

"There are always uncertainties," Karn said. "But the danger posed by that rift is not one of them. You are no coward, Lord Windgrace, but you are overcautious with regards to your home as well as overestimating your own importance. Urborg will endure."

Windgrace made a sound that was half growl and half roar. Almost as a reply, the rift over the Stronghold let out a thick, jagged stroke of lightning.

"Tell me the truth, construct. Will this actually work?"

"It will. It has before, and it will again."

"You make no sense to me," Windgrace said. "None of you do. The last time I followed someone else's grand scheme, nothing went as planned and everyone died."

"You speak of Urza and his Nine Titans' raid on Phyrexia proper. That was a long time ago, my lord, and things are even more dire now than they were then. Yes, this is someone else's grand scheme. But you know it's the only real option."

"I don't accept that."

"Then consider this: The last time, when everyone died, was the outcome worth the cost? Was stopping the Phyrexian Invasion and killing Yawgmoth once and for all a noble cause worth dying for? Urza thought so. And so did countless others. Many of them died here, in Urborg, under the shadow of that cursed mountain.

"I put it to you, Windgrace. This is still the same threat you agreed to meet all those years ago. The Invasion helped cause this current strife, created your hole in the sky. That battle is not yet complete and never will be as long as remnants of it continue to spoil Dominaria. It's time to finish it once and for all."

Windgrace felt tired. He was tired of arguing, tired of fighting with no hope of victory. "So be it," he said. "But if Urborg is left without protection, I will return from the grave and punish you severely."

"And I would deserve it. I trust you to survive. Do you trust me if you do not?"

Windgrace shook his head. "No. I will make my own arrangements." The panther-god crouched on his powerful hind legs and slammed his claws into the soil. He concentrated, summoning up the totality of forest and swamp mana that was his to command. The broad muscles in his arms and shoulders bulged, and a crushing jolt of pure magic thumped into the ground, making it ripple and undulate like liquid.

Windgrace rocked back, pulling his hands free. He stiffly rolled his neck and rose to his feet.

"What did you do?"

"I have infused a part of myself into the land. I may not return, but my spirit will continue to watch over Urborg. Your rift solution will have to work with whatever portion remains."

"Thank you, Lord Windgrace. I pray it will be enough."

The panther-god showed Karn a toothy smile. "Pray harder." Without giving Karn the chance to fill his head with more words, Windgrace settled back down to his haunches, every bit the mighty predator. He let his body slip into the soil, through the thin veneer of ice and the layers of rich, black mulch below. For a brief, shining moment, he was Urborg, every blade of grass, every rock, every last pine needle. It felt right. It felt proper. It felt like the fitting last act of a stalwart and noble protector.

Windgrace gathered himself, collected his ultimate force, and set his sights on the crackling circle of purple light in the sky.

Then he pounced, surging up with his jaws spread wide. He was gigantic, his head larger than the Stronghold itself. The rift responded as he approached, reacting as the Tolarians said it would, reaching for him, striving to absorb his power. It was laughable, he thought. All this clamor and commotion over something so small?

He engulfed the rift in his jaws, clamping down on it with his sharp fangs and his short, crushing molars. It burned him, ripped his flesh, blistered his throat, and broke his teeth. His jaw split, and his skull cracked. The pain was terrible, crippling, but Windgrace kept on. For a dreadful moment he felt the balance shifting, felt the rift tearing parts of him away and devouring them raw. He responded, pouring more of his limitless might into the task of breaking the disk and swallowing the bitter blood that gushed forth.

In the end, he outlasted it. The rift's force was spent before his own, and he felt the brittle disk shatter between his jaws like an overbaked cracker. As his consciousness drained away, and his life force was sucked into the shattered hole in the sky, Windgrace celebrated his victory. He roared, a hurricane wind of triumphant fury.

Then the panther-god vanished, taking the Stronghold rift into oblivion like a trophy between his teeth.

CHAPTER 25

The Weaver King watched Windgrace's final effort through the eyes of a thousand Phyrexian puppets. He felt a disquieting tug deep within when the purple disk winked out, but that was soon replaced by the warm, satisfying sense of a job well done. Windgrace was gone. Urborg belonged to the Weaver King.

There were no more Phyrexians to master, but he could make do with the multitude he already had. The cold remained unabated, but it would deepen no more. He had done all that his unseen patron required, and though he had not succeeded in besting his enemies, they were dead, and he remained.

He wondered, would that earn him praise or rebuke? For the first time he understood Dinne's recalcitrance and sullen moods. It was hard indeed to live for another, to be bound to another's will. Now that the most obvious obstacles before him had been removed, the Weaver King could focus on reestablishing his own autonomy. For that he needed Venser, and perhaps Dinne too.

Abandoning his army to their own devices, the Weaver King skated free along the silver threads that bound his subjects to him. He was unstoppable now. All he needed to do was wait.

Sooner or later, they would let themselves become vulnerable. When they did, he would own them all, body and soul.

* * * * *

Venser stood inside his workshop still half-dazed and exhausted from the day's events. Freyalise's death had come as a shock because he didn't know it was happening. It was far worse being a partial witness to Windgrace's final act of heroism. He understood that the panther-god was not a god at all, but that didn't change the lifelong awe and respect he had felt for Urborg's champion. Losing him was like losing his father all over again—along with his grandfather, his uncles, his mentor, and everyone else he had ever looked up to. He had lived his life in fear of seeing Windgrace and his gladehunters, but now that Windgrace was gone, Venser was even more afraid of the Urborg he left behind.

It had happened faster than any of them could process. Teferi had been working his way through a bowl of thin soup when he let the spoon clatter to the floor. On the bald man's urging, the three of them went outside just in time to see the great, black cat's head seize the Stronghold rift in his teeth and shake it to death. When the purple light went out and Windgrace went with it, Venser, Jhoira, and Teferi could only stand and stare silently.

Now they were back inside, and Venser's appetite had dwindled to a dull, manageable ache that was almost totally eclipsed by the shock and horror he felt. He could almost understand Teferi's renewed energy—they had succeeded in fending off the end of everything for another short while—but their successes were more costly with each step forward they took. Teferi, Freyalise, and Windgrace had been among the few planeswalkers gifted, driven, and noble enough to give their lives for the sake of others, and now they were all dead, missing, or disempowered. They had achieved their immediate goal of fixing the most dangerous time rifts, but they were changing the magical balance of Dominaria as radically as the rifts themselves.

Jhoira said nothing after Windgrace's display. She simply watched with a probing eye as the ex-planeswalker slurped his soup.

Karn materialized outside Venser's open door. He stood politely as Venser stared and Teferi happily chewed on the last piece of bread.

"May I come in?" the silver man said.

"Please." Venser was so numb that Karn barely registered as a singularly complicated artifact. Any other day of his life would have found Venser full of questions and a desire to examine the silver golem's mechanical innards. At the very least he would have peppered Karn with questions. Today, however, Karn was just another unfathomable player in this game of dangerously high stakes.

"Karn, my old friend," Teferi said. He mopped up the last of the soup with a piece of stale bread. Chewing and crunching as he stood, Teferi stepped back from Venser's humble table and circled around to greet the metal man. "You're arrived just in time to help us form the next steps in our plan."

"Lord Windgrace is—" Karn said.

"Gone," Venser said. "We saw."

"His spirit remains," Karn said. Venser must have visibly expressed the doubt and exasperation these words dredged out of him because Karn added, "I'm not speaking poetically, young man. Windgrace refused to go until he had seen to Urborg. He would not have gone if he didn't think this place was protected."

Venser caught the fluttering ray of hope before it passed his lips. "He's not dead then?"

"He is gone, as you said. But he may well return when Urborg needs him most. He will always be the ultimate protector of this dark and troubled place."

"Oh." Venser glanced around the shabby interior of his workshop. "Would you like to sit down?"

"Thank you, no."

"Karn is never tired," Jhoira said, causing Venser to realize he hadn't heard her voice since Windgrace had sealed the rift. "Even before he ascended he could walk across the bottom of the ocean without pausing for rest."

"And now there is an even greater task before him." Teferi coaxed Karn deeper into the room with a gentle hand. "Jhoira has outlined your idea." He turned toward the Ghitu. "Briefly. I would like to hear more."

Karn also glanced at Jhoira before saying, "The time rifts are aptly named," Karn said. "They are rife with temporal energy. They might have been even without the contributions of Urza's wayward experiment, but that experiment did happen. It was an unprecedented and unrepeatable event. Tolaria remained permeated by time magic for thousands of years, and when Barrin razed it down to the bare rock he opened the Tolarian rift wider and released that chronal energy into the larger network."

"And you intend to travel back to a time before the island was leveled."

"Yes. I intend to arrive just long enough to do what I have to, a matter of minutes before Barrin cast that terrible spell."

"I see. Why?"

"My experience tells me the journey will not be an easy one. Every backward tick of the clock will require major effort and expose me to incredible strain. The impact on Dominaria will also be considerable, and I intend to minimize it."

"How?" Teferi did not even bother to hide the keen interest that invigorated him. "How will you do it?"

"It was Jhoira's position that we should ask you."

"Really? I am humbled."

Cold silence reigned for a few moments until Jhoira said, "Can you do it?"

"No," he said cheerfully. "But I believe I can show Karn how."

Jhoira scowled. "I don't understand."

"There is nothing about a planeswalker that allows him to move through time, but Karn is special. He was made to be a time traveler. Silver is the only substance Urza found that was well suited to the rigors of the temporal stream. Provided Karn's body is still made of silver and not some ersatz silvery alloy concocted by his own brilliant mind—"

"I can be pure silver again," Karn said.

"Then all we need is the method."

"Wait," Venser said. "How will sealing the Tolarian rift reverse the cold here and in Keld?"

"The unnatural winter is a result of time's being bent by the rifts," Teferi said. "You recall the alternate worlds we saw when we were in the network? I believe the cold comes from one of those, from an alternate version of Dominaria where Freyalise never cast her World Spell and the Ice Age never ended. That world's Phyrexia must have invaded thousands of years before ours did, so its creatures have adapted to the cold." Teferi shrugged. "That part's just a theory, but it's a solid theory from where I'm standing."

"And will our theory kill Karn too?" Jhoira had risen silently and crossed the room on the far side of Venser's table. Teferi's good cheer grew strained.

"I doubt it," Karn said. He turned to Venser and said, "I am special inside as well as outside. Though I am functionally identical to a naturally born planeswalker, structurally I am very different. My being was comprised of a series of powerful, integrated artifacts called the Legacy. Among other things, within me now is a planewalking engine, a vast store of arcane knowledge, and several major powerstones." He turned back to Teferi. "I may be able to bring more power to bear than I need. Even if it drains me completely and reverts me back to my original status as a sentient golem, I will still contain the Legacy. I can use it to 'walk back here."

Venser spoke up, intrigued in spite of himself. "How will you return through time if your power is spent?"

"Returning to one's natural place in the time stream requires no effort," said Karn. "Rather, all of the stress and strain comes from taking one's self out of that natural place. If I lose most or all of my abilities, I will be drawn back to this era like a pea through a straw."

Teferi dusted the last of the bread crumbs from his robe. "The sooner we start the better. I will need a short time to gather my thoughts so I can suggest a method. Would an hour be acceptable?"

"Perfect," Karn said. "I have preparations of my own that will take at least that long. He turned to Venser. "I'd like you to come along if you're willing."

"Me? How? Why?"

"Because you are also unique. If Dominaria survives, you and people like you will be the new vanguard that leads it into the future. I'd like you to see the past just for your own edification, but I also want to see your power in action. If you're agreeable, we can consider this a research mission as well as a rescue. We will travel together, I'll observe you, you'll observe me, and we'll both come out with a stronger understanding of our roles in the multiverse."

"But I'm not made of silver," Venser said. "I can't go through time."

"Ah, but you can go to the Blind Eternities. I know because I've seen you there. Come with me as far as that and I'll make sure you're aware of my progress with every step I take along the rest of the way."

Venser looked at Jhoira, but her face was inscrutable. When he spoke his voice was low and solemn. "I've already seen Tolaria burn," he said. "I didn't like it."

"You misunderstand," Karn said. "I want you to be exposed to the multiverse itself. Not just to the wide range of people, places, and things it contains but to its essential structure, its very nature.

What happened on Tolaria and what we're about to do there are both extraordinary. You'll never have a better chance to see how vast it is and how complicated, or how easily it can all be thrown into chaos."

"All lessons worth learning," Jhoira said, "especially if you plan to travel from plane to plane."

"I don't, actually."

Teferi smiled. "But this adventure might just change your mind, eh?"

Venser started to rebut the planeswalker but stopped when he realized he had no honest retort. To travel across time and space with a one-of-a-kind sentient artifact as his guide . . .

"All right," Venser said. "I'll do it."

"Good man," Teferi said. "And with your permission, I'd like to come along too."

Venser could almost hear Jhoira's jaw clenching in the silence. At last Karn said, "You're also not made of silver, Teferi. And you are no longer capable of surviving in the Blind Eternities."

"But the ambulator is. I've been itching to try Venser's machine anyway. And you both could use my help, at least as far as the point where the planeswalk ends and Karn's timewalk begins."

"The machine may not work for you," Jhoira said. "It may not work at all. Since it brought me here I haven't even been able to turn it on. It was roughly treated in Skyshroud. It may need major repairs."

Teferi was undaunted. "Still, I'd like to try. With your permission, of course." He nodded to Venser.

He noticed both Karn and Jhoira were watching him intently. Did they know he had removed the ambulator's powerstones? Were they signaling him to keep them hidden?

"By all means," Venser said. "I'll show you how to operate it. Oh, and there's the control rig to put on, that's very important." He glanced back and saw relief in Jhoira's expression. Relief and amusement that Venser had instantly sought to saddle Teferi with the rig that he himself hated to wear.

"Thank you," she mouthed.

Venser nodded. "Right this way, Teferi." He felt light and exhilarated. He had not forgotten the sacrifices of Freyalise and Windgrace, could not and would never, but this was many of his lifelong dreams combined. To learn from a master, to see the universe, to do the right thing even though he was afraid. The fact that doing so made Jhoira smile was an unexpected bonus.

He put the rig on Teferi's shoulders, seated him in the chair, and ran through the ambulator's basic operation. He stepped off the dais and let Teferi sit anxiously for a few minutes before he confirmed Jhoira's diagnosis. Something was missing or broken from the ambulator, and it would take time to find and more to fix.

Teferi responded as Venser knew he would. "Time is something we don't have to spare," he said.

Venser nodded, the look on Jhoira's face behind Teferi filling him with warmth and purpose. Teferi asked him for a slate and some chalk to lay out his thoughts, and Venser provided them. Karn lumbered off behind the workshop and stood as still as the statue he appeared to be, strange lights flickering behind his warm, black eyes. Left more or less to themselves, Jhoira came to him, and they walked to the edge of the marsh.

"Thank you," she said.

"You're welcome. Between you and me, I would rather have you for company than Teferi anyway."

"Teferi and I should stay behind," Jhoira said. "We need to talk."

"Will you be all right?"

"Of course. Worry about him, though. He's not going to like what I have to say."

Venser let his thoughts wander for a moment. "Will this work?" he said.

"I think so. For better and for worse, Teferi's more like his old self. He's got his shortcomings, but he's also brilliant. No one understands time better than he, except maybe Karn, and that's a maybe. We've never combined his insight and Karn's power in the past, but it's a natural pairing. I expect grand results."

"What about you? What will you do?"

"I'm already looking forward to our next challenges. There are still rifts to close, and I don't know any more planeswalkers on whom to call. If you and Karn succeed, the whole situation could change all over again. Maybe you'll create some new opportunities that we can pursue."

"Jhoira?"

"Yes?"

"Thank you."

She laughed and waved her hand dismissively. "For what?"

"For everything. For helping me cope and spurring me on. For being refreshingly straightforward . . . though I do wish you had mentioned the extra bits you built into the ambulator."

"I am sorry about that. I was looking for a reason to tell you rather than not to tell you. One never came up."

"It's all right," he said. "The ageless part too. You might have mentioned that. I spent the first few weeks thinking you were an especially precocious and driven young girl."

Jhoira laughed, a light, honest sound that made Venser smile. "Who says I'm not?" she said. She stretched up and kissed him on the cheek. "Stay close to Karn," she said. "Do what he tells you. If he says run, don't ask why, just run."

"I promise."

Back at the workshop door, Teferi emerged with a slate full of small, cramped notes. He scanned the marsh and waved excitedly when he saw them.

"I think Teferi's ready," Venser said.

Jhoira nodded. "Are you?"

He looked into her endlessly fascinating eyes and nodded.

"Good," she said. "Then it's time to go."

CHAPTER 26

Teferi assembled them outside Venser's workshop and went into full-blown lecture. Back in Shiv, Jhoira had told him Teferi apprenticed with a famous Jamuraan storyteller named Hakim, and it was clear Teferi had worked hard to hone his oratorical skills.

"As usual," Teferi said, "we start with Urza. Some of us have intimate knowledge of his time travel experiment, though no one has ever been able to repeat it. I think I know why—and it's not simply because Urza was mad.

"Urza's mistake was the same one he always made: he overthought and overprepared. He made his machine entirely too vast and complicated, mostly to deal with any number of unexpected occurrences. But the more working parts a machine has, the more likely something will go wrong. Would you agree, Venser?"

"To a point."

"Absolutely. So I have gone in just the opposite direction. There is no machine. There isn't even a spell. Karn has traveled through time, and he has the power to do it again. He will serve as both vessel and pilot. His own inherent strength, guided by his mind, is all that he needs.

"We'll leave the future aside for now, as we're heading into the past, but in both cases the mind is the key. Thoughts and memories are not constrained by time. I can recall experiences and emotions from a thousand years ago and see them as clearly as the day they happened. All of us remember our most hated enemies and our most beloved friends, and those memories don't create the memory of emotion but new emotion, raw and fresh and powerful.

"Planeswalkers are nothing more than minds and magic. Minds are thoughts and memories and emotions. Magic makes them real. Once I made a work space for Jhoira by combining her ideas with my magic to create a physical form. Karn must use his memories and his magic to create motion, a direction and the impetus to travel in that direction. You must meditate, old friend. Isolate and organize those thoughts that will lead you back to Tolaria, back to the era of the Invasion. Focus on each successively older memory in turn. Use them as stepping-stones. Keep your progress slow and deliberate, at least at first. Start with what happened this morning, then move on to last night, yesterday noon, then yesterday morning. Treat each memory as a link in a chain and pull yourself along that chain. When you reach the link that is Tolaria at the moment Barrin cast his spell, make one more link, take one last step. The rift will be there and so will you. You can seal it then and there. Afterward, all you have to do is let yourself go and the time stream will bring you back to where you should be."

Venser waited until he was sure Teferi had finished, then said, "This all sounds very esoteric to me."

"That's because you're so practical-minded. You're accustomed to measurable goals and reproducible results. Trust me that trial and error will not work this time. Karn knows where to go. He simply has to let himself follow the most reliable path back across his own memories."

Venser shrugged. "I still don't get it."

"But I do." Karn strode forward, his massive arms swinging at his sides. "I'd like to begin now."

Teferi bowed. "I am finished."

Karn extended his large, square hand to Venser. "With your permission," he said, "I will start us off."

Venser reached out but pulled his hand back before Karn could clasp it. "You're sure I'll survive in the Blind Eternities?"

"I am."

"Because there was an impostor there last time I went. He wore your face and tried to get me out of the ambulator. I think he was trying to kill me."

"If the Blind Eternities were a danger to you, you'd be dead now. The essential nature of planeswalking dictates that the 'walker go through the void on his way from here to there. If it were capable of killing you, you would have arrived dead the first time you 'walked." Karn turned to Jhoira. "Did he arrive dead?"

"Hardly," she said.

"There you have it. If they could have harmed you at all, the Eternities would have certainly finished you off then. There are extreme stresses and primal forces that destroy anything and anyone who feels them. You've never felt them. You are entirely safe." He stretched his long arm out. "Trust me," he said.

Venser puffed out his cheeks as he blew air through his lips. He took Karn's hand.

"Now," the silver golem said, "we go."

* * * * *

Karn brought Venser to the edge of the void, where they both became solid. The young man actually held his breath for as long as he could before he finally relaxed. Eyes full of wonder, Venser said, "I'm alive."

"And so you shall stay. I will ask you to wait here and not 'walk farther. Distance and location mean nothing here, but it will be easiest for us to find each other if you stay put and I stay in contact." The golem's thick, square lips pressed together. *Is this comfortable?*

"Tolerable," Venser said. "Wait. Should I have said that out loud?"

It doesn't matter. What matters is you can hear my thoughts and I, yours. I shall move away from you now so that you do not get swept along with me when I go. Stay alert, my young friend. You are in no danger, and this is going to be extremely interesting.

"Good luck, Karn."

Thank you, Venser. Karn drifted out into the larger expanse of emptiness and color, his hands open at his sides.

Teferi had advised him to start small, with the freshest memory he had. Karn had not said so in front of the others so as not to embarrass Jhoira, but he had already chosen the milestones that would carry him back to Tolaria. If he was forging links in a metaphorical chain, each and every one would be inscribed with her name.

Karn pictured his dear friend's face at the moment she watched him leave Urborg, not moments ago. She seemed sad, even angry, and he did not like to see her so. He thought back to when he first arrived outside Venser's workshop to find Jhoira on the ambulator. The momentary spark of joy she showed when she recognized him was familiar and comforting, but it didn't last long. She was wise to suspect him of being the Weaver King in disguise, a small crime for which Karn would never forgive the mind raider.

Farther back now, to the strangely metallic sound of Jhoira's voice being broadcast through the ambulator. It was not her voice, not even really words, but Karn heard the coded signal and recognized his oldest friend. A machine himself, he found it an easy matter to translate and configure the piercing sonic waves into actual words that could have come from Jhoira's mouth. "Karn. Please come at once. Catastrophe brewing. Follow the sound of my voice."

And he did feel himself moving, following the memory of Jhoira's call for aid and comfort. Careful not to break the meditative state he had achieved, Karn nonetheless paused to mentally congratulate Teferi. His method was working.

A much longer gap existed between this memory of Jhoira and the next, so Karn concentrated on the times he had thought of her over the last few centuries. He had come close to calling out to her over the years, even considered searching for her as he and Jeska explored the multiverse. Jhoira never seemed to be available when he was, and vice versa, but that didn't stop him from imagining her, what she was doing, and her irrepressible vitality. There were viashino scattered all across the planes, and each time Karn saw one he thought of Shiv, then the Ghitu, then Jhoira herself. In an empty, blasted desert plane, Karn had carved a small boulder into a bust of Jhoira's face, leaving it as a welcoming monument to whomever visited next. The inscription across the base of the stone read, in elegant Old Thran, "Jhoira is my friend."

His progress grew swifter and more sure. He considered calling out to Venser but instead redoubled his efforts to root out memories of Jhoira, or things that reminded him of Jhoira between now and Tolaria's fall.

A beetle-shaped toolbox that Jeska used to keep her whetting tools organized. He had forgotten if Jhoira had given it to him or if he had conjured it to remind him of her, but every time the beetle clicked across the stone floor, he thought of Jhoira.

A precocious little girl from Rabiah playing with a clockwork bird. Her hair, skin, and eyes were all light brown. She looked up at the robed, hooded stranger and smiled at him. Karn thought of Jhoira.

His own reflection in a clear pond of still water. The inscription on his chest, the name she had given him. He thought of Jhoira.

A small powerstone-processing plant on the metallic planes of Mirrodin. It had been modeled after the Shivan Mana Rig that Urza found and refurbished, a foundry where goblins and viashino worked together under the observation of Tolarian students. For a time the rig was managed by Jhoira.

An elegant, metal sculpture of a woman and a man embracing.

The piece had been fashioned from Thran metal, so carefully crafted that as the amazing substance expanded, the figures in the sculpture aged and grew. They started as children, but when Karn saw it they were both middle-aged. Who first brought Thran metal to Urza, then helped him pioneer its large-scale production? Jhoira.

He was hurtling through the Blind Eternities now, surging upstream against the tides of time like a spawning fish, slipping past the forces that tried to bear him back.

He remembered standing on the decks of the great skyship *Weatherlight* as it soared through the clouds, trading spells and cannonfire with the Phyrexian armada. The ship had been constructed almost a millennium before the Invasion began. Its maiden interplanar journey was to the exalted home of angels. Its first captain had been Jhoira.

He had now crossed the biggest gap in his personal memories of his friend. There would be more for him to choose from, stronger, more vivid memories, but they would be grim and painful, images and emotions from the Invasion itself. *Getting close now,* he sent to Venser. *Be ready to observe and learn.*

I'm ready.

The sight of the hole that had once been half of Shiv. The anger and despair he felt when he realized that Teferi had taken her out of the world. Urza had been outraged that they hadn't stayed to fight, the *Weatherlight* crew had been amazed by most of a continent's simply disappearing, but Karn had simply and quietly mourned the loss of Jhoira.

Tolaria. The hidden island that Urza made, then wrecked, then made again. Karn had been born there and had met Jhoira and Teferi there. He had reached his destination, and though there was nothing of Jhoira that called him to the scene of Barrin's last stand, Karn's memories of the place were completely intertwined with thoughts of Jhoira. With the final internal utterance of her name, Karn forced his mind to go blank, and he felt himself come to a sudden stop.

I'm here, he sent, but the moment the thought left his mind he felt the almost irresistible pull of time upon him. He was no longer a fish swimming upstream. He was an elderly man struggling up a steep hill with forty-pound stones lashed to each limb. He didn't dare try to move forward to the shores of Tolaria for fear of falling and rolling back the way he'd come. Until he gathered his strength and got his bearings, it was all he could do to hold his ground.

He strengthened his heavy, silver limbs and added strength to his frame. The pressure eased somewhat, and he was able to stand straight.

Venser? he sent. *I have arrived. I am but a few steps away from Tolaria in the year AR 4205.*

Venser replied, *I hear you. My eyes and ears are wide open. Tell me everything you see.*

Karn reentered the material world, his heavy feet splashing through the low tide. Tolaria was aflame, overrun with ugly, iron insects that spat poison and exhaled disease. The academy buildings he remembered so fondly were broken, burning, and spattered with blood.

I'd rather not, he sent. *Wait a moment. I'll signal when I'm ready.*

Screwing up his courage, Karn stepped onto the shores of his birthplace. He cast a shroud of invisibility around himself, clenched his jaw, and prepared to witness a massacre.

* * * * *

I'll signal when I'm ready.

Venser exhaled, relaxing slightly now that this first step was complete. Karn was everything Jhoira said he was. He felt much more confident than he had with Teferi.

Venser. I think it's time you and I had a heart-to-heart chat.

The Weaver King's voice startled the artificer, but his fear soon gave way to anger.

"Go away," Venser said, "or I'll—"

Oh, leave it. We've been here before, my friend. You can't harm me, and you can't leave. Your metal friend told you not to. Why don't you just decide now—will you listen to me or disappoint the big silver ape?

Venser stood his ground. "What do you want? Why do you keep following me?"

I'm a part of you now, the Weaver King gloated. *I can't "follow" you any more than your hair, or your skin, or your left foot. I am you.*

"Liar. If that's the best you've got you must really be desperate."

Oh, I am that. I need you, Venser. I need your power. I have problems of my own, and most of them are planeswalkers. There's very little I can do against a god. But a man like you, with powers similar to theirs—you I can handle. If I had you with me always, I could go where I pleased. And if the planeswalkers came after me and I didn't feel like playing with them . . . I could leave.

"I'm not available," Venser said. "Get yourself another pet."

Pets are all I have. I don't want another pet. I want a host.

Venser's spine tingled at the way the Weaver King pronounced that last word.

I am going to hollow you out, Venser. I will burn out your mind . . . no, that's a bit of hyperbole. Your power resides somewhere in your mind, and I want to preserve that. How about this: I will shred your will and devour your personality. I will turn you into a living meat-robe that I can slip on or doff at my leisure. And you're going to let me do it.

Venser ground his teeth. He was not a warrior and had rarely thrown a blow in anger, but he knew how angry warriors talked.

Right now he understood how they felt too, and so without irony or shame Venser snarled, "Prove it."

If you insist. Dinne, the Weaver King's voice rose as if calling across the room, *kill the Ghitu and the afterthought.*

Venser choked on outrage. He sputtered and tried to say something that would forestall the Weaver King's order.

That is, the Weaver continued, *unless Venser puts aside his newfound bravado and opens his mind to me. Let me in, little builder. Close your eyes, tilt back your head, and let it happen. Rest now.* The Weaver King giggled. *Rest and relax. Soon it will all be over.*

* * * * *

"Teferi," Jhoira said, "I'd like to talk to you."

"At last." The bald wizard was sitting on the floor of Venser's shack. He dusted his hands on each other and got to his feet. "I was beginning to think you had disowned me."

Jhoira waited until he was balanced and steady on his feet, then said, "It's about Corus."

She watched his jovial mask freeze. It cracked, ever so slightly, and he said, "What about Corus?"

"You killed him. Didn't you."

Teferi turned his head away. "I don't remember."

"I think you do. And until you convince me otherwise, things will never be right between us."

He faced her once more, his expression tight, his eyes wide and dry. "Then that is a disappointment we'll both have to live with."

"What happened to you, Teferi?"

"I thought it was obvious."

"I'm not talking about the rift, or your planeswalking, or what you did to Corus."

"Or didn't do to Corus."

Sadness rolled up into Jhoira's throat. "You have fallen so far, my old friend. Urza was delusional. Urza was obsessed. Urza treated entire nations like tools in a box. But even Urza—"

"I'm not Urza."

"No. Because even Urza would blink when confronted by a friend with the truth."

"Barrin would disagree. Maybe when Karn returns you can ask him about it."

"I will." Sorrow quickly evolved into anger, and Jhoira felt her face grow hot. "But right now I'm asking you: Do you still want my help if this goes forward? Do you expect me to tag along to Zhalfir and Madara and all the other places that are on our itinerary, to trust you with my life and the lives of our companions when you don't trust me?"

Teferi shifted uncomfortably on his feet. He muttered something unintelligible.

Jhoira strode past him toward the workshop door. Her hand touched the latch, and Teferi said, "Wait."

She stopped, stock-still, with her hand on the exit. She did not turn.

"Corus attacked me," Teferi said. "But he couldn't touch me. My thoughts were unclear, but time phasing is as natural to me as blinking. If I were catatonic and you waved a torch in front of my eyes, I would shut them. If an eight-foot tall viashino warrior came at me with a mana star in his raised fist, I think I would phase myself out of harm's way."

Jhoira lowered her hand. "Is that what happened?"

"I don't know! I remember him striking at me with the star. I remember it passing through me. I remember him roaring in frustration."

Now she did turn. "And?"

"And he vented his frustration on the star. He took two of its points in each hand and folded it like a stale piece of bread. It cracked."

Jhoira knew to let him continue. His eyes were tearing, and his throat was clogged with emotion.

"I reacted instinctively. I couldn't let the mana release harm you, or Venser, or me. The first rays of light had just started to spill out from the crack. So I phased him and the star away." Teferi cleared his throat and wiped his face. "I wasn't fast enough. He went away for a few seconds, but enough of the star's power had leaked out to melt the sand where he stood. I thought I had shunted the blast aside, that he would be safe in the phased state. But when he came back he was dead, burned, and broken. I hadn't moved, not really, so I was still sitting on the ground where you found me. Corus sank into the molten glass before it cooled. By the time you and Venser returned, it had hardened." Teferi bowed his head. "That's it," he said. "That's what I remember."

"And it's horrible," Jhoira said, "but not unforgivable. Why did you keep this from me, from everyone? Why did you try to swallow it and make it disappear? Did you think I would just forget?"

"I didn't think. I didn't want to. I saved Shiv at the cost of three loyal Shivans whose only crime was to throw in with me." Teferi lifted his face. "The glass storm went awry. More Shivans died, and even if they had formed an angry mob to dismember us, I thought you hated me." His voice dropped to a whisper. "And for all I knew, Corus had already murdered you and Venser."

Jhoira opened her mouth, but it was the Weaver King's voice she heard.

Dinne, the gibbering harlequin commanded. *Kill the Ghitu and the afterthought.*

A thick, round spike bloomed from Teferi's shoulder. He hissed in pain and staggered back, knocking Venser's table on its side. Jhoira whirled in place to find a tall, reed-thin man in motley armor glaring at her with white eyes nestled deep within his pointed helmet.

Dinne's arm shot out, his fingers tight around Jhoira's throat. She gagged, and her eyes bulged. She battered his arm with her fists and tried to force a single gulp of air through her compressed windpipe.

That is, the Weaver King continued, *unless Venser puts aside his newfound bravado and opens his mind to me.*

The pressure on her throat stopped increasing but did not ease. Jhoira's brain began to tingle, and her vision went blurry and red. Her mind raced, her thoughts ticking off her companions. Teferi was injured and bleeding. Karn was a full four hundred years in the past, heading for the epicenter of one of the most destructive spells ever known. Venser was alone against the Weaver King. And this gaunt assassin was choking the life out of her.

Crazed from pain, she thought, Which of us is going to die first?

CHAPTER 27

Leading up to the Invasion, Karn had spent almost twenty years as a nonviolent pacifist. He was haunted by an accidental death he had caused, tormented by guilt to the point of near-paralysis. To salvage what he could of himself, he forswore aggression and tried to make amends.

Twenty years of hell. Twenty years of standing by and letting people hurt him, attack his friends and comrades. Of letting foul goblins swarm over his body and carry him away. Letting half-Phyrexian sadists torture him with his own moral imperative. It took the full-on world war to shake him from his inertia, to remind him that sometimes action is better than nonaction.

Revisiting Tolaria during the height of the slaughter was infinitely worse. The school had not been Urza's primary research and testing facility for decades, but Phyrexia singled it out for total destruction just in case. Where there had once been mana-bred soldiers and masterpieces of artifact-killing machines, there were now aged academics and fresh-faced apprentices. They were not soldiers. They were students. And Phyrexia didn't care.

It was possible to change the past. He had proven that himself. The consequences were unimaginable, however, and once history had been changed he found he could not escape the feeling that everything that happened from that point forward was his fault. Everything everywhere was affected by the smallest alteration in the way things had been. A single life spared, a single enemy dispatched, could give rise to far greater horrors.

These rationalizations meant very little on the killing grounds of Tolaria. It had been centuries since Karn had revisited the barbarity of the Invasion in his thoughts, but now he was here in the flesh. The agonized screams he heard were genuine. The blood that spattered the rocks and trees was real blood, fresh from the mangled bodies of teenage children. The buildings he had frequented, the pastoral glens and beaches he had strolled through, everything was covered in a ghastly veneer of blood, soot, and glistening oil.

The plague spreaders were the worst. They stalked high above the fray on legs as long and sharp as spears, venting blackish purple clouds of contagion. The gummy smoke seethed and rolled as it spread, and those whom it touched died screaming as their bodies dissolved and rotted out from under them. Those who breathed it in died faster but no more mercifully. A single gasp was enough to bring their insides out, liquefied organs and blood vomiting up from their bulging throats, their viscera dyed black by the caustic disease.

A doglike Phyrexian with elongated legs and a crocodile's snout stumbled into him. Before Karn could withdraw, the beast bent its flexible spine and snapped its foaming jaws around his forearm. Jagged teeth dug into his silver skin and acid smoke wafted up from the wound.

Without thinking, Karn brought his huge metal fist over and drove it into the dog-beast's narrow skull. The metal shell crumpled under the blow, and the brute's bottom jaw separated and fell to the ground. With its teeth still deep in Karn's arm, the Phyrexian thrashed and flailed to tear itself free. Karn regained his composure, concentrated, and seared the monster into ashes under a blinding-white light from his eyes.

Dozens of other Phyrexians turned on this new threat, this new potential victim. They snapped and slavered as they closed in on him. The screams had stopped, and Karn realized he was probably one of the only few non-Invaders left alive. His heavy brow furrowed. Karn did not often get angry, not even after he had renounced his pacifism, but he felt the strange sensation of ice-cold rage boiling up inside.

There was nothing for it now. They had seen him and attacked him, and he had responded in kind. They recognized him as an enemy, and they would not rest, would not stop until he was dead and in pieces.

"So be it," Karn said. He cast off the burden of protecting the history-that-was and prepared to fight.

* * * * *

Hold still, said the Weaver King. *I promise it won't hurt much.*

Venser calmed himself and considered the situation. The Weaver King hadn't paralyzed him as he had in Skyshroud. Why not? If he wanted Venser still and quiescent, all he had to do was take control of his body and force it to go rigid. What had changed between here and the forest?

He could flee, he realized. He could go back to Urborg and help Jhoira and Teferi escape from the Weaver King's shadow cut-throat. Karn had brought him here to observe and to learn, but he observed now that their lives were in danger, and he had already learned that such trials were beyond his ability.

Your friends aren't dead yet, the Weaver King said sweetly. *But they will be if you leave.*

"They will be if I stay," Venser said. He felt a cold, sharp length of wire stabbing into his forehead, and the Weaver King's voice came through it, straight to the center of his brain.

Rest, Venser. Let it take you. Your troubles will soon be over. All you have to do is lie down and die. . . .

Venser teleported. He shifted himself away from the Weaver King's probing mind and reappeared behind the screeching apparition. It was difficult to gauge distance or direction in this trackless void, but he no longer felt the sting of wire in his head. Wherever the Weaver King was, Venser had just avoided him.

That's the spirit. The more you flex those muscles, the less I'll have to train them. More icy needles stabbed into his head, digging into his temples, his eyes, the top of his head. The Weaver King seemed to be everywhere at once.

Pain and panic and his disorienting surroundings confounded Venser. He tried to pull back, to run away physically, but his legs found no purchase here. The Weaver King's uproarious laughter rang in his ears, more dolorous and humiliating than a thousand silver wires in his skull.

He did not want to die. He did not want to die this way, in this place, to this foe.

Silly boy. Haven't you been listening? I'm not going to kill you. I'm going crawl inside you and wear you.

Venser started to 'walk, trying to make it back to Urborg, but some of the wires in his head wouldn't break. He screamed as he started then abandoned his efforts, yanked back into the Weaver King's clutches like a child's toy on a string. His left eye went blind. His nose began to bleed, and he inhaled some blood, coughing it back out in a grisly, red spray.

The Weaver King couldn't stop him from teleporting—or planeswalking. He could tether Venser to him and prevent his escape, but he no longer had control of Venser's body. If he had, he would have used it by now. That was the thing that had changed between here and Skyshroud: he understood his true power.

He was not a titan, nor a goddess, nor an omnipotent wielder of infinite magic, but Venser was both planeswalker and mage. Whatever he had that made him so was an integral part of him, something that the Weaver King couldn't touch. The rest of his body and mind were fair game, but the ability to move through the multiverse was his and his alone. It wasn't much of a weapon, but it was a useful tool, and Venser had been using tools all his life. He needed to figure out an offensive use for this one or he was doomed to become a mindless husk.

Venser stopped struggling, stopped trying to pull his head free of the Weaver King's snares. Sometimes tools were not useful at all unless used in concert with other tools. Nothing he had done so far had changed things for the better. The Weaver King was still upon him. Jhoira and Teferi were still at the mercy of a soulless killer. Giving into the Weaver King's exhortations would not save him, would probably not save Jhoira, but it would give them all a moment of respite. If he stalled long enough, Karn might even return, and so far the Weaver King had always run from planeswalkers.

Except for you, dear boy. I run toward you every chance I get.

Venser felt his strength vanish, his body go limp. There was no gravity to pull him down and no ground to hit. Semiconscious, Venser's eyes rolled up in their sockets, and he listlessly floated, one arm cast awkwardly out beside him and the other jammed into his thick, leather belt.

Much better. And I like the recent turn your thoughts have taken. You can end this. I will spare your friends and call Dinne off. But you must surrender to me. Now.

Venser's eyes fluttered. More of the Weaver King's sharp, invisible wire burrowed into his skull, further clouding his thoughts.

Do it, he thought. *Do it now before I change my mind.*

With pleasure. But don't flatter yourself. You don't have much mind left to change. A new salvo of needle-sharp pain stabbed into his mind. *And soon you won't have any at all.*

The Weaver King giggled as he closed in for the finish. Venser could almost see him through the fog of pain and drowsiness, a skeletal figure with a wild shock of braided, orange hair. His skull-like features were twisted in a slavering grin of hunger and triumph.

Venser drew his hand from his belt, his fist clenched. He brought the fist up between him and the Weaver King. The Weaver King certainly saw Venser's action, but it only increased his mirth.

Oh my, he chortled. *It's come to fisticuffs, has it? Oh dear, oh dear. Whatever will I do when the mighty Venser punches me in the nose? My stars.*

Venser opened his fist, displaying two round, yellow stones. They were his greatest secret, the most valuable things he had ever owned, and he had kept them to himself for all of his adult life.

A present? A token of your esteem? The Weaver King now struck a fey and feminine tone. *But I didn't get you anything.*

The artificer's eyes rolled back down and locked on the phantom. Venser smiled. "That's all right," he said. "These are for you."

He hacked and spat a wad of bloody phlegm into the Weaver King's face. The gobbet passed through the phantasmal maniac, but for the first time ever Venser heard uncertainty and fear in the Weaver King's voice.

What are those?

Venser concentrated, clearing his mind and focusing on the stones, on the cold facets touching the skin of his palm. He pushed aside the pain and confusion brought on by the Weaver King's presence in his mind.

Then Venser teleported, careful to take only that portion of the stones in direct contact with his skin. He had to be quick. He had to be precise. Venser was both.

As the titanic energy contained by his powerstones spilled out into the Blind Eternities, Venser disappeared. He felt a surge of heat and force, and he heard the Weaver King scream as enough raw mana to level a city exploded in his face.

Venser reappeared roughly ten miles from the blast by the physical world's measurement. In the Blind Eternities he had no way to gauge how far away he was and so had no idea how large the great yellow ball of seething energy was. He watched and waited, mopping his bloody nose until the blast had paled and dissipated into the void. Then he returned to precisely the same spot he had been, blind in one eye and in utter agony from head to toe.

In his hand he held two flat facets of powerstone, the coinlike remnants of his most treasured possessions. He clutched them tight in his fist, waiting for the insipid giggling to start again or for a new icy needle to stab through his skull.

There was no sound, no pain, and no Weaver King. Venser let his body go limp, and he floated, unable to anything more than breathe, ache, and worry about his friends.

* * * * *

Dinne was still half-throttling Jhoira and waiting for further instructions when he felt the Weaver King vanish from his mind like smoke in the wind. He blinked, his blank, white eyes flickering in the shadow of his visor. Jhoira coughed, and Teferi groaned.

Dinne looked at them without recognition. The bleeding man on the floor and the woman in his grasp meant nothing to him. He opened his fingers and dropped Jhoira to the floor. She curled up and wriggled away from him, coughing all the while.

The Vec raider checked his belt to make sure the spike he had thrown into Teferi was his once more. Then the shadow warrior turned and melted through the wall.

* * * * *

Karn followed the shoreline, gouging a deep, wide furrow in the Phyrexian horde. He quickly realized that the normal course of events would cover up any trace of his actions here today. Barrin's spell would leave nothing but bedrock and ashes, and history would never know how many Phyrexians had been already dead when that spell took effect.

Karn could not bring himself to witness Barrin's final moments firsthand. The master wizard had been good and kind to him, but he had also come here bearing the body of his daughter Hanna, a hero of the Invasion and a much-admired fellow crewmember of the *Weatherlight*. Karn could not and would not intrude on his old mentor's grief. Barrin meant to carry Hanna's plague-stricken corpse to the grave of Rayne, the woman who had been wife to him and mother to Hanna. Barrin meant to die here, wanted to die here. He chose Tolaria as the place to build a grand pyre for his family and throw himself on it.

From the terrible upheaval that shook the island, Karn reckoned he had to act quickly. He stared up into the sky and spotted the rift, the time-steeped phenomenon that Barrin's last act would enlarge and expand beyond all control.

He knew what to do, but now that he was here it seemed perfectly obvious. The rift itself was like an explosion, and one sure way to stifle an explosion was with a larger explosion. The Tolarian rift at this stage was small and shallow compared to the nightmare over the Stronghold. Karn didn't think it would take all of his power to seal it, perhaps not even most of it. Still, he knew it was not a matter to take lightly.

Karn teleported directly into the center of the Tolarian rift. The fissure tugged and pulled at him like quicksand, but he asserted himself and shook off its clutches. He would survive this. Diminished, perhaps, but he would survive. He looked deep within, bringing forth the power of the world-stone that he contained as well as a significant measure of his own near-limitless might.

Like the Phyrexian dog that had latched onto his arm, the rift snapped at him, sank its fangs into his being. He gave the rift similar treatment to the beast-dog: He balled up his transcendent energy into a fist and rammed it down the thing's throat.

Though he was prepared for the struggle, Karn was still caught off guard by how difficult it was. The rift did not die easily, choking back each new wave of magic and mana with which Karn hit it. He felt his essential being draining away, his power flowing into the crack in the multiverse, filling it like mason's mortar. He was nowhere near the end of his reserves, but he knew he was weakening. He hoped he had enough strength to planeswalk back to Venser before Barrin's spell took the entire island.

Karn? The artificer may have responded to Karn's thoughts, or vice versa, but either way Venser's timing was almost perfect.

I'm here Venser. I am almost through. It has not been easy, but—No. Urza's eyes, no!

Karn? What's happening?

The silver golem felt the rush of corruption spreading out across his body and into his deeper self. This could not be happening. This was worse, far worse than any of them could have imagined.

Venser, he said. *I have to go now. I won't be back. Tell Jhoira I'm sorry.*

Karn? Karn! What went wrong?

I did, Karn thought. Long ago. An enemy I created has finally destroyed me. Then, to Venser, he sent, *Never give up, Venser. Nothing is impossible. You have much to do. I regret that I will not be there to assist you.*

Karn? Wait! Tell me what—

If you see Jeska, Karn said. *Tell her not to follow me. None of you should. Not ever.*

Who's Jeska? Karn? Karn, please!

Karn did not reply. Instead, he fled Dominaria as fast as he could, flickering in and out of the Blind Eternities so that no one would ever be able to pick up his trail.

Seconds later, Barrin set off his spell, and Tolaria died by fire, never to rise again.

Two days later, Venser teleported back to Urborg under his own power. He had revisited the threatened places he had been with Teferi and Jhoira, to the rift sites at Madara, Otaria, Yavimaya, and Zhalfir. He had been back and forth across the globe, from the edge of the Blind Eternities to Skyshroud and Shiv, and finally back to the empty, silent Stronghold. There was no sign of Karn anywhere.

Jhoira and Teferi waited for him outside his workshop. Jhoira had kept herself busy with the ambulator, refitting the powerstone couplings to accommodate her mana star. The machine would work again as soon as she adjusted the power flow, perhaps better than ever.

Teferi wore his arm in a sling, a bloody stain over his shoulder. Dinne's spike had cut deep and Teferi was taking a long time to heal. Jhoira's throat was much improved, and after two days she was finally able to swallow without pain and speak above a whisper.

Jhoira wiped her hands on a rag and came down off the dais. "Anything?"

Venser shook his head. "There is some good news. The thaw is here as well as in Keld. I think we've avoided another Ice Age for now."

"Always count your blessings, no matter how small," Teferi said. He spoke through the searing agony in his arm. "How are you?"

"I'm good. My vision is almost completely restored and my headache's been gone for a full day now. I think I'm almost fully recovered."

"Good news. Excellent news."

Venser cleared his throat. "I was wondering," he said, "now that we're all almost fully mended . . . and since we can go anywhere we need to, between me and the ambulator . . . where do we go next?"

"Zhalfir," Teferi said. "My home. It was always meant to be the second stop on our journey, but as you know . . . other matters took precedence."

Venser nodded. "This is the other continent you phased out?"

"It seemed like a good idea at the time," Teferi said. "But yes. Zhalfir and Shiv were both my doing."

Venser noticed the Ghitu was deep in thought, and he said, "Jhoira?"

"Hm? Sorry. I was just wondering where we're going to find more planeswalkers to help us from here on. I used to think I knew too many, but it seems we don't know enough."

"There are more," Teferi said. "Some will help willingly. We just have to find them." The wizard stepped out between Jhoira and Venser, his orator's voice rising. "I have something to say. I'm sorry. I've been acting more like the kind of planeswalker I've always despised—which is ironic because I'm technically no longer a planeswalker. I swear to you both: No more secrets, no more hidden agendas. We need more planeswalkers to seal the rest of the major rifts, but we also need each other. I would be honored if you would continue to accompany me."

"Accompany you?" Jhoira said. Her face was mild, but her tone was arch. "Who says we're going to let you accompany us?"

Teferi laughed, but Jhoira did not.

"I accept your apology, and I'm grateful to get it," Jhoira said. "But too much has happened to sweep this aside with pretty speeches. Venser and I have talked, and we're still dedicated to our purpose."

"As am I."

"No doubt. But our purpose has not always been yours, Teferi. If you wish to keep us together as a team, you will have to live up to your promise. Just because we need you doesn't mean we can't do it without you."

"Of course. And I look forward to restoring myself to your good graces."

Jhoira nodded. "I'd like that."

"Agreed," Venser said. "So when will we be ready for Zhalfir?"

Lightning flashed from the clear sky, stabbing down into the ground beside the ambulator. A cloud of smoke and dust billowed up. Venser could see a figure moving inside, and he stepped over beside Teferi and Jhoira, within arm's reach of them both.

The woman was short but fierce, with thick, red hair. She was dressed in dusty, leather armor and she wore a short, thick sword. She stepped out of the cloud and took them all in with a firm, defiant stare.

Venser muttered from the side of his mouth. "Planeswalker?"

Jhoira kept her eyes on the wild-eyed woman "Almost certainly."

Teferi nodded. "Definitely."

The woman put her hand on her sword. "My name is Jeska. I'm looking for Karn," she said. "And I know this is the last place he came. Where is he?"

Venser clenched his fists and teeth tight. His life had indeed been much simpler before he met Jhoira and Teferi.

R.A. SALVATORE
ROAD OF THE PATRIARCH
THE SELLSWORDS, BOOK III

Jarlaxle and Entreri have found a home in the
monster-haunted steppes of the Bloodstone Lands,
and have even managed to make a few new friends.
But in a place as cruel as this, none of those friends are
naive enough to trust a drow mercenary and a shadowy
assassin to be anything but what they are: as dangerous
as the monsters they hunt.

OCTOBER 2006

SERVANT OF THE SHARD
THE SELLSWORDS, BOOK I

Powerful assassin Artemis Entreri tightens his grip on the streets
of Calimport, driven by the power of his hidden drow supporters.
His sponsor Jarlaxle grows more ambitious, and Entreri struggles to
remain cautious and in control. The power of the Crystal Shard grows
greater than them both, threatening to draw them into a vast web of
treachery from which there will be no escape.

PROMISE OF THE WITCH-KING
THE SELLSWORDS, BOOK II

Entreri and Jarlaxle might be strangers in the rugged, unforgiving
mountains of the Bloodstone Lands, but they have been in difficult places
before. Caught between the ghost of a power-mad lich, and the righteous
fury of an oath-bound knight, they have never felt more at home.

NOW AVAILABLE

For more information visit **www.wizards.com**

FORGOTTEN REALMS and its respective logo is a trademark of Wizards of the Coast, Inc.
in the U.S.A. and other countries. © 2006 Wizards of the Coast

HOUSE OF SERPENTS
By The New York Times best-selling author
Lisa Smedman

VENOM'S TASTE
The Pox, a human cult whose members worship the goddess of
plague and disease, begins to work the deadly will of Sibyls' Chosen.
As humans throughout the city begin to transform into the freakish
tainted ones, it's up to a yuan-ti halfbood to stop them all.

VIPER'S KISS
A mind-mage of growing power begins a secret journey to Sespech.
There he meets a yuan-ti halfblood who has her eyes set on the scion
of house Extaminos—said to hold the fabled Circled Serpent.

VANITY'S BROOD
The merging of human and serpent may be the most dangerous
betrayal of nature the Realms has ever seen. But it could also be the
only thing that can bring a human slave and his yuan-ti mistress
together against a common foe.

For more information visit
www.wizards.com

FORGOTTEN REALMS, WIZARDS OF THE COAST and their respective logos
are trademarks of Wizards of the Coast, Inc. in the U.S.A. and other countries.
© 2006 Wizards of the Coast

ENTER THE NEW WORLD OF

THE WAR-TORN

After a hundred years of fighting the war is now over, and the people of Eberron pray it will be the Last War. An uneasy peace settles over the continent of Khorvaire.

But what of the soldiers, warriors, nobles, spies, healers, clerics, and wizards whose lives were forever changed by the decades of war? What does a world without war hold for those who have known nothing but violence? What fate lies for these, the war-torn?

THE CRIMSON TALISMAN

BOOK 1

Adrian Cole

Erethindel, the fabled Crimson Talisman. Long sought by the forces of darkness. Long guarded in secret by one family. Now the secret has been revealed, and only one young man can keep it safe.

THE ORB OF XORIAT

BOOK 2

Edward Bolme

The last time Xoriat, the Realm of Madness, touched the world, years of warfare and death erupted. A new portal to the Realm of Madness has been found — a fabled orb, long thought lost. Now it has been stolen.

IN THE CLAWS OF THE TIGER

BOOK 3

James Wyatt

BLOOD AND HONOR

BOOK 4

Graeme Davis

For more information visit **www.wizards.com**

EBERRON, WIZARDS OF THE COAST and their respective logos are trademarks of Wizards of the Coast, Inc. in the U.S.A. and other countries. © 2006 Wizards of the Coast

FOLLOW MARGARET WEIS FROM THE WAR OF SOULS INTO THE CHAOS OF POST-WAR KRYNN

The War of Souls has come to an end at last. Magic is back, and so are the gods. But the gods are vying for supremacy, and the war has caused widespread misery, uprooting entire nations and changing the balance of power on Ansalon.

AMBER AND ASHES
The Dark Disciple, Volume I
MARGARET WEIS

The mysterious warrior-woman Mina, brooding on her failure and the loss of her goddess, makes a pact with evil in a seductive guise. As a strange vampiric cult spreads throughout the fragile world, unlikely heroes – a wayward monk and a kender who can communicate with the dead – join forces to try to uproot the cause of the growing evil.

AMBER AND IRON
The Dark Disciple, Volume II
MARGARET WEIS

The former monk Rhys, now sworn to the goddess Zeboim, leads a powerful alliance in an attempt to find some way to destroy the Beloved, the fearsome movement of undead caught in the terrifying grip of the Lord of Death. Mina seeks to escape her captivity in the Blood Sea Tower, but can she escape the prison of her dark past?

AMBER AND BLOOD
The Dark Disciple, Volume III
MARGARET WEIS

February 2007

For more information visit **www.wizards.com**

DRAGONLANCE and its logo are trademarks of Wizards of the Coast, Inc. in the U.S.A. and other countries. ©2006 Wizards.

ELVEN EXILES TRILOGY
PAUL B. THOMPSON AND TONYA C. COOK

The elven people, driven from their age old enclaves in
the green woods, have crossed the Plains of Dust and harsh
mountains into the distant land of Khur. The elves coexist
uneasily with surrounding tribes under the walls of
Khuri-Khan.

Shadowy forces inside Khur and out plot to destroy the elves.
Some are ancient and familiar, others are new and unknown.

And so the battle lines are drawn, and the great game begins.
Survival or death, glory or oblivion — these are the stakes.
Gilthas and Kerianseray bet all on a forgotten map,
faithful friends, and their unshakable faith on the
greatness of the elven race.

SANCTUARY
Volume One

ALLIANCES
Volume Two

August 2006

Volume Three

June 2007

For more information visit **www.wizards.com**

DRAGONLANCE and its respective logo is a trademark of Wizards of the Coast, Inc.
in the U.S.A. and other countries. © 2006 Wizards of the Coast

R.A. SALVATORE'S WAR
OF THE SPIDER QUEEN

THE NEW YORK TIMES BEST-SELLING SAGA OF THE DARK ELVES

DISSOLUTION BOOK I
RICHARD LEE BYERS
While their whole world is changing around them, four dark elves struggle against
different enemies. Yet their paths will lead them all to the most terrifying discovery
in the long history of the drow.

INSURRECTION BOOK II
THOMAS M. REID
A hand-picked team of drow adventurers begin a journey through the treacherous
Underdark, all the while surrounded by the chaos of war. Their path will take them
through the heart of darkness and shake the Underdark to its core.

CONDEMNATION BOOK III
RICHARD BAKER
The search for answers to Lloth's silence uncovers only more complex questions, allowing
doubt and frustration to test the boundaries of already tenuous relationships.

EXTINCTION BOOK IV
LISA SMEDMAN
For even a small group of drow, trust is the rarest commodity of all.
When the expedition prepares for a return to the Abyss, what little trust there is
crumbles under a rival goddess's hand.

ANNIHILATION BOOK V
PHILIP ATHANS
Old alliances have been broken and new bonds have been formed. While some finally
embark for the Abyss itself, others stay behind to serve a new mistress – a goddess with
plans of her own.

RESURRECTION BOOK VI
PAUL S. KEMP
The Spider Queen has been asleep for a long time, leaving the Underdark to suffer war
and ruin. But if she finally returns, will things get better... or worse?

For more information visit **www.wizards.com**

FORGOTTEN REALMS and its respective logo is a trademark of Wizards of the Coast, Inc.
in the U.S.A. and other countries. © 2006 Wizards of the Coast

IN THE WAKE OF
THE WAR OF SOULS...

The power of the Dark Knights in northern Ansalon is broken.

The Solamnic order is in disarray.

And in a shrouded mountain valley, an army of evil gathers.

Against them stand a mysterious outlawed warrior, a dwarf, and a beautiful enchantress. With the aid of two fugitive gnomes, they will hold the banner of Good against the forces of darkness. And from the ashes of war, a new Solamnia will rise.

THE RISE OF SOLAMNIA TRILOGY
BY DOUGLAS NILES

Volume I
LORD OF THE ROSE

Volume II
THE CROWN AND THE SWORD
June 2006

Volume III
THE MEASURE AND THE TRUTH
January 2007

For more information visit **www.wizards.com**

DRAGONLANCE and its respective logo is a trademark of Wizards of the Coast, Inc. in the U.S.A. and other countries. © 2006 Wizards of the Coast